RESURRECTION

RESURRECTION

Tucker Malarkey

RIVERHEAD BOOKS

a member of Penguin Group (USA) Inc.

New York

2006

RIVERHEAD BOOKS
Published by the Penguin Group
Penguin Group (USA) Inc., 375 Hudson Street, New York, New York 10014, USA ·
Penguin Group (Canada), 90 Eglinton Avenue East, Suite 700, Toronto, Ontario M4P 2Y3, Canada
(a division of Pearson Penguin Canada Inc.) · Penguin Books Ltd, 80 Strand,
London WC2R 0RL, England · Penguin Ireland, 25 St Stephen's Green, Dublin 2, Ireland
(a division of Penguin Books Ltd) · Penguin Group (Australia), 250 Camberwell Road,
Camberwell, Victoria 3124, Australia (a division of Pearson Australia Group Pty Ltd) ·
Penguin Books India Pvt Ltd, 11 Community Centre, Panchsheel Park, New Delhi–110 017, India ·
Penguin Group (NZ), Cnr Airborne and Rosedale Roads, Albany, Auckland 1310,
New Zealand (a division of Pearson New Zealand Ltd) · Penguin Books (South Africa)
(Pty) Ltd, 24 Sturdee Avenue, Rosebank, Johannesburg 2196, South Africa

Penguin Books Ltd, Registered Offices:
80 Strand, London WC2R 0RL, England

Library of Congress Cataloging-in-Publication Data

Malarkey, Tucker.
Resurrection : a novel / by Tucker Malarkey.
p.   cm.
ISBN 1-59448-919-X
1. Archaeologists—Fiction.   2. Apocryphal Gospels—Fiction.
3. Cairo (Egypt)—Fiction.   I. Title.
PS3563.A424R47   2006   2006044274
813'.6—dc22

Printed in the United States of America
1   3   5   7   9   10   8   6   4   2

BOOK DESIGN BY CHRIS WELCH

MAP BY MEIGHAN CAVANAUGH

This is a work of fiction. Names, characters, places, and incidents either are the product of the author's imagination or are used fictitiously, and any resemblance to actual persons, living or dead, businesses, companies, events, or locales is entirely coincidental.

While the author has made every effort to provide accurate telephone numbers and Internet addresses at the time of publication, neither the publisher nor the author assumes any responsibility for errors, or for changes that occur after publication. Further, the publisher does not have any control over and does not assume any responsibility for author or third-party websites or their content.

Author's Note

This is a work of fiction. The gospel excerpts included are from existing translations of *The Gnostic Bible*, the Nag Hammadi, and other ancient texts. Where the translators are known, they are credited in the acknowledgments to this book.

For My Grandmother,

Sister Mary Monica

Contents

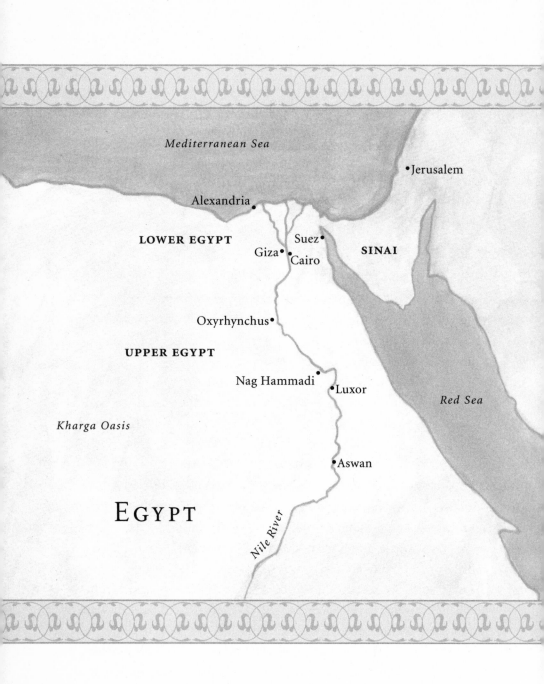

Author's Note

My fascination with the Nag Hammadi gospels was sparked when I read an account of the accidental discovery in 1945 of more than fifty ancient papyrus texts. The Second World War had just ended, and the evidence of a Christian God was thin. How miraculous that in December of that year the lost words of several overlooked apostles were unearthed by a Bedouin in the silence of the Egyptian desert.

The reappearance of gospels as authentic as those of the New Testament should have been a momentous event, with much fanfare and attention. Instead, only a few people took note. The texts themselves slipped into obscurity, languishing for years unopened and untranslated. Decades passed before they became available to academics, and still more time before they entered mainstream theological discussion. As I write this in 2005, the public remains largely unaware of their existence and the light they shed on the little-known story of Christianity.

Resurrection is a novel based loosely on real events. Gemma Bastian and the Lazar family are my own creations, but many of the ancillary characters actually existed. The portraits I draw of them, however, are fictional. The historical, archaeological, and biblical material is real, as are the gospel quotations and fragments.

As the words of these lost gospels make their way to you across oceans, deserts, and even time itself, you may find in them the resurrection of a story that has long been buried—the story of a great faith.

If you bring forth what is within you,

What is within you will save you.

If you do not bring forth what is within you,

What is within you will destroy you.

—*The lost gospel of the apostle Thomas*

PART ONE

CHAPTER ONE

London, 1947

A s GEMMA BASTIAN left the hospital reluctantly for two days' leave, a flurry of sparrows wrested her eyes from the pavement. Her eyes followed the birds across the sky, lingering on the weak and setting sun. Though she was cold, she made her way slowly through the East End, taking an unfamiliar route that might prolong her return to a flat empty of people but filled with possessions that were not hers, the wardrobes of ghosts she could neither inhabit nor dispense with. One did not throw such things away. One gave them to the needy, or traded them at secondhand stores. But she could not bear the possibility of their reincarnation, that someone else wearing her mother's yellow dress might one day pass her on the street.

She glanced briefly at a crumbling brick house, its bomb-struck side newly hung with scaffolding. She had staunchly ignored the city's meager attempts to rebuild itself. Here, in the East End, it could never be enough. It was one of the war's many cruelties that the bombs of the Luftwaffe had done their worst in the poorest part of London. Now, as dusk grew close, working people were arriving home to their demolished neighborhoods and switching on their lights. It could still surprise her. During the black-outs, an amber glow had meant fire, not the warmth of a lamp-lit home.

Gemma's eyes moved from one window to the next. Life, for some, had moved on.

She let herself into her flat and wandered in the half-light to the spare room. Clutching her jacket around her, she stood in front of the closet that held her mother's clothes. On the floor was a box with her stockings, some packages still unopened. Wear them, her father had urged. Stop drawing stocking seams on your legs. It's too cold for that. But Gemma had forgotten the feeling of a stocking. Like most women in London, she had learned to draw quite a straight line down the back of her calf. She knelt on the floor and with a finger tipped the lid off the box. Three unopened packages. She took one to the bed and tore the cellophane. For a long time she sat with the stockings unrolled across her lap, her hands resting lightly on the translucent fabric. Without thinking about what it meant, she pulled them on, allowing herself to remember the luxury of their soft, gloved protection.

It was only six o'clock. She lay back on the bed, her arms rigid at her sides. She had lost a patient that day. Death, too, was changing, resuming a normal proportion that, strangely, hurt more. It carried her back to the beginning, when the death had just started, when it was still possible to feel something. She sensed the same shift in others at the hospital. They were emerging from a kind of collective shock, like survivors of a shipwreck bobbing up in a calmer sea, and looking at one another perhaps for the first time beyond the gasping emergency of near drowning, past the mere physical survival that had become their single reduced goal. Now, in the halls of the ward, she felt glances that flashed with a query: Who were you before? Who were we all? Where do we go now?

Gemma raised her arms and pressed her clenched, overwashed hands into the air, spreading her fingers. We go forward, she thought. Taking one stroke and then another, away from the scene of devastation. Toward dry land, toward something that did not give way. She both wanted and feared it. She thought that once she finally reached stable ground, she would inhabit her exhaustion completely. She would not be able to remain standing. And beneath that fear, another one. The houses were being bricked back together, but it did not seem possible that the scorched place inside her would heal.

She thought again about the letters she had received a week ago, the two envelopes she now carried with her, both sent to her by her father from Egypt. She had long held the bright word inside her, using it like a weapon against the inviolate gray of London. The first letter had made her laugh out loud. She could almost feel her father's excitement. He wrote that he had made an unexpected find, a find her rebellious spirit would appreciate. It would also leave him with quite a bit of money. Enough money for him to buy a house and bring Gemma to Egypt to live in decent style.

Don't worry, he wrote, *it's all aboveboard. The reason there's money involved is that no one likes change, particularly venerable old religious institutions. People will give, pay, sacrifice almost anything to prevent it. But this is change that will benefit us all, a change I have been hoping for all my life. I think I have rediscovered a God that even you will believe in.*

Maybe it was possible, she thought. If anyone could resurrect a God that had died a hundred times, her father could.

The other envelope had contained a strange, thick paper covered in letters she didn't recognize, letters that looked ancient. The envelope had borne another name before hers but it had been scratched out. She could just make out "Anthony Lazar." David Lazar was the name of her father's closest friend in Egypt. She didn't know an Anthony. She only half cared that she didn't understand what this piece of paper meant. Her father would explain it to her later. She dared to hope that he would do so in Egypt.

She had fallen asleep when the doorbell rang.

A tall man stood on the other side of the peephole. Through the magnified circle, she could see only his clean-shaven jaw. His voice was strong and deep through the door.

"My name is Bernard Westerly," he said. "I'm here about your father, Charles Bastian." Gemma unlatched the door but not the chain. "I know him through the museum," he added.

"You know him from Egypt?" She closed the door and unhooked the chain.

He looked down at her as he passed her into the tiny hall, where in his bulky winter coat he was altogether too big. "I know his work."

Bernard Westerly was taking off his gloves and surveying the flat as if it were a newly conquered territory. He made no attempt to put her at ease. Gemma maneuvered around him, deciding not to offer him tea.

"I came to ask if you had heard anything from him."

"Like what?"

"Anything."

Gemma turned and walked into the sitting room. She stood at the window. Above the chimneys and charcoal rooftops she found the silver curve of the new moon. "What might I have heard?" she asked.

"Are you familiar with his recent project?" Westerly asked.

She shook her head slightly. "I'm a nurse," she said evenly, "not an archaeologist."

He began looking around the flat. Gemma turned to watch him, keeping her hand from pressing against the letters in her pocket. "Are you looking for something?"

Westerly had paused at the bookshelf. "Are these books yours?"

"Yes."

"Then you are a nurse who speaks many languages," he said. "Like your father."

Gemma was silent.

"So he hasn't sent you anything out of the ordinary? Something to do with his current work?"

"Why would he do that?"

The man smiled and shrugged. "For safekeeping, maybe."

"Safe from whom?"

He looked at her with what might have been amusement but did not answer.

"No," she said, moving to the door. "I've received nothing out of the ordinary."

He looked at her closely and then smiled with sudden ease. "It's just museum business, you understand. Nothing to worry about. I'm sorry to have disturbed you."

I T WAS LATER that the peculiar detail registered. He had taken off his hat but had not unbuttoned his coat. But he had bent his tall frame to look at her books. She remembered now, something that had briefly struck her as odd. Beneath the buttoned collar of his coat, she thought she had seen the stiff white band of a priest's collar.

In the night she woke twice, feeling herself begin the familiar and numbing work of imagining the worst.

I T WAS NOT the next morning but the morning after that the telex came. When she opened it, Gemma fell against the wall, unable to breathe.

There were a few short incontrovertible sentences in brutally broken English. She stumbled to the bathroom and fell to her knees to retch. Afterward, she pressed her cheek to the cold tiles. When she finally opened her eyes, she stared up at a painted tile of roses until they blurred into a bloodstain. She stayed there until night fell, until everything fine and fragile inside of her had been crushed.

When it was over, she stood and stared at her gray reflection in the mirror. Her father was dead. He had been found in his office. The words said his heart had failed him. Money would be wired to her bank account. She was to use it to make her way to the house of David Lazar in Cairo.

P ROFESSOR ANTHONY LAZAR had climbed up to Gabal Al Tayr late in the day. Too late, his assistant Zira warned. But he had wanted to see something before the sun set. Sometimes it could be urgent with the professor. Zira could see it in his face, feel it in the tension of his silence.

He watched now as his employer tucked a flashlight in his belt and bounded up the mountainside like a goat.

Professor Anthony had not been settled since they arrived, since the sudden departure of his elderly friend Charles Bastian from their last site in Upper Egypt. It was an unusual friendship. Zira had never seen Anthony so impassioned by conversation, had never witnessed the miracle of his speaking uninterrupted for nearly an hour. They might have been father and son. Then Bastian had left, it seemed, in the middle of the conversation. Anthony was not satisfied with the way his friend had broken off, or with the hastily written note he had found pinned to his tent.

Restocking in Cairo, they thought they might see him. But Bastian had not been in Cairo. Because something about his friend's disappearance disturbed Anthony, they had waited as long as they could. Finally, there had been nothing to do but return to their base in Kharga. Soon he and Zira were days away, folded back into the silence of the Western Desert.

Zira squatted and waited for Anthony to return. It was getting dark in the sudden way of the desert, and though his employer had grown up on the edge of the Sahara, navigating the loose rocks and pitch of Gabal Al Tayr in the darkness was perilous, even for a nimble man.

The day had begun as it was ending, with a restless roaming of ruins they both knew well. That morning they had visited the Temple of Hibis, a pagan temple that had been built over by Christians in the fourth century. Then they had gone to the Necropolis, another site of pagan abandonment. Sand and wind had uncovered an almost equal number of pagan and Christian temples, chapels, and burials. "The desert does not discriminate, thank heaven," Anthony had said. "It preserves all gods."

Last Anthony wanted to see the Cave of Mary at the top of Gabal Al Tayr, the mountain of birds. Its walls were covered in ancient etchings, one of the Madonna and Child. The lore was that the infant Jesus and his mother had stopped here after fleeing the Massacre of the Innocents.

Zira stared up at Gabal Al Tayr and lit a cigarette for the illusion of warmth. He hadn't eaten that day and his hunger made him cold. He thought about other things. He thought about his family in Cairo and money and what to cook for dinner. Above him, on the ridge of the hillside, the outline of a man had appeared. Zira did not know how long he had been there. He was standing stock still. Zira rose and ground out his cigarette. His employer could move as quickly and as quietly as a cat. It was unusual for the son of an Englishman. Anthony was at home in the desert, unlike the other Europeans who clustered in Cairo like a maladapted flock of birds. Why all these people had decided to live in the desert in the first place was a mystery to Zira.

Maybe, like Professor Anthony, he was becoming a little strange. There were moments in the violet silence of the desert evening when Zira was aware of a deepening of his spirit. It was an obscure life he was leading out here on the edge of nothingness, but he was satisfied with it. Perhaps it was at the edge of nothingness that true meaning began. Everything once known had been forgotten, Anthony said. It had only to be rediscovered. Unearthed.

Zira had forgotten his hunger. He lit his lantern to show his location in the darkness and resumed his squatting position. Anthony would come when he was ready.

It was later, while he and Anthony were sitting by the fire, that a bare-chested boy on a horse quietly entered the pool of light. In his hand was a letter. Anthony reached for the folded and stained envelope and motioned the boy to sit. He slid off the bare back of his horse, and Zira gave him some bread and *fuul*. His eyes were huge and luminous. Anthony noticed he was missing a thumb. He poured him a cup of tea, stirring in two spoons of honey.

Anthony read the letter, tilting it toward the firelight. Then he folded it and continued to sit without speaking. The boy drank his tea in silence. When he set down his empty cup, Anthony dug into his pocket for a coin and watched as the boy and his horse slipped back into the night. With his eyes on the darkness where the boy had been, he said quietly, "Zira, we have lost a friend."

Zira's eyes locked on Anthony's face.

"Charles Bastian is dead."

Zira crossed himself quickly. He waited until the fire dimmed into ember, then leaned forward and agitated the logs. In the brighter light, he studied Anthony's face, reading it like an oracle. He pulled his burnoose tightly around him and waited.

"We will return to Cairo," Anthony said. "The khamseen is coming anyway. Maybe this year we will avoid being buried in sand."

CHAPTER TWO

Seek and do not stop seeking until you find.
When you find, you will be troubled.
When you are troubled, you will marvel
and rule over all.

The Gospel of Thomas,
from Nag Hammadi

EMMA OPENED HER eyes. The desert was coming toward her, the plane dropping through a sky that had two colors only. They were leaving the blue for a relentless and inhospitable beige. How will I exist in such a color? she thought. I could be flattened between the sky and the sand like a leaf, like an insect. She closed her eyes again, shutting out the light of the desert, clutching her knees as the plane lurched and touched down in Cairo.

Like a great sundial the plane turned and taxied to something that might have been an airport—a small, low building the color of sand, the color of everything she could see of Egypt. Gemma touched her hair, fastened her hat by feel, found her lips in a tiny smeared mirror and colored them red.

The door to the plane opened and stairs were affixed. She could see the wind in the hair of the pilot as he stood at attention in a shaft of light. She put on her gloves and readied herself. It will be hot, she told herself. There will be dust. She could see it now, like a film. Remember this moment, she thought. Remember what the world looked like before.

During the war, when it seemed every strength had been scooped out from inside of her, Gemma had learned a trick. Around her hollow

11

interior she had shaped a façade of confidence, the mask of a woman who was unafraid of pain or death, who could not be fooled or taken advantage of. A woman who had nothing left to lose. She dropped this mask over herself now like a shield and searched her memory for the words she had taught herself in this strange language. When she reached a taxi, she forced herself to say them with conviction. "Take me to Garden City. I have two English pounds, no more."

The driver smiled and found her in the rearview mirror. "You have learned our language."

Gemma shook her head and looked out the window. "You have learned mine."

"It's better to know the language of the captors," he said. "Then you have a chance at freedom."

"I think that's wise."

"You are going to Professor David Lazar's house."

Gemma leaned forward. "How do you know that?"

"Because he told me to look for you."

"How nice of him."

"He is a nice man."

"I don't know. I've never met him."

"You will like him. He has paid your way to Garden City."

Gemma stared out the window of the only motorized vehicle on a street crowded with donkeys and tented vendors. *Your country killed my father.* She clutched her purse, her knuckles white. Women walked with wide, shallow baskets balanced on their heads, carrying vegetables, garlic, eggs. Gemma's eyes passed over them, briefly locking onto the gaze of a woman whose face, everything but her scornful eyes, was covered in black cloth. Gemma thought wearily, This is not how I wanted to come here. She leaned her head back on the worn leather seat. Above her, the sky was no longer as painfully blue. It was more like skies she had known. She needed a decent night's sleep.

As if in protest of this urge for rest, the first call to evening prayer blared from a minaret high above. Gemma stared wildly into the sky as other calls sounded after it and the city was filled with harsh, dissonant melodies. She remembered now. Her father had called them "angels' caterwaul." For the Western ear, it was hard to discern anything godly in the discordant wailing. To Gemma, it sounded more like a call to war than a beckoning to prayer. She shivered. The sun was setting and the air had gone cold and dark as suddenly as if a plug had been pulled. The taxi had entered a leafy neighborhood with large houses, but she could no longer see much of anything. She pulled her jacket around her and moved her toes inside her shoes. She was ready for the journey to end.

GEMMA SET HER suitcases down and looked up at the Lazar house. It was what you called a grand house, elegantly solid with marble pillars at the entrance and balconies on both floors. She knocked on the door, which was shaped like a keyhole. When it opened, light spilled out but did not quite touch Gemma where she stood. Against the brightness of the hall was a young man with a cane. She saw a head of neatly combed brown hair and a strikingly handsome face that was temporarily confused by the darkness that met him. Gemma waited, extending the moment of disconnection so she could observe this man who was as of yet unknown to her. His face was youthful but lined. She wasn't sure of the combination that had carved its character, whether it was pain or compassion, politeness or empathy. Underlying all of it was a bedrock of despair. This she could clearly see. She knew this face; she understood it. Her heart cracked open at the unexpected sight. The war had followed her, even here. She stepped into the pool of light on the doorstep.

Like an animal trained to fear, he stepped back. There was the right distance then for them to both guard themselves and look at each other, which they did in concentrated silence, a silence that would not have existed before the war. In the light, he turned and she saw the burn on the side of his face that had been in shadow. It crept up from inside his shirt collar like a vine, branching at his jaw into two angry molten fingers, one touching his cheekbone and the other curling into the corner of his mouth like a scimitar, like something that could gut him. The disfiguration was all the more jarring because of the beauty of the face. Had it almost been perfect? His eyes were on her, and as she met them Gemma thought, The wound is new; he still doesn't know how it looks. I am a mirror.

"Gemma Bastian," he said. "I've seen pictures of you."

"You have me at a disadvantage." She held out her hand, boldly bridging the space between them as if meeting another wounded soldier was easy for her. She was the unvanquished, after all, the one who had not gone to meet war but had stayed at home to wait for it and then gone at it with every weapon she knew how to use.

He took her hand in his loose, cool grip, which tightened slightly before letting go. "I'm Michael Lazar," he said.

"Michael," she repeated. Not Anthony.

"David Lazar is my father. He's not here, I'm afraid. But you are expected. Please come in." His voice was light and educated and easy and did not at all belong to the face; it did not belong to the eyes. He moved aside as she carried her bags past him into the echoing silence of the spacious hall.

"I'm sorry about your father."

"Thank you."

"And you've come all the way from London." He attempted a smile. "I'm sure you'd like a drink." Gemma nodded but Michael Lazar didn't move. He stood there staring at her shoes.

Gemma set her bags down again. "Could I possibly put my things somewhere?"

"Yes, of course. Forgive me." Michael Lazar shifted his weight on his cane. "My manners are worse than rusty. I think they've put you in the red room."

"Red." She smiled. "Lovely. Do you think I might have a glass of water? Then I'll freshen up and join you for a drink."

"Lovely," he echoed. Still, he didn't move.

Gemma looked up the curved staircase. "What a beautiful house."

"It is."

"Have you lived here long?"

"I partly grew up here. Now I'm just a guest. Like you." He turned to the stairs and looked at them.

Suddenly she understood. She picked up her bags and started up the stairs. Over her shoulder she said, "Just point the way."

He looked up at her gratefully. "To the left, third door on your right. I'll have your water and whatever else you might like in the den." He indicated the direction with his cane. "Take your time."

The red room was a salve. Her eyes drank in the deep colors, the richly patterned rugs. She pulled the door closed behind her and leaned against it. The room was, like the house, grand. The bed was high. A mosquito net hung from the ceiling, draping the four corners of the bed, enshrouding it like a tomb. She wanted to be inside its gauzy softness, behind a filmy barrier, to lie just for a while hidden from the world.

She crossed the room to the velvet curtains framing the balcony windows and stood inside them. Against a sky still stained with color was the clear outline of the city. Then, in the distance, she saw the massive shapes of Giza, one pyramid behind the other. She stared without comprehension as the shapes faded into the night. She had not imagined their enormity, though her father had shown her photos, even sketched them to scale. She opened the balcony door and stepped outside.

Leaning out over the railing, she saw that it was jasmine that perfumed the air. It climbed the walls of the house along a trellis, wrapping it in sweet white blossoms. Somewhere in the garden below was a fountain and the soft melody of water. She drew a deep breath, allowing the dry air to fill her lungs completely. So this was it, she thought. This was the spell.

She stepped back inside and drew the curtains closed. Turning up the flame of the lantern on the bureau, she surveyed her new domain. This is the room I will sleep in, she thought. The walls that will hold me while I find a way to bury my father's ashes.

DOWNSTAIRS IN THE den, Michael Lazar was lighting a fire. He leaned close to blow on the kindling. Gemma stood in the doorway and thought, How brave to come so close, to almost kiss the beast that had tried to devour him. Though the thick carpet allowed her to enter silently, Michael raised his head. "It's surprising, isn't it?" he said, blowing again on the bundle of kindling. "This is the desert after all. But the nights can be so cold."

"Yes, I noticed that."

Michael rose and turned to her. "You've changed."

Gemma looked down at her dress. "I have."

"Here's your water and most every alcohol known to man. Sorry it's only me here. I know you've got pressing business with my father."

"Pressing?" Gemma smiled quickly. "I don't know that it is, really. As far as I know, the dead stay dead forever. I'd love some sherry, if you've got it." She sat in one of the chintz armchairs that flanked the fireplace. "You were in the war," she said.

Michael smiled joylessly as he limped with his cane to deliver her sherry. "What makes you think that?"

She looked up at him. "So was I."

"A WAC, were you? Got to drive the likes of me around in an ambulance?"

"I was a nurse, actually."

"You've been in London?"

"Yes."

"You've been bombed to kingdom come."

Gemma sipped her drink. "Yes."

"Well, we've all had quite a party." He tipped a large glass of neat whiskey to his lips and swallowed half of it, dribbling some on his shirt from the burnt corner of his mouth, which made him curse. He remained standing, glowering above her. His anger was sudden. She could feel it like a wall of heat. She got up and went to the bookshelf. The war was over; his wounds were not her problem. She looked at David Lazar's books and pretended his son wasn't there. On her knees she could see the titles more closely. She knew some of these books from her own father's bookshelf. The pain of the recognition was unexpected. She held her hand to her mouth and bit her knuckle. It was like seeing his shoes on the bottom of his closet or smelling the shirts of his she had already forced herself to give away.

She could feel Michael watching her. Finally, she turned to face him. "Nothing in England can really prepare you for this place, can it?"

"If you ask me, we Brits belong on our sodden island." He finished his drink and set the glass on the mantel. "I met your father. I liked him."

Gemma picked up her sherry and returned to her chair. She wasn't prepared to talk to this man about her father. "What happened to your leg?"

Michael tapped his calf with his cane, making the hollow sound of wood on wood. "Seems I've lost it. But I've got a new one now, just today in fact. It's not half bad, just half wood."

She stared at him from across the room. Both his forced cheer and his bitterness were mockeries. They were smoke screens. The man himself was nowhere to be seen. She did not have the energy or interest to find him. She returned to the fire and her drink. Michael refilled his glass and settled into the chair next to hers. They sat for a long time without speaking. The room was warm and comfortable, and with its dancing tongues of flame, the fire held their eyes like a stage.

"The truth is," Michael finally said, "I don't know the last time I had a proper conversation. Somehow one's family doesn't count. I used to be quite good at this sort of thing. Maybe I was even charming. Now you've been here less than an hour and you're already running from me." He looked at her and almost smiled. "It's in moments here and there that I realize how much I've changed. I know it sounds asinine, but I haven't been in the presence of an intelligent pretty girl in a long time. I'm sorry to have been rude. I'm sorry to have made you run. The time for running should be over."

"It depends on what you're running from."

"Wounded soldiers, in this case. Nice ones."

"I've suffered considerably at the hands of nice wounded soldiers."

"Have you? I'm sorry."

"Don't be."

"On behalf of my fellow soldiers, I apologize for any and all mistreatment."

"You have no idea what you're apologizing for."

"I know soldiers can be a raucous lot."

Gemma lapsed into silence. He glanced at her before returning his gaze to the fire. She felt his counterretreat, elbowing his way back down the hole he'd ventured out of. The minutes passed. Gemma could feel the distance between them growing. It was absurd. *The war was over.* She leaned toward his chair and briefly covered his hand in hers. It was meant to be a gesture of comfort, a wedge in the widening breach of isolation. But Michael grasped her fingers tightly, locking their hands together. Suddenly she was back in an ambulance with a man ripped open and bleeding. Michael's grip rippled through her, electrifying her. It all came back. She did not need to see his eyes; in the wordless exchange she understood him perfectly. The war was not over, not here.

The sudden and harsh sound of laughter echoed down the hall, and Gemma realized that the interruption she had been waiting for and wanting was now unwelcome. She and Michael had created a fragile camaraderie and she was reluctant to expose it, even to laughter. "That would be my father." Michael released her hand and gripped his cane tightly, preparing to rise. "Come, I'll introduce you."

As they moved toward the door, she wanted to take his hand again, feeling instinctively that they needed each other's protection. She walked closely to him, letting him set the pace.

Gemma thought it was her presence that silenced the two people in the hall, but their eyes were fixed on Michael. They were in evening clothes, faces flushed from the night air. Gemma quickly studied the man who must have been David Lazar. Unlike her calm, cerebral father, this man was restive, with a strained exuberance. Gemma's immediate impression was that he was attempting to cover up a great loss.

"Good Lord," he exclaimed, looking at Michael. Then he laughed. "Look at you! You're walking!"

The woman next to him was dark and petite and dressed in layers of pale green silk. Nothing, not even a strand of hair, was out of place. Her hands were clasped together in a tight economy that conveyed a precise balance of containment and joy. "It's marvelous," she said. "How does it feel?"

Michael said, "Like I've got a stick for a leg. It's not a smooth transport."

"Not yet," his father said. He turned to Gemma. "Gemma, welcome. We're delighted to have you. I only wish it was under better circumstances."

While David Lazar looked nothing like her father, there was an unmistakable resemblance. She tried and failed to identify what it was, ignoring the poignant reminder that her father had spent a great deal of his life somewhere else, with people other than herself.

She stood there in front of him and did not know what to say to the man who felt both like an old acquaintance and a complete stranger. She finally held out her hand, wondering if she should instead hug her father's closest friend. He grasped her hand in a strong, warm grip.

"I'm so glad to meet you," he said. "Your father was right, you're perfectly lovely. This is my wife, Nailah."

Nailah did not hesitate. She stepped forward and embraced Gemma. Gemma closed her eyes against the smaller woman's shoulder and pressed her cheek against her silk dress. She smelled of oranges. For a moment Gemma missed her mother fiercely. Nailah's embrace tightened as the younger woman's body started to softly shake. It had been a long time since someone had held her close. Nailah stroked her hair. "Poor lamb," she said.

"I'm so sorry," Gemma said, pulling herself away. "I don't know where that came from."

"I do," David Lazar said, offering her his handkerchief. "It was probably long overdue. Come, let's have some dinner and I will distract you with stories of days gone by."

Nailah was smiling at Michael. "Really, I can't believe how well you're getting around!"

Her spirit was infectiously warm, but Michael seemed impervious. "I deserve a medal, don't you think?" he said. "Do they have medals for gimp achievement?"

"We'll make one," his father said. "We'll melt down some of Nailah's necklaces and pour a mold. We'll make you a handsome medal for bravery and loss and—thank God—survival."

Michael's eyes found the floor.

"My son is a hero," David continued. "Shot down in a Spitfire and lived to tell the tale."

Michael was failing to smile. The four of them stood in the hall, too loosely connected to move forward as a whole. Gemma realized that the gaiety, forced as it was, was better than this brittle paralysis. Nailah's eyes returned to Michael. David watched them both, lost in sudden melancholy. Michael had removed himself completely. Nothing remained of the man Gemma had glimpsed by the fire. He avoided her eyes, shifted his weight uncomfortably.

"We've been at the museum," David said. "He should have been there tonight. Your father should have been there."

Gemma started to speak but faltered. For once, the impulse to comfort was misplaced. For once, she was the one in need of comfort.

"Well, I'm ravenous," Nailah said. "One never gets enough to eat at these functions." Her light, melodic voice was meant to be reassuring. But nothing, at the moment, was right with these people.

"Yes." David stared abstractly at the floor. "I'm paying for it now, swimming in memories. Drowning maybe."

"Come," Nailah urged. "Let's eat."

She steered them all to the safety of the dining room. Her command and social grace made Gemma think Nailah was older than she looked. Her accent was hard to place. Part British and part, Gemma supposed, Egyptian, though her eyes were lighter than those of the women she had seen on the street. Gemma stared after her, waiting for Michael, who moved haltingly now, an occasional grimace of discomfort contorting his features.

"There was a tribute to Mariette," Nailah explained as they entered the dining room. "The founder of the Egyptian Museum. David gave a presentation on the museum's first years."

"It didn't feel right without your father. Sit close to me, Gemma, I don't hear as well as I used to."

Nailah leaned to touch a long match to two half-burned ivory candlesticks. Between them was a glinting crystal bowl filled with pomegranates and tangerines. Triangles of color winked across the circumference like beacons.

"My father didn't like to talk about Mariette," Gemma said. "I don't think he liked him."

"Understandable." David laughed, guiding Gemma to the seat next to his with hands that were large and warm. "Mariette was unscrupulous, ambitious, and wily," he went on. "Ironically, he was also responsible for the preservation of this country's finest antiquities."

The dining room table had been set for three. David settled himself at the head while Michael circled the room slowly to the empty place opposite Gemma.

As Nailah smoothed a napkin in her lap, a tall, distinguished-looking man in a white robe and skullcap swept soundlessly through a swinging door. His eyes appraised the situation at the table, lingering on Gemma and coming to rest on Michael's empty place setting.

"Amad," David said, "this is Gemma Bastian, Charles's daughter."

Amad bowed his head. "Miss Bastian. I am honored."

"I've known Amad almost as long as I knew your father."

Amad began setting another place in front of Michael. "Amad is a member of my father's new family," Michael said, tipping back in his chair. "Family number two."

Gemma hesitated and then asked, "And who is Anthony?"

After a moment of silence, David said, "My other son."

"Where is he?"

"A question often asked in this household," Michael commented dryly. "Anthony would teach us that the key to popularity is absence."

"Anthony is in the Western Desert," David said. "A few days away. I sent him a letter telling him about your father. They were colleagues—and friends. I imagine he is on his way to Cairo for whatever memorial service you wish to have."

Gemma lowered her eyes. The border of her plate was painted with very tiny, very English fruits. Apples and quince and raspberries.

"Maybe it's not time for that yet," Nailah offered quietly.

Gemma kept her eyes on the tiny fruits. "Tell me more about Mariette."

After a brief silence, Nailah said, "Amad knew Mariette, didn't you, Amad?"

"Yes," Amad said. "He was my first Frenchman."

"You didn't like him any more than Gemma's father did," David said.

"He was a very . . . French Frenchman. And he moved quickly, like a rabbit."

David laughed. "Mariette was a dervish when it came to getting his hands on antiquities. No one had faster fingers."

"Once, I saw him laugh," Amad said. "In that moment he seemed almost like a man."

Amad placed a colorful chopped salad in front of Gemma. She closed her eyes and inhaled. "Garlic," she said. "And something else."

"Coriander," Amad said. "And mint."

"Mind the dark green bits," Michael warned. "They're hot peppers. And if you're worried about your breath, pass."

"I know it's not very British, but I love garlic," Gemma said. "My mother often cooked with it."

"I once had the pleasure of tasting her cooking," David said. "It was when you lived near Hyde Park. You were just a little towheaded thing."

"So I have met you."

"I'll try not to be insulted that you don't remember." David smiled. "Fiona was a lovely woman."

Michael drank half his glass of wine. "Was your mother abandoned in England while her husband went off to dig up buried treasure in Egypt?"

"Michael," his father warned.

Michael looked directly at his father. "Like mine?"

"No," Gemma said evenly. "She could have come."

"So she was actually invited?"

"I think my father would have been delighted."

"But he moved here anyway. Without her. Like my father."

"No," Gemma said, looking between the candles to confront the dark insolence of Michael's face. "He moved here after she was killed in the

Blitz." The table fell silent. Gemma put down her fork. "I'm sorry. That was uncouth."

"No," Michael said, "it was honest."

"Dear Gemma," Nailah said. "What a time you've had."

"Yes, well," Gemma said. "I've found that people can adapt to just about anything. The problem turns out to be when things go back to normal."

Michael raised his glass to her. "Whatever normal is."

Gemma found him again across the table. "I suppose we rise to unknown heights when we have to, don't we? Then we come back down to our peacetime selves. But nothing feels the same."

"War is enormously confusing," David said.

"I found it fairly straightforward," Michael said.

"The clarity of war," his father mused, "is false."

"Is that so?" Michael said.

"War's most dangerous consequence is its seeming simplicity. It reduces conflict, people, and countries to their basest parts, makes you believe there is a definitive good and evil. There isn't. Oversimplification is why we get into wars in the first place."

"Is that the view from a distance?" Michael asked. "Because as far as I know, you've never been even close to a war."

"All I'm saying is the world is more complicated than good and evil. When you begin to understand that circumstances can explain most things, it becomes harder to judge—harder still to kill."

"I know millions of people who would disagree with you. Were they alive, they would argue that evil is alive and well."

"Evil is the absence of good," David maintained. "It is not a force of its own."

"Explain that to the citizens of Hiroshima," Michael countered. "Or Dachau."

Amad entered carrying a white porcelain tureen. For a moment, peace reigned.

"Amad makes the best curry soup in Cairo," Nailah said. "Gemma, you must tell us how we can help you while you're here." There was a softness to Nailah's demeanor that made her seem slightly out of focus. It was matched by her almost impressionistic beauty, a beauty that was too graceful to overwhelm. Gemma followed the line of her gentle, wavy hair, the barely detectable trace of makeup, and the silk dress that was not so much a color as it was a suggestion of a color. Beneath Nailah's symphonic grace was a strength that did not mind being mistaken for something else.

It made Gemma feel sharp and awkward. She became aware of her tailored dress and her bluntly cut hair. She felt that even in candlelight the colors on her face were too bright. Her lipstick was too red, her eyes too blue. She felt pasted together, like a collage.

She looked down at her hands and realized she didn't care. It was an accurate reflection of who she was: shattered, pieced back together, held together by old glue. "I'll need to sort out my father's things," she said. "I suppose I'll need you to take me to his apartment."

"It was just a room, really," David said. "And he let go of it some time ago, without a word, which is just like him. I dropped in on him once and the place had been relet."

"Then where was he staying?"

"In the old days he stayed here. I'm afraid I don't know where his recent digs were. He had been gone so much I figured he just moved his things into his office and slept there when he was in Cairo."

"Then my first stop will be his office. I have to go through his papers anyway."

"That will be a job," said David. "His handwriting is worse than mine. He'd leave me these notes that looked as if he'd given a pigeon some ink and made it walk around on paper. Then he'd be miffed that I didn't meet him for lunch."

"Don't worry," Gemma said. "I can read most of it."

"Well," Nailah said, "don't be in a hurry. Stay with us for as long as you want or need to stay."

"Absolutely," David said. "This will be your home in Cairo. Don't even think about going anywhere else."

Gemma smiled and reached for her wineglass. She was unaccustomed to staying in other people's homes. "So," she said, "Mariette was a very French Frenchman."

David laughed. "Back to Mariette?"

"I'd like to hear more."

"Let me see." David tasted his soup, lost in thought. Even downcast, his eyes dominated his features. They were large and expressive and in memory brought to life a spark that had since been doused. Gemma watched his face with interest. At some point, he had clearly understood the requirements of holding center stage. She could see in the injured face of his son that performing was a regular affair for his father. "I should go back to the fourteenth century," he began. "When an insidious little book called *The Book of Buried Pearls* started circulating in Egypt. It was, in a sense, the first guidebook of Egypt. It told of tombs and treasure and where to find buried antiquities. That nasty little volume was responsible for most of the looting of ancient Egypt. Looting, after all, was not yet illegal. It took hundreds of years to make a law against it and then decades more to enforce the law. That was where Mariette proved useful. He created a place to put all these things."

"His own loot too, I imagine," Gemma added. "Or so I heard."

"As I said, he was unscrupulous. Now we've got antiquities dealers to mediate."

"My father called them thieves," Gemma said.

"Watch what you're saying," Michael warned. "You're enjoying the spoils of an illustrious career of pillaging."

"Oh Michael." Nailah's sigh was like a breeze.

Soup bowls were removed and a platter of grilled prawns and couscous was passed around.

"To some it's an unpleasant reality that in a land that lost most of its ancient history, it is the graceless—and in some cases godless—Europeans who have made the most headway in its recovery," David said. "It is we who have locked statuaries, mummies, sarcophagi, urns, masks, jewels, gold, silver, and even obelisks safely behind the doors of the Egyptian Museum. Michael will tell you that it's not all that well organized yet."

"That's putting it mildly."

"Somewhere amidst the chaos you'll find your father's office."

"I'll take you, if you like," Michael offered. "And maybe we can hear about England for a while. News from the current empire."

"Yes," David said, frowning at his son. "I've gotten carried away. I'm sorry if I've bored you."

"You haven't," Gemma said. "It's fascinating. I'd much rather talk about Egypt. Anyway, I'm too tired to contribute anything halfway interesting."

"You've already disproved that," Michael said.

Gemma folded her napkin and placed it on the table. "My father sent me something," she said quietly. "But the envelope had another name on it before mine. Your son Anthony's." She fished into her pocket. "Trouble is, I'm not sure what it is."

David put on his glasses and peered at the addresses on the envelope. "He could have found a new envelope, you'd think."

"Do you recognize what's inside? I think it's papyrus."

David removed the paper from the envelope and held it in front of him. "Hmm."

"What?"

"It's not old papyrus, for one." David held the paper up to the light. "The letters are Coptic."

"Why are there so many spaces between them? It doesn't seem as if there are actual words."

"There aren't. And I have no idea why. There was no explanation?"

"None."

"Maybe it was just a souvenir."

"Knowing my father, that would be unlikely."

"So you've got a little mystery to solve. I could show it to someone, if you like."

"That's all right." Gemma extended her hand.

David replaced the paper in the envelope and handed it back. "Coincidentally, it's Anthony, your co-addressee, who will be able help you with this. If your father trained him, as I expect he did, he'll be able to make something of it."

"What do you mean, trained him? Trained him how?"

"Sometimes I think he trained him to look for what wasn't necessarily there." Gemma studied the older man's face as it collapsed into humorless fatigue. "Charles had an astounding imagination."

It was an effort to keep her tone light. "You're making him sound unacademic."

"Perhaps the word is 'unorthodox.'"

"I take it you disapproved?"

"At times. At other times it yielded remarkable results."

"So you weren't overjoyed by your son's friendship with my father—by his training."

For a moment, David didn't respond. From across the table, Michael laughed harshly. "I didn't think it was possible," he said, "for Anthony to disappoint."

"It's not that I'm disappointed." David glanced at Gemma. "Maybe it's just that I wish I saw more of him. In recent years, Charles had that privilege."

"When the war ended, Anthony got traded for me, you see," Michael said. "The inferior model."

"Oh Michael." David batted the air weakly.

Before silence could reclaim the table, Gemma moved her chair back. "Well, I think the day finally caught up to me."

"I'm tired as well," Michael said. "Let's hobble upstairs and collapse on our respective beds, shall we, Gemma?"

Gemma didn't want to hobble anywhere with Michael. From the moment his father had entered the house, she felt Michael had forced her to choose between them. Somewhere during the course of the dinner conversation, Gemma's allegiance had shifted to David.

At the top of the stairs, Michael touched her hand, as if to reclaim her. "I'm glad you've come. It's done me good to see another face. I hope you'll let me show you some of Cairo."

"I'll be quite busy, I think."

"You're cross with me."

Gemma turned to face him. "You treat your father badly. It's hard for me to watch. Particularly now."

"You think I'm rude."

"I think you're unkind."

"You don't know him."

"And I don't know you." Gemma turned to the door of her room.

"Let's start over again tomorrow, shall we? Don't cross me off your list yet."

"I haven't crossed you off my list. I'm just tired."

"Sleep well, then, Gemma. Give me another chance in the morning."

Gemma closed the door behind her and sank her gaze with relief into the colors of the room. She sat on the side of her princely bed, her feet not quite touching the ground. Too dazed to unpack, she listened to the sounds of the Lazar house. Shadows from her lantern trembled on the wall. Somewhere there was a draft. She flattened her palms on the fine muslin bedspread. She had no real right to be angry with Michael. Now that she had arrived, her nerves were exposed. The momentum of travel could no longer protect her. The buffer of physical motion was gone, as her father was gone—as his body and face and voice were gone, as even his room was gone. She could not lie on the bed he had slept on, or sit at the table where he'd taken his tea, or look out the window he'd looked out of. There was to be no comfort, nothing to make it more real.

Gemma sat very still and strained to hear something other than her own breathing. Her sense of isolation was cavernous.

She rolled onto her stomach and lightly traced the embroidery she could feel like Braille under her fingers. She could barely make out clusters of roses. English flowers. Had her father once slept here? She laid her cheek against them. She didn't know how long she had been there before she heard the rustle of palms in the garden; the wind was pressing against the thin windows of her room.

Finally, she pulled off her clothes and lay in her slip under the mosquito net, bereft but safely afloat on the pale vessel of her bed. She did not even have the energy to dread the coming days. When she finally closed her eyes, sleep came almost instantly.

CHAPTER THREE

Thomas said to them,
If I tell you one of the sayings He spoke to me,
You would pick up rocks and stone me.
The Gospel of Thomas,
from Nag Hammadi

ANTHONY LAZAR ROLLED along easily on the wavelike motion of his camel. The scorched desert before him was domed by a porcelain blue sky, cracked only by a single strand of cloud. This was how weather began here. A chord, a bar. Then the crashing symphony. He tried not to think about Charles Bastian. Knowing as little as he knew about the circumstances of his death, thinking would do no good. As he fixed his eyes on some unspecified point ahead, other thoughts came and went. He did not stay with any of them for long. He thought briefly about how late their start was, and how far they had to go, and that the winds were coming early this year and they might catch them. Sometimes he thought he could hear them gathering strength behind them. But he did not turn to look. They had been caught before. Looking did not help.

There was no place for fear in the desert. Or impatience. Neither got you anywhere other than where you already were. Once it had been hard to fend off the temptation of these unravelings, to fall into the chasm they offered with the hope of escaping. It was no more of an escape than madness. Wanting something other than what had robbed you of your life. This was something he had learned well in the desert, from men who lived more than a thousand years ago. His professional achievements, he knew, were the effortless fruit of a deeper discipline he had absorbed from this cluster of strange, reclusive men, the earth's first hermits. He had devoted his life to understanding them, and translating from the Coptic their profound, frugal verse.

Recently, he'd made the trip to Cairo more frequently, because, with the aid of Charles Bastian, he'd helped garner the money to build a Coptic museum in Cairo. It had been a challenge to raise money for such a quiet time in history, a time that boasted no gold, no monuments, no burials with untold treasure. A time of no visible splendor.

Splendor was his father's arena, and it had been covered and recovered, and now the spoils from pharaonic Egypt gleamed from inside the finest museums and palaces of the Western world. Much of Egypt had been stolen from her.

His father still didn't understand his friend's change of archaeological course. Anthony did.

THEIR FRIENDSHIP HAD begun at Oxyrhynchus, in Upper Egypt. Anthony was translating writings unearthed at the site of a Christian monastery that had not been inhabited since the third century. A few miles away, Bastian brushed away layer after layer of sand from the arid waste heaps of Oxyrhynchus. The city's infamous mounds of rubbish had quietly preserved treasures since the time of Christ. Bastian worked with a focused intensity that made Anthony wonder if he knew exactly what he was looking for. Once he had asked. Bastian had responded by dipping his eyes into the shelter of his broad-brimmed hat and lapsing into silence.

Anthony, as comfortable with silence as he was in the older man's presence, spoke more freely than he ever had, sharing how he was tracing the wanderings of a handful of holy men, men who, in the fourth century, had struck out away from the cities into unknown territory, forging into the stark, unyielding sands of the desert to find a God that had been stolen from them.

When he first described his hermits, Bastian's eyes grew bright with interest. "Tell me," he had asked, "do you know why they left?"

"Because men who declared themselves the fathers of the new church told them there was only one God and one way to find him—through their church. Because they believed there was more than one way, they were branded as heretics."

Bastian had beamed. "I'm so pleased that you know this. So few people do."

"I think of it often. Imagine one day waking up and being told you cannot worship as you had all your life."

Bastian had stared into the fire for a long time. Finally he spoke. "What would you say if I told you that it was not only your hermits who lost their God?"

"What do you mean?"

"I mean that there were once more than thirty beloved gospels circulating the land, written by apostles who have since been forgotten. When only four were chosen for the New Testament, the others were ordered by the Church Fathers to be destroyed. Even reading them became a crime punishable by death. I ask you, what in those books created so much fear?" Bastian didn't wait for an answer. "Imagine a Christianity that has been lost to us, a Christianity that celebrated the wisdom of all sacred texts, all religions, that valued women, and that believed God existed inside all of us, that there was no need for mediation, no need for priests or rabbis. That we could each find God on our own, without a church. *That's* the Christianity that has been lost to us—*that* was why there was fear." Bastian had arched back to look at the stars. Anthony remembered losing sight of his face. When he returned to the fire, he looked at Anthony with a fervor the younger man had never seen. "I can show you written proof."

"There would have to be a lot of it."

"I would give you gospels, gospels enough for a new New Testament."

Anthony looked at the other man across the fire and did not know if he saw inspiration or madness.

"Do you know why we are both here, in this particular place?" Bastian asked. "It's because this was a place of monasteries, of holy men. Do you know what I believe? I believe those holy men loved those gospels. I believe that when the gospels were outlawed, they hid them."

"Why?"

"Because it's what I would have done."

They had spoken long into the night about the fragments that had been found over the years. There had been many copies of the gospels, most of them written in Coptic. Some of them had survived. Occasionally an entire gospel surfaced in some antiquities shop and quickly vanished into private ownership.

"But don't you see, they belong to everyone?" Bastian demanded. "Had they been included in the Bible instead of being tossed on a rubbish heap, these accounts of the story of Jesus would have changed the course of history." Bastian launched a branch into the fire and watched a small explosion of sparks. "The more I find, the more angry I become."

It was months later, after many such conversations, that Anthony learned that the older man had once been in Catholic seminary. "It was in England and I was young," Bastian said in explanation. "And the truth had importance. I was not given the truth. In God's house, I was not given the truth. I had no choice but to leave."

"Are you still a Christian?"

"I am the oldest Christian. I am the forgotten Christian. My apostles have been buried."

Anthony came to know about these lost apostles, whom Bastian referred to as Gnostics. He agreed with his friend that God existed within everyone, that the way to him was through the wisdom of self-knowledge, through gnosis. Bastian gave words to a belief Anthony had never spoken of, that had come to him quietly but firmly in the peace of the Western Desert. In time, he began to feel that he and Bastian were fighting together their individual wars for that spark of divinity that lay buried inside each of them.

Then Bastian made his first big discovery at Oxyrhynchus. It was only a scrap of papyrus, but through it Anthony glimpsed the world Bastian had described. It was a fragment, a beautiful thing. Bastian established quickly that it was from the lost Gospel of Thomas. Holding it, he was quietly overcome. "This, my friend, could change everything."

"Change what, exactly?" Anthony asked.

Instead of answering, Bastian handed him the fragment. Much of the script had faded completely from the browned papyrus, but some was surprisingly clear. The Coptic lettering was curved and elegant, penned by a scribe who had lived nearly two thousand years ago. Bastian traced the legible script with his finger and read,

> "...to
> Of.....................hi...........................go in,
> ......they.........................trying to go..........
> However, b............se a.................nnocen...........v...."

"I will find the complete text," Bastian said, walking away. Over his shoulder, he added, "And when I do, the apostle Thomas will rise again."

It was Bastian's tone that made Anthony believe him. Studying the fragment, Anthony understood for the first time what his father's friend was trying to do. He understood why he was waiting, hovering like a hawk. Bastian had spent years gathering the pieces to a story he would one day offer the world. A story that might, as Bastian had said, change everything.

Before long, Anthony began to feel Bastian's impatience. He offered to help him in his search. But the older man declined. Soon thereafter, Anthony felt his friend distance himself. He ceased discussing his work. When Anthony asked him why, Bastian answered, "Because it's not safe material, Anthony. And you're young yet. I keep my silence because you are my friend."

Then came the day Anthony woke to find Bastian and his man Bashir gone. Bastian had left a brief note pinned to the flap of Anthony's tent: *Sorry to leave so abruptly, but we never know when God will come calling. We will meet again in Cairo.*

✛　✛　✛

W HEN HIS TRANSLATIONS were completed, Anthony left Oxyrhynchus for the ruins at Kharga Oasis, stopping briefly in Cairo to replenish
his supplies and see his parents. His first question was about Charles Bastian. The inquiry prompted a now familiar discomfort in his father. No,
they had not seen him. Then, as Anthony settled in for lunch, David Lazar
lamented as he often did that he had lost his son to the desert. His mother
did not make such pronouncements. After lunch, she sat with Anthony in
the garden as the shadows swept across his face and waited for her son to
find his way to her.

That afternoon they took their tea under the shade of the date palms.
She worked on her embroidery while he drew figures in the gravel with a
branch. It was when he ignored Amad's cake for a quarter of an hour that
she put her embroidery down.

"Anthony," she said.

"I am learning," he began.

"Tell me."

"I am learning that history is told by the winners. That is why it is
uncontested. But every story is a story told by man. Even stories about
God." Anthony snapped his branch in half. Then he snapped the halves
into quarters. Then he threw the bundle into the bushes. Nailah resumed
her needlework.

Anthony said gently, "Don't worry about me, Mother."

Nailah paused with her needle. "I want you to tell me what you've
found," she said.

"I can't. It's not mine to tell."

"Then you cannot tell me not to worry."

That evening, she found him back in the fading light of the garden
bent over a New Testament Bible.

"Tell me," she said, taking it from him and holding it in both hands like
a brick, "why are you always reading this book?"

Anthony did not answer. He picked up a flower that had fallen from
the hibiscus tree and laid it on her skirt. "Some find it important." He

smiled because his mother had configured her own hybrid religion that resolutely ignored texts. "You're welcome to borrow it."

"I want to know what you've been doing, Anthony."

"What have I been doing?" he repeated absently. "I've been listening to a friend," he said. "A friend who has told me a different story about Christianity." He tapped the Bible. "Not the story we've been given here. He may find proof of this. Until then I don't know if he is mad or sane."

She was not listening as carefully as she was watching. "You're afraid."

He took her hand but would not look at her.

"Are you in danger?" she pressed.

"No. Though I have a feeling"—Anthony paused—"my friend might be."

"Charles?" She took her hand from him. "The fear you're trying to hide is spreading to my heart."

"No, Mother. This is a time for courage. Before our eyes, history may change. We must be prepared to watch it."

He now thought that his mother, with her fine intuition, had understood before he had. She had sensed the danger. And he had not been prepared.

Anthony pulled his camel's reins and waited for Zira, who had dozed off balanced on the back of his camel. They were nearly there.

At times his life between Cairo and the desert felt like a strenuous dance between the secular and the sacred, between the material and the spiritual. Then sometimes, on journeys between the two worlds, like this one now, he experienced the rare and wild spin that dizzied the separate parts into one. And for an immeasurable instant, it was all effortless and beautiful. The desert and Cairo were painted into the same extraordinary picture. It was in those moments he thought he was coming closer to what the desert fathers had identified as God. The only person he knew who understood this was Charles Bastian.

Anthony and Zira slowed as they neared the top of the al-Takir dune. Cairo lay in the distance under a reddish haze. Giza shimmered in the heat. From here it looked like a city a child might build, whimsically replacing squares with triangles.

The wind was rising. Anthony covered his face with his headscarf. He wondered where Charles Bastian had died, and how. He hoped he had been prepared, that his final emotion had not been fear.

Anthony did not go home to Kit Kat, where his houseboat rocked on the edge of the Nile. He went instead to East Cairo, to the City of the Dead. He stood at the entrance of the Tomb of the Caliphs. Jacket flapping in the dry wind, he stared out at the rooftops that sheltered the unimaginable graveyard below and searched for the spirit of his friend.

Traveling back through the city, past the mosques and palaces of Ed Darb and El Muski, he allowed himself to miss the city he had abandoned, the swirl of heat and color and always, in the raised dust that covered the worn stones of the city like talcum, the presence of God. When the minarets wailed for afternoon prayer, Anthony leaned in a doorway and watched as men flowed in tributaries to the mosques, remembering well the confused sense of belonging and isolation when these people left to worship a God he was not born to know.

Anthony stopped for a coffee at an outdoor café where he could watch the street as he read a newspaper. What he read told him that Cairo was changing more quickly than he thought. Putting the paper down, he observed a group of men sitting at the far end of the café. In the bits of conversation, he could hear in their voices a discontent that, like a fever, climbed higher and higher.

An hour later he found himself not at home but in front of the Egyptian Museum, the place where Charles Bastian's body had been found. Instead of entering, he sat on a bench, watching people come and go. Finally, disallowing thought, he rose and strode quickly to the entrance of the building. Inside it was unnaturally cool and dark. Anthony was aware of the dampness of his shirt, of the lost heat of the afternoon. He started down the empty hallway, slowing as he passed Bastian's office. He paused to press his hand briefly against a door that had never been locked to him.

He stood in the doorway of his own office, which seemed uninhabitable. He had lost his sense for what was in it. The overhead light was out.

He flicked it back and forth absently, standing in the blue-gray dimness. Finally he moved to switch on the desk lamp. He leaned against the desk for another long moment before committing to the chair, realizing he would not stay in Cairo longer than he had to. There was nothing for him here, not now.

He had just finished going through his office mail when there was a knock on his door. He rose when he saw who it was. Togo Mina, the director of the new Coptic Museum, did not often drop in on people. Anthony had met him only a few times and had observed only that Mina had an open, intelligent face and the quick, precise movements of a small man.

"Lazar," he said, "we need to talk."

Mina lowered himself to a chair and settled into a state of nervous suspension. He put the briefcase he was carrying on his lap and rubbed his hands together, his lively brown eyes surveying the room. "As you know, Cairo is a city of rumors," he said. "Some of them reach me. I have heard talk of a finding, a finding so monumental that at first I dismissed it. One rumor does not a finding make. But there have been more rumors since, and now it seems we are on top of perhaps the millennium's most important archaeological discovery. I'm afraid in my skepticism I've lost valuable time." Anthony waited as Mina rearranged himself on the unforgiving wooden chair. It's Bastian, Anthony thought. It's Bastian's find.

"You knew Charles Bastian," Mina said, as if Anthony had spoken out loud.

"We were colleagues."

"You were friends," Mina said. Anthony waited until the other man scowled. "I'm not used to stumbling around in the dark in a museum I am supposedly directing. We may be talking about the lost gospels here. Missing since the fourth century. I think Charles Bastian had seen them."

Anthony looked impassively at Mina. "Why do you think that?"

"Because, man, he was right there! I have his expenses. Two months ago he was in Southern Egypt, near Luxor. A place called Nag Hammadi, where these gospels were supposedly found." Mina opened his briefcase and removed a file. "He took three camels for two weeks. He paid his felucca captain well. He ate cheaply. He also paid someone in Nag

Hammadi, a Mr. Bashir." He looked up at Anthony. "Come on, man, there isn't time!"

"What do you want from me?"

"Stephan Sutton from the British Museum died near Nag Hammadi a few months back. Some sort of rock slide. A strange coincidence, don't you think?"

Anthony shrugged. "It happens."

Mina rose abruptly. "It strikes me as odd that you should be so indifferent to the future of the museum you and your friend Bastian helped to build."

Anthony's eyes locked onto Mina's. "They said it was his heart. Is that true?"

Mina turned away. "Because Christendom might be upended by this find, there are a number of parties in pursuit. No one will talk to me, of course. Quite rightly. If in fact these gospels exist, and if I find that any portion of them is headed out of the country, I will initiate legal action immediately. I will do anything I can to keep them from leaving Egypt. I think some of them are in Cairo as we speak—and may have been here for months. They might have already passed into private ownership, which would be a travesty."

"How do you know they're in Cairo?"

"Because the people who were chasing them in Nag Hammadi are now here. Because your friend died here, in Cairo."

"I suppose you went through his office."

"And found nothing. Will you help me?"

Anthony hesitated. "My work is in Kharga."

"Kharga can wait."

Anthony looked at the ceiling. "I need some time."

"Listen to me, Lazar, there is no time. I know you and Bastian were friends, and I know you prefer to work alone. I'm asking you to do something that is perhaps uncomfortable for you."

Anthony held Mina's eye for a moment longer. "All right," he said. "Tell me what you know."

Mina sat down again. "Here's the rumor: It appears that some desert outlaw got his hands on a number of these manuscripts—somewhere in or around Nag Hammadi, I'm guessing. The next step would be to sell them to someone in Cairo. Once they're here, transit out of the country is all too easy. I can't allow that to happen. You grew up here, Lazar. You've got contacts through your father. See if you can find out something before they're smuggled out. In the meantime I'm sending a man to Nag Hammadi to see what he can find."

"I would consider going."

"I know you would, but I need you here." Mina stood with finality. "I am happy to have your compliance, reluctant though it is."

"You have an enviable style of negotiation."

"That is why I direct. Now, you know this business well enough to tread carefully." He paused at the door. "And there's the Bastian girl."

"The Bastian girl?"

"His daughter. She's just arrived in Cairo and will be rummaging around in his office any day. That makes me uncomfortable. Her father was working on very sensitive material and he was found dead. I don't believe in coincidence, not in Egypt. Do what you can to hurry her up and get her out of Cairo."

Anthony smiled in slow incredulity. "How could I possibly do that?"

"Exert gentle pressure. It shouldn't be too hard. She's staying at your father's home."

"Mina," Anthony protested, "my plate is now full."

"All right, all right. At the moment I'm relieved to have you as an ally. I'm not a man without instinct. I think I can trust you."

Anthony inclined his head in slight acknowledgment. "I don't know if you should. I don't know if you want the help of a man who knew Bastian as well as I did, who does not believe it possible that he had a weak heart."

Mina studied the younger man and stepped back into the room. "If we are to be a team, perhaps you should tell me more about what your friend Bastian was working on. Unless, of course, you find trusting me an impossibility."

Anthony remained silent.

"Are you protecting someone?" Mina asked, coming closer. "Yourself, maybe?"

Anthony looked up. "I'm protecting Bastian," he said simply.

"Bastian is dead."

"And I fear what the world will do to his memory. I myself did him the dishonor of thinking he was mad." He paused.

"His work was controversial," Mina said.

Anthony pressed his fingertips together and realized he could not prevent Bastian's conjectures from one day spilling out into the world. The most he could now do was offer his own, hard-won understanding. He glanced at Mina, who was doing his best to look patient. "Bastian claimed an entire branch of Christianity had been buried. He said that Christianity had been cleaved, like a man from a woman, that we would war and destroy and be incapable of understanding ourselves or God until it was made whole again."

Mina stared. "Is there more?"

Anthony looked past him to the wall, his eyes wandering the terrain of a map of the Western Desert. He half smiled and sat back in his chair, keeping his eyes on the other man as he spoke. "Bastian believed that everything that ailed Christianity today would be healed by these hidden teachings. He was looking for the texts to prove this. He once said that he was going to find enough evidence to make a new New Testament. He said he would bring back forgotten apostles, apostles who would resurrect an old religion—and the true Jesus." Anthony inhaled. "Mad or not, if this find is what I think it is, I can understand why he is dead."

Mina sat for a long moment and then slowly rose. "As soon as you know anything, you come to me straightaway."

"I will do what I can."

"Good. Because we're not the only interested parties." Before he let himself out, Mina turned. "This is a race, you see. A bloody race."

AFTER MINA LEFT, Anthony sat in his office for a long time thinking. He had been back only a day and already a web was weaving itself around him. After a while he gathered his things and prepared to return home, wondering if this race was his to run. He would do what he could to help Mina. But this had been Bastian's realm—and there had been too much death already. His world was far from here, far from murderous races.

A trip to Nag Hammadi would have been the best thing for everyone, he thought, locking his office. He was thinking not just of his own comfort. Anthony had seen his brother once since he'd returned from the war. Michael had been thin, weak, and venomous. The distilled essence of his worst self. Anthony was the first place he directed the bile and fury of his pain. It had been a regrettable outcome, the amputation. Staying away from Cairo was the most generous gift Anthony could offer his brother. Michael, predictably, chose to willfully misunderstand, adding his brother's long absences to his list of transgressions. There was nothing for Anthony to do but fight to keep his love for his brother free of pity, which Michael could smell like a dog and hated more than he hated his now detestable life. A life he had once held with pride and a certain glory, as if to say to his brother, *Even after you took everything from me, I survived.*

Mina didn't know what he was asking. Frequenting his family home was a sentence, a trial he wasn't sure he could, at this point in time, gracefully endure.

CHAPTER FOUR

Jesus said, As for you,
be on guard against the world.
Arm yourself with great strength . . .
for the trouble you expect will come.

The Gospel of Thomas,
from Nag Hammadi

GEMMA AND MICHAEL left the house in the effulgent light of mid-morning. The fissure that had opened up between them the night before seemed to have been bridged by the light of day. Michael found her in the kitchen drinking coffee, skimming the English newspaper of the week before. He seemed almost happy. He announced that he was going to show her the river of life.

"Before it gets too bloody hot," he added. When she offered nothing more than a fleeting smile, he said, "It would help me if you came. I'm not entirely sure about this leg of mine."

Gemma looked up at him as if to measure the weight of his need.

"I'll take you to the museum," he offered.

She laid down the paper. "Let me get my hat."

THEY WALKED ALONG narrow, tree-lined streets shaded by arching branches. The sidewalks were bordered with neatly manicured shrubs sprinkled evenly with blossoms. The morning air was cool and abhorrently damp. As they walked, Michael pointed out various embassies and residences of note. Gemma listened, paying attention more to his gait, which was too fast for someone with a new leg. The wooden legs were hard, she knew, jamming the joints like a piston. She kept her own pace leisurely, pausing to look at houses and flowers, aware that he was already straining; his brow was damp and there were violent spots of red on each sallow cheek.

"One day I'll take you to the Citadel," he told her, "the highest point in Cairo. From there our little Garden City looks like a pathetic smudge of green."

"Surely it's prettier than that."

"Not from there. What it is is a monument to British determination. And denial. You don't feel like you're in the desert here, do you?"

"No, it feels more like England."

"Exactly. In the mid-nineteenth century, every inch of this elite neighborhood was planted with some kind of greenery. Then the soil was saturated with so much water that it turned into a veritable greenhouse. As intended, the little enclave sprouted and started to look almost like home. I suppose it was meant to remind them of their green isle—maybe more to distract them from whatever madness possessed them to live in the desert in the first place."

"Where does the water come from?"

"They steal it from the Nile. The problem is that when they leave their oasis, they still find the desert. It will always be there. The inhabitants of Garden City are as rarefied and doomed as a bunch of hothouse flowers. I know because in a short period of time I've become one of them."

"Come," Gemma urged. "Let's escape the greenhouse."

On the west, Garden City was bordered by the Nile, and it was this general direction Michael and Gemma took when they left the house. By the time they reached the river, Michael seemed spent. They had left the shade of Garden City and entered hot, vibrant Cairo. The city had clashed like a cymbal around Gemma's head as they made their way down a street crowded with donkeys and camels. Thick bands of illuminated dust rose around them as sunlight pressed through slats and roofs and the narrow spaces between buildings. Above them, chickens perched noisily in the windows of open-air homes. Robed men and women carrying baskets and bundles elbowed their way through throngs of vendors setting up tents cluttered with wares. Gemma coughed against a cloud of dust churned up by a clanging herd of black goats.

"I'm trying to scare you," Michael said, offering her a handkerchief, "so we don't have to do this again."

She shook her head and waved away his handkerchief. "I'm fine."

"Here's the river." He led her to a bench on Sharia Corniche El-Nil. The languid, colorless Nile flowed slowly past and the sails of feluccas flapped in the windless morning. Across the river two women wrung out their washing on the shore, twisting the moisture from long sheets held between them. A man and a boy stood barefoot in the shallows and threw a fishing net. Above them the palms were high enough to stir with a breeze Gemma could not feel. She was uncomfortably damp and inexplicably dirty, but she smiled from under her hat. "I think it's beautiful."

"So I failed."

"Believe me, I was prepared not to like it, but I do. I like all the life. It's exciting."

"You can have it. I'll take soggy old England any day."

Gemma rolled up the sleeves of her blouse. "Will you go back?"

"To what?"

"To your country. Life must go on, I've been told." Gemma tilted her head to the sun and closed her eyes. "Have you ever seen such a sun?"

Michael leaned over and kissed her quickly on the lips. Gemma's eyes opened in alarm as she touched her mouth.

"What was that for?"

"You just look so pretty."

"But you don't just kiss somebody because you like how they look. You don't."

"I enjoy your company."

Gemma shook her head. Michael rose without his cane, stuffed one of his hands in his pocket and jingled some coins. He looked down at her abjectly as she handed him the cane. "You're right," he said and began walking away. Gemma let him walk for a while and then followed him, quickly catching up.

"Let's forget it, shall we?"

"I used to know what the right thing was," he said. "Now, without trying very hard, I bungle things."

They stood aside as an impatient old man passed, pulling a laden and rebellious donkey.

"You haven't bungled anything."

"I've upset you."

"You surprised me. It's not the same thing."

He pressed her hand and held her in front of him. His eyes probed hers with quiet intensity. She was momentarily entranced by the boyish sweetness of his face. She felt she was looking at the ghost of the man who lived before the war. "You see"—he took her hand and put it on the scar at his lip—"I didn't know if I could kiss with this."

Gemma closed her eyes to his beautiful, ruined face. Then she stood on her tiptoes and pressed her mouth against his. His lips were soft and held her for longer than she intended. She returned to her feet, dropping from his altitude with some relief. "I don't think you'll have difficulty."

He had caught her hand. "Gemma," he said.

Gemma smiled, invoking her bright nurse's professionalism. "Let's go, shall we?"

They resumed their walk. He had inherited a full allotment of his father's charm, she thought; it lay beneath his bitter shell like a deep, cool reservoir. No wonder he had ventured a kiss. He had probably never been turned away by a woman in his life.

"Here we are." Michael gestured to a pinkish marble building with pillars and a congregation of miniature palms at the entrance. "There's a café across the square," he said. "I'll buy a newspaper and post myself there. Take your time."

"I'll just take a quick look. You don't mind?"

"Of course not."

Gemma did not enter the vast exhibit hall of the museum. She followed David's instructions straight to the lower level and her father's office, using the key David had given her to open the door. It had been her father's key. At first it didn't seem to fit. Gemma swore and jiggled it until it finally turned. Then the door itself seemed swollen; she had to push it open with her shoulder.

She froze when she saw there was someone already there. A middle-aged man looked up at her from her father's file cabinet. A thin layer of ginger-colored hair had been combed over an otherwise bald head. They stood staring at each other. "Is this Charles Bastian's office?" Gemma asked.

The man continued to look at her without answering. His eyes were pale and held hers in a vague, watery focus.

"Is it?" she demanded.

"And you are?"

"His daughter." Gemma watched as a smile deepened the lines around his eyes and the round face took on the semblance of warmth—familiarity, even.

"Yes," he said, "I see the likeness." The accent was English and university-educated.

"Do I know you?" she asked.

"We've never met. I was an acquaintance of your father's."

"Do you mind if I ask what are you doing in his file cabinet?"

"Just a quick perusal." He smiled fleetingly. "Museum business."

"What does that mean exactly?"

"It means it shouldn't concern you."

"Everything about my father concerns me."

"Your father was involved with material that didn't belong to him. I don't know that it should concern you."

"Does this material belong to you?" Gemma demanded.

For a moment, the composure slipped from his face.

"I think you should leave," Gemma said.

The man took his coat from the chair, moving with unrepentant slowness. "If I were you, I would finish your business here quickly," he said. "It may not be the safest place to be."

Gemma kept the door open and stood against the wall. She did not take her eyes off him. "If you could tell me your name and where to find you, I could contact you if I found anything important."

"Just take my advice, and close his office as quickly as you can."

Gemma held out her hand. "Unless you want me to notify security, I think you'd better give me your key."

She stood there as he placed the key in her open palm. "Forgive me," he said softly. "I should have offered my condolences." Before she could pull her hand away, he grasped her hand with his cool, damp fingers. "He will be missed."

Chilled, she locked the door behind him and dropped both keys into her pocket. She leaned against the door and breathed down a rising apprehension. This was the second man looking for something her father had had. She remained leaning there until her apprehension was replaced by irritation. These men were interfering, coming between her and her father, not letting her be alone with him. She did not move until she could feel him again.

Her father's office was small, with a high ceiling. It looked unnaturally neat for him, but it had probably been tidied up by either the police or the museum staff. She circled the large leather office chair, the chair where he'd been found. She kept her distance from it, pacing around the small space, glancing at the stacks of material. She touched nothing. Among the maps on the wall hung a dark image that Gemma took to be the Virgin Mary and Jesus. Her father, ex-seminarian, categorically opposed to religious iconography, had decorated his office wall with an image of the Virgin Mary. He had never hung anything but maps on his walls.

Gemma turned away from it. His appointment book lay on the desk like a souvenir. She opened it and glanced at the life he had been leading, the extended arrows connecting the days and weeks of travel, the cryptic notations of his time in Cairo. A few dates to ride at the Giza Stables. She put her fingertip on the initials *A.D.—p.m.*, which appeared almost every day for a month before his death. After Death, she thought, postmortem. There was an appointment with a bank manager and a realtor's card folded into a flyer of a house for sale. She studied the sketch of a handsome house, the details of the property. There were gardens, a small orchard. Was this the house they were meant to live in? Holding the card in front of her, she reached for the phone and dialed the realtor's number.

"I'm calling on behalf of Charles Bastian," she said when a Mr. Ascomb answered.

"Bastian?" The man was slightly frantic. "He was meant to meet me weeks ago. Now the house has sold. I had no way to reach him, you understand?"

"I understand," Gemma said. "So he wanted to buy the house?"

"We had already completed the paperwork. Who are you, his secretary?"

"No. But I apologize on his behalf."

"Have him phone me if he's still in the market."

"Thank you."

Gemma replaced the receiver. She flipped through to the end of the appointment book. Nothing. But wedged in the front she found a newspaper article, folded twice over. It was a story about a man who had perished in a rock slide, a British archaeologist. He'd been found in Southern Egypt near a place called Nag Hammadi. Stephan Sutton. Gemma wrote down the name and the place, pronouncing the unfamiliar syllables out loud. She copied the address of the bank and added underneath *A.D.—p.m.*

Finally, she sat down in the chair and swiveled, letting her eyes wander the room. She assumed the position she imagined he'd been in and laid her head down on the desk. How had he possibly died here? She needed the details; she needed to talk to David Lazar, to someone who knew what had happened. At the moment she couldn't believe her father, seldom sick with even a head cold, had simply sat down one day in his office chair and died. Finding a scavenger in his file cabinet made her believe it less.

She realized she had failed to get the name of the ginger-haired man. *What happened to you?* She closed her eyes and silently entreated her father to speak to her.

A moment later, she raised her head and stared again at the picture of the Virgin Mary on the wall. She rose and stood in front of the age-chipped frame. Then she lifted it to see the inscription on the back. *Isis and Horus, (second century), Virgin Goddess and child.* It wasn't the Virgin Mary after all. But the likeness was uncanny, down to the posture of the baby and the way the mother held it. She replaced the frame and went to the bookshelf, removing the most concise volume on Egyptian mythology and stashing it in her purse.

I NEED TO go to the bank," she told Michael when she rejoined him at his café. "The Bank of Egypt. Is it far?"

He folded his newspaper and finished his beer. Gemma noticed his color was better. He pointed across the square. "It's just there."

"Do you mind?"

"Of course I don't. We're here, aren't we? I hope it's good news."

The bank was supported by ivory-colored pillars and planted with hibiscus. Inside, the veined marble floors and soaring panels made it feel colossally empty. She was quickly seated in front of the manager her father had named. He looked at her kindly now, ignoring the jangle of his telephone. She tried to see his eyes behind the smudge of his bifocals as he leaned toward her, one hand extended. She felt suddenly like crying. "My father was Charles Bastian," she managed to say. "I believe he had an account here."

"Miss Bastian. I'm so sorry."

Gemma fixed her eyes on the desk. "I've come to take care of his affairs. I know he was meant to meet with you the week before he died."

"And he did. He was in the process of purchasing a house. We set up a transfer of funds. Only, on the day of the transfer, your father's account was nearly empty. Needless to say, when we didn't hear from him, we could not go through with the purchase."

"Where was the money coming from, do you know? Where did it go?"

"I don't know. He was quite confident that it would be here on the day of transfer."

"Did he say anything else? Anything at all?"

"It was a short conversation, I'm afraid."

Gemma sat in silence. Around her, she could hear no voices, only whispers. The bank felt like a tomb. "If you think of anything, if anything else comes up, will you contact me? I'm staying at this number."

"Yes, of course, Miss Bastian. You'll let me know what you'd like to do with the remaining funds?"

"I suppose you can make me out a check."

Good news?" Michael asked when she rejoined him. He was finishing a second beer, and he seemed almost chipper.

"My father was a poor man. It's not really news."

"Oh dear."

"I would have been shocked to find money, to be honest."

Michael left some bills on the table and they began walking.

"There was someone in his office at the museum," she said. "A man. I didn't get his name. He was looking for something. I didn't like him."

"That whole museum lot is monstrously unscrupulous and competitive. So my father says."

"I don't think he was from the museum. But he had a key."

Michael glanced at her. "It scared you."

"A bit."

"Well, you were in your father's office, where he died. You weren't expecting to see anyone there. It was a shock. Perfectly understandable."

Gemma looked over her shoulder as they walked away from the museum.

"Well, the world is still turning," Michael reported. "The news of the day is that Israel has formed something called Sherut Avir, a tiny air force that's meant to protect them from the big bad Arabs. It looks like Egypt is going to have another war. If they let me fly in it, I'd even consider becoming a bloody Egyptian."

Gemma tried to listen, keeping her eyes on the street ahead as they wound their way around mounds of fragrant tobacco and tiers of glass water pipes. She began doing financial calculations, absently watching the eyes of passersby fix on Michael's marred face with both fascination and repulsion. The street narrowed and became an alley. Michael was forced to walk behind her. She deliberately slowed her pace, feigning interest in the textiles and weavings hanging above them from ropes. She stood on her toes to inspect the intricate geometric patterns and scenes of ancient Egyptians communing with gods that were horned, fanged, and winged. Then she touched Michael's sleeve. "Maybe you need work," she said. "A job."

"There's nothing for me to do here."

"Don't be silly. You're an educated, intelligent young man."

"I was a pilot."

"Before you were a pilot, you were something else."

"No," Michael said. "I was nothing else."

She turned to him. "You were," she insisted.

He leaned heavily on his cane. "I don't remember. I'm not sure it even matters, or that I care one way or the other." He was looking over Gemma's shoulder.

She followed his gaze. They were at an intersection of two main avenues. "Where are we?" she asked.

"Very near to the Grand Hotel." Michael motioned. "Where we could have a drink and cool off."

"Right, then. Let's go."

The sight of the hotel relieved them both. Michael was suddenly talkative. "It's an infamous old watering hole, the Grand, built in 1869, to mark the opening of the Suez Canal. But really Ismail Pasha built it for Empress Eugénie. He wanted to impress her."

"It looks like a palace."

"Yes, well, men will do anything, it seems."

They arrived at an outdoor restaurant surrounded by a garden and a maze of graveled pathways. Guests strolled under parasols and perched on benches next to carp-filled pools that burbled and swelled as the fish fought over invisible bits of food. The maître d' led them to a shaded corner table where the sun filtered down between large canvas umbrellas and the fronds of date palms that bent in the wind. Michael ordered mint juleps. The day's warmth and the walk eased Gemma's nerves. She rested her head back on her wicker chair, happy to be in a beautiful place with someone who was able, even temporarily, to transport her from her own life.

When their drinks arrived, she pulled her father's book on mythology from her purse. "What do you know about the goddess Isis?" she asked Michael.

"I pride myself on knowing next to nothing about my father's country."

"How absurd."

Michael smiled.

"Well, you might be missing out. Listen to this." Gemma read, " 'Isis married the god Osiris, who was murdered by jealous rivals, among them the god Set, who sealed him in a coffin and sent it out to sea. In a state of profound grief, Isis recovered the coffin and vowed to bury her beloved properly. When Set discovered the coffin Isis had recovered and hidden on the banks of the Nile, he opened it and murdered Osiris all over again, this time dismembering him into fourteen pieces, which he scattered for the crocodiles. With the help of seven scorpions, Isis searched for Osiris's body, joining each piece she found to reform him and eventually bringing him back to life. Osiris was Egypt's first mummy.' " Gemma paused. "Here's an intriguing postscript: 'Isis and her scorpions found everything but Osiris's penis—and so it was magically that Isis conceived her son, Horus. With this act, Isis earned the status of Virgin Mother and for thousands of years was known to embody the greatest female power of all, the ability to bring life from the lifeless.' "

"What a sordid little tale."

"My father has a lithograph of Isis on his wall."

"Your father was a man of sordid tastes."

Gemma lowered the book. "What do you know of his tastes?"

Michael laughed. "He befriended my brother, for one."

"Your brother is sordid?"

"My brother is not what you would call easy company. Who knows what they got up to out there in the desert, no womenfolk for miles. Sordid might be just the beginning."

Gemma plunged her gaze into the carp pool. "I like that you don't treat me like porcelain."

"Well, you're clearly made of tougher stuff."

Gemma let her mind drift. Half listening to another conversation, she heard a word she vaguely recognized, a word that interested her. She thought for a moment, tried to chase after it to see if it was a place or a name or just a word. Whatever it was, it was gone. She realized she was tired.

She straightened, returning to Michael. "I'd like to hear what happened."

"What happened?"

"In the war."

Michael shook his head.

"Your father told me you flew a Spitfire. I saw one once. It had red circles painted on its wings. They looked like targets. At the time I wondered why anyone would want to paint targets on their airplane."

"It's so we can recognize each other. Don't want to shoot down the wrong plane."

"Ah. That seems sensible."

Michael laughed.

"So what was all the brouhaha about the Spitfire?"

"The brouhaha is that they're remarkable airplanes. During the war, they kept improving on the original. The first engine, the Merlin, became faster with the Griffon, the most powerful engine ever made. It could be adapted for low or high altitudes—it could be tropicalized, navalized. It was a brilliant plane."

Gemma listened, twirling a sprig of mint between her fingers. For a moment she thought about the lithograph of the virgin goddess and child in her father's office. Really, it was quite strange. A waiter brought a bowl of salted nuts. They ordered two more juleps. "So you fly around up there in a group? What do they call it, a squadron? Forgive my ignorance, but I dealt with fliers after they left the air."

"Yes, it's called a squadron. And yes, you often fly in formation with other planes. But sometimes you fly alone. It depends on the mission. If you fly a lone mission, you usually have a wingman." He smiled. "I had a good wingman."

"And a wingman flies on your wing?"

"He watches your back. A guardian angel. Mine was Frank Sturgeon. Great flier. We had hand signals. There were official hand signals. But we had our own. We broke the rules."

"Can you really see each other's hands up there?"

"We could. But Frank and I were different from the other pilots."

"You were better fliers."

"Better fliers or daredevils, I don't know. Our skill didn't do us much good in the end, did it? Now I think I should have taken a desk job like my friend Timothy. I thought he was a pansy to request it, but he had a wife and baby. Said he didn't want to risk it. He had responsibility. Not me. I was the idiot. My head was filled with dreams of glory. I wanted to be the best."

"It sounds like you were."

"It's not for war, that kind of thinking. It's for sports and school."

"I would think that's exactly the kind of thinking you want in a war."

"It isn't."

"Why?"

"Because"—Michael tapped ice into his mouth—"it isn't just you out there."

Before he finished his second julep, Michael ordered a third. Gemma ordered tea and surreptitiously studied his scar. The tissue was a smooth band that curved like a crescent into his mouth.

"I miss it," he said. "I miss the war."

The tables around them started to fill with more Europeans. "Everyone's so nicely dressed," Gemma commented.

"Oh yes, Cairo's very glamorous. They're living in a fantasy, these expats. I find their company tiresome."

Gemma dropped a cube of sugar into her tea. "Isolating yourself won't help," she said.

"Won't help with what?" Michael asked hotly.

Gemma raised her eyebrows. "With getting back to the world. With moving on from the war."

Michael leaned back in his chair, his mouth pressed in a bitter seam. "I don't know that I'm isolating myself. I just don't have much in common with these people."

"It's taken me a while to realize that I'm not alone. So many people lost so much."

"Not these people."

"You don't know that."

"Gemma, you're sermonizing."

"I'm sorry."

"Don't sermonize. It's boring."

"I can't help it. I've had two mint juleps. It's my training."

"What exactly?"

She paused. "To bring people back."

"It's a bit late for that."

"Is it? I don't see a corpse. I see a man who lost a leg."

"I know about the leg." He smiled tentatively. "It's the man bit I'm not sure of." He stared straight ahead. In profile, she could see only the perfect side of his face, the proud cheekbone and jaw, the long tapering eyebrow. "Maybe you could help me with that."

She closed her eyes to remember the other half of his face. "Maybe I could."

He spoke without turning. "Tell me, with all you've lost, do you consider yourself lucky?"

"No," she answered quickly. Then she corrected herself. "Yes."

"Well, you're further along than I am. I'm still wallowing in self-pity, as you can see."

"It takes time."

Michael looked at his watch. "You lost your father only weeks ago and already you're feeling lucky. I'd say that's pretty fast work."

Gemma pushed her tea away. She felt suddenly stranded under their umbrella, marooned on an island of memory and loss. "I think I'd like to walk now," she said. "Shall we call you a taxi?"

"That was brutish. I'm sorry, Gemma. I lost a leg. You lost your family. I'm feeling small. Do you understand?"

Gemma cautioned him with her hand. "Let's not speak about it anymore. Please."

"Frank died," Michael said quickly. "I left him. I went after a German. I didn't even look to see if he was there."

"It happens," Gemma said flatly. "Millions of people died in the war. I'm sure most of them had friends who lived and feel like you do."

He pressed her hand to his lips. "You're quite beautiful. You don't seem to know it. Not like some girls."

"My father used to say never mind how you look because it all goes to hell in a handbasket someday."

Michael smiled. "For some of us sooner than others."

Gemma pushed her chair back. "Let's go to the market."

"The market?" He squinted up at her. "That's the Islamic part of the city."

"I know."

"It can be unpleasant."

"I don't care."

"All right, then. To the market."

"We can get a taxi."

"No, you wanted a walk, so we'll walk."

"You're sure you're up to it?"

"You want to see Cairo, that's the way to do it."

BEING SLIGHTLY DRUNK did not help Michael's agility. It did make him garrulous. He limped unsteadily down the street, lifting his cane for emphasis as he passed judgment on the current state of Egypt, effectively masking his physical discomfort with bombast.

"You may not have noticed yet, but this country is in shambles. They've got themselves a king who's spending all their money. Apparently, the natives are getting restless. King Farouk might not last the day. Ask me, I don't know if self-rule was the best idea for this place. They haven't managed very well. Besides, they're accustomed to being told what to do. They've been overrun and occupied and dominated for thousands of years. For three hundred years they were ruled by an army of Turkish slaves. The last time they were able to rule themselves was before Christ. I can assure you, the British aren't the worst thing that's happened to them."

"That sounds frighteningly imperialistic."

"Yes, well, I'm from the empire. It's we who built the roads that you are now enjoying, and the communication systems that allow this place to function."

"And the canal that almost bankrupted them."

"That bloody canal." Michael jabbed his cane into the air and lost his balance. Gemma gently steadied him. As he leaned against her she felt the warmth and strength of his body. She felt the physical attraction. She didn't yet know what to make of their chemistry. They were like two ships in parallel navigation over shoals and sandbars, at times needing to watch only their own passage, at times safe enough to watch each other.

"Wasn't it more in England's national interest to get the canal built?" Gemma asked.

"What do you know about it, the articles you've read in some liberal newspaper?"

"What I know I learned from my father," she said.

"Who had his liberal leanings."

"He was sympathetic to the people of Egypt."

"He was an Englishman, first and last," Michael declared. "A Christian too, or started that way. I don't know how he ended up. As I heard, he ventured into some of the darker realms."

Gemma stopped. "What darker realms?"

"I have no idea. This is just dangerously idle gossip, I'm afraid."

"Don't bait me, Michael."

"All I know is that according to my father, yours changed."

They continued walking. "I think Egypt did change my father," Gemma conceded. "I don't know that darker realms were involved."

"Children often know precious little about their parents. This I can say from personal experience."

"No, my father talked to me quite a bit."

"You mean he told you what to think."

"He educated me! And I've been known to form my own opinions."

"A true modern woman. I've heard about your type."

Gemma was as repelled as she had been attracted. "I don't like you nearly as much when you condescend to me."

"I'll remember that before I try another kiss."

"The way you're going, you won't get close enough."

Michael caught her around the waist and drew her to him. In the same instant, Gemma felt a hand slip into her pocket. She grabbed the fabric of her jacket, trapping the hand inside.

She stepped away from Michael, gripping the hand of a young boy whose face was torn between fear and contempt.

"Did you want something?" she asked. The boy shook his head, his eyebrows hooding his eyes. "You could just ask," she said.

"He can't understand you," Michael said.

"He understands."

Michael laughed.

Gemma put a coin in the boy's hand and released him. He ran from them, ducking behind a stall heaped with garlic. They continued walking. The day had grown hot. The clouds had been chased high and burnt into an ashy ceiling. Gemma could not tell how high they were, or if they were still even clouds.

"I don't need your protection," she said.

"I can see that."

"I have been managing on my own for some time."

"It must be tiring."

She looked at him sideways. "Are you being sardonic?"

"Not at all."

Gemma stopped. A beggar with withered legs and cataract eyes held out an empty brown hand. "I am tired," Gemma said.

Michael glanced at his watch. "Listen, I don't know about the market today. Some other time?"

"Some other time."

"You don't mind heading home?"

Gemma looked at him to see which man she was talking to. It was neither. His complexion was gray and waxen, but he was perspiring. She had pushed him too far. "Home sounds like a perfect idea." Gemma raised her hand to the cars in the street. "Let's take a taxi."

"Don't do it for me. No," he added, "do it for me."

A taxi slowed and pulled over.

When they settled themselves in the back, the cane between them, Michael seemed revived. "Is it impolitic to ask if you are a Christian?" he asked.

Gemma smiled and looked out the window. "Am I being interviewed for a position?"

"Just curious."

"I suppose I am, technically."

"Do you go to church?"

"I used to, with my mother, though I don't know how religious she was. She was a great one for bake sales." Gemma tapped her fingers on the window. "It's the one sure way a woman can help. While men pontificate and direct and decide the fate of the world, a woman can bake a cake."

"That's a bit harsh."

"Is it? Religion is different for women, full stop. Did you know that because I'm unmarried, the Church of England registers me a 'spinster'? I found that out when I applied for a passport. That's what I am to them. Not a nurse or a daughter or a friend or a useful person, but a spinster. And no, I don't go to church anymore. The war cured me of that habit. In case you're wondering, my father and his dark realms had nothing to do with it."

"I shouldn't have said that."

"Yes, well." Gemma turned her attention to the street and tried to memorize landmarks so she could find her way back to this part of the city again alone.

WHEN THEY ARRIVED back at the Lazar house, Michael went straight to his room for a lie-down, wordlessly passing his father on the stairs. David stared after him and then settled for Gemma's eye. His expression had lost both the warmth and the candor of the previous night. He looked older, and unmistakably sad. "Won't you have tea with me?" he asked.

"I'd love to. Give me a moment to wash up and get myself in order. I haven't even unpacked."

"No rush at all, my dear. I'll be in the garden."

Gemma went to her room and resisted the temptation to flop down on her bed and sink into mint julep oblivion. She was more interested in talking to David Lazar. She had been collecting questions for him.

She washed the grime from her face and ankles and changed into a clean dress. She had not packed enough clothes. She did not own enough clothes. Not for the amount of perspiration and dirt one accumulated simply walking down the street. She hung her few skirts and blouses and two dresses in the wardrobe, shaking out the worst wrinkles from the fabric. She stared at the lifeless clothes, unable to imagine how she looked in items that identified her as so unmistakably female. A nurse was different from a woman; a uniform was not a dress. She stood on tiptoe in front of the small mirror to see below the neckline. The dress was pretty—that was its function. She did not feel its prettiness.

She found David Lazar sitting in the garden shaded by a newspaper. When she moved a chair next to him, he folded his paper and held the back of her chair. "So," he said, "how are you finding Cairo?"

"It's strangely charming."

"I agree. Was Michael a good guide?"

Gemma turned her face to the sun. "We had a nice day."

"I'm glad he took you around. He hasn't been very active lately."

"That's understandable, isn't it?"

"Of course. I only worry when he stays in bed until dinner."

"Well, I think he's genuinely tired now. We walked a long way."

"Did you? Good."

"Really, he's doing remarkably well with his new leg."

David took out his pipe and packed it with tobacco. "Michael doesn't like it here much. Sometimes I think he's angry at the country itself." He lit his pipe and puffed on it until the ember was strong. "When I married Nailah, he chose to stay in England with his mother. He was forced to come here when she died. Now he's trapped. In his eyes, I think, I must be both a killer and a jailer."

Gemma shielded her eyes and looked at him. "It's sometimes best to think the worst. Then one's own heart can't be broken as badly."

He smiled. "We all have our ways of surviving. Those of us who survive have learned them. You must have done the same."

"I don't know." Gemma forced a laugh. "Am I surviving?"

"Dear girl."

Amad appeared and moved a table between them and set up a tea service. He came back with a plate of toasted pita and hummus and a bowl of black olives. The light pierced the breaks in the tall fence, banding his white robe with rich afternoon sunlight.

"Thank you, Amad," David said. "I hope you don't mind a savory tea."

"Amad isn't Muslim," Gemma said, looking after him. "Is he?"

"He's a Coptic Christian. Very devout." David sipped his tea. "Amad liked your father very much. He was with us on all our digs. When his wife died, he chose to remain in my employ when I came to the university. I argued with him; he's enormously capable. But he argued back. He says the domestic life suits him fine; he likes the peace and the work isn't heavy. So he's become as indispensable here and at my office as he was in the field." David smiled. "Also, he is my good friend."

"Do Copts speak Coptic?"

"Some. Some just read it. The language is as old as the religion. Many of the old texts come to us in Coptic."

"And Amad, can he speak Coptic?"

"Amad can speak most languages."

"And you?"

"No. Hieroglyphics are the extent of my linguistic achievement. Your father had the gift for languages."

The sound of the fountain filled the silence. Gemma watched a swarm of tiny insects move in and out of the light.

"I have his ashes, Gemma. It's up to you to decide what you want to do with them. You're free to take them back to England, of course."

"I'm not ready to think about that. Not yet."

"There's no need to rush. I just wanted to let you know what we had done."

She turned her chair to face him. "Before we talk about ashes, I need to know what happened. I need to understand how someone like my father just dies."

David rubbed his temples. "I'm afraid I don't know much more than you do. As you know, they think it was his heart."

"They found him in his office? Just sitting there?"

"I'm afraid so."

"Had he been there long?"

"That's the problem. He had been there for some time. So it was hard to determine the cause of death."

"Was there an autopsy?"

David smiled sadly. "This is Egypt, Gemma."

"Do you understand why that's not enough of an answer?"

"Of course I do."

"He was a healthy man."

"I know he was."

"How do I know the ashes belong to him?"

"Oh dear. I have his ring, if that helps."

Gemma sat back. "I wish you could have waited."

"It was a matter of— I'm sorry, Gemma. We were given no choice."

"It makes it hard to believe he's dead."

"I can understand that."

She reached down for her purse. "I don't know if you knew, but he had come into some money. He wrote me about it. And now it seems to have vanished. He was going to buy a house." She handed David the realtor's drawing.

"So that's why he gave up his room."

"You can see why I'm curious. That's not all. There was a man in his office today. He was looking for something. I was too startled to get his name. He clearly wasn't supposed to be there."

David's brow furrowed slightly. "That's a bit disturbing."

"This man said my father had something that didn't belong to him. Do you know what that might have been?"

David thought. "Offhand, no. I have no idea."

She pressed the toe of her shoe past the fine layer of gravel to the dirt below. "Do you know what he was working on?"

"Oh, Charles had a few pots in the fire."

"So you don't know."

"I know some things. He had been asked to present a paper on the mask of Tutankhamen. He was compiling his notes from that dig and putting them in order enough to publish."

She asked with some disbelief, "He was writing a book on King Tut?"

"He was gathering material."

"Then what was he doing in Upper Egypt?"

"You should ask Anthony when he comes. He was with him there at a site near some monastery that Anthony was excavating. I'm afraid we lost Charles to early Christianity. It's been years now since he made the jump over to A.D. I blame his time in the seminary. We left him there too long." David smiled dryly. "But even so, your father's mind was unique. He wasn't like the rest of us, delighted just to unearth things. He was more interested in what the things meant. You're talking to a simpler man, I'm afraid. Anyway, it's Anthony you want. They had offices near one another. I think they talked quite a bit."

"Did he have other friends?"

"Of course, though I think they were mainly social acquaintances. Charles was a private man." David lit another match and held it to his pipe.

"And Stephan Sutton?"

"What about him?"

"There was an article about his death. Father kept it."

"Sutton worked for the British Museum. He was also an archaeologist."

"Did my father know him?"

"Probably. The archaeological world is small."

"Strange that archaeologists should be dying all of a sudden."

"I have chosen to believe the tragedies are a coincidence, because I know nothing to the contrary. Sutton had an accident. It happens. Your father's heart was perhaps not as strong as one might think."

"Stephan Sutton was found under a pile of rocks."

"Rock slides are common in the mountains."

"I knew nothing of my father's weak heart."

"Nor did I. But that's what it looked like to the doctor who performed the postmortem, cursory as it was."

Gemma inclined her head and stared at the sky. Clouds were forming, joining together like lost continents. "Did your son Anthony go to war?"

David raised his eyebrows. "No, actually. He didn't have to. Technically, he's not a British subject."

The smoke from David's pipe thickened and billowed into a tiny storm cloud about his head. Gemma watched as it rose and dissipated. "The last thing my father wrote me," she said, "was that he would soon have the money to send for me, enough for me to stay for a while. He was finally going to show me this country." She thought about the woman and the child in the lithograph. "He has a framed image of Isis and Horus in his office. Maybe I'm silly to think it's important, but he made such an issue of banning religious iconography from his life. 'Another form of preaching,' he always said."

"Yes, he came out quite against the Church," David said sharply. "Didn't he."

"But not against God. Only if you find him yourself do you have a relationship. Letting someone else tell you what and how and why to believe is the road to fanaticism."

"I'm afraid you sound just like him."

Gemma chewed her lip. "Did he have someone here?"

"Someone?"

"A woman."

David laughed. "Not that I know of."

"Would you tell me if he did?"

"You're an extraordinary girl, Gemma."

"No, really, you've got to understand how little I know about his life in Egypt. Now that he's gone I want to feel I at least know what he did. If he loved someone, I'd like to know that too. I'd also like to know what could have made him enough money to bring me here to live."

"I can't tell you, I'm afraid. I don't know. We're all lost in our own labyrinths here. Charles and I have often shared paths, but for some time we've been going in different directions." David leaned forward to meet her eyes. "For a long time, he was my closest friend, Gemma. I miss him terribly. I miss his humor and his intelligence. He had such fine observations, such good instinct. That counts for a lot here. Sometimes I thought he had divine guidance, the way he could find things. The way he put things together. He was a great man. You've got every right to grieve and be angry and want to know more. It's part of the process. As I said, I will help in any way I can. When and if he ever gets here, I'm sure Anthony might be able to offer assistance as well."

A moment passed. "Michael said he thought my father ventured into dark realms. What do you think that means?"

"Michael likes to stir things up. Pay no attention, especially when he drinks." David visored his eyes to watch a plane pass overhead. Gemma could tell he was tiring of her questions. "A Mustang," he said with sudden energy. "When Michael joined the RAF, I learned all their names."

Gemma watched the plane disappear behind the dense magenta blossoms of a bougainvillea tree. "Michael hardly mentions his brother. Are they not close?"

David glanced back toward the house. "They have been. They're both remarkable young men. But then fathers tend to think highly of their offspring. Sometimes they want too much for them." He shook his head as if to clear it. "Shall we go inside? I'm feeling a little chilly."

Gemma stayed seated. "We'll scatter his ashes here in Egypt," she said. "This was his home."

CHAPTER FIVE

NTHONY STAYED UP half the night finishing an article he had promised to write for a British archaeological journal. It was an overview of Kharga and his work there. The area was little known to the archaeological world, much less to the public. He briefly explained that Kharga had been not only an ancient monastic site but also a place of banishment for early Christian leaders, when their views conflicted with the doctrine of the new church. It was meant to be a punishment, this exile to the Western Desert, but Kharga had become a haven of peace and meditation; it had become a place of liberation.

Anthony wrote about his most recent excavation, a site ten kilometers away—the Christian Necropolis of Al-Bagawat, which contained 263 mud-brick chapels with Coptic murals. Preserved by the arid climate, the Necropolis was hardly a ruin. One still could walk beneath its mud-brick ceilings, weave between the arches and pillars. He described the Chapel of Peace, and the images of Adam and Eve and Noah's Ark on its dome. He worked as much as he had the patience for, feeling that the final product was adequate but not transcendent—a failure, really, because Kharga itself was transcendent for him, belonging to no era or culture. Desert and oasis, host to both the living and the dead, and the dead were a kindly presence that still lived, at least for him.

He wanted to tell Bastian what he had seen on this last trip to Kharga. He wanted to share the phenomenon of witnessing a moment in time when many religions had occupied the same soil, the moment when the Christian idea of God had formed and congealed, and other ideas of God were forcibly abandoned. He would have liked to have taken Bastian to the Chapel of Peace on the western slope of the Necropolis and shown him walls covered with testimonies in Coptic, Arabic, Greek. Ancient graffiti recording the single, urgent fact: *We were here. Our Gods were here.* The Egyptians' saints Paul and Thecla were painted alongside the names: *Adam, Eve, Abraham, Isaac.* The walls were a record of the myths and stories that spanned four hundred years.

After sleeping for a few hours, Anthony showered, shaved, and made himself some coffee. He sat for another hour on his balcony in front of the Nile and deliberately thought of nothing. The great blue-green river soothed him as it always had, with its swirling eddies that rose and disappeared, surging up again and again from the deep. When Anthony left his chair on the balcony, he felt rested as he rarely did from sleep.

He spent the remainder of the morning unpacking and sorting his laundry. He then left Kit Kat with his canvas shoulder bag, making his way to the market to restock his kitchen.

It was noon by the time he got home and pulled from the closet his boxed files from Oxyrhynchus. He removed a folder marked *Bastian.*

He spread the notes from the folder on his bed and stood above them, wanting to review from a distance the things he had written when he and Charles Bastian had been at Oxyrhynchus together. It had been a time of both profound learning and of profound shock. The things Bastian had told him did not all register immediately; some were deflected and temporarily lost. But at one time or another, Anthony had written most of it down.

His eyes now passed over what Bastian's beloved Gnostic teacher, Monoimus, had written in the second century:

Abandon the search for God and the creation and other matters of a similar sort. Look for Him by taking yourself as the starting point. Learn who is within you, who makes everything His own and says, "My God, my mind, my thought, my soul, my body." Learn the sources of sorrow, joy, love, hate. . . . If you carefully investigate these matters, you will find Him in yourself.

This was the essence of Bastian's work, and his central belief. It was what he wanted most to impress upon Anthony—*God is within all of us.* Anthony wondered now if Bastian's efforts to educate him had been out of friendship or something more. Was Anthony the only person who had known the extent of Bastian's theories? Had he made Anthony a guardian of knowledge that might otherwise be lost? Had he in some way anticipated his own death? Finally, what would he have wanted Anthony to do now? Anthony knew the answer: Whatever he could to secure the gospels and get them somewhere safe, somewhere the public could at some point have access to them. But what of Bastian's grand theory? Christianity cleaved by the Church Fathers and fatally wounded for more than a millennium. And now there was a chance that the crippled faith could be fused back to wholeness with its lost half, by the very gospels the Church Fathers had banned, the lost gospels of Nag Hammadi. It was a lifetime's work. But it had been Bastian's life. Anthony had borne witness, that was all. He had borne witness to a fantastic story, a story he wasn't sure he believed. At this point, he could do no more than pay Bastian the respect of remembering his vision. But then the vision might have to die with the visionary.

And there was the visionary's daughter, about whom Anthony was strangely incurious. Bastian's only child had lived far from Egypt and would have little understanding of his work here—or the danger he had courted. Anthony would do as Mina asked, and encourage her to leave the country where her father had died, as soon as possible. It was a place of civil unrest and foreign beliefs and dust. A place far from the comfort and greenery of London. He did not imagine he would have difficulty persuading her.

CHAPTER SIX

GEMMA SPENT THE afternoon with her father's book on Egyptian mythology, finishing the chapter on the goddess Isis, whose cult was so popular and widespread that instead of fading with the other Egyptian gods and goddesses, it stayed alive to be embraced by both the Greeks and the Romans. The "Mother of Life" and "Crone of Death" were supposedly still worshipped in the twentieth century, with temples as far north as Paris. And when Christianity gained a foothold in the fourth century, the worshippers of Isis founded the first Madonna cults in order to keep the goddess alive. Her influence was visible in the Christian icons of the Virgin Mary and Child.

Gemma made some notes and closed the book. Her father, once a devout Christian, now had an ancient goddess on his wall. He had exchanged one virgin for another. She had no idea what it meant. She had no idea why she was taking the time to read about it. The fact was that her father never did anything without a reason. Even hanging a picture on a wall.

THAT EVENING AT the Lazar house there was music in the courtyard. Gemma paused in the doorway to see Amad sitting cross-legged on the painted tiles. She was watching another man who had known a part of her father she hadn't. Behind him was a fountain with an ice-blue porpoise spouting a stream of water. Inlaid gold flickered between the turquoise tiles as the sun struck it. Lying across Amad's lap was a string instrument that looked something like a lyre. His eyes were closed as his fingers slid up and down the neck of the instrument, making a strange, inexact melody. She stepped forward quietly and sat on the edge of the courtyard under a small lemon tree. The tiles beneath her were smooth; their stony coolness easily penetrated her thin dress. After he had played a while longer, Amad motioned her to come closer.

"Please," he said. "Join me."

"What is it?" she asked.

"It is called an oud." The instrument gleamed with inlay of mother-of-pearl.

"It's beautiful," Gemma said.

"They say it was invented by Lamak, a direct descendant of Cain. When Lamak's son died, he hung his dead body in a tree. As it dried out, it began to look like an instrument. This instrument became the oud."

"An oud," Gemma tried out the word. "At home I play the piano."

"A somewhat larger instrument."

"Yes." She laughed. "Difficult to travel with."

"You like music?"

"Very much."

"And what songs do you love?"

Gemma paused. "You may not know them."

"I may surprise you. Your father taught me many songs."

"Did he?"

"And I taught him some."

"Can you teach me?"

"If you are able to learn."

"I think I'm able."

Amad plucked his oud and moved his finger down to its head, jiggling it slightly to make the instrument ululate. "You make me remember your father. A man always able to learn. If he has given you this, he has given you a gift."

Gemma held her hands in her lap. "Thank you for saying that." After a moment, she said, "May I ask you something?"

"Of course."

"How do Copts differ from other Christians?"

"Ours is one of the oldest Christianities, brought to us by Saint Mark."

"I don't know anything about Saint Mark."

Amad smiled. "He brought his teachings to Egypt only a dozen or so years after the death of Christ. But there have been many prophecies about the Christian faith in Egypt. In the Old Testament, Isaiah said, 'In that day there will be an altar to the Lord in the midst of the land of Egypt.'" Amad set down his oud. "And the Lord said, 'Out of Egypt I called My Son.'"

"But Egypt is a Muslim country."

"The Prophet of Islam had an Egyptian wife, the only wife to bear him a child. 'When you conquer Egypt,' he said, 'be kind to the Copts, for they are your protégés and kith and kin.' So we are safe here, though we must pay a tax, Gezya, which qualifies us as Ahl Zemma, or protected."

They sat for a moment in silence. "I'm sorry," Gemma said. "I didn't mean to stop you from playing."

Amad's fingers returned to the strings of the oud. "The music we make with the oud is different from what you know. You are accustomed to harmony. With our music, harmony as you understand it does not exist. If you look for it, you will be disappointed. Instead you have melody and rhythm. It is also an instrument with imprecise notation. It does not have the frets of a guitar. We musicians hear notes differently. The same song can sound different but have the same notations."

"So you can't learn it on your own."

"No, in fact, one should never play from notation if one has not heard the piece of music first. There's no telling how badly one might interpret the notes."

"So you will teach me, at least a little?"

"In the evening before dinner I sit here most days with my oud. I would be happy to have you join me."

"Thank you, Amad."

He rested his hands on the strings of the oud. "I am sorry you lost your father." Amad began to play.

Gemma looked around the courtyard. It was a peaceful little place, with only the gentle disruption of the fountain and a square of sky above. "When did you last work with him?"

"It must be ten years now." Amad played a short song that made Gemma shiver. "In the Valley of the Kings."

"Do you have children, Amad?"

"I have a son, Zira. He works with Anthony. They have become a team, like their fathers once were."

"I know my father was working on something when he died. You don't know what it was, do you? Maybe Zira mentioned something?"

"Zira works for a man who is at home in the desert. Over the years he has grown quiet. While we enjoy each other's company, we do not often talk."

"I hope to meet them both someday."

"I'm sure you will. Anthony will come as soon as word reaches him. He liked your father very much. As did I."

MICHAEL LAZAR SEEMED to arrive at the dinner table already drunk. His words were slightly slurred and his eyes were glassy with inattention. He made no attempt to keep up with the chitchat of the first courses, instead entertaining himself by smiling and laughing at private jokes. By the time the main course was served, he had nodded off. Nailah and David talked around him, ignoring his soft snoring. When Michael's head rolled to the side, Gemma rose.

"He's all right," Nailah said calmly.

"Michael?" Gemma raised her voice. "Would you like to lie down?"

Michael's eyes opened and idly wandered the room, searching for Gemma. "Too much walking lately," he said. "I do think I need a little lie-down." He stood and stumbled, kicking his cane out from under him. It skittered across the floor and smacked into the wall.

Gemma watched as David and Nailah glanced at each other. For some reason they neither moved nor spoke. Gemma pushed her chair back and retrieved his cane. "Come," she said to Michael. "I'll take you upstairs."

"Lovely." He refused her offer of the cane, holding up his palm, which was blistered and red.

"We'll have to bandage that."

Nailah stood up. "Gemma, we can attend to it."

"I'm a nurse," Gemma told her. "Bandages are my specialty."

"You're sure?" Nailah asked.

"Of course."

"Thank you, dear girl," David said.

They both seemed relieved to have her take over. She felt all at once sorry for this man, this son, who had become a burden to his family. Gemma took Michael's cane in one hand and circled his waist with the other. They paused at the bottom of the stairs while she adjusted her hold. He gripped her shoulder tightly.

"My brother is coming home," he mumbled. They began their laborious ascent. He seemed unaware of how heavily he was leaning on Gemma, who struggled to support almost his full weight.

"Yes," she said as they took another step. "Your father told me."

"My little brother, Anthony. He comes by now and then to remind us of what he looks like."

"I'm eager to talk to him about my father."

"Yes, they were quite cozy, holed up like mice in their little offices. God knows how they spent so much time there. No windows, dust everywhere."

"Why are you and your brother not closer?"

"Hard to be close to Anthony."

"Why's that?"

"Don't know really. Different mums maybe. Little brother's half Egyptian." Michael grabbed the banister to steady himself. "Born with a bit of sand in his head."

"What do you mean?"

"Nothing. Don't listen to me now. I've got worse than sand running around my brain."

They rested at the top of the stairs. "What do you have running around your brain, Michael?"

The saber of scar in the corner of his mouth twitched into something that might have been a smile. "I have you, Gemma."

"Right." Gemma led him to her room, where Michael hopped over to the corner and collapsed on a chaise, where he watched her with half-closed eyes. By the time she had gathered her alcohol and gauze, he had dozed off again. She sat next to him on the chaise and touched his hand. Michael flinched but did not waken. He was deeply asleep. She leaned close to his ear. "Michael," she whispered.

He looked at her through slitted, indolent eyes. "Gemma," he murmured. "What were you doing with that god-awful instrument?"

She thought, then smiled. "Amad's oud?"

"You see, even the name sounds awful. It's just given me a little nightmare."

"I'm learning how it works. It's so different from any music I've heard. At home I play the piano. But while I'm here I thought it would be nice to learn to play the oud."

"Please, no. I'll buy you a piano."

Gemma dabbed his palm with alcohol. Michael winced and turned his head away. "I'm sorry, this won't last." She uncapped a tube of antibiotic ointment and dabbed the gel on the open blisters.

"That's better," Michael said.

"I'm going to make a thin, loose bandage so it gets some air tonight. But you're going to have to use your other hand for a while."

"It's not strong enough."

"It will get strong. As quickly as you formed these blisters, it will strengthen."

"That's heartening." He smiled at her. "Can I sleep here tonight?"

"No." She laughed. "You cannot."

"If I married you, you'd let me sleep on your chaise."

"Husbands, if I'm remembering correctly, share the connubial bed."

"I'd like that even more." He held her eyes until she blushed.

She dismissed him with a laugh. "You can't imagine the proposals a nurse gets."

"It's been such a long, lonely war," he said.

"Sadly, I'm quite inured."

"Perhaps I should take that as a challenge."

Gemma reached for his good hand. "I think we're challenged enough, you and I. Come on, then, let's get you to your bed."

She helped him to his room and hoisted him onto his bed, removing his single shoe. "There, now. Shall I take off your leg?"

"No, leave it. But sit with me, just for a moment."

"All right."

"Did you find some company, these past years, or were you as lonely as I was?"

"I had company, of a sort. Nurses do."

"Gemma."

"Yes?"

"Did you offer up that gorgeous body of yours to a wounded soldier?"

Gemma remained silent. Then she looked away from him.

"Did you?" Michael persisted.

She put her fingers over his lips. He kissed them. He held her hand to his cheek. She would not look at him.

"I try to hide from the war too," he said. "I try to hide but it manages to find me. Lie with me just for a moment. I want to tell you a story." Gemma looked down at him. Before she could refuse, Michael entreated, "Please, it's important." She wordlessly arranged herself next to him and together they looked up at the canopy of the bed.

"There was an old Frenchman. He was trying to help me. I had crashed a landing in his field. My leg was crushed. I thought I was on fire. I couldn't think straight. He said something to me in French. Came out of nowhere. He surprised me. I got my gun out and he started shouting, putting his hands up. He was making so much bloody noise. You don't shoot some- one to shut them up. But that's what I did."

Gemma was silent. She turned to watch Michael's profile, the side of his face that was a scarred theater of pain.

"Now I keep seeing him," he said. "Waving his hands around. He was old, as old as my father. He was wearing a white nightshirt."

For a while they lay without speaking. Then Gemma leaned over and kissed the smooth, raised tissue of his burnt cheek. "You can't keep these things locked up inside. They only fester." She got off the bed and paused at its base.

"Thank you, Gemma. Thank you for the day. For the conversation, for the challenge. It was worth every blister."

In her own room Gemma moved in the dark to the curtain and slipped inside its thick softness. The night was gauzy with heat and the dimmed lights of the city. She could not be Michael's nurse. Her heart yearned for a home too desperately for her to take on that role, a role in which she easily lost herself. It wasn't why she had come. She had come to lay the dead to rest. Before love, there had to be peace, a peace she could not yet imagine finding in this country.

CHAPTER SEVEN

I am the knowledge of my search,
The finding of those who look for me,
The command of those who ask about me,
The power of powers . . .

The Gospel of Thunder,
from Nag Hammadi

THE NEXT MORNING Gemma asked Michael to take her back to the museum as soon as he finished his breakfast. He looked up at her and pleaded with bloodshot eyes. "Come, it will be good for you to get out," she urged. "Are you ill?"

"Didn't sleep much. Seems to be another feature of my marvelous new life."

"I'll take a taxi, then."

"And I will hold the fort."

She turned at the door. "Try to get out, Michael."

"I need my nurse for that."

"Don't be ridiculous."

He smiled wearily and wagged a finger. "Teasing."

As GEMMA WAS driven through the city, the memory of the ginger-haired intruder returned to her. Perhaps another reason she had wanted Michael's company. It was disconcerting; she had not felt the need of a man for years. But this was a different country. She straightened in the back of the taxi and concentrated on learning the streets. It was always better to know more, her father said. Which is what bothered her about both Bernard Westerly and the ginger-haired intruder; they would not let her know more. Worse, they seemed practiced in the way they did not answer questions, as if they had been trained in vagueness, in prevarication.

The museum came into sight and Gemma searched for bills in her purse. What could the ginger-haired man do to her anyway? If she saw him again, she wouldn't let him slither away. She started to hope he would be there. It would be satisfying, she realized, to have someone to confront.

She entered her father's office with a battle-ready ferocity that bounced off the walls of the empty room. She stood in the silence and searched the objects around her to see if anything had been removed or disturbed. It all looked the same.

Her eyes returned to the lithograph. She lifted it off its hook and laid it on her father's desk. After a while she turned it over. Later she couldn't remember what compelled her to unlatch the frame.

Between the lithograph and the back of the frame was a folder, fitted into the grooves of the frame. She pulled it gently free and opened it. In front of her was an image of a woman with her foot on a lion. On the bottom of the page was a page number. It had been ripped from a book. The woman was identified as "Inanna." Behind that was another ripped page, and another woman, but this one was fornicating with a man on some kind of altar. The image was titled "Entu priestess." Behind that was yet another page of a woman titled "Ishtar of Babylon . . . a prostitute compassionate am I." She was riding on the back of a lion, her breasts and loins exposed.

Gemma held her breath and looked at an image of a woman with four arms and a stringed instrument. She was young and dark and beautiful. "Saraswati, the master of the 64 Arts from which the art of loving is considered as first and most important. . . ."

Another woman and man were locked together in ceremonial dress in what looked like a temple. Their faces were ecstatic. "The Kama Sutra; the 64 arts, India."

Gemma turned to the final page, where an Asian man and woman were entangled in a circle of limbs. Their mouths were clasped on each other's genitals. "Increasing Yin and Yang leads to everlasting life," the description read.

Gemma closed the folder and pushed it away from her. The folder might have belonged to someone else, someone who had owned the lithograph before. Reluctantly, she reopened it and looked at the headings on the ripped pages. She wrote them down and then went to the bookshelf. It did not take her long to find the book. She sat down and spun the leather chair away from the desk, away from the folder and the book. Was this her father's dark realm? She spun back and rested her head on her arm. She stared at the room sideways.

I came to bury you, she thought. But when that is done I have to find out what you were doing here.

THAT AFTERNOON SHE told David she'd decided on a short, simple ceremony at Giza in the late afternoon, when the sun was descending between the Pyramid of Khafre and the Great Pyramid.

"It sounds like a photograph," David said.

"It was. The first one I saw of Egypt."

"Fitting. Who would you like to be there?"

"Your family and anyone else who knew him well enough to care that he is dead."

David paused. "Would you like anyone religious to say something?"

"No," Gemma said. She had pinned her hair the way she'd worn it at the hospital and found it gave her a sense of control. "No one from the church. I'll say something. I'd like you to, as well."

"I'd be happy to. And I'll make a list of people. You know, Nailah's cousin has a stable at Giza."

"The Giza Stables?"

"Yes."

"I think my father rode there."

"I know it for a fact. They've got lovely Arabians. And I'm sure they'll help us arrange transport. You need a four-legged beast to get around those parts."

✝ ✝ ✝

GEMMA INSISTED ON visiting the Giza Stables by herself. She reassured the Lazars that she wanted to be alone. Her father had made the Arabian horses of Egypt into the stuff of legend. He had fallen in love with them when he first came to Egypt, declaring them more beautiful than most women, and certainly easier to handle. This was a joke, because he appreciated difficulty in women. He thought it was a sign of health. "Women are going to reclaim the earth someday," he told her. "It will be a happy day for all of us."

And hidden images of naked and fornicating couples? How did that figure in? How dare he leave something like that for her to find and not be around to explain it?

Making her way through Cairo, she realized that there had to be an explanation: She had known her father. He had not had a secret, perverse life. As if to outstride any objection to this, she began walking faster. She almost took a wrong turn and had to stop to get her bearings. Across the street was a small mosque. She paused outside a three-story house with carved doors. Reaching out, she touched the wood and followed the swooping groove of what must have been an Arabic letter. She looked up and recognized the spire from a church she knew. She continued to walk, but more slowly, taking in the details of houses she passed, the sudden cat flashing from a hidden alley, the roughness of the stones beneath her feet. The afternoon was cooling, the sunlight mellowing into amber. There were still hours of daylight left. There was no reason to hurry. She could try to enjoy herself.

Cairo was a different place without Michael, who moved with claustrophobic anxiety between European watering holes. That he lacked curiosity, Gemma could tolerate. But his swings of mood, which were both sudden and disproportionate, bewildered her. She grasped that he was in psychic pain, and his physical discomfort was evident. But the nihilistic black moods that fell on him like an anvil were something she had seen only in dying men, in men who knew they had lost their own private wars.

✝ ✝ ✝

GEMMA ENTERED THE stables at Giza silently and watched a man pitch forkfuls of hay to a half circle of white horses. Pools of water shone beneath the immaculate animals and steam rose from their haunches. She looked beyond the realm of the man and his horses to a long row of stables; there were at least thirty stalls. A few white heads craned from their stalls, surveying her with their sharp ears bent forward.

Aside from this man, the stables were empty. He rested now on his fork and wiped his forehead with his sleeve. He seemed tired, at the end of his day. When his eyes found her, he raised his eyebrows. "You are quiet for a European."

"I didn't want to interrupt."

"Also unusual for a European. You know, I could sense you before I could see you."

"Are you Mohammad?"

"I am Umar, Mohammad's partner."

"Did you know my father, Charles Bastian?"

"I knew him. He came here to ride."

"Alone?"

"Sometimes." Umar stabbed his fork into a bale of hay. "Sometimes with David Lazar, though it has been a long time since I've seen them here together. The last few times he came with a woman."

"Who was she, do you know?"

"Mrs. Dattari. An Italian woman. Exceptional, how do you British say, *seat*." Umar smiled with teeth that were even and white, and Gemma wondered if his family had money.

"Do you know her first name?"

"Yes. Angela."

A.D., Gemma thought. "Do you know how I could find her?"

"I believe she has returned to Italy. But she keeps a house here."

"Where?"

"In Garden City, Ismail Pasha Street, I believe."

"I see," she said, curious that a man who ran a stable would know her address. "Umar, is it too late for a ride?" she asked.

"That depends where you want to go, and if you can ride."

"Over there." Gemma pointed. "And I can ride."

"It's not too late to go to the pyramids."

"I'm staying with Nailah, Mohammad's cousin," Gemma offered. "She sent me here."

"Then you shall ride for free." He wiped his hands with a rag. "You are lucky. We have the finest horses in Cairo."

"They look beautiful. I've never ridden an Arabian."

"Come," he said. "I will give you a nice mare."

Umar led her down the row of stalls. As she followed his light step, he seemed the human manifestation of the taut animals that peered out at them. He was as upright, as bound with latent energy. "You will see," he said. "Arabians are different from other horses. They could carry you across a desert of dragons, but they can also be afraid of their own shadows."

"I like that," Gemma said. "I understand that."

He opened the door to one of the farthest stalls. The horse he bridled nuzzled his chest. He saddled and bridled a second horse and both horses tossed their heads with anticipation. "These have not been out today. They will want to run."

"Good. I also want to run."

Umar smiled and wove his fingers together to make a step for her foot. "Her name is Yoolyo, the month she was born. And maybe like you, she was born wanting to run. You'll wait for me?"

Gemma's horse was already trotting toward the stable entrance. She barely waited. They tore across the desert. Yoolyo had a smooth, fast gait. She was easy to ride and needed virtually no guidance. She seemed to know just where they were going. Gemma simply held on while the horse pounded across the firm sand toward the pyramids. Gemma felt tears streaming down her face. She wasn't sure if they'd come from the wind in her eyes or from the grief that had caught her in the chaos of movement. She did not want to stop. She did not look back at Umar. She leaned forward and touched her mare's neck. "Yoolyo," she said, "you are almost fast enough."

Umar rode a few lengths behind her. When he whistled, Gemma drew the reins and brought Yoolyo to an unwilling stop. "Don't leave us here," he said. "The Sahara is long."

Gemma turned her horse to look at the sun descending between the pyramids. "Just a bit farther," she said. Umar followed her at a trot. When she finally stopped, she walked Yoolyo in a large circle, inspecting the ground and the distances to both tourists and the pyramids. "We can go back now," she said.

Umar asked no questions. As his horse turned restively and pranced backward, his dark eyes locked onto Gemma's face and then moved over her form in a more languorous scrutiny. She met and defensively returned his stare. Then, when she sensed no affront, she began studying him as she felt she was being studied, noting both virility and femininity in him, in the intelligent curve of the eyes. It was because of his eyes that his attention was not insulting. No one had ever looked at her this way.

Later, at the stables, Gemma washed her hands at the outdoor sink. She was pressing a damp handkerchief to her face when Umar came up behind her. She could feel him there. She did not move when he briefly touched the nape of her neck with the back of his fingers. "This is the most beautiful part of the horse, and, I think, some women."

His touch immobilized her. It was the touch of supreme confidence, the touch of a man who knew without question that some things on earth belonged to him. She thought, I have never been touched this way. She had been touched furtively, drunkenly, ineptly; she had been groped and worse.

He said gently, "I find European women to be as skittish as Arabians. Ideas alone can make them bolt."

Gemma ignored the blood rushing through her and held his eye. "That place out there," she said. "It is where I will scatter my father's ashes."

"I see."

"My father and Angela Dattari, were they—?" Gemma faltered.

Umar lowered his thick eyelashes. "A great Persian poet said, 'All particles in the world are in love and looking for lovers.' Maybe even you, Miss Bastian."

They stood there in the quiet dusk. Part of her wanted to stay in this world of his, where one could say such things, where such things were true. The next moment the sun was gone and she shrugged her jacket over her shoulders. She was remembering that she didn't understand the first thing about him or his country. "Can you arrange transport for twenty people on Wednesday?"

"Happily."

She paused. "When did you last see my father?"

"Oh, it has been some time now. I thought he had left Cairo."

Gemma took a fold of bills from her jacket pocket. "I don't know if this is enough."

"Don't worry, you can pay the rest later."

She looked back toward where they'd been. "I will remember this afternoon."

"Of course you will." Umar smiled. "You've ridden your first Arabian."

BACK AT THE Lazar house, Gemma found David in his office, dozing in an armchair. When the click of the door woke him, he motioned for her to sit.

"Who is Angela Dattari?"

"Angela Dattari?" David blinked. "She's an Italian woman who lives here in Cairo. I know her socially. Why?"

"She spent time with my father."

"I wasn't aware of that."

"I want to know what happened between you and my father. Don't tell me the nice story, tell me the truth."

David straightened, reached for his tea, and winced at its temperature. Then he sat back and closed his eyes. "The truth is that your father got himself into territory I found unpalatable."

"Unpalatable."

"Offensive."

"Please explain. He's dead. There's nothing to protect me from."

"It was because of the seminary." David hesitated. "He knew the scriptures so well. Too well maybe. I think that's why he made a link."

"What link?"

"Well, that is a good question. Frankly I don't think there is one. But as you know, we disagreed." David waved his hand in the air as if in disagreement with himself. "It started with the Gospel of John. Your father was right that John gives a different order to things." David paused. "He tells about events the others don't mention. Not Matthew, Mark, or Luke."

"What things? What are you talking about?"

"I'm talking about the gospels in the New Testament. I'm talking about the Bible. Only John wrote about Jesus turning water into wine at the wedding at Cana—or raising Lazarus from the dead. Only John speaks of these things. Your father was obsessed by this inconsistency. He couldn't leave it alone."

"Is this the reason you disagreed?"

"No. We disagreed because John was just the start, because your father never could leave anything alone." David stared, trancelike, at the floor. "In my father's house are many mansions. John, 14:2. These words, your father pointed out, come directly from *The Egyptian Book of the Dead.* Your father was making a link. He was creating a theory."

"A theory," Gemma repeated.

"A theory that the cult of Christianity borrowed considerably from Egyptian religion. Your father thought this was so partly because while Jesus was a Jew, he was raised in Egypt, where the Holy Family fled after the Massacre of the Innocents."

"So?"

"He thought that Egyptian religion had a great influence on Jesus—that he learned much of their magic."

"What do you mean, magic?"

"The Egyptians had a retinue of tricks they used to conjure proof of their gods."

"Like what?"

David ignored the question. "Your father thought that this information was suppressed by the Church Fathers. He believed there was some kind of cover-up."

"Cover-up for what?"

"To hide the man Jesus had really been. That's as far as I was willing to listen. But that was years ago. There, then, that's more than enough information."

Gemma absorbed this in silence. She thought about the folder behind the lithograph. "And that's all?"

"That was enough."

She said, "My father had many theories."

"This theory went too far."

Gemma cast back to a conversation she had once with her father about why he had left the seminary. He had said, "Imagine the founder of the Roman Catholic Church not liking women. Not liking them at all. How could I possibly stay? My life rests on women's strength."

Her father had left the patriarchal, celibate world for Egypt, an ancient land of goddesses. He had started excavating history, digging up pharaohs and queens and, in private, the powerful women behind the lithograph, women David Lazar had probably never heard of. To what end? To compensate for some lack? To prove a point? What point? She turned back to David. "So you severed ties?"

"We didn't sever ties. Gemma, you have to understand. Personal faith almost precedes our consciousness. Sometimes we don't know why we believe, or even that we do. Until someone like your father comes along and turns the world and heaven and everything in between on its collective head. I kept thinking, Dear God, this is blasphemy—or worse. Then we stopped talking. Frankly I'm glad. That silence preserved our friendship."

"So when he stopped talking to you, he started talking to your son?"

"It was natural, I suppose. They had more overlap. But I don't know what they shared. At times it worried me; Anthony was brought up Christian."

"So was I. And my father raised me to believe in God. I don't think he was a heretic."

David avoided her steady gaze. He picked up his teacup and then replaced it badly. It wobbled noisily on the raised border of the saucer. "In my opinion," he said, "he was questioning the unquestionable."

"Is there such a thing?"

"Absolutely."

"If he upset his closest friend, I wonder how many other people my father might have upset."

"Do you really think people want to hear anything different from what they were taught as children?"

"I don't know about 'people.'" Gemma rose. "Do you?"

"*People*"—David smiled—"are not interested in such challenges, take my word for it."

Gemma managed to smile back. "I think you'd be quite surprised if I took your word for it." She rose and headed for the stairs.

"Hope springs eternal," David called after her. "But please don't let it concern you. These academic disagreements are common—and it's all in the past now. It shouldn't taint your memory."

"I have no memory of my father in Egypt," she said. "That's the problem."

Upstairs, Gemma penned a quick letter.

Dear Mrs. Dattari,

My name is Gemma Bastian. Charles Bastian was my father. I think you knew him. I don't know if word reached you in Italy that he passed away, but I thought you should be informed. The address below is where I will be staying for the next month or so, if you happen to return to Cairo and would like to meet.

I would.

Sincerely,

Gemma Bastian

At dinner, Gemma masked the residual discomfort from the afternoon's conversation with impeccable table manners as she watched the patriarch of the family drink too much and begin to orate. She had seen something in David Lazar that afternoon that she had seen in men at war, a kind of vicious fear. Her father had threatened something at David's core. While David might not be a bad man, she realized she couldn't trust him. She focused her attention on Michael, whom she did trust in a way—he, as far as she knew, had nothing left to fear, lose, or lie about.

IN THE MORNING she was up before dawn, posted inside her curtains. She unfolded a map of Cairo and watched as the sky lost its pigment and turned a beautiful and fragile shade of white, glancing up just as the sun, glinting like a weapon, mercilessly shattered it.

She dressed and moved quietly through the house and out the door. Once enveloped in the cool morning, she made her way to Ismail Pasha Street on the other side of Garden City. Angela Dattari's house was large and white and shuttered. It was set back from the street like a weather-battered ship. It looked abandoned. Gemma rang the doorbell anyway and leaned with her back against the door. There was a beautifully tended garden. Angela Dattari must have had a team of gardeners. Gemma dropped the letter into the mailbox and walked around the property, stopping at a dry fountain. At its center, a naked woman of marble arched her back and, with finely molded hands, released a dove into the sky. Gemma stared for a long time at the sculpture, finally accepting the woman with the dove as a proxy for Angela Dattari. Before she left, she addressed the woman silently. *Who were you to him?*

CHAPTER EIGHT

Where the beginning is, the end will be.

The Gospel of Thomas,
from Nag Hammadi

T HEY PREPARED TO scatter Charles Bastian's ashes at the place Gemma had found at Giza. David and Nailah had contacted the people they thought would want to be there. Michael had volunteered responsibility for the food and drinks for the reception at the house. And in her room, Gemma scoured the Lazars' copy of the New Testament and her father's copy of *The Egyptian Book of the Dead.*

No one mentioned the fact that Anthony had not yet arrived, but it seemed as if the house itself was waiting.

T HE DAY BEFORE the event, Nailah helped Gemma alter her black trousers, which no longer fit. It had been years since she'd worn them. Gemma had gone into a panic, partly because she had nothing else to wear and partly because, like everything else, her body had changed. Nailah had her stand on a stool in front of a long mirror and, with pins in her mouth, deftly took in the waist. After the fitting, Gemma lay on their bed and watched Nailah's nimble fingers manipulate the fine thread. This quick, fluttering, iridescent woman was the backbone of the Lazar family.

Incomprehensible to Gemma was that she never betrayed even a note of impatience with her often indolent stepson or her distracted husband. Gemma thought she was glad for female companionship, perhaps because only another woman could appreciate the internal labor required for such external harmony. She herself felt incapable of the smallest harmony. She did not think she could even manage the one thing that had brought her to Egypt, the day that, as it approached, she felt she might lack the strength for.

In the end, it was not hard. She simply invoked the man she remembered her father to be and let him guide her. On their way to Giza, she addressed him in her mind: *This formality is for your ashes. I will do something more for the man you were. I will find out what happened to you, even if it means not understanding what you did with your life.*

In addition to the Lazar family, a cluster of colleagues and friends joined her at the Giza Stables in the late afternoon. Gemma moved among them, introducing herself and accepting condolences. All the while, she looked for the man with the ginger hair, who, it seemed, was not even an acquaintance.

Umar was not there. Mohammad led guests to the mount of their choice, horse or camel. It was a country in which one learned how to ride such animals.

They traveled in a meandering train to the pyramids. Against a sky that was uniformly blue, the pyramids were creamy and startling. As they approached, their geometry became craggier. Gemma stared at the guests hypnotically and thought how tiny they all were, how insignificant their secret furies. Passion and belief and God were projects to keep them busy while they passed through a landscape in which they were little more than insects. Ants with their ant gods.

Far off, she could see the stake tied with a white scarf that whipped in the wind. Umar had marked the place. The air was not as clear as it had been on their ride. It held more color from the afternoon sun, making the air seem dense, as if they were breathing the desert itself in.

There was convivial murmuring as the guests dismounted, and Gemma had the bizarre sense that they were gathering for a picnic. She waited for Mohammad to lead the animals away and then raised her hand to silence the small group.

"My father sent me a photograph of himself, standing almost in this same spot. The sun was setting between two pyramids and he was standing there in front of these amazing monuments looking completely at home. And happy. So this is where I always thought of him. He loved this place, as many of you know. He loved his work here." Gemma let her eyes travel over the audience of expectant faces. Had these people known him? Would he have called them his friends?

"He lost a lot in his lifetime," she continued. "Egypt was healing him. I could sense that in his letters. I'm sorry I won't be able to see it through his eyes. But I'm glad to know he had so many friends, and that so many of you were able to bid him farewell. Thank you for coming today." Gemma unfolded a piece of paper and read, "'Homage to thee, O thou lord of brightness, Governor of the Temple, Prince of the night and of the thick darkness. I have come unto thee. I am shining, I am pure. My hands are about thee, thou hast thy lot with thy ancestors. Give thou unto me my mouth that I may speak with it. I guide my heart at its season of flame and of night.'" Gemma looked up. "A reading from *The Egyptian Book of the Dead*."

The small congregation was silent. David Lazar cleared his throat and stepped forward, dignified, as always, in a burgundy ascot and dark linen suit. He took off his straw hat and held it behind his back.

"Charles Bastian was my good friend for many years. He was a man we shall all miss. I shall miss him most for his companionship, and for how much he saw. Sometimes I was shocked when I read his account of some excavation or journey we had shared. It reminded me of how important it is to have friends who see things differently from the way you do, or who just see more." David glanced at Gemma. "When we were excavating Tut's tomb, I remember the most amazing vase. It was made of alabaster, perfectly plain on the outside and inside. But there was something exquisite and mysterious about it. Every other object was covered with such ornate detail; that this vase was simply what it appeared to be didn't seem possible. It was Charles who suggested lighting it from within. We were all speechless when Amad put a candle inside and an intricate painting of Tutankhamen and his wife appeared. It was the loveliest, most delicate rendition, with detail and color you simply can't imagine. To this day, I don't understand the physics of it. Of all the things we found, it was the most beautiful. I often think of it. I was lucky to know Charles. Luckier still to have called him my friend."

It was both an explanation and an apology. Gemma nodded to David as he rejoined the group and gestured to Amad, who stepped forward with his oud. He picked out a haunting melody that offered no comfort. The strange song ended on a seemingly arbitrary note, resolving nothing. When he finished, he bowed his head to Gemma, who walked a short distance away from the group carrying the pewter urn that held her father's ashes. Though small, the urn was remarkably heavy and cool to the touch. She walked until she could no longer hear the voices behind her and then she turned toward the sun and removed the lid. The top layer of ashes lifted like talcum. Slowly, she spilled the remaining ashes and watched as the silver cloud was caught by the wind and rose in the sky. She turned in a half circle, following the expanding, glinting blizzard as it dissipated and then vanished. Returning to earth, her eyes rested on two figures she had not noticed before. They were standing slightly apart from the others. She studied a face she had not yet seen, a man with skin brown from the sun. She stared abstractly at his light-colored eyes, which were striking, and his disheveled clothes. Next to him was a man in a white robe and skullcap. A Copt. The wind fluttered his robe, and for a moment that was the afternoon's only discernible sound.

Michael was coming toward her, walking without difficulty. He encircled her shoulder with his arm and led her back to the others as if she were the cripple, not he. She had never seen him move with such ease. Gemma focused on the sand beneath her feet, recognizing in his gesture both the act of ownership and that this dust-covered stranger must be Michael's brother, Anthony.

✝ ✝ ✝

ANTHONY LAZAR LEANED against the wall of his father's house, a point of stillness, unmoved and seemingly unaware of his surroundings. Dressed now in immaculate white and tan, he was a citadel of calm rising above a sea of darkness and mourning. He watched Gemma approach.

"You must be Anthony."

"And you are Gemma, Amad's oud pupil. It seems you have charmed even extended members of my family."

"It's the other way around, I'm afraid."

"My brother looks happy." Anthony turned his eyes to her, and in them Gemma saw his mother, Nailah.

"You knew my father," she said, changing the subject.

"He was my friend."

Gemma waited but he did not continue. Nor did he offer condolences. He just stood there looking at her with his great green eyes. She studied the planes of his unmarred face, and for the second time since she had arrived in Cairo, felt she was in the presence of a foreigner. But he was neither European nor Egyptian. His silence was not rudeness. It was something else, something she wasn't presently equipped to identify.

"The other day I paid a visit to Angela Dattari," she said. "But it seems she's gone back to Italy."

"I don't know who that is."

"Then maybe you weren't as close to my father as you thought."

Anthony's eyes were on her. "Your point?"

"No point. It just seems my father was a man of secrets." Gemma accepted a glass of wine from a passing tray. "I'd like to talk to you about his work."

"What about his work?"

"Your father said you might know what he'd been doing these past months. He said you could read Coptic." Anthony sipped his whiskey and watched her. "You do read Coptic?" Gemma said.

"Yes."

"Well, recently my father sent me something. I'd like you to take a look at it. Principally because your name was on it before mine."

"My name?"

"Yes, on the envelope. It's some sort of papyrus fragment." Anthony seemed to be studying the pattern of the rug. "You don't mind looking at it?" she asked. He did not answer. Now he was looking at someone over her shoulder. She did not let herself turn around to see who it was. Her efforts to communicate felt extravagant.

Finally his focus returned to her. "No," he said. "I don't mind."

She straightened her back to dispel the sensation that she had tripped and fallen in front of him, and that instead of helping her get up, he was studying how she had fallen and why.

She freed herself and stalked away from him, glad for other people and light conversation. The rest of the room was an oasis of ease. She furled around guests like smoke, never staying in one place very long. Periodically her eyes returned to the wall, where Anthony Lazar had not moved. She was at times aware that he was watching her. At first it embarrassed her. She didn't know whether she felt insulted or flattered. Her face grew hot. The conversations she attempted did not take flight.

Gemma allowed her glass to be refilled again and again. She was aware that she laughed too loudly, that she was becoming graceless. Finally she turned to him and met his eye with drunken courage. Who was he anyway? A man who didn't know how to make conversation, a man with sand in his brain. A man who had not, like his brother and her father and almost every man she knew, been touched by war.

AT SIX O'CLOCK, Nailah shepherded her family and Gemma away from the party and into the den. It was a signal for the remaining guests to leave.

Gemma was tipsy and cheerful, her most dreaded task accomplished. Her father had found the wind and was everywhere now, even above this house. She thought he would have wanted that.

In the den she bantered with Michael and deliberately ignored his

brother. As her drunkenness progressed, she felt less capable of interact-
ing with Anthony Lazar. In Michael she found shelter. He performed a
savage postmortem on the guests at the party, reenacting inane bits of
conversation he'd been forced to endure. "You wouldn't have known this
was a sad occasion," he said. "In Cairo a funeral is just another party.
Some of those people weren't even at Giza. They probably didn't know
your father from a crocodile."

"Michael," Nailah said, "Gemma's had a long day."

But Gemma was laughing.

Anthony had shed his jacket and unbuttoned the top button of his
shirt. He and his brother moved around each other with an unflagging
awareness of the other. It wasn't until a fresh round of drinks had been
poured that they spoke.

"So, Anthony, how is Kharga treating you? Met any nice girls?" Michael
continued, "though no one's as nice as Gemma here."

"I'm sure you're right."

"Nice is the worst insult," Gemma protested.

"Forgive me," Michael said. "She's horrid."

"She's delightful," Nailah said, rising. She left the room to arrange dinner with Amad. Silence followed. Gemma swallowed some of her drink.
She turned to Anthony. "I was reading in the paper today about the civil
unrest here. I'm not sure I understand it. Is there going to be some kind of
revolt?"

"Anthony might not be able to explain," Michael asserted. "Desert man
that he is. Like I told you, it's that Farouk. He's spending his people out of
house and home."

"I think it's a bit more complicated than that," his brother contested
quietly.

David Lazar entered, his cheeks crimson with wine, his eyes bright from
the people he'd charmed. He had been immersed since the service, moving from one guest to the next, transfixing them like a beam of light.

"Gemma," he said, "how are you faring?"

"We're talking politics," Gemma said. "At my request. Maybe you can
explain what's happening in Cairo."

"Only at great length," Michael interjected.

"Perhaps it's time for a short lesson in Egyptian history," David suggested.

"Please no," Michael protested.

"Why not?" Anthony asked. "I doubt Gemma would object."

"Of course I wouldn't."

"Because she's polite," Michael said.

"Because I'm interested."

"I'll limit it to the Suez Canal," David said, crossing the room to the bar. "How's that?"

"Yes, please, the canal. Michael goes apoplectic at its mention."

"Lies!" Michael boomed.

David poured himself a drink. "The problem with the canal is that it was so damned expensive. Egypt ended up needing an international fund to support it. As you may know, the British set one up for them. Ismail, who was governing Egypt at the time, was given forty-four percent of the shares. Six years later he was forced to sell them off to British subscribers. Then he was faced with bankruptcy and more or less had to agree to let the French-British consortium help him manage his finances."

"The Egyptians aren't good with money," Michael said. "That's evident."

"In 1882," David continued, "the British sent forces to calm unrest in Alexandria. It was the beginning of the British occupation."

"Influence," Michael corrected.

"Skip forward to the First World War, when thanks to rogues like your father and myself, the Egyptians started to become aware of the history they had lost. Some of their identity was returned to them. There was a newfound nationalism. So, understandably, they grew unhappy with the British presence."

"My father, rescuer of nations," Michael said.

"Stop it, Michael," Gemma said.

Michael raised his eyebrows and took a swallow of Scotch. But he remained silent. Anthony watched them both with an expression Gemma could not begin to read.

"About the same time," David resumed, "the British turned Egypt into a full-fledged protectorate so they could deal with the threats from Germany and Turkey. In 1919, the king of Egypt tried to win independence from the British. An independence of sorts was granted in 1922. But the military defense of the country and the canal fell into the hands of the British."

"That was not independence," Anthony insisted quietly.

"Some don't think so," David agreed.

"Please go on," Gemma said.

"In 1936, Egypt and Britain signed a treaty that allowed British forces to carry out their North African campaign. Two years ago, the Arab states met in Cairo and created the Arab League, which was meant to create a united front to pursue the interests of the Arab world. Suffice it to say, the British were not invited to join. Meanwhile, the extravagance of King Farouk had created problems. He is now facing what you could call leadership challenges."

"The Egyptians are ready to rule themselves," Anthony said.

"They haven't been ready since pharaohs ran the place," Michael said. "I doubt they remember how."

"So Farouk is allied with the British?"

"He is supported by them, rather like an indulged child with distant parents."

"What do you think is going to happen?"

Nailah entered, smiling like a beneficent goddess, transferring the focus of the room in a seamless coup.

"I think it's time for dinner," David said. "Nailah doesn't allow politics at the table. So we'll continue this later, shall we, Gemma?"

OVER DESSERT, Gemma finally spoke to Anthony. Although he was sitting next to her, they had not yet addressed each other directly. She glanced at him now, remembering that she needed him. "I understand you have an office at the museum."

"Yes, a few doors down from your father's."

"Amad says you worked with him in a place I can neither remember nor pronounce."

Anthony hesitated. "At one point we were excavating in Oxyrhynchus."

"That's it. What an astonishing name. It sounds like Greek for some African mammal."

"It's a rubbish heap," Anthony said shortly.

"What fun," Gemma said dryly, put off by his pith. "Do I have to beg you for details?"

"I'd be happy to tell you anything you'd like to know."

"I don't know how to begin to ask about an unpronounceable rubbish heap."

"Some other time, then."

"No," Gemma insisted. "Now."

"Very well. Once upon a time, there was a magnificent city. It was bordered on the east by quays. On the west, the road led up to the desert and the camel routes to the Oases and to Libya. All around lay small farms and orchards, irrigated by the annual flood—and between country and town, a circle of dumps where the rubbish piled up. The place was ideal for preservation; the drifting sand covered these mounds in what is luckily a rainless part of Egypt."

Gemma was now concentrating. Talking about this ancient rubbish heap had unleashed an unexpected poetry in Anthony. She accepted coffee from Amad and began sipping it quickly.

"In 1898, two Oxford men published the first volume of their findings from this rubbish heap."

"What did they find?"

The rest of the table had grown quiet. Michael yawned loudly. "I'm finding myself exhausted," he said. "I think I'll retire to the den. Gemma, would you care to join me?"

"Yes, of course. In a minute." She turned back to Anthony.

"What did they find?"

"Ancient private letters, shopping lists, everyday scribblings."

Gemma frowned. "When I first went to my father's office, there was

someone there, going through his things. He said my father had something that didn't belong to him." She leaned toward him. "What do you
think that was, some everyday scribbling?"

Anthony held her eyes with unwavering calm. "I have no idea."

"I know he discovered something important. I want to know what
it was."

"That might be a misplaced curiosity."

"Why?"

"Because he's gone. Proximity to his work won't bring him back."

"He was going to buy a house. But you know, his bank account was
nearly empty. Where do you think that money was coming from? Where
do you think it went?"

"I don't know anything about your father's financial affairs."

"But he talked to you more than anyone."

"Only about some things. Listen, Gemma, there was a reason your
father didn't share what he was doing."

"Clearly."

"I know it's not what you may want to hear, but I'd stay out of it."

"Out of what?"

Anthony remained silent.

Gemma continued. "Maybe I should tell you that I was visited by
someone in London who wanted to know if he had sent anything unusual
from Cairo. I think he was from the Church."

"What did you tell him?"

"That I received an envelope bearing both of our names? No. I told
him nothing. But I can't stay out of it. What an inane suggestion."

Anthony folded his hands in his lap. "I'd like to see what your father
sent you."

"Will you help me?"

"I don't think you've been listening: He wouldn't have wanted you
mixed up in his business."

Gemma frowned. "What are you, his proxy?"

"Of course I'm not. I'm just trying to do what I think he would have
wanted."

"Well, it's too late. I already know at least one of his theories came between him and your father. Jesus grew up here in Egypt! Who knew? How many other offensive theories were there?" She watched the effect her words had on his face and said, "So you see, you can't shake me off so easily."

From the den, Michael bellowed, "Gemma, they're playing our song!"

Anthony escorted Gemma to the den. She whispered vehemently in the hall, "I have a right to know what happened to him."

"I don't know what happened to him."

"Then you must tell me what you do know. There are too many unanswered questions. Why, for instance, would he have imagined some kind of ancient cover-up by the Church?"

"Who told you that?"

"Your father."

"We'll talk tomorrow. Now, please, go dance with my brother."

Michael had opened the French doors to the garden. The night air was cool and fresh and the scent of jasmine mingled with the wood smoke of the den. Gemma smiled at him. Michael switched on the gramophone and set the needle. "Night and Day" started to play. He turned to her and bowed deeply. "Madam, may I have this dance?"

Gemma looked over his shoulder to his brother. "How I miss dancing."

"Allow me the pleasure, then." He took her hand. "I have been known to tread on delicate toes, only now I won't feel it. Please tell me if I crush your foot."

"I won't mind if you do, not tonight."

ANTHONY WATCHED FROM the doorway as they twirled into the garden, Michael the stable point around which Gemma spun. He had not expected her father's features to be beautiful on a woman, and he had not expected her to be his contemporary. Somehow he had envisioned her as a child, as his friend's daughter.

Anthony moved farther into the room. That Gemma was chasing after her father's theories did not necessarily pose a problem. She could spend months at it and still remain at the periphery of his most incendiary work. Because she did not have months, there was no reason not to share with her some of his earlier ideas and musings. It seemed only fair. But he did see the reason in keeping her from her father's biggest theory of all, the theory of which all the others were mere strands, a theory that Anthony was in no position either to evaluate or to defend. If she were his daughter, he'd want her nowhere near it. She'd already had two disagreeable encounters because of it.

He could hear her humming as the light caught the edges of her dress, reminding him of the only ballet he had ever seen. Behind the music, he could hear the unfamiliar sound of his brother's laughter. In the dappled light, they moved in and out of sight. Pausing theatrically in front of the door, his brother kissed Gemma lightly as she returned from a twirl. In her response was both surprise and pleasure. Anthony stepped away from his vantage point, picked up his jacket, and silently left the room.

CHAPTER NINE

If the woman and man had not come apart,
They would not know death.

The Gospel of Philip,
from Nag Hammadi

THE NEXT MORNING Michael didn't appear for breakfast. Gemma waited until ten drinking coffee, half reading the English newspaper and half thinking about the inscrutable Anthony and what he wouldn't tell her. She stared out at the flickering morning light in the garden. A rose brushed against the window, a rose of astonishing beauty; she had never seen the color combination, a pale pink that seeped into a fringe of yellow. It looked painted. She toyed with her coffee spoon and wondered again what for David Lazar might constitute a "dark realm."

By eleven, the light outside had been rounded by heat; the flowering bushes and roses swelled with color. Gemma gave up on Michael and searched for someone else who could give her directions to the museum. She found Nailah in the dining room, arranging a new centerpiece; this one was grapes and figs. Even in casual dress, the older woman was elegant. Her wide black slacks were cinched at the waist; her red blouse was flecked with bursts of white flowers. How, Gemma wondered, had she escaped the cloaked fate of most Egyptian women? By marriage to a European? Gemma realized that Nailah had finished with her directions, that she herself was staring.

"Did you know my father well?"

Nailah smiled. "Enough to miss him."

"But it seems he left this house long before he died. I still don't understand what happened between him and David."

Nailah turned back to her centerpiece. "They quarreled. It's what men do. They don't know how to make peace. David was stubborn—and your father was a man of principle."

Gemma watched as Nailah's manicured fingers rested on the edge of the bowl and then fluttered to move a fig into better balance. It was a perfect still life. "Is David not a man of principle?"

"He is. His trouble is that he thinks he's not. Michael accuses him of not knowing war. But there is war inside of him, a brutal little war."

"The antiquities," Gemma said. "Michael accused him of pillaging."

"Everyone pillaged. Everyone but your father."

The two women stood in silence. "What god were you raised with, Nailah?"

"I was raised with money." She frowned. "God was not necessary."

"The antiquities business?"

"What else?" Nailah bit her lip softly. "Sometimes I regret my father's enterprise. He gave me many gifts, but he did not give me the gift of faith. Faith can pass from generation to generation for centuries and then suddenly be broken. From some it's stronger than death. In our family it was like a daisy chain."

"And in this family?"

"In this family, God changes shape. Stay long enough, and you may see Him come and go."

As Gemma left, Nailah called after her. "There's a lovely party a week from Saturday, an annual dance. I hope you'll come."

Gemma turned back. "Yes, of course."

Nailah's hands pressed together in brief consort. "Michael will be so pleased."

As SHE WALKED to the museum, Gemma raised her eyes to the women she passed, the girls who met her eye and the covered women who, after an intense moment of scrutiny, cast theirs away. In what, Gemma wondered. Disgust? Shame? What happened to them in the journey to adulthood? When were they instructed to hide themselves? She became conscious of her own body and how, unlike the robes of the Egyptian women, her clothes contoured her shape; they were bright and colored and completely without mystery. She was conscious of the bareness of her legs, the feel of open air and sun on her skin. It was a strange context in which to be reminded of her essential femaleness, but she realized she was grateful. It wasn't a bad body; it had done what she asked, more or less without protest. It had survived a war. And, she thought now, it had been too long forgotten, exiled to a region of her mind she rarely visited. After years of tending to wounded and lonely men, she had lost all sense of her sexuality. As a nurse, one could not afford to think of such things; these poor soldiers were tormented enough. One had to be careful not to encourage them.

She thought again about the images her father had collected. The graphic illustrations of the sexual act had shocked her, but they were not indecent. Rather the shock came from the fact that the depictions of copulation seemed to be portrayed as sacred.

As she strode down Sharia Qasr el-Aini, strands of memory returned to her. It was time, perhaps, to let some things come back. An affair with a young captain whose hand had been blown off by a grenade. She thought it might have been love. Or something even more. His infection was severe; the remaining limb was ragged, a mess of bone and tendon and seared flesh. Gemma watched through the weeks as the doctors kept cutting the gangrenous arm; watched the soldier's silent pleas of protest, watched until there was nothing left. The captain was there longer than most. She learned his name, read to him when the pain woke him, sat silently with him as the infection spread to his blood. The last week of his life, the captain's eyes were misted with morphine and the painless understanding it allowed him. As he felt his time slip away, he began talking to her. She became his confessor, his family, the world he was leaving. He said he had never given his heart to a woman; he said he thought he could imagine what it would be like to love. She had held his hand as he suggested marriage. They both laughed. Then he turned his head from her and he cried. Something simpler, then, he suggested. Some night they could pull the curtains and marry their bodies. He wouldn't make a noise.

Gemma could hear his drug-softened voice, see his tormented, glassy, blue-gray eyes, his long fingers that caressed hers with surprising strength. She could feel again the tingle and creep of her own buried desire. What harm? she thought. Maybe a gift for us both. It was not a time for false morality. It was not a time for withholding.

So one night they touched with trembling fingers and left the world and its war behind. It was almost an answer. She remembered how gentle they were with each other, how something fragile and fluttering was coaxed into life. Something she had forgotten.

It was so lovely with her captain she knew there would be a cost. She had not known how great. She should have. She should have known there were no secrets in the ward, that everything was heard, even the faint vibration of a moth's wings beating against a lantern, that in the stillness of disease and dying, all ears strained to hear life.

Nurse Bastian, you give it away.

The first accusation was hurled from a young soldier who felt betrayed. Others did too. They backed her into a corner. Why not us? *We might live.*

That's just why, she said. Now leave me be. She snapped and tucked the clean sheets for the new arrival who was waiting for her captain's bed.

But they hadn't let her be. One night after two bottles of whiskey and a raucous card game, two of them crowded her into the linen closet and pressed a pocket knife to her throat. *Don't scream; we are not criminals.*

She had stared at the bare bulb above. If she tried now, she could remember their names, but not their faces. Her memory had painted them into something theatrical, turned them into actors on a stage.

The first had tried to be gentle but his excitement made him violent. He pushed and failed to get inside of her. She remembered the wetness on her thigh. The second had wept, dropped his knife, and begged forgiveness.

She forgave them because it was easier. At the time, she thought they needed their forgiveness more than she needed her anger. Where would anger get her? Far worse things happened every day. Every day.

✝   ✝   ✝

S HE DUG IN her pocket for her father's office key and tried to get back
to her captain. After they had made love, he shone with defiance, his eyes
full of meaning. The spoken words were few: She had healed something
in him, he said. He was not afraid to die.

She sat down in her father's chair and spread her hands on the desk.
These hands have healed, she thought. Why can't I love them more?

She turned to a stack of archaeological periodicals and began scouring
them. She searched for a pen to make some notes after reading an article
about the unpronounceable rubbish heap, Oxyrhynchus. Then, without
thinking, she pulled out the book from which her father had ripped the
pictures. The volume was *Sex and Mythology: The Divine Transformation.*
She turned to the place where Inanna had been and began reading.

> The Sumerians, whose culture dates back to 5000 B.C., were the first lit-
> erate people. Of all the deities, Inanna, the goddess of love and procre-
> ation, was the most revered. Her influence lasted far longer than that of
> any other god or goddess. Inanna openly rejoiced in her own sexuality.
> From clay tablets and fragments of text, we hear how, for instance,
> when she leaned back against the apple tree, "her vulva was wondrous
> to behold." And with her consort, the shepherd Dumuzi, Inanna
> describes
>
> > *He shaped my loins with his fair hands,*
> > *The shepherd Dumuzi filled my lap with cream and milk,*
> > *He stroked my pubic hair,*
> > *He watered my womb.*
> > *He laid his hands on my holy vulva.*
> > *He caressed me on the bed.*

Of all the deities, Inanna was the most revered, Gemma wrote, thinking
of Isis and how in both the Sumerian and Egyptian cultures the female
goddesses were the most powerful and enduring.

As the representative of the goddess, the priestess would, through sexual union with the king, bestow her divine power upon him, thereby making him fit to rule. . . . The ultimate power was in her keeping.

Gemma closed the book and pulled out *The Catholic Encyclopedia,* which was wedged like a forgotten bookend at the far side of the shelf. She went to W, for *woman,* reading first about Aristotle's designation of woman as an incomplete or mutilated man. The encyclopedia text then read, "The female sex is in some respects inferior to the male sex, both as regards body and soul." Corinthians said that (xi 7), "The man is the image and glory of God; but the woman is the glory of man. . . . Man is called by the Creator to this position of leader, as is shown by his entire bodily and intellectual makeup."

How sure they were, Gemma thought. How unshakably sure.

Her eye was caught by an observation by Herodotus that Egyptians were unusually respectful of women—more so than other nations in the fifth century. Because of their goddesses, Gemma thought.

Behind her there was a light tap on the door. Gemma closed the book and covered it with another. "Come in."

"How are you making out?" Anthony asked.

Gemma swiveled to face him. "Just starting, really."

"I'm afraid I can't help you just yet." Anthony swung his bag over his shoulder. "I have a meeting, but come down the hall later. I'd like to take a look at the papyrus fragment your father sent you."

She waited one long hour. In that time, she uncovered the book she'd been reading and put it back on the shelf. Then she took it out again and reread the section on Inanna, the Sumerian goddess. "My holy vulva," it had said.

She put the book away again and leafed through some dog-eared periodicals. She scanned the marked articles and then sat for a while, thinking about what she had read. She then forced herself to sift through layers of various piles of paper stacked around the office. They provided a sampling of her father's early research materials, from the time he worked with David Lazar. Maybe David was right and he was compiling material for a book on King Tut, because she could find nothing current. But she didn't believe it. Chewing on her lip, she walked to the corner and opened a file cabinet and flipped through the labels. She lingered awhile with his old financial records, receipts, and requisitions for excavations and trips he had taken for the museum, remembering some of them from letters he had written her. Then there was nowhere to go but back to his chair. Because the desktop had been cleared, there was no way to tell what he had been doing when he died. It was the complementary offense to his cremation. It was as if someone had wanted to obliterate every trace he had left on earth. There was no one, no one but her, to bring him back.

On impulse, she reached under the desk and felt around. Set back under the lip was the knob to a drawer. She pulled it, but like his desk at home, it was locked. She searched for the hidden catch and when she found it, released it. The drawer popped open. Before her in a small stack were his journals. She picked up one and then another, first smelling them and holding the smooth leather covers to her cheek. He had shown them to her before, to give her an idea of his life in Egypt. He had shown her sketches, pressed flowers. She paged through them quickly. A cursory look showed her the familiar narrow columns of notes. Written diagonally in the margins were sketches and quotations. Between a few blank pages were leaves and flowers. She pressed the binding open further. Wedged deep inside were grains of sand. She tipped them out and let them collect in her lap. Then she began turning the pages in sequence, one after another, feeling closer to him than she had in months.

She looked at his most recent journal and searched for his final entry. It was a single line written wildly in the middle of the page: *Between Isis and Mary is proof of woman lost.*

What did that mean? Was he talking about the women in the ripped pages? What woman was lost?

One journal had pages she couldn't read at all. It seemed to be the oldest. Interspersed with the incomprehensible lettering of some other language and different-colored inks was her father's scrawl, which she couldn't always decipher. It was a different scrawl than she had taught herself to read, a younger version perhaps. Her sense of frustration returned as her father's presence lifted and floated away, leaving her alone again with someone she wasn't sure she knew.

Next to the journals was a New Testament, which, along with the journals, Gemma slipped into her bag.

THE DOOR TO Anthony's office was ajar but the room was empty. There were signs of recent occupation—a mug of tea, a half-eaten sandwich. She stared at the crumb-filled plate, trying and failing to imagine the regal Anthony eating such ordinary food. She lifted the piece of bread to see what was inside. Cheese. The presence of a cheese sandwich somehow made Anthony seem more human, more like someone she could talk to.

She lingered a while longer, reluctant to return to her own unimaginable task. Anthony rounded the corner as she left his office. In self-defense, she held up the envelope her father had sent her. "I brought this."

"Yes, please come in. Forgive the disorder. We Coptic scholars are in transition."

Gemma reentered the office and stood awkwardly while he cleared a chair for her. She observed and quickly deflected the beauty of his unscarred face, realizing she was more comfortable with deformity than an unreadably handsome mask.

"So," she began, "in Oxyrhynchus, did they also find an item called 'Sayings of Jesus'? A piece of papyrus that corresponded to the time when all material except the chosen four that now constitute the New Testament was deemed heretical and mostly destroyed?"

Anthony paused before meeting her eye. "I believe so, yes."

"You believe so." Gemma stared at him. "The Bible was edited. I suppose I shouldn't be surprised. It didn't actually fall from heaven."

"May I ask what you've been reading?"

"Periodicals my father saved."

Anthony almost smiled. "Why don't I get us some tea."

"Would you like me to come?"

"No need. I won't be a moment. Milk? Sugar?"

"Nothing, thanks."

Anthony made his way to the cafeteria, somewhat stunned by the progress she'd made overnight. It was as if her father were speaking to her from the grave. She was not going to be put off, that much was evident. He decided there was nothing to do but have the conversation, but carefully.

When he returned with the tea, she began speaking as soon as he walked in the door.

"So," she continued, "these gospels were voted out and tossed."

"It wasn't as simple as that. There were hundreds of copies; they were like best-selling books, as popular and widespread. Getting rid of them was nothing less than a military operation."

"It seems extreme."

"I think it was quite a violent process."

"What, exactly, made them heretical?"

Anthony shrugged. "They might have contradicted something the new church said, or wanted people to believe."

"That sounds like something my father would be interested in. Tell me, how would the Church feel about such fragments surfacing now?"

Anthony looked at her sharply but did not answer.

"This is what you were working on together," she guessed, "isn't it?"

"We didn't work together. We worked alongside each other. My area of research is quite different."

"Fine. I still want to know everything."

"I don't know what you mean."

"Really?" she said, turning away to look at a map. "So what is it you've been doing in Kharga?"

"Excavating the dwellings of the earliest Christian communities."

"Where is the Western Desert, exactly, apart from being in the west?"

"Three days' camel ride, if the weather is cooperative."

She paced around the office, looking at books and pictures. Like her father, Anthony hung nothing but maps on the walls. "But surely it doesn't rain in the desert."

"There are winds."

"Winds," she said lightly.

"Herodotus reported that in 525 B.C. the Persian ruler Cambyses II sent fifty thousand men into the desert past Kharga. They were never seen again. Yes, winds."

Gemma pivoted away from him to face the wall of maps. Anthony continued, "The same ruler murdered his brother out of envy, thinking that somehow his brother was a threat to his own absolute power."

Gemma did not turn. "So sometimes you come to Cairo?"

"Regularly. We are in the process of building a Coptic museum here. Until it's completed, we are housed here."

"So these early Christians lived out in the desert. Weren't there easier places to live?"

"Any place would have been easier. But that was the point."

"They wanted to suffer."

"Some of them had been banished. Some of them wanted to be alone."

"That's interesting."

"Is it? I'm not sure it's interesting to anyone but me—and maybe your father."

Gemma finally perched on the edge of a chair. "My father could stir my curiosity for just about anything. But you must have known that about him."

He looked at her. "Yes, I think I did."

His eyes were a remarkable, reflective green. To Gemma they seemed distant with appraisal. But in moments they flashed with something else. After looking for a moment more, she decided that Anthony's behavior was intentionally remote, his aloofness effortful. It made her want to shock him, tell him she had lifted the bread from his sandwich and found out it was just cheese—that she would find him out eventually. Instead she held out the envelope and watched his eyes pass quickly over the fragment of papyrus. Then he handed it back to her and gathered his things to leave.

"Where are you going?"

"To the market. I told my mother I would buy her spices."

"What about the fragment?"

"It's a fragment from the Gospel of Thomas. A copy of the original your father found at Oxyrhynchus."

"It's a fragment from a lost gospel?"

"A copy. Yes. The Gospel of Thomas."

"Who is Thomas?"

"He was an apostle."

"I'm ashamed to say I don't know anything about him."

"You and most of the world."

"And the rest of the gospel?"

"As far as I know only fragments exist."

Gemma stared at the papyrus. "Why would he send it to me?"

"I can't tell you. Nor can I tell you why he might have first planned to send it to me."

"You said these gospels were outlawed because they might have contradicted the Church. How?"

"Now you're asking for a dissertation. This was your father's area of expertise, not mine. I study hermits, not apostles."

"Why are you rushing away?"

"Because it's later than I thought." Anthony moved toward the door.

Gemma stood up. "Can I come with you?"

Anthony shrugged. "If you don't mind the walk."

"No. I'd love the walk."

"It's not an easy time of day to get through the city."

"I don't mind."

WHEN THEY PASSED through the doors of the museum, they were struck by a sun that had reached its full and painful strength. Half blind, Gemma pulled her hat over her eyes. "If you were to guess, why do you think he sent the papyrus fragment to me?"

"I don't know."

"You must have some idea."

He started down the museum steps. "Shall I tell you about Cairo?" Before she could answer, he continued. "Now here's something." Anthony stopped in front of a large window covered by an intricately carved grille and what looked like a water trough where the windowsill should have been. "A sabil, or fountain," he explained. "It was kept full of fresh water. Copper cups were attached to the grille so that thirsty passersby could help themselves to a drink. Wealthy warlords and nobles would often build a sabil to win over both the local population and their god above." He pointed to an upper floor above the sabil, where a small terrace was open to the breezes. "That terrace was set aside for the teaching of the Koran. It is called a kuttab. Mohammad was well pleased by the combination of a sabil and a kuttab."

Gemma did not comment but let him continue to describe the city that was clearly his home. His words painted the air before her, and in this way he reminded her of her father, who had held huge, light-filled quantities of knowledge so easily inside of him.

They passed into another neighborhood, this one riddled with smaller streets and side alleys. "This is Fatimid Cairo," Anthony said. "Once the imperial capital of Egypt. There are still remnants, hidden palaces and mosques. Up here is the madrassa and mausoleum of Sultan Qalawun, built in the thirteenth century. Three hundred Crusader prisoners built it, in only thirteen months."

"Can we go in?"

"We can look, but we shouldn't enter."

The mausoleum was an octagonal configuration of columns, some of which were massive granite pillars. The walls were covered with brightly detailed geometric mosaics and Arabic lettering. "It says 'Allah,'" Anthony whispered. From everywhere it seemed that gold glinted, lit by the rays of pure color falling from hundreds of stained-glass windows. It was quite easy to believe that God dwelled in such a place. It made Gemma think of her father and the God he had pursued for most of his life. Would he have felt him here, in this place? Did Anthony? Had they shared gods? Gemma stared at the gilded words and the air with colors that wove and unwove themselves, and could find nothing to say to this man who said he knew her father well.

They continued walking, but soon Anthony stopped again, this time pointing to a rather ordinary-looking residence. "The palace of Qasr Beshtak, a notorious rake who managed to marry the sultan's daughter and then was murdered by the Mamluks, because they were a violent and jealous people and could not stand to see the wealth of others."

Gemma paused in front of a façade with panels of various-colored blocks of marble, arranged together like some sort of puzzle.

"It's called 'joggling,'" Anthony said. "A decorative technique."

"I like that word," she said. "I'd like to find another way to use it."

"Her heart was joggled with love and desire and grief."

Gemma stopped and looked at him. "That's beautiful. It happens to be true."

"Did you think I was talking about you?"

Gemma turned and began walking.

"I was talking about Beshtak's wife, the sultan's daughter. She was quite distraught by her husband's violent death."

A flock of birds fell like a carpet from the sky, frightened by a demonstration of chanting protesters moving in a slow river down the street.

"What are they saying?" Gemma asked.

"They are saying, 'Egypt for the Egyptians.'"

"I think you agree."

"I think it seems fair enough."

"Do you think Farouk will be ousted?"

"Probably."

"Is he really so awful?"

"Relative to other Egyptian rulers, no. There was Al-Hakim, the third Fatimid caliph, who came into power at age eleven. When people refused to substitute his own name for Mohammad's name during Friday prayer, he burned down their neighborhoods. He was also no lover of women. He outlawed the manufacture of women's shoes so they would be forced to stay at home." Anthony glanced at his watch. "We must hurry. It's almost prayer time."

Anthony lengthened his stride; Gemma ran sporadically to keep up with him. The route was incomprehensible. Anthony stayed slightly ahead of her. She followed him like a stray dog, like a Moslem woman. They twisted and turned, and soon she was disoriented and damp with perspiration. She wondered if he was deliberately confusing her. Over his shoulder he asked, "Are you hungry?"

"If it means sitting down, yes."

She thought she heard him laugh.

He led her to a small restaurant, and as soon as he sat down across from her, he performed a terrible trick. He hardened his features and carried himself far from her. His eyes lost their light, became flat, without message or meaning. Gone was the storyteller. Gone was the repository of information that had entranced her for the last hour. The bridge to her father was broken. Gemma unpinned her hat while he ordered for both of them. "You're very confident of my tastes," she said.

"I ordered things I'm sure you've already eaten."

"Can we talk about the fragment?"

"There's not much to talk about, is there?"

"I don't believe you."

"You don't have to."

Gemma rested her chin in her hand, refusing to attempt conversation, refusing to give him the advantage by losing her nerve and babbling like an idiot.

"*Aish*," he said, holding up a piece of pita. "Bread."

Gemma mimicked him, pointing to the butter.

"*Zibda*."

Two glasses of mint tea and a small bowl of olives were delivered. "*Zeitun*," he said. He pressed his finger into the bottom of the bowl and held it up. "*Zeit*."

"Oil," she said.

"Yes."

Then he sat quietly, his eyes cast downward. She laughed irritably. "Is that the only conversation you're capable of?"

He looked at her like she was a tree or a horse, something he didn't expect to speak. Finally he said, "You seemed like someone who likes to know the names of things."

She put an olive in her mouth and stared out onto the street, determined not to lose her composure. She would play his game and wrap herself in silence. He wasn't the only one capable of moving through the world in a cocoon. She clenched her jaw. The minutes passed. Other sounds filled the silence. Outside on the street, two men were arguing. In the kitchen, food was frying in oil. There was the faint static of a radio station. A fly circled her head, alit briefly on her cheek. She batted at it and swore.

"Do they serve beer here?"

"It's not the habit of Moslems to drink alcohol."

"Are you Moslem?"

"No."

"Well, this Moslem city seems to be saturated with alcohol."

"Only the European establishments."

"And your house."

"Not mine."

"You don't associate with your family?"

"No," he corrected. "I live on the river."

She drank her whole glass of water. "Where on the river?"

"I don't think you know the river well enough for me to explain."

"So?"

"So."

She ate another olive. "You're different from your brother and your father."

"Yes."

"They're good at conversation."

Anthony smiled. "It was said of Abbot Agatho that for three years he carried a stone in his mouth until he learned to be silent."

"Lovely." She forced a smile. "I suppose he's your hero."

"In that he was trying to be an ordinary man, yes."

"With a stone in his mouth for three years? That's hardly ordinary."

"One of the most difficult things in the world is to be an ordinary man."

"I suppose you think you're ordinary."

"I'm trying."

"Well, it's not working."

"I will have to try harder."

"I don't know if being ordinary should involve so much effort."

"So you see the challenge."

She laughed and continued laughing. It felt good to make some noise. Anthony raised his eyebrows in silence. The food arrived. She did not know the names of anything on her plate and he did not offer to tell her. She copied him, eating with her hands, scooping grains and dips with circles of flat brown bread. Anthony concentrated wholly on his food. It was like eating with a domesticated animal. She decided that she would use the time to think about something else. She mentally reviewed what she had seen in her father's office and felt her face grow hot.

"Why are you unwilling to talk to me?" she finally said.

Anthony gestured at the table and the plates of food between them. "Am I unwilling?"

"He was your friend. I would think you might want to help me."

"As his friend, I have a responsibility to do what he would have done. He did not speak to you of his work, so I don't think I should either."

She ignored his refusal. "Let's start with the Gospel of John. I've read it. In fact I've reread all the gospels. And I see why he was so interested in John. John was different from the others, wasn't he?"

Anthony leaned back and watched her.

"Was something in my father's work questioning the Bible? Does it have to do with these lost gospels?"

Anthony picked up his tea and held it in both hands. "It's complicated."

"We have time."

His eyes were following the slow rotation of the fan. "I'll tell you this. Your father felt the New Testament was not a reliable source of information. He was right. The gospels don't always agree. Sometimes they blatantly contradict one another. Really, skepticism is healthy when one considers that no one has been able to establish when, where, and by whom the books were even written."

"But my father was more than skeptical."

Anthony tipped his chair back. Then, for the first time since they sat down, he rested his eyes on Gemma. "It's time we got to the market."

"We're not finished." Gemma followed him to the door.

"No, I imagine not."

"Why would my father have an image of Isis and Horus on his wall? He's never tolerated religious iconography."

Anthony paused before going out onto the street. "If I were to guess, I would say it was symbolic."

"How?"

"There is an emerging school of thought that maintains that Christianity wasn't unique, as some would believe. The myth of Isis, widespread at the time of Christ, shares remarkable similarities with the Gospel story. The virgin birth, the murder, the Resurrection—the Ascension to heaven. The main difference is that the Egyptian cycle is an allegory, and the Gospel tale is considered by many to be historical fact."

As they made their way along a crowded sidewalk, Gemma fell behind. Anthony waited. Gemma touched his arm. "Go on."

"It wasn't just in Egypt that Christian-like myths existed," he said. "The most popular religion in Rome at the time Christianity was spreading was based on Mithra, a god thought to be the son of the sun, sent to the earth to save humankind. Two centuries before Jesus, the myth of Mithra held that he was born on December 25 in a cave and his birth was attended by shepherds. He sacrificed himself and had a last supper with twelve of his faithful, whom Mithra invited to eat his body and drink his blood. He was buried in a tomb and after three days rose again."

"You're not serious."

"Perfectly. Then there was the Greek cult of Dionysus, another myth in which a man born of a virgin died as a martyr and became a god. The thesis is that Christianity absorbed elements of other popular myths at the time. Because the story was familiar to the people, it was that much easier to accept. The point is, Christianity was put together by men, not God. It did not, as you say, fall from heaven."

"Why isn't this common knowledge?"

"Because history is told by the victors. Everything else falls away. With pharaohs, they chipped out the names of those who had come before and destroyed their temples and statues. It was every ruler's greatest fear, because they knew if there was nothing to remind people they had lived, they would be forgotten. Not only forgotten, erased. What upset your father the most was when the truth was hidden. When we have truth, we have a chance at understanding. Through understanding we can reach freedom. When the truth is hidden, we are all wounded. We are all crippled. He told me this once in the desert and I have never forgotten it."

As they entered the spice bazaar, the crowds grew thick. Anthony reached back for her hand and held it behind him, weaving through tents with burlap bags filled with saffron and ochre and powdered indigo. She stopped thinking then and for a moment she was happy. A girl, not a woman, being led by someone else.

Her eyes passed over the crowds of people and were caught by a face of a lighter color. Some distance behind them was the pale, ginger-haired man. He was wearing a hat now. She involuntarily tightened her grip on Anthony's hand. As she watched, the gap behind them closed. Then the face and hat disappeared.

"What is it?" Anthony asked.

"The man I saw in my father's office. He was just over there."

"Are you sure?"

"He's English, reddish hair." Gemma looked at Anthony. "Who is he? Do you know?"

"I don't know. Your father mentioned once that he thought he was being followed. But you should know he stopped talking to me about many things these past months." He turned away and added, "I hadn't seen him for some time."

"Had you fought?"

"No, no."

"He just disappeared from sight?"

"I didn't think it was personal."

"You thought he had found something."

"It's what we archaeologists do."

"The man in his office insisted he had something that wasn't his. Had he stolen something, Anthony?"

"That's not really an operable verb in our line of work. Finding is another matter."

She grasped his hand to stop him from walking. "Will you help me?"

"Help you how?"

"Help me find out what happened to him. Help me find what he found! Don't you want to know? He might have died for it."

She watched his eyes flicker. His voice dropped low. "It is precisely because your father is dead that I do not want to lead you any further into this."

"You don't even know me. How can you care so much about my safety?"

Anthony turned from her and began walking.

She followed, disconnected. They walked for over an hour in silence, returning to the Lazar house in the late afternoon. It was enough for Gemma. She was ready to lie on her bed until the heat and dust and conversation unwrapped themselves from her suffocated being. At the front door, Anthony stepped back and let Gemma precede him into the hall. When she turned at the foot of the stairs, he was gone. She trailed up the stairs, counting them as she went. At the top she glanced at Michael's door before turning toward her own and closing it firmly behind her.

The tall windows blazed with light. Beyond the trees of Garden City were the afternoon's sunbaked shades of gold, brutal and unvaried at this time of day. The sun seemed to cast no shadows to help determine shape or distance. And lying over everything, a soft, impenetrable haze. The pyramids and the minarets of the mosques looked as if they'd been washed by the same brush. They seemed far away, lost under a patina that would never rise.

Gemma left the window for her bed and stared at the ceiling. Her father had sent for her because he had found something that had changed his life, something that had restored his faith—and might restore hers. They were going to start a new chapter, in a new country, together. To the endless war, to the bottomless loneliness and loss, there had almost been a happy ending.

She could not let it go.

She rolled onto her side and studied the brocade pattern on the chaise longue. The possibility that she might never know why her father had died, or what he was doing when his life ended, made her despair. She could not let it happen. She thought instead about practical matters; the problem of money was a good place to start. She did not want to overstay her visit with the Lazars, but a hotel would quickly dry up her funds. She was, for the time being, trapped. At some point there would be the question of what she would do when she had cleared out her father's office. Go back to London? The prospect twisted her insides.

Stop wallowing, she told herself.

"We must be like architects," her father had said. "We must construct our own happiness."

It was the year that half their house had been blown to bits. They had moved into a new flat, and sat side by side at the piano they had dragged with them. Only some of the keys played. Her father had just returned from Egypt. He told her about his work at the museum, and some of the places he'd been, places that sounded unreal to her. Later she could neither visualize them nor remember their names. Perhaps, she thought now, one of them had been called Oxyrhynchus. As was their ritual, she had chatted to him about her work at the hospital and then flatly recited a list of the people who had died. Lastly she related another list, this one of amusing stories she had saved for him, doing her best to make him laugh. She told him about their friend Poppy Collins turning her husband's wardrobe into her own; she'd stayed awake all night while he was out carousing, altering his suits to fit her. There were no clothes to be had anywhere, and she should have some compensation, shouldn't she? Or the soldiers who romanced the local girls and fornicated with desperate passion in the rubble of the East End, unaware of the boys who would sneak up from behind and steal their trousers from their ankles. The shortages were everywhere. It seemed the fewer things that were available, the more humorous life became. But the fact was, there was nothing left and it wasn't at all funny. People laughed because they had taught themselves how.

Gemma remembered then that it seemed impossible that the war would end. No one even thought about it. But her father was, as always, stalwart.

"Even in such a world," he said, "we can build the lives we want."

"With what?" Gemma asked. "Shrapnel?"

"In Egypt the Bedouin weave tents from goat hair. The fellahin make houses out of mud. We will use whatever God gives us."

She had looked at him in surprise. "God?" she repeated. "I don't think I've ever heard you mention him."

"Don't worry, I'm not talking about some graybeard up in the clouds. The word is just an abstraction."

"Have you been finding God in Egypt?"

"Let's say I see signs of God. More signs than there are here."

"What sort of God?"

"A different God from the one I was raised with. A God I might be comfortable with. Someday I hope to introduce you. I am working toward that."

"In Egypt?"

"In Egypt."

"Promise me. Then I will promise you to do my best at constructing happiness."

He had laughed then, and pulled her close. "I got lucky with *you,* Gemma."

Gemma wrapped her arms around herself and rolled onto her side. Don't wallow, she told herself. Do something. Start constructing your happiness. Go look for your father's God.

THE NEXT MORNING she was up before the dawn. She watched the sun rise, splitting the night like a fruit. She jotted a note and left it on the kitchen table, wanting to escape the house before conversation, before her quieted mind could be disturbed by the beleaguered communication of the Lazar family.

She walked quickly from the house, feeling the small thrill of escape. The morning air felt gloriously fresh, and when she turned the corner, she paused to breathe it in more deeply. There wasn't a single human sound. The wealthy residents of Garden City had no reason to rise at dawn.

Gemma took off her sweater and folded it over her arm. It was in this peaceful, settled state that she had often walked the streets of London, before a shift at the hospital, when the stillness of the morning preserved a clarity lent by night and the distance of sleep—when, for minutes at a time, she could perceive a faint harmony that might have once existed, or existed still, but underneath everything else, like a tentative melody overwhelmed by timpani. Rippling softly through her was the fragile memory of the way things had been before the war. Then, as she walked in the morning that was still hers, this memory and its pain were shed and replaced by a tentative imagining of the way things might be again.

When she reached Angela Dattari's house, she stood staring up at the balconied bedrooms like a suitor. The pale paint was peeling in leprous patches. Someone who could afford such a house could afford to keep it up. Perhaps Angela Dattari was never coming back. Gemma wandered into the garden. The marble statue of the woman looked more lifelike in the thin light of morning. Gemma circled her, scrutinizing the curves and angles of her shape. Then she sat on the edge of the fountain pool, wondering what woman had been able to hold such a pose for the artist.

Nearby, a door closed. Gemma straightened. A small elderly man rounded the corner of the house holding a rake. He did not see Gemma, did not look away from the leaf-strewn path in front of him, as if calculating the exact number of motions it would require to clear it.

Gemma watched him pass her and cleared her throat. She did not want to startle him. "Good morning."

The man gripped his rake and turned. "And you are?"

"I am a friend of Angela Dattari's."

"I do not know you."

"My name is Gemma Bastian. I think Angela Dattari knew my father."

"She is not here."

"I know."

"May I help you?"

"I was taking a walk. I'm sorry to intrude. It's such a lovely garden. Very peaceful. You are the gardener?"

"I take care of the house when Mrs. Dattari is away. And the garden, yes."

"Do you know when she'll be back? I am waiting for her."

"I think you will get hungry waiting there."

"When will she be back?"

"She said three weeks. But she has been known to change her mind."

"Why did she leave?"

"Because that's what she does, from time to time."

"Did you know my father, Charles Bastian?"

"No."

"Are you sure?"

"Would you care to leave Mrs. Dattari a message?"

"I already wrote her a letter. I put it in the mailbox."

"A good place for a letter. Now, if you'll excuse me."

Gemma sat for a while longer in silent rebellion. She believed she had every right to be here. A territorial gardener wouldn't know the details of his employer's personal life, wouldn't necessarily know her father. Before she left, Gemma approached him once more. "Did you see anyone coming to visit the last weeks Mrs. Dattari was here?"

"I am here all day. Mrs. Dattari is a private woman. I saw no one."

"But at night?"

"At night I am asleep."

Gemma left the garden. *A.D.—p.m.* Had her father come at night? Is that what the notation meant? It was the only explanation that made sense so far. Why at night? Was Angela Dattari a secret? He had visited her for more than three weeks straight. Then he had died.

And now Angela Dattari was also gone. Gemma caught a final glimpse of the sleek form of the statue, releasing her dove to the four winds, and started back to the Lazar house.

Chapter Ten

I disclose my mysteries to those
who are worthy of my mysteries.

The Gospel of Thomas,
from Nag Hammadi

Togo Mina took a sharp breath. Outside his office, a youth lay slumped. His arms were thin and bare and streaked with dirt. Mina bent down and touched the boy's brow. He seemed to be asleep. He gently shook his shoulder until the boy roused himself from what seemed to be a drug-induced slumber. As the boy pulled his arms out from inside his tunic, Mina saw that he hadn't been drugged. His hands shone red with blood. "Who has done this to you, Ali?"

The youth stared vacantly and, as Mina tried to get him to his feet, whispered something almost inaudible.

"Maback?" Mina repeated. "Is that what you said? We need to get you into my office and I'll phone an ambulance."

The boy shook his head in protest, rolling his eyes back as if there were something behind him. "Maback," he said again.

Mina was now ripping the boy's tunic so he could stanch the bleeding. As he felt for the wound, he found that strips of material already circled the boy's torso. Mina followed them around to the boy's back, where he could feel that a rectangular shape was being held in place. *My back.* Mina could feel the smooth leather of the book. God in heaven, Mina thought.

Anthony received the urgent summons in the library. After entering Mina's office, he stopped abruptly. In Mina's armchair, a human shape lay under a rough and sodden tunic.

"He's dead," Mina announced. "He arrived with a knife wound. He said it's because he stole. I think he might have tried to steal this." Mina held the leather-bound book.

Anthony glanced at the book and went instead to the boy. He held his hand to the boy's brow. "I know this boy."

"He sometimes runs errands for the museum. It's barbaric."

"Had you sent him on an errand, Mina?"

"I told him about the texts, yes. I told him there would be a reward for any information that could lead us to them."

"I see." Anthony covered the boy's face. "Did he tell you anything else?"

"He wasn't able to. God help us, if these are the people we are dealing with."

"We don't know who we're dealing with. The texts might have been hijacked by a gang of boys—and they might have fought amongst themselves."

"This book was tied to his back. He couldn't possibly have tied it there himself. Nor could he reach it, not with that wound."

"So someone sent him here like this. It communicates a certain message." Anthony covered the boy and turned his attention to the book. "Is that what I think it is?"

Mina held it out. "I am sure it is from Nag Hammadi. We are lucky. The French Egyptologist Jean Doresse is here in Cairo. He can authenticate it. I have telephoned Doresse at his hotel. I want him to come to the museum at once."

"Shall we take a look?"

Mina took the oversized book to his desk and gingerly opened it. As he did so, there was the profoundest silence between the men, settling even the disturbed air of death in the room. Bastian had often described to Anthony the phenomenon, the tactile experience of seeing such an ancient treasure, touching it with one's own hands.

Mina turned the page and a small white envelope glared up at them.

It was addressed to Togo Mina. Mina slid his finger under the seal and read,

A minor book,
but the museum should have something.
Especially if it is desperate enough
to send boys to steal.

"I didn't send him to steal, for God's sake!" Mina's voice rose. "Who would do such a thing?"

Anthony held up his hand for silence. He did not want to discuss the matter further with the overwrought Mina. He focused on the book, following the Coptic lettering with his fingers. "It's titled *The Exegesis of the Soul.*"

Mina leaned over the text. "I never knew such a writing existed. Can you read it?"

"It will take time."

"Please start, then, will you, Lazar?"

Anthony went to the table in the corner that held a crystal decanter and glasses and poured the other man a whiskey. "Try to calm down, Mina."

Anthony took the next two hours to translate the beginning of the text. When he finished, he pushed his glasses onto his forehead and looked at Mina, who, while waiting, had supervised the removal of the boy's body and drunk his whiskey and two cups of tea.

"Tell me," Mina said.

Anthony held up the translation. "It says:

"Wise men of old gave the soul a feminine name. Indeed she is female in her nature as well. She even has her womb. As long as she was alone with the father, she was virgin and in form androgynous. But when she fell down into a body and came to this life, then she fell into the hands of many robbers. And the wanton creatures passed her from one to another

*and . . . her. Some made use of her by force, while others did so by seduc-
ing her with a gift. In short, they defiled her, and she [. . .] her virginity."*

The men sat for some time in silence. Then Mina reached for the page
of translation, speaking slowly. "The soul is female and pure and sexless,
but when put in a female body on this earth, is seduced, defiled."

"Safe only with the father. Virginal, androgynous."

"To me, this is no minor book. What are they, Lazar? What are these
books?"

"Perhaps they are an extension of our known Christianity. Or maybe a
different version of it."

"That passage alone is enough to ponder for a lifetime." Mina's toe began to tap. "Maybe the person who wrote this note killed the boy simply
to prevent him from talking about where he got this." Mina dropped the
note in the waste bin. "I don't know whether to be furious or thankful."

"Both. It's a gift, just seeing it."

"What I would do for the gospels we suspect are there, the gospels we
have seen only fragments of. I would do anything."

"The gospels of what Bastian called the inner circle of apostles."

Mina looked up. "What inner circle?"

"He believed that there were two levels of Jesus' teachings, one for his
ordinary followers and one for an inner circle of disciples, men and women
who seemed to have a more intimate knowledge and a deeper understanding of Jesus' teachings. It was their gospels that were outlawed."

Mina fell into a chair. "The questions abound."

"Indeed."

"What did this inner circle see and understand? How different and how
much more than their brothers in the New Testament? Why were their
words so inflammatory—and their beliefs so dangerous?"

"If Bastian were here, he could tell you."

WHEN ANTHONY GOT back to his office, his thoughts returned to the
boy. It was the third death possibly related to the gospels, but unlike Sut-

ton and Bastian, this death had been blatant and cruel. The boy had been an innocent. Anthony gathered his things and felt his anger rise. How much death would there be? He was strangely without fear. Walking home, he felt the fire lit by Charles Bastian had been rekindled. Like Mina, he wanted these books; he wanted them for the world. He wanted others to feel as he had felt that afternoon, the piercing of lassitude, the cracking of the hard shell of cynicism. He wanted to rip open all false heavens in favor of the one he was imagining now, in which women and men were intertwined and both part of something greater. As agitation began to gnaw at him, he remembered something Bastian had once said: The hardest thing in life is wanting something.

Once home, Anthony poured himself a glass of wine. If he were to be honest with himself, he would have to say there were other things he had begun to want. His world was changing and he only half understood how.

CHAPTER ELEVEN

Peter said to them, Mary should leave us,
Females are not worthy of life.
The Gospel of Thomas,
from Nag Hammadi

I N H E R R O O M, Gemma was reading something fairly astonishing in one of her father's history books: It took Christians a long time to agree on what Christianity was supposed to be. Nor was the religion born in Rome, as she had assumed. When the apostles spread, Peter went to Rome, others went elsewhere—Thaddeus went to Armenia, Paul to Greece. The first community to call itself Christian was in Syria. James the Just, Jesus' brother, whom many considered the head of Christianity, remained with the Jews in Palestine. These were all equal centers of Christianity.

It was only after the Roman conversion, when Constantine made Christianity the official religion, that the Roman branch declared itself the official branch of Christianity, and the lineage back to Peter became the only lineage with official credibility. Jesus' "disposyny," or blood relatives, were not taken into account.

She had not considered that Jesus had relatives. His disposyny were the Jews who fought the Romans in three wars over the claim that their own son, Jesus, was the Messiah. They believed that he did not fulfill the prophecy. He had not brought world peace, or a universal knowledge of God. He had not brought all the Jews back to Israel.

Then the gospel texts themselves were chosen, edited, and purged for the first two centuries of the Christian era. Various theologians and Church Fathers admitted attempts to rewrite and compile them. Clement of Alexandria disclosed in the second century that there were two versions of the Gospel of Mark. One was suppressed because it contained "sexual" passages unfit for the public.

At the end of the second century, one man sealed the fate of the New Testament. Bishop Irenaeus of Lyon declared for the first time that the four gospels were dogma. There had been no previous mention of this anywhere. No rank had been given to the gospels; they were all considered equally authentic, equally valuable.

Gemma wrote, *Bishop Irenaeus effectively codified Christianity—and he did it all by himself.* She found herself balking over his declaration.

The heretics boast that they have many more gospels than there really are. But really they don't have any gospels that aren't full of blasphemy. There actually are only four authentic gospels. And this is obviously true because there are four corners of the universe and there are four principal winds, and therefore there can be only four gospels.

When the four chosen books became dogma, all others were ordered destroyed—and all competing branches of Christianity were outlawed, persecuted. And Mithra, Isis, and Dionysus were stamped out as pagan cults.

GEMMA WASHED HER face and sat down at the desk with her father's New Testament. Looking for the passages she had already read and reread in the Lazars' Bible, she saw that her father had made faint notations in the margins.

At John's version of the wedding at Cana, where Jesus performed his first miracle, turning water to wine, written in the margin were the words *Whose wedding? Jesus'?*

Gemma stared at the words. Had her father gone mad?

She flipped to John's version of the raising of Lazarus. Her father had written:

Mark's and Luke's versions omitted—Only reason story of Lazarus is in the Bible is because John too powerful to censor.

Reasons to censor others:

LAZARUS = BROTHER OF MARY OF BETHANY

MARY OF BETHANY = MARY MAGDALENE (Church confirms this.)

So, Gemma thought, Lazarus was the brother of Mary Magdalene. Why would this be a reason to omit the story of Lazarus from Mark and Luke—simply to avoid the mention of her name? At the bottom of the page there was a notation in pen.

MARY MAGDALENE = ANOINTING PRIESTESS

(See Luke 7:36–50, John 12:1–8, Mark 14:3–9, Matthew 26:6–13.)

Gemma ripped a piece of paper from her notebook and marked the sections. She found they all referred to the same event: the anointing of Jesus' feet.

But the versions differed.

Luke's version described a woman—"in the city, which was a sinner"—who intruded on their meal with the Savior and anointed his head and feet with the ointment, spikenard. She then dried him with her hair.

Mark and Matthew described the same event and said it took place at Bethany. Neither of them named the woman.

John was explicit: The anointing happened at Bethany at the home of Lazarus, Mary, and Martha. It was Mary who performed the anointing.

So, Gemma thought, only John was brave enough to name Mary Magdalene and the town where she lived—and tell a story about her brother, Lazarus. John, because he was too powerful to censor. Because he was not afraid of her?

She turned the page to find another strange notation: Christ comes from the Greek *christos,* which means "anointed one."

The person who "Christ-ened" Jesus was a woman.

Below this was the line: *Anointing priestess becomes unnamed sinner; disciple becomes repentant whore. Women marginalized in New Testament. Women erased. The proof is with the others.*

The others?

Gemma closed the book. The other gospels?

Then she closed her eyes. She ached for her father's company, for his mind. He would have made it all perfectly clear; she was quite sure that it had been clear for him.

But she was alone and stumbling, her head now saturated with information that she knew she couldn't discuss with the men of the Lazar family: one member who had branded her father as blasphemous, another as a dweller of ominous "darker realms," and a third who seemed bent on not speaking about him at all.

For all this, she felt strangely uplifted by the vision of this powerful woman. And more, a feeling of admiration for her father.

Had he been there, he would have told her to stop thinking. Too much thinking could destroy the thought, he had said.

A t t e a t i m e , Michael found Gemma in the den, reading one of the books from his father's collection. He bent to see the cover. "Boning up on the new land, are you?"

"Did you know that the body of the Great Sphinx was only fully uncovered in 1858? It was just a head up until that point. Your father's friend Mariette dug it out of the sand. They didn't even know it was a lion."

"Who knows what the bloody thing is. It's probably some mad pharaoh's idea of a guard dog."

Gemma studied the photograph. "Is it as huge as it looks?"

"I'd say it qualifies as big, yes."

She closed the book and looked up at him. "I'd like to see it."

Michael laughed. "Of course you would."

"Will you take me?"

"Sometime, before Christmas. Let me get up my nerve."

"Let's go now."

Michael smiled. "You really are refreshing, you know."

Gemma glanced up at the clock on the mantel. "We can go and be back by dinner."

Michael pivoted on his cane and made his way to the liquor cabinet. "A drop or two of fortification first. We're not walking, mind you."

"Of course we're not."

"And a bottle of wine for the sunset. No arguing. It's part of the deal."

"I'll get the glasses."

THE FIRST VIEW of the Great Sphinx unleashed a giddiness in Gemma. The scale of the beast made her want to whoop and run, make herself known to whatever god had inspired such a creation. It was insane and glorious. She was not even as big as a single claw. She made a quick dash toward the statue.

"Human beings are astounding," she called back to Michael. "Don't you think? I mean, imagine building this! What's it for? What's it doing?"

"Come back here, you crazed harpy," he said, laughing. They sat on a hillock and Michael opened the wine. "I don't believe it. The bloody sphinx has put you in a good mood."

"It has. But I've had a good day."

"Did you? Tell me why."

"Some days things make sense. Even the awful things."

"I heard Anthony took you to your beloved Islamic Cairo."

"He did."

"And how is the work going in your father's office? Is Anthony helping out?"

"In a way. But let's not talk about that, not here."

"All right. As long as you don't start preferring my brother to me, we'll talk about whatever you like."

Gemma accepted a glass of wine.

"The first time I came here was a long time ago," Michael said. "In fact it was the only time until now."

"But it's so marvelous, how could you resist?"

"Listen, child. I was ten. My father brought me to this very place. It was before I—before we—knew that he had two lives."

"What do you mean?"

"Quite simply, he had a mirror image of us, here in Egypt. Another woman, another son. On that day he introduced me to my half brother. Not far from where we're sitting, in fact. 'Meet Anthony,' my father said. 'Maybe someday you two will be friends.' I didn't know why he said it or who Anthony was. He was younger, with these huge eyes. I remember finding it strange that he stood so close to my father. Who did he think he was? Didn't he have his own father?

"In those days I loved my father deeply. He was— Well, you've had a taste of him. Sometimes he was more magician than father. He took me out of school and brought me here. We rode camels! Can you imagine, an English boy taken out of public school midterm to ride a camel in the Sahara?

"The day I met Anthony I knew something had changed. I didn't understand it at the time, but soon enough it became clear. My father didn't want to pretend anymore. He was no longer mine, no longer my mother's. The sad ending to the sad story is that since that day the thought of coming back here has turned my stomach."

"I don't blame you."

Michael pointed at the Great Pyramid. "I used to climb to the top."

"Did you?" Gemma visored her eyes and looked up. "I can't imagine."

"Yes, you could. Never love someone because you pity them, Gemma," Michael said. "It's an act of cruelty. I had a girl once who said that to me. She was poor as a beggar. And she was right, I did feel sorry for her."

"Does it matter how one comes to love? Isn't it enough that the love is there?"

"Do you believe that?"

"What I believe is you never know how much time you have." Gemma shook her head at the offer of more wine. The sun was setting, indigo seeping into the edges of the blue sky. The air had already cooled. "The night my mother died," she said, "I ran outside to the shelter. My father was standing in the front yard staring at a fire across the street. He was like a sleepwalker. When I looked back at the house, I saw a whole side of the house had disappeared. Their bedroom was gone. He'd been working downstairs in his office. Both of us were on the other side of the house.

"We walked through the night. We walked till morning. It didn't seem to matter if more bombs dropped, or if we were hit by one of them. I remember thinking we might find her, out there somewhere. We walked through the ruins of other people's lives—shredded photographs, staircases going nowhere. I'd seen it all for weeks. Before, I remember, every time I passed a bomb site, I felt lucky. I had this feeling it wouldn't happen to us. It's ridiculous, but I thought that because we were good people who loved each other, we would be protected somehow."

"God, Gemma. What a hell you've endured."

She let her shoulder touch his. "You know how it was. Death became like all the things we adapted to and decided not to think about. Like making overcoats out of wool blankets, or carrying those bloody gas masks around. I remember when they started making purses with false bottoms that fit the mask inside. I thought, how sensible!" Michael put his arm around her and pulled her closer. Gemma bent her head. It felt good to be held. It felt good to talk. "I worked at St. Anthony's. Some nights I had to choose whose hand to hold. They always knew when they were dying, you see; they would plead with their eyes for you to come to them. It seemed like being alone was more frightening than the dying itself. Sometimes I felt closer to those people than to anyone; it was as if their souls came rushing out for a last embrace.

"My mother didn't die like that. There was no time for her. It hurts to think about it. Where was I? Why was I not with her? Why was she not with us?"

"It's not your fault, darling. The Luftwaffe was dropping bombs on your heads."

Gemma was shaking her head. "She was different from my father. She was silly. And beautiful. And a brilliant, wild pianist. She liked to sing popular tunes at the top of her lungs. She could figure out the melody after hearing it just once on the wireless. She used to get us to dance. My father adored her." Gemma pressed her eyes with the back of her hand. "For a long time I didn't understand their relationship. She seemed to be from another world from him, a world that wasn't as real somehow, a lighter place. But once I overheard them talking and he was telling her what he'd been working on. He was asking her what he should do, the way a child would ask. I hadn't known how smart she was, or how much he respected her mind. She didn't need to prove it to anyone, you see."

"She sounds like you."

"No. I don't have her grace. I'm a bumbler."

"I think I like bumblers."

Gemma turned to him. "Do you?"

"Very much. Tried to kiss one once. That was a mistake."

Gemma turned and briefly touched her lips to Michael's cheek. "We bumblers can overreact."

"I'll keep that in mind."

On the horizon was a faint glow where the sun had been, a delicate shade that was being crushed by the weight of the darkness above. Gemma pulled her knees to her chest and buried her face. Her voice was muffled. "You were right about the soldier. There was a captain in my ward."

"Go on," Michael said after a pause.

"He was dying. I think we fell in love."

"Don't tell me, you had sex with a dying man." Gemma didn't answer. Michael laughed lightly in disbelief. "What did he do to convince you?"

"I'm telling you because I want you to know you're not the only one who's done things that feel out of character."

"Really, Gemma, to consort with a dying soldier."

Gemma pulled herself away from him. "I'm sorry I told you."

"Ah well, I suppose illusions aren't meant to last. Gone is the innocent Gemma."

"What is she now, a whore?"

"I'm not complaining, believe me. Maybe you'll oblige me someday— or do I have to be dying?"

Gemma rose and walked away. She hailed the first taxi she saw, leaving Michael to find his own.

✝   ✝   ✝

THAT NIGHT SHE took dinner in her room, drinking most of the carafe of wine Amad had brought and bolstering herself up with pillows so she could eat and read in comfort. She was not going to reconcile her feelings of rage and humiliation with Michael—or herself—not tonight. Tonight she would allow them to tear her from tip to toe. She was not whole anyway. She was not even two halves. She was shattered, not like fabric, like glass. She was not going to occupy her body, it was too sharp. Not tonight or tomorrow or until it felt softer. Her heart hardened, a round stony thing that lay heavily in her chest. You weigh me down, she told it. I wish I could live without you.

MICHAEL KNOCKED SOFTLY before he cracked open the door and waved a white napkin. "Will you hear my terms of surrender?"

"I don't know. Were we fighting? It seemed to me that you were passing judgment, like God."

"Like a jackass." He stepped into the room. His skin had gone gray again. "I've thought about it. I've spent all evening thinking about it. With the help of some whiskey, I've come to an understanding of my behavior."

"How very modern of you."

"I think I'm jealous of your captain. I wish it had been me. But I didn't die. I lived"—his voice trembled as he raised his wooden leg—"and this has made me a bit of a monster."

Gemma marked her place in her book and put it down. "That's not what I see."

"Yes, I know that about you." He walked unsteadily to the bed. From his pocket he removed a velvet box. "I've had this for a long time. I didn't think I'd give it to anyone. Now I'm quite certain it belongs to you." He opened it and took out a chain and a gold, heart-shaped locket. "It was my mother's. She would have thought you were the bee's knees. She would have told me not to foul it up. So here I am, trying not to foul it up." Michael was trembling, as if even his charm was a weight he could not support. With difficulty, he unfastened the clasp and held it in front of her. It was inlaid with tiny rubies and diamonds. She touched the locket gently and shook her head.

"It's too lovely."

"Take it."

She held his eyes to steady him. "It's not necessary, Michael."

He stared at her mutely, his face more torn than burnt, the locket dangling from his fingers. Finally, he dropped the necklace back into the box.

"Do you think, Gemma"—he faltered—"do you think you might help this monster love again?"

"I think," she said slowly, "there are things we must all relearn."

He sat on the edge of the bed and reached for her hand. She held his firmly, to calm the flutter, if only for a moment.

CHAPTER TWELVE

The Pharisees and the scribes took the keys of knowledge.
They hid them. They did not go in,
nor did they allow those trying to go in to do so.
You, however, be wise as snakes and innocent as doves.

The Gospel of Thomas,
from Nag Hammadi

B
ECAUSE ANTHONY'S NUMEROUS visits to Cairo's legit-
imate antiquities shops and collectors had yielded no results,
he prepared himself to delve into the shadowy underworld
of Cairo's less scrupulous antiquities dealers. These unsavory characters
were not unknown to him; they had frequented the family home when
Anthony's father was swimming in treasure—not all of which, thanks to
them, made it to the museum. One man in particular stood out in his
memory. Phocion Tano was the most charming, the most unprincipled,
and by far the most successful of the lot. Anthony remembered watching
him laugh blithely as he snapped an ivory artifact in half after he and
Anthony's father had reached an impasse. He recognized Tano's style in
both the wounded errand boy and in the gesture of the package tied to
the boy's back. The boy was a warning. The text and the note were a nod
of respect to the men of the museum he had successfully partnered with
in the past, men he could not afford to lose. Men like David Lazar, and
now, perhaps, his son.

The fact that Zira had heard a rumor that Tano had been in Nag Hammadi convinced Anthony further of the antiquities dealer's involvement.
Stephan Sutton had died there—at a strategic place, and a crucial moment.

Anthony hailed a cab to Giza that evening, feeling there was little time. Gemma Bastian was making rapid progress. Though she was not necessarily looking in the right direction, there was no guessing where her attention would turn next.

Phocion Tano liked to lose himself in one of the many bars and restaurants at the endless and elegant Oberai Hotel, close to Giza. Once a lavish hunting palace, the Oberai suited Tano, whose tastes were extravagant and hours irregular. The Oberai catered to hotel guests, and one could arrange almost anything at any hour with as much or as little privacy as one wanted.

Tonight Anthony found Tano in a candlelit corner of the Khan El Khalili restaurant, sitting like Ali Baba, mopping up a saucer of baba ghanoush with pita. A water pipe rose like a minaret next to a little bowl of *sheesha*. Sitting across from him was a long-haired young woman who might have been his daughter, if he weren't Phocion Tano. When Tano saw Anthony approaching, he waved her away and pulled out a chair for Anthony.

"You've put on weight," Anthony said.

"I can afford to." Tano drained his glass of wine.

"You can afford anything the black market can buy."

"Not one for pleasantries, are you?"

"Let's stick with money."

Tano eyed Anthony across the table. "How's your father?"

"Getting older."

"I miss the old days, when the world was ours."

"For the stealing."

"For the taking!" Tano signaled imperiously for more wine. "So, a man who, to my knowledge, has never been bought wants to talk about money?"

"I want to talk about your money. Or more accurately, money that might soon be yours."

"And suddenly this attracts your attention? Are you considering a change in career? I don't blame you!"

"The Nag Hammadi find, Tano."

Tano scratched his head. "Yes, I've heard about it."

"It belongs here, in Egypt."

"I've never known you to take sides, Lazar," Tano mused.

"No, you're right. I've been a witness. But the world has changed."

"Has it?"

"Those texts should not go into private hands. They belong to the people of Egypt."

"You are speaking for the people now?" Tano laughed. "I've hardly heard you speak for yourself."

Anthony remained silent. He could feel his tiredness. Tano poured two glasses from a fresh bottle of wine. "You're not at all like your father. He transmits like a beacon. He could never keep a secret. Beware of a man who is not large enough to contain a secret. Also beware of a man who contains too many, who has perhaps an abundance of space, who enjoys floating above the world. This is not a man who enjoys dictating morality, as you are attempting now."

"Nor is he a pawn."

"Tell me, then, what you are playing for? What matters so much to a man like you? Revenge? I imagine you're above that too. A woman? Forgive me, but you don't strike me as the passionate type."

"It's incredible that you know anything, given your aversion to listening."

"I don't need to listen. I *know*."

"Then I have no need to tell you."

Tano popped a dolma into his mouth. "You can't bear to be seen, can you, Lazar?"

"It depends by whom."

"And I was enjoying the fragile tendrils of a new friendship."

Anthony shifted his weight. The restaurant was nearly empty. A busboy hovered in the far corner by the cutlery and water glasses. "The untimely death of Stephan Sutton," he said quietly, "might require a formal investigation."

Tano raised both hands. "Now, now."

"And your messenger. Have pity on the young, Tano."

"I pity no one. What do you want, Lazar?"

Anthony looked up at the painted ceiling. "And there's Charles Bastian."

"Now you're getting carried away."

Anthony leaned forward. "What I want is an end to the death. And the books belong in Egypt, Tano."

Tano regarded him soberly. Then he laughed. "If you were the Second Coming—if you were the Messiah himself, no, no I don't think I could oblige you even then. Sorry." He began gnawing on a kebab.

"The museum will have the backing of the government to litigate any sale outside the country."

"The government! Ha!"

"Try me."

"You're bluffing."

"Try me," Anthony repeated.

"I'll take my chances against the Egyptian government. If I blew on it, it would disintegrate. Like an artifact! Like something that belongs behind glass!"

"The museum is prepared to make an offer."

Tano snorted. "How much?"

"We can't negotiate until I have proof that you are in possession of the Nag Hammadi texts."

"Haven't I done that?"

"*Exegesis* might have been an isolated finding."

"You know it wasn't."

"Do I? How many are there?"

Tano sat back and rubbed his globe of a belly. "More than enough. A small library, in fact." He watched Anthony's face. "You have mastered an expression of indifference. I'm sure it serves you well." He plowed a slice of pita through the dish of hummus. "But not here. That you can do any negotiating at all with a government on the verge of collapse is perplexing. I can't say I feel threatened."

"You should. I have known you for a long time. Unlike you, I have been listening and watching. Until now, it didn't matter to me who had blood on his hands."

"Blood on these hands? Never." Tano leaned forward and smiled, his gold fillings glinting. "You forget I am the player here, Lazar, not the pawn." He sat back and pushed his plate away.

"People prefer not to deal with murderers, Tano, even in the antiquities business."

"Let's stop with the saber rattling, shall we?" Tano wiped his beard with a napkin. "I'll share something with you. This find fascinates me. Do you know why? I am being offered as much money to make it disappear. What do you think of that?"

"Who is making that offer?"

"That's the most surprising thing of all. Don't push me, Lazar. If you set the dogs on me, especially that terrier Togo Mina, you do nothing but make my choice easy. What do I care about the people of Egypt? So let's keep this between us. No histrionics, no saving the world. Just two grown men negotiating. Playing a little game of chess." Tano raised his hand for the waiter. "I believe the next move is yours."

"I think that somewhere below that hedonistic façade, you care about your place in the afterlife, Tano. I think you have a healthy reluctance when it comes to 'disappearing' sacred texts. When you give me proof of this library, you'll have my next move."

ANTHONY WOVE HIS way back to the entrance of the Oberai. He decided to walk instead of taking a taxi. The night was moonless and warm and stars pierced the sky, lending a flickering yet constant light. He dug his hands into his pockets and kept his eyes on the empty road ahead. He missed the desert. He missed the space and the time and the endless opportunity to think. The distance he'd had from his life was gone. He was in it now, up to his neck.

As he suspected, *Exegesis* had come from Tano. And Tano had been unnerved at the mention of Stephan Sutton; the shadow of anxiety had crossed the big man's face. The accusation had indeed given Anthony some leverage. But unless Anthony was misreading clues, the mention of Charles Bastian had not. He thought now that unless his friend had died a natural death, there had to be someone else involved.

CHAPTER THIRTEEN

There are forces that don't want us to be saved.
They act for their own sake.

The Gospel of Philip,
from Nag Hammadi

T HE NEXT MORNING Gemma went to Anthony's office in the museum. He gestured to the empty chair. Gemma sat and drummed her fingers on the arm of the chair. "I found his journals."

Anthony raised his eyebrows but said nothing.

"He kept them in a hidden drawer similar to one he has at home." Gemma crossed her ankles and stared at the pattern of tiles on the floor. "In one of them he made a list. He wrote, *Evidence of Another God,* and then he gives what seem to be dates." Anthony waited. Finally she looked up at him. "In London, he once told me he had found a god he might be comfortable with. He said he'd introduce me one day." She leaned forward. "I think he was following a trail."

Anthony leaned back in his chair. "What kind of trail?"

"A trail of ancient texts. The dates are discoveries of sacred writings. They've turned up in the strangest places."

"How do you know?"

"Because you people report these things in your archaeological journals—and my father saved the issues. He's even got a copy of an article from a journal over a hundred years old. In 1773, one was found in a London bookshop. It was the record of a dialogue between Jesus and his disciples. Then, in the middle of the last century, a Scotsman purchased another near Thebes." Gemma consulted the list of dates. "The manuscript wasn't published until 1892—it was a record of conversations Jesus had with his disciples, a group that clearly included both men and women. Finally, in 1896, a German Egyptologist who knew about these other finds bought a manuscript in Cairo that contained four more texts that now reside in Berlin. These proved to be actual gospels." Gemma opened the journal on her lap. "Berlin," she repeated. She turned the first page to show Anthony. It contained the single word written in small, neat script. "Berlin is the only word I could read. The rest is in some kind of gobbledygook language."

Anthony rubbed his eyes. She was too clever by far. And she had found something he knew nothing about. He looked at her. She was sitting like a bird poised for flight.

"Did your father have a relationship with Berlin?" he asked.

"All I know is that he spent time there when he was young. It was after he left seminary. He would have been twenty-three."

Anthony closed his eyes. "That puts it very close to 1896."

"Yes. I am wondering if he saw Carl Schmidt, the German who bought the four gospels."

"Interesting thought." Anthony looked at his watch. "I've got to get back to work. See you at dinner?"

"What about 1945?"

"I don't know what that refers to. We were working in Oxyrhynchus. But there were no major discoveries."

"I wish I knew why he bothered to write in some kind of code. It's hard to imagine him being that secretive—or that afraid." Gemma rose. "Though I've been reading about Bishop Irenaeus of Lyon, who seems quite frightening. In defense of his new church, he wrote five volumes entitled *The Destruction and Overthrow of Falsely So-Called Knowledge*. I laughed when I first read that, but you know, who devotes his life to destroying sacred material? A fanatic, my father would have said. A frightened fanatic."

When she was at the door, Anthony spoke. "Irenaeus was waging war. He had no choice. At the time, these 'heretical' gospels had already made their way from Gaul through Rome, Greece, and Asia Minor, jumping like wildfire. People were hungrily reading them. He was in danger of losing control of his fledgling church."

Gemma came back into the office and sat down. "It's about control, isn't it? The potential loss of control of a world and an order men had created in the name of God."

"The new church."

"The new church," she repeated. "Thank you for talking to me about this. Anyway, the reason I came is to tell you I think my father discovered something in the trail of texts."

"Do you?" Anthony put his glasses on and reached for his pen.

She leaned forward, circling her knees with her arms. The tiles on the office floor were arranged in no apparent pattern. She let her eyes follow the chaotic lines and for a moment thought of absolutely nothing. "Be honest," she finally said. "You're not sure if his death was natural."

Anthony hesitated. "I don't need to be sure. Nor should you. He's gone, and our job now is to honor his memory by remembering his spirit, which we shall both miss."

Gemma looked up. "Why didn't you go to the war?"

"Because I'm not a soldier."

"Don't you learn to be a soldier?"

"Some men are born to it."

"Men like your brother."

"Yes. My brother was a fine soldier."

"I know he was." Gemma stood. It was only when she looked back from the door that she saw the figure of a woman in the floor tiles.

"Who is that?"

"Isis, actually."

"Yes, I see her now. How curious that she adorns your office too."

"Not really, considering we do what she did—bring the dead back to life."

✝ ✝ ✝

GEMMA WENT BACK to her father's office and took his address book from her purse. The book was so worn some of the pages were falling out. A yellow piece of paper fluttered to the ground as she made her way to the *Rs*. She looked at it briefly before returning it to the book. It was some kind of receipt, though it was impossible from the scrawl to tell for what. Printed quite clearly on the top, though, was the name *Albert Eid: Antiquities Dealer*. There was an address. Gemma folded the receipt and put it in her pocket. Then, with her finger marking the name in the address book, she copied the address of Carl Schmidt.

Before she left she drafted a short letter.

To Carl Schmidt:

My name is Gemma Bastian. My father was Charles Bastian. Did you know him? I am curious if he ever visited you in Berlin and read the manuscripts you purchased in Egypt. What were they? Were there any in particular he was interested in? This would of course have been a long time ago. Please tell me anything you might know—he is dead now and I find I want to know as much as possible about the life he led. (Please forgive me if I am mistaken and you didn't know him—I'm sorry to take up your time.)

Sincerely,

Gemma Bastian

THAT NIGHT GEMMA came to dinner late. It had taken her some time to compose herself after finding that the notes and books in her room had been disturbed. She had been careful to leave them in exact positions. They had almost been replaced correctly, but now the neatly aligned papers were slightly askew and two books were stacked in reverse order. Someone had been there. She found Amad in the kitchen.

"You didn't tidy my room today, did you?"

"No."

"Has anyone been here today?"

Amad paused. "Aside from family members, no."

"Which family members?" Amad turned back to the food he was preparing. "Nailah? David?" she said. "Did they go to my room?"

"David, but surely he was visiting with you."

She stared at Amad's back, choosing not to say that a visit with David would have been impossible. She had not been in her room all day.

HER ENTRANCE TO the dining room did nothing to interrupt a conversation that was unusually lively. It might have been because Anthony was there.

She leaned toward David and asked quietly, "Were there any visitors today?"

"Why do you ask?" David said.

"Because I think someone's been in my room. My papers have been disturbed."

David picked up his glass of wine. "Was anything taken?"

"Not that I could see."

"Well, then, what's the worry?" David kept his glass raised and took another swallow. "We were just talking about the war," he said, dismissing the subject. "It seems an Arab invasion is inevitable."

"It's quite strange," Nailah said, "to have a fixed date set for a war."

Gemma quickly decided to reject the possibility that her host had invaded her privacy. "What do you mean," she asked him, "a fixed date for war?"

"Israel will be made a state on May 14. The war should start on the fifteenth. Israel has been raising an air force," Michael said. "They've collected a motley crew of pilots: Jews, Gentiles, even ex-Nazis. So I hear."

"I don't believe it," Nailah said. "Ex-Nazis?"

"I can tell you firsthand that they can fly planes." Michael shook his head. "Sometimes I even miss those bastards," he muttered.

Gemma tilted her head so she could see Michael around the candles. She could tell by his voice he'd already had more than his share of wine. Her impulse, again, was to bring him back. "What was it like," she asked, "being up there against the Germans?"

He did not chide her for being artless. He lit a cigarette and spoke quietly, as if they were alone. "There were good days and bad days." He inhaled deeply. "Imagine feeling more alive than you've ever felt—and so close to death you could practically smell its breath. Sometimes it was the best feeling I've ever known. Sometimes it was terrifying."

"Bloody incredible what you boys did up there," David said. "What was it Churchill said? You turned the tide of the world war."

Michael leaned back and exhaled. "Father," he said, "that song is getting worn out."

Amad entered and started clearing the plates.

"It's hard for those who didn't fight," Anthony tried, "to know how to thank those who did."

"How do you thank someone for giving their life?" Michael asked. "I couldn't begin to tell you."

"You're still here," Anthony said quietly.

"Is that right? Every time I hear the propellers of an airplane, I feel like I'm in some hellish afterlife." He ground out his cigarette. "I was the best in our squadron, but that counts for nothing now. Sometimes I think I already lived the best moments of my life."

"There will be more," Anthony said.

"Will there?" Michael sat back and studied his brother. "You've always done the right thing, haven't you, Anthony? Even staying out of the war, which I thought was criminal. But look at you and look at me. It was the right thing to do."

"Not my war."

"It was a bloody world war! Are you no longer in the world?"

"Yes," Anthony answered. "I am."

"What I want to know is how it feels to stay so good and clean. Are you ever tormented by the distance you keep from the rest of us? Don't you ever want to make a mess?"

"Leave it, Michael," his father warned.

"Sorry, can't do that. You see, when we won the war, I lost my enemy. I've been fighting all these years and—poof—the devils are gone. So now you're it, little brother, just like you used to be. Don't tell me you don't understand."

"I do."

"Bloody disgraceful, that."

"I think I'll excuse myself," Gemma said, rising.

SHE ESCAPED TO the garden and stood at the far end with a cigarette, angrily blowing white clouds into the night. She didn't know how much time had passed before Michael spoke from behind her. "I've misbehaved again."

Gemma exhaled. "Is that what you call it?"

"Whatever it is, it seems you bring it out in me. Come over here, will you? I need to reenchant you."

Gemma didn't turn. She looked up at the trillions of stars above her. It was a massive universe, but men shut themselves into tiny windowless boxes. She did not want to live in a box.

"I'm not going to stay behind," she said, pointing at the ground. "I'm not going to stop here."

She could hear him coming closer, dragging his leg the way he did when he'd had too much to drink. "What does that mean?"

"That means if you want to know me, you're going to have to pull yourself together." Gemma turned. "Because your behavior is juvenile."

"Dear Gemma." He smiled in the darkness. "You know, it's the strangest thing. I believe I need you."

Gemma said nothing.

"There was a bloke in our squadron," he continued. "Brave as they come. Never bailed out, not like some of us. Finally he was hit. The cockpit was in flames. He was forced to jump. What he didn't know was that his parachute had also caught fire. I watched him fall all the way to the sea, like a match being snuffed out." They stood there in silence. "Come here, will you?"

"I'm quite happy where I am."

He took another step toward her. She could feel the warmth of his body. Still she didn't turn. "Churchill said, 'Never in the field of human conflict was so much owed by so many to so few.'"

"You feel you're owed?"

"Sometimes I feel I should get something out of all this, yes."

"You feel you should get me?"

"Word has it you've been got." Gemma flinched and spun as Michael reached out for her wrist and held it tightly. "I shouldn't have said that."

Gemma tried to pull her arm from him, but he was too strong. "Let me go, Michael."

"I've lost too much, you see. I can't have you slipping away."

"Let me go."

"If you'll listen to me. For God's sake, I need you to *listen* to me."

Gemma let her wrist go limp and turned away from him.

"Late in the war they put these cameras on our guns," he said. "They only recorded when we shot the guns. They showed us the films. One dogfight we thought we'd shot down three Germans. Two of the planes were our own. We became discouraged, paralyzed. They stopped showing us the films. It didn't matter how incompetent or bloody mad we were, as long as we could get back into the plane. Six or seven times a day, every day. One day I had off. I drank myself into a stupor. Every man died. Every one. I'm still here, filled to my eyeballs with ghosts."

"You're not the only one, Michael."

"Reassure me, then. Tell me I won't lose you too."

"Reassure you?" she asked in disbelief. "You're as manipulative as a child."

He pulled her to him roughly and started to kiss her neck. When she tried to push him away, he held her viciously by her hair. "Is it so hard to kiss a gimp?"

"It's not that and you know it," she said evenly. "You're hurting me."

"I disgust you." He released her suddenly, pushing her away so abruptly that she fell to the ground.

From the direction of the house, Anthony cleared his throat. "Everything all right here?"

"We were having a private discussion," Michael called back.

"And Gemma seems to have fallen." Anthony walked quickly to her and offered his hand.

"So gallant, my little brother," Michael said. "I really might swoon. Will you carry me upstairs?"

"No. But I'll walk with you. I think bed is a good idea all around. Good night, Gemma."

"Yes, good night, Gemma." Michael yawned. "We had no joy tonight, darling. I'm sorry."

GEMMA STAYED IN the garden and burrowed into her thoughts, away from the Lazars. When Anthony rejoined her, she was far away. They sat next to each other in silence, the specter of Michael wedged jaggedly between them. "Are you all right?" he asked.

"Yes, of course."

"He has a temper."

"Is that the word for it?"

"I know it's hard to feel it sometimes, but he's quite taken with you."

Gemma hugged her arms around her and pushed the idea of Michael away like a boat from a jetty. "There's something else I want to talk to you about," she said. "It's my father's work, I'm afraid."

"Go on."

"It's a note he made in his New Testament."

"What note?"

"In Romans 16:7, Paul refers to a female apostle as 'outstanding among the apostles.' Her name was Junia. I have learned that every Greek and Latin Church Father until the year 1000 acknowledged that Junia was a woman. After that, something happened. Her name was changed to Junias, a man's name. There was subsequent total denial that this outstanding apostle had ever been a woman." Gemma glanced sideways at Anthony. "I'm starting to see something. Maybe it's what my father saw," she faltered. "I know you don't like talking about it."

"I'm listening."

"For thousands of years women had power. All over the world—and not just in the home, but in society and myth and religion. For every god there was a goddess, for every priest a priestess."

"And?"

"In Christianity she disappears. But I've been finding traces of her, Anthony, in the New Testament. It's like she's hiding between the pages. They couldn't take her out altogether. You said my father was looking for what was lost. I think that's it. I think the woman was lost and that's what he was looking for."

"You've developed a theory."

"Let's take the example of Mary Magdalene, whom he was without question tracking. Aside from the Virgin Mary, the only woman in the Bible who is not a sister or a mother or a wife to anyone—who is simply herself—is Mary Magdalene. Clearly she is someone important, and close to Jesus. But why is she not talked about more, why is she only brought up when she happens to be present? Why don't Matthew, Mark, or Luke name her?"

"There's another theory that prostitutes weren't worth writing about."

"I think, like Junia, she was edited out of those gospels. I think she wasn't edited out of John because the Church Fathers didn't have the nerve. But you know, I read that at the end of the second century, a core of Roman Church Fathers wanted the Gospel of John excluded. Because it told too much. I think Mary was more than we've been led to believe. Much more."

"You are your father's daughter, without question."

"Sometimes," Gemma said softly, "I think about how lonely she might have been."

They walked inside together. The house was quiet; all lights but the hall chandelier had been extinguished. Gemma opened the door for him.

"I'm not leaving just yet," Anthony said.

"Well, good night, then. Thank you for listening."

"Good night, Gemma."

ANTHONY STAYED UP late and watched as the fire in his father's hearth cooled and then died. In the gray dawn he realized that he could not play the role of policeman with Gemma. She was too determined—and she had too little regard for her own life. If she weren't the daughter of his friend, he would be glad to have her on his side. The trick would be to keep her away from Tano, away from Nag Hammadi. Away from people and places that could harm her. If not that, he had to at least get to them before she did. He realized he did not want anything to happen to her; not just because she was Bastian's daughter, but because Bastian lived on inside of her. She was as smart and reckless and alone as he was. And like him, she had the dangerous gift of vision.

Walking home, he admitted to himself that he had taken a risk with Tano. The man was savvy. He might outmaneuver Anthony. Anthony might have already blown his chance.

When he reached Kit Kat, he lay on his bed and waited for morning. He dozed after a while, thinking of Charles Bastian, of Gemma and her fragment. When he opened his eyes again, it was ten o'clock. An idea had woken him, jolted him from a dream of the desert. Had Bastian been in it? He splashed water on his face and headed for the museum. It didn't matter that he couldn't remember his dream. The idea was there. There was something he had missed, something Bastian had meant him to see. The only problem was that he needed Gemma's cooperation. He needed her fragment. There would be a price to pay for it; he would have to answer her inevitable questions. He would have to tell her more of the truth.

PART TWO

CHAPTER FOURTEEN

Anthony found Gemma lying on the floor of her father's office reading, her head on a stack of books. He sat down and looked at her. In front of her, he held up a piece of paper so old it didn't look like paper. "It's a remarkable material, papyrus," he said. "They're still not sure how it was made."

"I was reading that the word 'bible' comes from the Greek *biblos,* which means 'papyrus.'" Gemma reached out to hold the papyrus. The ceiling light shone through the thick paper, making it glow. "It's beautiful."

"Your father showed me a trick when we were camped at Oxyrhynchus. The Egyptians were great ones for magic. He made a point of learning some of their tricks—for the challenge of it, he said. Now I think he might have had other reasons."

"Because he thought Jesus was a magician from Egypt?"

Anthony stared at her. "The fact is there is little to no biographical information about Jesus before he appears in Galilee, a grown man. It is remarked upon in the Bible that Jesus had no accent from that place, unlike his disciples. And your father believed that he learned magic in Egypt, where conjurors abounded and where religion and magic were one and the same, and so he was able to perform . . . tricks. Water into wine, raising the dead. There were a number of well-known sorcerers at the time who performed such feats."

"Does entertaining such a possibility make my father a heretic?"

"To some, maybe. Not to me. Anyway, he wasn't alone in this school of thought, Gemma. The Talmud, the oldest book of Jewish truth, states absolutely that Jesus came from Egypt—and the reason he was arrested was sorcery."

"Meaning he was a fake?"

"Meaning that the real miracles he performed might have been internal."

Gemma was silent as Anthony continued. "Consider the possibility that his miracles lived in the words of apostles that we have yet to discover."

"And will we discover them, Anthony?"

Anthony didn't answer. Instead he wiped his glasses with a handkerchief. "Do you have your fragment?"

She retrieved it from her purse but then held on to it. "Why are you helping me?"

"I'm helping both of us." Gemma studied his face as he spoke. "I think he might have used one of his tricks on that fragment. I think the envelope was first addressed to me because your father thought I would remember it. What he didn't know was how long it would take me." He held out his hand. "In English these letters read something like:

"...to
Of.....................hi...........................go in,
......they.........................trying to go..........
However, b...........se a.................nnocen...........v...."

"Is it all right if I wet it?" Anthony asked.

"I suppose so. Yes."

Anthony dabbed his handkerchief in a glass of water and pressed it to the papyrus. The missing letters between the spaces that began to form words were faint at first. "What does it say?"

"Jesus said, The Pharisees and the scribes took the keys of knowledge. They hid them. They did not go in, nor did they allow those trying to go in to do so. You, however, be wise as snakes and innocent as doves."

"And you will get the keys of knowledge," Gemma said.

"If you are both wise and innocent."

"Is it possible to be both?"

"I think you're an example."

Gemma thought. "Innocent how?"

"Innocent to danger, to begin with."

"I'm not at all innocent to danger. I've lived with danger for years. Danger is survivable."

"Which is not so wise, really."

"Yes, yes." Gemma waved her hand. "I know. Now, what does this fragment trick mean?"

"Your father has filled in the missing letters and words of this fragment with his own hand, completing the text from the Gospel of Thomas."

"Meaning what?"

"Meaning that he has seen an uncorrupted copy of the Gospel of Thomas, suspected by some to be one of the closest disciples to Jesus."

"Why exclude Jesus' closest disciple from the New Testament?"

"Think of it. Thomas has been called Jesus' twin."

"But Jesus' brother was James."

"That's right," Anthony continued slowly. "Jesus was also said to have called Thomas his equal."

"Twin, equal." Gemma paused. "I see. It doesn't really work for the son of God."

"Exactly. But no one has ever seen a complete Gospel of Thomas. Plenty of suggestive fragments, but no one can substantiate this claim that Jesus had a disciple he considered his equal."

"No one—except maybe my father."

"Maybe. Interestingly, Thomas was one of the most popular texts at the time your Bishop Irenaeus decided to exclude him."

"What unbelievable power that man had."

"Irenaeus also proceeded to rewrite history a bit, claiming that Mark and Luke were eyewitnesses, which they weren't."

"Doesn't that qualify as flat-out lying?"

"It's the making of a story. Irenaeus and the Church Fathers were struggling against competing forms of Christianity, and were trying to come up with the best form. It was important, then, to have the gospels agree on who Jesus was, and what happened in his life—and what his teachings were. The synoptic gospels of Matthew, Mark, and Luke provide a relatively consistent version of Jesus' life and deeds. John is a more complicated case. But in general, the gospels of the New Testament are complementary stories."

"And Thomas might have rocked the boat," Gemma said.

"Thomas might have overturned the boat."

Gemma tapped her pencil. "Why send the fragment to me?"

"A letter posted to England would escape notice."

"But really, it was meant for you. The message was one only you could decipher."

"Yes."

"So I was a courier?"

"Perhaps."

"That only works if he knew he was going to die," Gemma said. "How else would I come here and show this to you?"

"Maybe he sent the fragment as an assurance that if the worst happened, someone would know he'd found what he'd been looking for, that he had accomplished something."

"Not just someone. You and me." Anthony stared at the fragment in silence. "Did it occur to you that he might have wanted you to help me?" Gemma asked.

"Help you what?"

"Help me find out what he died for."

"Not if it meant endangering your life, no. By now, I think you know my position on this."

Gemma picked up the papyrus. Through the damp paper she could see words on the other side. She turned it over.

Anthony was watching her. "What?"

"He's written something on the other side."

In a moment, he was next to her. There were four short words written in a language Gemma didn't know.

"Do you know what this says?"

Anthony held the fragment closer and, not for the first time, lied to her. "No."

"Damn it! There's too much that I can't read!" She looked at her watch and began gathering her things. She had an appointment with Amad. "What would they look like, these gospel books?"

"Why do you ask?"

"Because I'm curious. What if I found one?"

"I would hope you would tell me."

"I'd have to recognize it first."

"That wouldn't be hard—you've never seen anything like them. They're quite beautiful leather-bound books," Anthony began, watching Gemma closely. "About yea high with script on both sides of the page. Script like this." He held up the fragment. "As I said, if you ever came across such a book, I hope you would tell me."

"Of course you would. Then what would you do?"

"Whatever it was, it would be for your own good."

"I don't know why you seem to know so much about my own good." Gemma stooped for her purse.

"For your own good, I would still strongly advise noninvolvement."

"I'm curious: Is all your strong advice because I'm a woman?"

"I don't know. Maybe."

"You think I'm a senseless, grief-stricken female who's going to go off and get herself killed."

"It has occurred to me."

"And you don't want it to happen on your watch."

"No."

"I like that you're honest. You don't trust me. Maybe you don't trust the female sex."

"I haven't had much experience with your sex."

"You haven't done the research out there in Kharga?"

"No."

Gemma stared at him. "So where does that leave us?"

Anthony inclined his head slightly. "It leaves me looking out for you—still."

WHEN GEMMA LEFT the museum it was prayer time. The minarets wailed. In the middle of Tahrir Square, men laid down their prayer mats and knelt facing Mecca. She was moved by this sidewalk prostration. These men prayed to a God who didn't care where they were praying, only that they prayed.

And her father's god?

Gemma resumed her walk slowly. The glimpses she was catching both thrilled and frightened her. She was gaining ground on her father, skimming over the years he'd spent determining what had been lost—over the many more spent in the process of recovery. She was making up the distance between them.

She headed away from the museum. She had a name, Albert Eid. She had an address. But there were things she had to do first. She crossed Tahrir Square and headed for the river. The sight of water instantly calmed her nerves. She realized she needed the integrity of solitude more than she needed the help of any man. The solitude, though wearing, was familiar to her. She had learned it from her father.

Walking briskly along the Nile toward the Lazar house, she knew she had far from lost her soldiering instinct. She remembered quite well what it felt like to go on the offensive, to tread soundlessly close to the enemy. To live fearlessly under a sky of falling bombs.

By the time Gemma reached the Lazar house, she felt she had summoned the power of Isis, an unbreakable goddess captured in tile, strong enough to be trod upon daily by mortal men.

Amad was in the garden, cutting chives. He nodded as Gemma sat near him and tilted her face to the sun. "Amad," she began, "do you know of anyone who might help me with running errands, doing odds and ends? I will pay of course."

"I know any number of boys."

"One with street smarts, who speaks some English."

"That narrows it down. It will probably end up being a relative of mine."

"Good. Then I know I could trust him."

"How soon?"

"Soon."

"I will find you someone by tomorrow."

"Thank you." Gemma turned. "I'll see you this afternoon for my lesson?"

"If you still have the time," Amad said.

"I will have the time for as long as I'm here. It's more than the music, Amad."

"Very well, then, I will see you at four." He rose and reached into his pocket. "Though I doubt it's necessary, I have this for you." He handed her a key to her room. "It locks the door from the outside. Perhaps just having it will ease your mind."

CHAPTER FIFTEEN

B EFORE TURNING TO the pile on his desk, Anthony copied down the four words Bastian had written on the back of the fragment. He was trying to ignore the fact that not only Gemma's perceptions but her whole being unsettled him. It was hard to get back to his own lengthening list of things to do, not just for Mina, but for his own all-but-forgotten work. In the end, he left the pile and the list and made his way to Mina's office to tell him what he had learned.

"So Charles Bastian had seen the Gospel of Thomas," Mina said. "I knew it."

"What intrigues me is that on the back of the fragment he wrote something else. A list of names—written in Aramaic, of all things. The list reads: Thomas, Philip, Mary, and, strangely, Thunder."

"Could he have just been making notes?"

"I don't think so. It wasn't his style. Because Aramaic is the language Jesus and the apostles spoke, I am going to make the wild conjecture that this is a list of the books Bastian had chosen for his testament. Four to illustrate the four main principles of the Gnostics—the most important tenets he felt were lost. This is a guess."

"But an educated one."

"The list might also tell us what to expect to find, if we ever get near these texts." Anthony pointed a finger to the last name on the list. "What puzzles me is 'Thunder.' It's not a name, it's not even a place. It's a noun— a sound, a weather phenomenon. If it weren't for that, I would say definitively these names are books he had read and evaluated and deemed worthy of his new New Testament. Four new apostles for the four old."

"It borders on lunacy." Mina put his head in his hands. "Let's assume that Thomas, Philip, and Mary—and even this Thunder—are out there. How do we go about finding them?"

"I suggest that you let me make the inquiries. I'm not as noticeable as you are. We don't want to draw attention to our efforts; there's enough competition as it is. Your man should be returning from Nag Hammadi any day. We will have his information soon. Something will surface shortly, I am confident."

"Hopefully not the news that we are too late."

"Hopefully not."

Anthony returned to his office. He did not question his instinct to keep his information about Phocion Tano to himself. Mina was too excitable— and Tano was too flammable. They were like unstable elements that should not be mixed.

CHAPTER SIXTEEN

T HE NEXT DAY Gemma donned a sober dress with a
button-up collar. Her most practical shoes carried her across
the city as she rehearsed lines to Albert Eid, antiquities dealer.

"Some people simply call them thieves," her father had told her. "And
many of them are. Thieves who profit by pillaging a country unable to
defend its own treasures."

She walked on the inside of the sidewalk, with her eyes trained in front
of her. When a shop door opened suddenly onto the street, she stopped.
In the reflection of the glass were the people behind her. One, brighter than
the rest, drew her eye. It was her ginger-haired follower. The sight of him did
not rattle her as it had before, because now he too was being followed.

When she reached Eid's shop, she glanced back and caught sight of
both the man and Amad's boy, Farrah, following him. As she put her hand
on the door of the shop, the man crossed the street. The boy ambled, his
hands in his pockets, his eyes on his shoes. Posting himself near to the
pale-eyed man, he leaned in a doorway and rolled a cigarette.

Countless thimble-sized bells rang as she entered Eid's shop. It was dark
and cluttered and smelled of must and furniture wax. Under a long glass

case were rows of statuettes: gods and animals and pharaonic royalty. Arranged in order of decreasing size was a row of scarabs. Gemma bent to inspect them and realized she would be no better at discerning what was real than the next ignorant tourist. Behind the case was a little man with a monocle that glinted like a coin.

"Are you Albert Eid?"

"I am."

"I was wondering, did you have any dealings with Charles Bastian from the Egyptian Museum?" The little man adjusted his monocle in an action that seemed to Gemma patently dishonest.

"And you are his daughter?"

"Yes."

"I see the resemblance."

"So you knew him."

"Cairo, in some respects, is a small city. What sort of dealings were you referring to?"

"Did he ever bring you anything?"

"He may have, at some point."

"You don't remember?"

"I deal with many people. I also see many people socially."

"Surely you can't be in this trade with a faulty memory?" Gemma smiled.

"How can I help you, Miss Bastian?"

"I have a receipt from your shop. It's dated November 2. What did he bring you?"

Eid held out his hand for the receipt and again adjusted his monocle. "I'll have to check my records."

"Okay," Gemma agreed. "I'll wait."

"I'm afraid I don't keep them in the shop. You'll have to come back another day."

Gemma studied Eid until he cleared his throat. "You know he's dead," she said.

The little man blinked. "I read it in the paper." His eyeglass caught the light, allowing Gemma to see only his left eye. "Now, if you'll excuse me."

Gemma waited until another man emerged. He was twice Eid's size and half his age. His skin was coffee-colored and his face pitted with scars. "Where's Mr. Eid?" she asked.

"I'm afraid he was called away."

"I don't believe it!" Gemma slapped her hand on the glass counter between them. "Your employer is a coward. And probably a thief."

The man smiled slowly. "That's one of the nicest things I've heard said about him."

Gemma pivoted and walked out the door. The bells jangled mockingly behind her. When she reached the street, she stopped. The follower was gone. After fingering the bills in her wallet, she removed half of them and turned back to Eid's shop, yanking open the door and striding to where Eid's stand-in was making a show of polishing miniature cat figurines. The little statues looked ridiculous in his big, meaty hands. Gemma laid down the small stack of bills. "Will you help me?"

"I don't know." The man glanced behind him. "Jobs are scarce in Cairo."

"Answer a question. Just say yes or no," she continued before he could object. "Do you have a thick leather book filled with pages of papyrus? They would have been covered with Coptic script, like this." She showed him her fragment. Eid's man laid down his feline statuette and looked at her. "How many questions?"

"Three."

"Then, yes."

Gemma inhaled. "The man who brought them, was he English?"

"No."

"And the man who came to pick them up? Was he English?"

"This is not a yes or a no. There was no man."

"One more, please." Gemma took out the receipt. "Is this the receipt for the book?" The man shrugged. "I've given you as much as I can," she said.

"And I only have one job."

"Blink if it's the receipt."

The big man fluttered his eyes like a girl, and Gemma smiled. "Thank you," she said.

A few blocks away, Gemma stopped at a newsstand. A moment later, Farrah joined her. They spoke briefly, facing newspapers in countless languages. An airplane droned overhead. Gemma looked up reflexively as she pressed a bill into Farrah's hand. Then she turned to hail a cab.

The follower was staying in a part of the city Gemma didn't know. She stood in front of the terraced hotel and saw that it had a wanton tilt. Inside, the lobby was clean but charmless. The walls were hung with faded posters from faraway places, places that had once been closer to her. There were skiers in Austria, a bridge over the Seine, even Westminster Abbey. Off the lobby was a small restaurant where a cluster of British guests were having afternoon tea. A young man watched her from behind the reception desk, where he joylessly guarded a wall of keys hanging from hooks. He was neither cheerful nor obliging. It took a smile and a brief description of her "friend" to extract a room number.

Gemma did not allow herself to acknowledge the fear that churned inside of her as she climbed the stairs to the second floor. She walked down the carpeted hall, her footsteps soundless, insubstantial. She stopped in front of room number 30 and rapped sharply. A moment later her ginger-haired man stood there blinking.

"Miss Bastian," he said, standing aside to let her in. He was in his shirt-sleeves. Facing the closet, he buttoned a shirt. "Shall I order tea?"

Gemma averted her eyes and walked past him. "I don't need tea." She positioned herself in a corner chair and held her purse in her lap. "At my father's office, I failed to get your name."

"My name is Roberto Denton."

"Are you Italian or English?"

"Half Italian, in blood only. I was raised in England."

"I noticed you today, outside an antiquities shop."

"Did you?"

"Yes. To commemorate my father's career here, I went out and bought myself an Egyptian brooch. Did you enjoy watching me?" Denton reddened slightly. She was almost sorry for him. "Mr. Denton, why are you so interested in my movements?"

"I was interested in your father."

"And something you think he had, you said at the museum. Something that didn't belong to him."

Denton moved the room's other chair to the middle of the room so it sat between Gemma and the door. Gemma looked away from the menacing alignment to the weak light falling from a single square window. Dropping her gaze, she found Denton's round face hovering like a moon. "Something that did not belong to him alone, I should have said," he replied. "The so-called lost gospels. I'm certain you know to what I refer. Holy words belong to the world, don't you think?"

"And the world has appointed you to retrieve them?"

Denton busied himself with his position in the chair, crossing one leg over the other. Gemma looked at him more closely. His thick fingers lay placid, but the fingernails were bitten to the quick. "How do you find Cairo?" she asked.

"I find it hot."

"You're very fair. You should wear your hat."

It took him a moment to smile.

"You were saying my father wanted the gospels for himself."

"I was suggesting that he might have fallen prey to a common temptation. Perhaps he meant to sell them for a profit. He was only human."

"Is that a crime punishable by death?" Gemma asked quickly.

"Of course not. In a world of skewed morality, such crimes have become commonplace."

"I see no evidence that my father committed a crime. And my father's morality was not skewed."

Denton laughed softly. "Because he was once a seminarian?"

"Tell me, Mr. Denton, where did you meet?"

"In England. Years ago. I believe it was at a lecture. Your father and I shared thoughts on religion. Over the years, we kept up a correspondence."

"Are you from the Church?"

Denton hesitated and smiled. "I am what you might call a bridge."

"I don't know what that means."

"Your father wanted to show me these gospels."

"Why?"

"He was a great intellectual. He liked to prove his points."

"What point was he trying to prove to you?"

Denton looked away. Gemma waited. The room was airless and hot. A wooden cross hung above the single bed. She wondered if Denton had hung it there. His eyes returned to hers slowly. "If you must know, I was worried for him."

"Were you? Why?"

"Because his ideas posed a danger."

"A danger to whom?"

Denton took his time choosing his words. "To a world in which people are easily confused."

"And you, Mr. Denton, were you confused by my father's ideas?"

Denton smiled and Gemma saw he was missing two side teeth. "Are you a Christian, Miss Bastian?"

"Is it relevant?"

As he stared past her to the wall, the features of Denton's face seemed to drift from one another. He seemed all at once fragmented, lost. She felt sudden pity for him, and reproach for herself. Denton was not necessarily her enemy—as Eid was not her enemy. These men were not out to destroy her. She was simply coming between them and the things they wanted.

We all want to be found, she thought. Gemma leaned forward. "You admired him, didn't you?"

Denton looked at her numbly, as if she were farther away than she was. "Your father was incredibly . . . bold."

"Bold," she repeated.

Denton hesitated. "He was like Moses, standing on the mount, thrashing a sword at heaven."

Gemma stared. "Thrashing at what?"

"Perceived injustice," he said calmly. "Something like that."

Gemma kept her tone even. "Are you saying God killed him for that?"

"I'm saying your father was making an argument that nothing in God's world is as we've been told it is. Even Jesus himself was a different man. Yes, your father was bold. Some would say foolish."

Gemma waited a moment. "What do you mean by 'God's world'?"

"His Church, his book."

"The Bible?"

"Yes."

"I've been learning about how the Bible was put together—it's the oddest story. Do you know it?" Gemma's voice was light. "A man called Marcion of Sinope, a man I've never heard of, a funny, inconsequential man, threw a lot of money at the Church and told them he thought the Jewish God was different from the Christian God, and he compiled some gospels in a book to honor the latter. Ultimately, he was rejected by the Church and branded a heretic. His book had a different fate. After hundreds of years of debate, Irenaeus and the Church Fathers decided to keep his selection."

"Irenaeus was a man of extremely noble character."

"But it's funny, don't you think, Mr. Denton, that God would work in such circuitous ways, accepting the gospel choice of a man who was ultimately rejected from his church. It makes you wonder if God was involved. It makes you wonder if the Church is, in fact, just an institution of men."

"Miss Bastian, you know too much and too little."

"Perhaps. But I am learning quickly."

Denton pressed a handkerchief to his mouth and coughed violently.

"Are you ill?"

"Dust," Denton said.

"Anyway," Gemma continued, "I've found nothing to indicate my father was in possession of any gospels, and I assure you, I've looked. So perhaps you should call off the hunt."

Denton lowered his handkerchief. "You do appreciate, Miss Bastian, the need to protect the flock."

"No, I'm not sure I do. Hopefully, it won't kill me." She straightened her jacket. "When will you return to England? I'm sure there are plenty of sheep in need of your prayers."

"When I've seen some sights."

"And will I be seeing you again?"

"Perhaps. But my job is almost done. I will soon be officially on holiday."

"What is your job, exactly?"

Denton spoke with sudden annoyance. "I told you, didn't I? Have you not been listening?"

"You told me you thought holy words belonged to the world. But you did not tell me who sent you."

"A layperson may not understand." Denton's smile was sudden and too bright. "A single man should not be in control of such material. You see that, don't you?"

"How vague you are, Mr. Denton. And history is full of such men. Where would we be without poor Marcion? Or your beloved Irenaeus?"

Denton uncrossed his legs. "I've enjoyed our little chat, Miss Bastian."

Gemma grasped her purse, her eye on the door. "In any event, following people is sinister. In the future, you might simply ask."

"But you would not have had an answer. Like me, you are searching."

"And like you, I am starting to believe there is nothing to find. Good day, Mr. Denton." Gemma glanced at the bedside where there was a worn New Testament. Curled on top of it was a string of rosary beads. Denton's eyes had followed hers.

"Do you know a man named Bernard Westerly?" Gemma asked. Denton blinked as if he hadn't heard. He was looking past her again, his face broken apart in some private confusion. "Mr. Denton?"

"Your father," he began, and then he faltered.

"Yes?" Gemma prompted.

"There was no one like him." He shook his head as if to wake himself. "Keep well, Miss Bastian. May you have a safe journey home."

Gemma reached the door and turned. "Did I say I was going home?" The last expression she saw on Denton's face was the first one she could read clearly. Whether it was of her, or of some abstract idea of God, the man was unmistakably afraid.

SHE WALKED BACK to the Lazar house through the Islamic part of the city, buying a headscarf on the way because she was sick of being stared at; sick of being so easily followed. As she increased her distance from

Denton, her thoughts became more lucid. In death, her father had opened not only a secret history of women but an enigmatic world of men. She did not yet know how to proceed, by which rules to navigate men like Roberto Denton or even David Lazar. She picked her way through the maze of small streets. As she found her way in the bright chaos of Cairo, she realized that in this new world she was without a role. Not daughter, not nurse. It was not worth panicking over. Instead, she found herself quietly excited. I do not know how this will come out, she thought. I do not know how it will end.

S HE ATE A late lunch in the kitchen, and when she passed Michael on the stairs, feigned tiredness. Really, she was reinvigorated by Denton's fear. He knew about the lost gospels. He knew her father had been making an argument. *Jesus himself was a different man.*

It was becoming more and more believable. This is what she needed to focus on. She needed to establish how Jesus was different—and why his being different was threatening. Gemma considered the women who had been hovering in her consciousness since she had seen the lithograph of Isis. She sat down and closed her eyes and pushed the theory further.

If Jesus was in fact Egyptian, he would have come from the land of Isis, and a culture that valued women, or at least tolerated them as deities; he would not have excluded them from his teachings—or his life, particularly if celibacy had been considered a sin. Mary's role would make more sense, particularly if Jesus came from a land where sex was considered sacred. Might she have held that undisputed power of opening the gateway to the divine? In any case, Mary's primary role was not something the Church Fathers would have wanted to popularize, not at a time when goddess cultures were being actively abolished. For some reason, women were too much of a threat to the new religion. The folder behind the lithograph was an extended illustration of their power through history, a power that abruptly stopped with the advent of Christianity. To the detriment of the world, Gemma thought.

She got up and knelt next to her bed, pulling out a very large, very old book. Sitting next to the window, she pressed the binding open so the humped pages would better catch the light. The book creaked dangerously. She had smuggled it out of the museum library. In front of her in the Queen's most imperial English was a description of how Coptic letters might be written. She traced them with her finger, trying to press them into familiarity, hoping they might help her decipher her father's earliest and unreadable journal. As she did so, Gemma reviewed again the events she imagined had occurred with Albert Eid. Someone, a courier or a messenger, had brought him a manuscript, to either evaluate or authenticate. Eid had made up a receipt and taken a look at the book. Meanwhile, the receipt was delivered to her father, who was supposed to get the book back, perhaps for the museum. But by then, Eid had determined that the book was indeed authentic and potentially extremely valuable. Eid never returned the book. Gemma thought suddenly of the fragment from Oxyrhynchus. The book in Eid's possession was the Gospel of Thomas; was that what the fragment was trying to say?

It didn't make sense. If Eid had the manuscript, her father possessed nothing worth dying for.

Except, maybe, his "argument," she thought, which he had made to at least one person. Gemma tapped her pencil. Why would he make an argument to Denton? For the sake of dialogue? A discussion with a representative from his old life, from the church he had left? Maybe her father had attempted a conversion.

Gemma stared at the Coptic letters and then turned to her father's journal. She tried to breathe past the irritation she felt at the sight of the notes and columns she still couldn't read. But as she continued to look, she felt she could almost see a pattern; there were rhythmic regularities and repetitions. Still, she couldn't figure out what dictated them.

Then she pulled out *The Divine Transformation,* the book that had once shocked her senseless. She was starting to see why her father owned it. She was starting to find it relevant.

Like two threads, her father's book on divine transformation and the

New Testament were beginning to weave together. It was a thin, mysterious tapestry, but Gemma was becoming quite sure that picture would be completed by the texts her father had spent his life unearthing.

He had found something in Upper Egypt that restored his faith in God, perhaps in humanity itself.

And Mr. Denton, man of God, wanted what her father had found.

Someone knocked on the door and her heart skipped. She closed the book and shoved it under a pillow. Michael stood in the doorway smiling subversively and holding up a note like a miniature pennant. "Here, you missed this when you came in—creeping like a secret agent, I might add. It's a note from Nailah. A reminder."

"Oh no. I completely forgot."

"You have." Michael crossed the room to the chaise. "I'll go if you go."

"I can't go to this kind of party."

"If it's because you've got nothing to wear, Nailah's got you covered. She has more clothes than the queen. She'd love to dress you up, I'm sure."

"I'm just not in the right frame of mind."

"Are you still angry with me?"

"No. But only because I'm not thinking about it."

"I get irritated. It's worse when I drink."

"I know."

"Don't ask me to stop drinking. Not yet."

"Just attempt civility when you do. If you can't be civil, then just hold your tongue. You drag everyone down with you otherwise. You're miserable to be around."

Michael held his cane in front of him with both hands and looked at Gemma over the top. "It's like this: I can get through a whole day, and sometimes a night, being civil. But there are times when my good will runs out. Then I don't give much of a damn what comes out."

"Clearly."

"Gemma, sweet, honest Gemma. I don't like many people these days. But I like you. It's become quite important to me that you like me too. What would you say if I said I'll do my best?"

"I'd say that would be a start."

"Maybe we both need a nice party. We *might* actually enjoy ourselves. To be honest, I don't think you have a choice. This falls into the category of houseguest obligations."

"Does it really?"

"For pity's sake, you're not going to jail. Come on, Nailah's in her room waiting for you to pick out something to wear. Unless, of course, you have some fabulous gown stashed away."

"You know I don't." At the door she paused. "You can be quite sweet when you want to be."

Michael pointed his cane at her and squinted one eye, as if holding her in his sights. "I want to be."

W ELL," Nailah said as Gemma entered her room. "I caught you in time. Come, you have some decisions to make." She led Gemma to the long, dense parade of colors and fabrics in her closet. There were glimmers and glints of beads and sequins and, hanging above, the arboreal bulk of feathers.

"I've never worn a boa," Gemma said.

"Then you must tonight. Nothing is softer."

Gemma looked away from the dizzying array. "Will you do me an enormous favor and decide for me?"

Nailah ran her smooth hands over the dresses and stopped midway at a yellow chiffon gown with thin draping layers. She took it out and held it up. It shifted and moved like water. The V-neck and the hem were woven with tiny crystal beads that reflected the light.

"It will be a bit short on you, but that's getting to be the fashion these days."

Gemma held the delicate fabric between her fingers. "I can't wear this. I'll destroy it."

"Then you'll destroy it. The idea is to have fun doing it. Before we get you dressed, let's take care of the rest of you."

Nailah seemed to understand that Gemma didn't mind being mothered. On the contrary, she felt comforted by the older woman's presence and didn't object when Nailah sat her on an ottoman and began vigorously brushing her hair. She watched her pin it into a loose bun at the nape of her neck. Then she offered Gemma her makeup case, which was filled with the pastel squares and circles of cosmetics Gemma hadn't seen for years. Nailah watched in the mirror as Gemma quickly powdered her face with a brush that felt like sable and dabbed on rouge. It was an intimate rite she realized she had shared only with her mother. Nailah chose a shade of lipstick that was softer and pinker than something Gemma would have chosen for herself.

Nailah walked her over to the full-length mirror and stood behind her. "You see, there's nothing wrong with being female."

Gemma stared at her reflection. "I don't know if I can do this. At one time in my life, maybe. But it's been so long."

Nailah pulled two tendrils from Gemma's bun. "Don't you think it might be time to enjoy yourself? There will be lots of young people there. Now, let's find you some shoes."

"Will Anthony be there?"

"I'm afraid he avoids these things. I tried for years to get him to attend. For a few seasons he obliged me but looked so unhappy I let him go home early. I think he was relieved when I stopped asking. Now you're ready. Off you go. I'll be down shortly."

Michael stared as Gemma came down the stairs. "I'm speechless," he said.

"Please talk. Or I won't recognize either one of us."

He offered her his arm. "You're going to be eaten alive tonight."

"I'd rather stay in one piece."

"Then stick with me."

"Happily, if you don't drive me away."

I T W A S A world she thought she'd lost. The marbled floors of Shepherd's Hotel shone with the reflection of three-tiered chandeliers. Languorous wood fans moved the air about, stirring the fronds of indoor palms that made the train of enormous rooms feel like a civilized oasis. Gemma could hear the band playing. She wanted to close her eyes and just listen; she hadn't heard a proper band in years. When they entered the ballroom, she smiled involuntarily. At least twenty couples waltzed on the dance floor; the clipped whirl of men in their black and white spun blooming clouds of color. Bouquets of white and pink and silver passed before her and she instantly wanted to be among them. She followed Michael to a table and knew it was an impossibility. This was no longer her realm. It was some afterworld for survivors, an Avalon for the untouched. She felt fraudulent and torn; she wanted to be five years younger; she wanted to disappear.

"I won't embarrass you by asking you to dance," Michael said, signaling for champagne.

"Good. I'd rather just sit."

"In my previous incarnation, I cut a decent rug."

Gemma sipped her champagne, holding the glass close enough to feel the bubbles on her skin. "I have no doubt."

"The numbers of women I seduced with my sheer agility were too high to count."

Gemma laughed. She was sitting as straight as she possibly could. In the gossamer-thin dress, she felt almost naked. She hummed softly to the music.

"Now I'm as shy as a spotted fawn."

"Please."

Michael raised his arm like a conductor. "Let them serve as our visual confections, something to rest our eyes on while we get quietly drunk on champagne, which is quite good, don't you think?"

Gemma smiled and lifted her glass. "To other people's parties."

A new song began, a liquid two-step. Gemma's foot tapped. "Look at you," Michael said. "You can't keep still."

"'Little White Lies.'"

"I should hire someone to spin you around a few times."

"I wouldn't object."

"No, on second thought, I like having you here."

Like a possession, Gemma thought. She sipped her champagne. Her thoughts strayed. She wanted to share what she was learning. She wanted to share it with Michael. She set down her glass. "Did you know that in Babylon, whores were not only respected but sacred? They were also rich and owned land."

"Something I like about you is that I never know what's going to come out of that pretty mouth of yours."

"It was because the sexual act was seen as transformative, particularly for the men. The transference of power made them fit to rule. But it came from women."

"The whores?"

"In some cultures sex was once sacred. It has become degraded—as evidenced in your tone of voice when you say 'whore.' Did you know that celibacy was considered a sin in Jesus' time? Geza Vermes in the second century compared 'deliberate abstention from procreation' with murder. Paul said that 'it was better to marry than burn.' So what are the odds that Jesus was celibate? He wasn't known for preaching celibacy. I think it's something the Church Fathers inserted, thinking it might be useful."

"Useful for what?"

"Keeping women in their place. Keeping them from power."

"I think it's a grand idea. Can't have a bunch of harlots running things, now, can we?"

Gemma turned away.

Michael squeezed her hand. "I'm teasing you, darling. Try not to get too serious about all this."

There were moments when she thought he was right, when all she wanted was the lightness required to fall in love. "Michael"—Gemma leaned forward—"would you come with me to Upper Egypt?"

"Why?"

"Because I want to see it."

"And what, pray tell, would you like to see?"

"Oxyrhynchus."

"That frightening rubbish heap where your father worked?"

"Come with me. Please."

"That would be both a bad and crazy idea."

"It would be good for you to get out of Cairo," she argued.

"So I can get even hotter and worse-tempered?"

"We'll be on the river. It will be interesting."

"The river does not at all interest me. It's infested with malarial mosquitoes and starved crocodiles. I can think of better bedmates."

"Right. So I'll go by myself."

"Don't be ridiculous."

"Is that what I would be?"

"Yes," he said affably, letting his hand float into the air. "You couldn't possibly manage."

"I didn't ask you to come for protection, I asked you to come for company. But never mind, I think I'd rather go alone."

Michael smiled. "I think I've discovered how to get your goat. Just insinuate that there's something you can't do alone and, kapow, fireworks."

"I'm glad you're so pleased." Her eyes wandered to the other side of the room and locked onto something that made her smile. Michael turned to look. "Good Lord," he said. "What have we here?"

From across the room Anthony was making his way to their table. "Quick, we can still make it out if we leave now."

"No. I'd like to stay."

"And be bored to tears by our resident desert hermit?"

"Maybe."

"Well, will you stop jiggling your leg? It's giving me the twitches."

"I can't help it. It's the music."

Anthony stood at their table. "Hello, Michael, Gemma."

"Anthony, I'm stunned. What in God's name are you doing here?"

Anthony held his hands behind his back. He looked elegant and surprisingly at ease. "I felt like a dance. Gemma, would you do me the honor?"

"Anthony dancing." Michael laughed. "Now this will be a night to remember."

GEMMA LEFT MICHAEL with a vague sense of betrayal. She was abandoning him to do something he couldn't. In a moment it passed. The music began and it rang through her like a struck bell; she vibrated. Every part of her sang.

Anthony held Gemma firmly, guiding her easily around the floor. She was unaware of his lead. They moved together, his eyes steady on hers. She looked over his shoulder and mouthed the words to another song she knew by heart, *I bought violets for your furs, and there was April in that December, the snow drifted down on the flowers . . .*

"That's a pretty dress."

"It's your mother's."

"She has good taste."

"So," Gemma said, "somewhere along the way, you learned how to dance."

"I have a few neglected skills. I haven't seen you at the museum."

"I've been doing other things."

"What other things?"

"A bit of my own excavating."

"Ah. And what have you dug up?"

"Oh, this and that."

Anthony pressed her hand with his and bent his head to her ear. "Not enough, Gemma."

"I'll tell you when there's something to tell."

"Tell me before that."

Gemma turned and smiled quickly at Michael, who was watching them. "Right now it seems everyone's hiding something. I feel like I'm in a shadow play."

"You are. Step out of it. There's nothing to be gained."

"So many things require your energy, Anthony. You needn't bother taking care of me."

"That's generous of you."

"You needn't bother because I'm not going to step out of it. I will only exhaust you."

"I've spoken to Togo Mina. He's given you a deadline, I'm afraid."

"For what?"

"For sorting out your father's office."

As they spun a rotation in silence, Gemma made her face go wooden, a trick her father had hated. "How long do I have?" she asked.

"Another week. They need the space, you see."

"I see."

"What is it you're looking for, Gemma?"

"What are any of us looking for? What are you looking for, here at a party you historically loathe?"

Anthony tightened his grip around her waist and pulled her closer. "Do me a favor, then," he said into her ear.

"Maybe."

"Tell me what you find, no matter how small."

"I'll consider it if you give me a good reason why."

"Because I've already lost one friend." He released his grip and pressed his thumb gently into her palm. "Tell me, how is Michael?"

"Happily drunk, as you can see. I haven't managed to save him from himself."

"You're wrong. He's coming back to life."

"How do you know? You never see him."

"It's in his eyes."

"Why don't you ever see each other?"

"Because it's better that way."

"Because he's still angry about his father?"

Anthony looked down at her. "Because he's lost enough."

MICHAEL FINISHED HIS champagne as Gemma and Anthony stayed for another song and then another. "East of the Sun" and then, fittingly, "Mandy, Make Up Your Mind." He cringed as his father approached his table, emitting an intolerable pathos for his lame son.

"Are you enjoying yourself?"

"Enjoying myself? I feel like an old man watching children play."

"Ah, Michael." David Lazar sat down. "You've been dealt a tough blow."

"I wish you'd stop making grand pronouncements."

"I'm trying to talk to you, Michael. I don't know how anymore."

"The problem is your son is gone and you're incapable of understanding the man who took his place."

David reached across the table. "Help me, then."

Michael looked at the extended hand and instead picked up his champagne glass. "It's useless."

David moved his chair closer and gripped his son's shoulder. "Tell me the worst of it," he entreated. "The blackest moment."

"In the midst of all this happiness and health?"

"I don't give a damn about that."

"Champagne's gone. You'd better go and save me from bathing in the pity of a hundred stares."

David left for the bar. When he returned with another bottle of champagne, Michael stared hotly at his brother and Gemma and began his assault. "Are you listening? Do I have your undivided attention?"

"Yes."

Michael laughed and toasted his father. "But your attention has always been divided, hasn't it?"

"Do you want me to leave or shall we continue with our conversation?"

"By all means continue. This is such fun to talk about. Imagine, Father, if you can, getting into a plane that may very well become your coffin—*every day.* You stay when everything inside of you is telling you to flee. You stay and stand in front of death, day after day, and you do not make a scene; you pretend it's a job like any other, though often your friends don't come back from work."

David Lazar watched his son finish his glass of champagne and mechanically pour himself another. "It's called bravery."

"It's called madness. They dress it up as something else to make it look pretty, to make it look like something people will love you for."

"You are loved for it, Michael."

"Am I? Shame I can't feel it. They don't tell you they take away your senses along with your fear. They don't tell you that while your body may survive, your heart turns to granite."

"This, I think, is the nature of war."

"It's betrayal. What separates you and me, Father, is the experience of extreme obedience. A soldier's will is bent until it's broken. Only then do we become useful. I think obedience has damaged my ability to think. And it has made me angry."

"That might be the morphine," David suggested.

Michael finished another glass of champagne. Then he looked at his father as if he were a blurred photograph of someone he might have known. "Did you know we were told to shoot down rescue planes? The bloody Red Cross: bang bang, into the drink. Kill the angels. But keep quiet about it—the public doesn't understand. Well, we didn't either. But our commander said they were a menace and we were good boys. So you know what I did? In my mind I painted swastikas on their big, clumsy wings and sent the angels to heaven. Where does that leave me? Where will I go when I'm dead, Father?"

David set down his glass and sat back in silence.

ANTHONY AND GEMMA returned from the dance floor looking very bright and young. Michael motioned for his brother to sit. "Tell me, brother. What have you been working on these days? Gemma's been creeping around like a spy with the secret to Enigma and you have been in Cairo far too long. I want to know what's happening."

Anthony glanced at Gemma. "I'm here to build a museum. Because I know something about what her father was working on, I've been helping Gemma sort out some of his things."

"Example."

Anthony looked at Gemma again, who shrugged. "Charles Bastian was interested in a collection of gospels that have been lost since the fourth century."

"Lost to whom?"

"To all of us."

"Why not keep them lost? Example."

"In short, they may redefine what we understand Christianity to be."

"Oh Jesus, Anthony. Can't you leave it alone? The poor bloody Church."

"The Church is indeed bloody. It always has been. That's part of the problem."

"And you're infecting poor Gemma here. She's going subversive on me." Michael turned to his father. "Isn't it a fact that some of us protect and some of us destroy?" he asked. "How do you feel, Father, having sired one of each?"

"The only destruction I see here is self-inflicted."

"Well, it smells like heresy to me," Michael said. "I should turn you in, little brother. You're a danger to world peace."

"I'd be happy to explain it in more detail, if you like."

"I don't like."

"All right."

"Is nothing out of bounds? Can't we have something to keep us warm at night? Must you take the Church too?"

Gemma took Michael's hand. "Let's talk about something else, shall we?"

David made his excuses, and soon after Anthony rose. "Thanks for the dance, Gemma. Good night, Michael."

"Good night, brother. Sorry to be a bore."

Anthony smiled. "Never a bore."

In the taxi home, Michael mumbled, "We should go to church, start laying a proper foundation, you and I."

"I think the last time I went to church was at my mother's funeral."

"Horrid lapsed girl." Michael yawned. "We'll save you yet."

Gemma looked out the window. "I remember the minister saying as he always does, 'Father of our Lord Jesus Christ, we confess that we have sinned in thought, word, and deed,' and for the first time it seemed all wrong. I asked him afterwards, This week I have saved lives. I lost my mother. What is my sin? He said we have all sinned, that we were born in sin. I asked him why, because Eve ate an apple? He said the way of Christ is not to question, but to have faith." The cool night air blew through the open windows of the taxi. Gemma pulled her shawl around her. "The fact is he did not give me an answer. He told me not to ask. I suppose I am like my father. I need to ask."

She looked over at Michael and saw that he was asleep.

When the taxi pulled up to the Lazar house, Gemma whispered to the driver to wait for her. After seeing Michael to his room, she quickly changed her clothes and grabbed a blanket and her toiletry kit. She slipped off her heels to tiptoe back downstairs and out the front door. "Take me to the museum," she told the driver.

"The museum is closed, miss."

"Not to me it isn't."

Gemma stared out the window, trying to remember the name of the security guard. If his office was going to be denied her too, she would spend every minute possible in the one place she knew for a fact her father had occupied.

CHAPTER SEVENTEEN

T HE NEXT DAY Mina marched into Anthony's office unannounced. He was too upset to sit. "The man I sent to Nag Hammadi. I have just received word that he is dead."

"What happened?"

"His head was smashed in by a rock. Poor man was just supposed to ask around, see what he could find. Smart fellow, half Bedouin and so spoke the language, mixed in well. I thought he could glean some information. Really, I sent him to his death."

"I'm sorry, Mina."

"I've been to see Phocion Tano again. I'm afraid I lost my temper. But I know his reputation. I can see he is fully capable of violence."

"I would steer clear of Tano."

Mina harrumphed and bent down to tie the lace of his shoe. "The real pity of it is that whoever has these texts probably has no idea of their value. Doresse has authenticated the text in our possession. Do you know what he said? He said this discovery will mark an epoch in the study of the origins of Christianity. He said history will need to be rewritten."

"So the lawless rogues may know they've got a good chance at becoming rich. Some people will pay whatever it takes to prevent history from being rewritten."

"To think that money even enters the equation—that a worldly value could be placed on such material! But I know better, naïve as I am." All at once Mina seemed to calm down. He clasped his hands behind his back and stared up at the ceiling fan. "I think I'm being followed."

"By whom?"

"By a man who is in no way remarkable. But I am someone who notices clothes and I think he owns but one threadbare jacket."

"European?"

"No, he looks Egyptian. As I said, he looks like everyman, save for the jacket. Here's what I think: There are more gospels out there. They are like a covey of flushed quail. Once they reach us, they are safe. But crossing the gauntlet between Nag Hammadi and the museum has already meant death. As we saw with the boy, Ali. And now another innocent has fallen. My question is this: Who else is out there?"

"We'll find out. In the meantime, I wouldn't trifle with Tano. We've got enough to worry about. I'm afraid we may be in the middle of a small holy war."

Mina turned to him. "You think the Church is involved?"

"Gemma Bastian was visited in London by someone she thinks was from the Church—inquiring about her father's work. So, no, I wouldn't eliminate the possibility."

"Are you talking about Rome?"

"I don't know. I think, certainly, that Rome has a lot to lose by letting these gospels reach the public. If they have been circulating for as long as we suspect, I'd be surprised if they didn't know about them."

"Good Lord."

"It's an ancient story, Mina. Old truth battling new truth. Defendants of both are willing to die—and, it seems, to kill. The catch here is that the new truth *is* the old truth."

Mina furrowed his brow. "You seem remarkably calm about the prospect of holy war."

"I'm fatalistic."

"Don't let that stop you from fighting this . . . *war* with me."

"Funny, I told someone recently that I wasn't born a soldier. But maybe I wasn't thinking of the right war. Now"—Anthony stood—"I'm in need of some tea." Mina rose. "In this war we are fighting for the lives of fallen soldiers, angels maybe," he said. "Really, these gospels couldn't have come at a better time."

"Mina," Anthony said when they reached the door, "we are probably in for more than a skirmish."

"Yes, my friend, I know."

ANTHONY MADE HIS way to the cafeteria, wondering not about what Church men might know about Bastian's work, but about how. When he returned to his office, he stopped in the corridor. There was a boy standing outside his door. As Anthony approached, he saw the boy was clutching a package to his chest. The boy regarded him with sullen eyes and extended the package. Anthony looked him over, thankful to see that he was very much alive. He gave him a bill and took the package, locking the door behind him. Inside the package was another wrapped package, and a letter. It was from Phocion Tano.

Your friend Togo Mina has been to see me twice now. You know my feelings on the subject. I don't like his manner. He makes threats like you, but unlike you, he has no bargaining chip. Don't let him become an annoyance. Enclosed find my next move, my queen to your pawn. Something to persuade you not to harass me. I have the texts, lots of them; I am simply waiting to see who is the highest bidder. Enjoy what I have sent you. It is a token of my respect to you and your family. My translator tells me that while not a major gospel, it could start a revolution. To me there is no name attached, and so no value.

Anthony carefully unwrapped the package, taking care not to damage what was inside. He stood staring at the text in front of him, reaching out at last to touch the pages with his fingers. Then he took out the lunch he had packed and positioned his tea and settled in for a long session. He knew as soon as he began translating that he would forget his hunger, his need for sleep. It did not matter then, how long it took. What mattered was the words on the page in front of him. What mattered was the feeling that, in this task, he was alive as he had never been.

CHAPTER EIGHTEEN

T HAT MORNING GEMMA woke rumpled and sore from a night on the floor of her father's office. Her head hurt from too much champagne. She stretched to loosen a knot in her neck, momentarily overcome by the memory of dancing. She sat up and for a moment the world tilted dangerously. The floor had been cold. The discomfort didn't bother her. It was how her father had spent many of his nights, many of his vigils. This was her vigil to keep.

She looked up at the room from her new vantage point, thinking she might see something she hadn't seen yet. The room looked both larger and smaller. She stood up and the room assumed its proper proportions. The only thing to do was continue the progress she was making with the journals, because she was sure she was getting somewhere. She smoothed her hair and skirt and ventured out of the museum to the café across the square for coffee and a pastry. She needed fortification before she re-attacked the nonsense of the first journal, before she pushed to the next word she could almost make out. The problem was the words didn't belong to the Coptic language, at least not completely. Sometimes, if she relaxed, she could see there was an order to the lines. But then it would be turned on its head. She had started to focus on the vowels simply because, after conducting a systematic hunt, she couldn't find any. Not one. This was too strange not to mean something.

THAT AFTERNOON SHE returned to the Lazar house. She had just washed up when Amad knocked on her door. In his hand was a letter with a foreign stamp. She recognized the language of the return address. It was from Germany. She tore open the envelope. Written in a shaky hand was a letter from Carl Schmidt. Gemma sat on her bed to read it.

Dear Gemma Bastian,

Though I am an old man who has forgotten much, I remember your father well. I remember his passion and his youth. I remember he was young to be in the seminary. What I remember most vividly was his face when he first read the Gospel of Mary Magdalene and how serious he became. I remember his blackened fingers from the ink of writing in his journal. He later told me that what he read had changed his life. He would not return to seminary. It worried me. I am happy to tell you this because I have always felt in some way responsible. Perhaps your existence absolves me. I am delighted to hear Charles went on to have a family. Before he left Berlin, he told me this: He could not be a part of a church that denied parts of itself. It was, he now believed, a church created by men, not by God. God would not have been so fearful of women. This is what he said, and I will never forget the conviction in his voice. I am sorry to hear he has passed on, but how nice that he had a daughter who loved him enough to want to know him. He was a good man.

Fondly,

Carl Schmidt

There was a gospel of Mary Magdalene.

Gemma got off the bed and went to the window. Before she was born, her father had read the Gospel of Mary Magdalene. Because of what he read, he left the seminary. Because of what he read, the direction of his life changed. He'd married. He'd had a child. Did Gemma have Mary Magdalene to thank for her life?

Her father had not known such a gospel existed, she thought. He had come from a world that did not even like to say her name.

The founder of the Roman Catholic Church did not like women, did not like them at all.

Down in the garden, Nailah was clipping flowers. Maybe it was Gemma's stare that made her turn and look up. The women waved at each other. Gemma tugged gently on the curtain sash, wishing it were she who was moving like a hummingbird between the flowers. Instead she prepared herself to reattack the Coptic alphabet, hauling the great musty tome to the light of the window.

THAT AFTERNOON AS Gemma passed Michael's door she heard a thudding crash, not the splintering of an inanimate object but of a person. Inside, Michael swore and then fell silent. She knocked softly and held her ear to the door. "Michael," she said, "are you all right?"

She waited and then turned the handle and gently opened the door. "Michael?" She could not see him. Then she saw his foot. He was on the floor, sprawled. His shirt lay in a pile next to him. His wooden leg was on the other side of the room.

Michael's eyes were closed. He seemed to be asleep. Gemma knelt next to him. In the hand that lay under the bed was an empty syringe. The glass vial of morphine was on the bedside table with its top snapped off.

Without opening his eyes, Michael smiled. "Gemma," he said. "I can smell your perfume."

"Morpheus," she said softly.

"Is that what it's called? I'll have to buy you some."

"Morpheus, the Greek god of dreams. Father of morphine."

"He's my friend."

"No he's not."

"You don't know him."

"Yes I do."

"Don't be alarmed, dearest. It's just something I do sometimes, for the pain."

"Are you in pain?"

"I was. I fell. I was angry. I threw my leg." He laughed. "Not many people can throw their own leg."

"Can I help you?"

"You can let me look at you."

"Do you need your leg?"

"Toss it in the fire. Useless piece of wood."

"Let me help you get on the bed."

"Aren't I on the bed?"

"You're on the floor."

"Ha!" he barked faintly. "So soft, the floor."

"That's the morphine."

"Lovely stuff."

"Addictive stuff." She angled her body under his, preparing to move him.

"I'm quite happy here." He opened his eyes a crack. "Love that dress. You look edible."

Gemma got to her feet. "I'll leave you, then."

"Righto. See you for cocktails."

Gemma went to her room and sat at her desk. After a moment, she let herself slump. She sat there until the light faded, until she could no longer make out the pattern on the rug. She knew that Michael was someone she could be with; she could walk by his side, listen to his stories, be charmed by his voice and manner. And she knew she could help him. What she didn't know was whether she could help him live, or help him die.

There was a light tap on the door and David Lazar poked his head in. "A letter's come for your father. Looking at the postmark, I'd guess it's from his brother in Australia."

Gemma looked up. "He doesn't know."

"Is there anything I can do to help?"

"No. I just need to sit down and write some letters. I've been avoiding it." She paused. "I'm not exactly sure what to say."

David stepped into her room and stood against the wall like a sentry. "How do you mean?"

"I don't know how to phrase the details. Details like, his death was suspicious."

"Surely that's unnecessary."

"Now that he's gone? You Lazars agree on one thing: He's dead, who cares why? What I find odd is that both you and Anthony have devoted your careers to learning about the lives of dead men. Why is this so different?"

"I don't know, Gemma. Maybe because he was of our world."

"Then can you explain from this world of yours how one day he thought he was going to have money, a house, and me in it—and the next day he's dead from heart failure with nothing in the bank?"

"This is Egypt, Gemma. The rules of England don't apply. Things happen, things you don't always understand."

"That's not good enough." She added impulsively, "Especially from someone who disapproved of his work."

"Dear Gemma, that's just part and parcel of the territory. We're academics! We squabble! When we came here, we stepped off the map. Living in this country has required us all to surrender old paradigms, cultural assumptions—things we thought we understood."

Gemma stared hard at her father's friend. She wanted to believe him and couldn't. To her surprise and his, she started to cry. David searched for a handkerchief. "I'm a miserable houseguest," she said.

"Surely you're more than a houseguest," David said gently. "I think you've won my son's heart." He placed a firm arm around her shoulder. "Try to relax. Try, for a moment, to relieve yourself of the weight of the world."

Gemma half crumpled into tears while David staunchly oversaw the torrent. "It's going to be all right," he said softly.

BEFORE DAWN, GEMMA woke from a dream about Mary Magdalene. She had been in the lithograph with her child, and as Gemma stood in front of it, Mary stepped out of it, assuming normal human proportions.

They were just the same height. Mary walked around her father's office as Gemma had so many times. She took a book from the shelf and sat down, motioning for Gemma to join her. It took Gemma a moment to realize that the child was gone. She woke before she could turn and look at the picture, to see if the child was still there. *You have left your child,* she wanted to tell Mary. She wanted to warn her: *Find the child.* Before you read a book, find the child.

The morning was uncharacteristically overcast, which made Gemma think about London, and how effectively she had put it behind her. She had managed an amputation of her own, dismissing London like a bad dream. She took coffee and toast in her room, setting herself up at the desk with stationery and pen. The first letter would be to her uncle in Australia. Gemma didn't know him well enough to judge whether she should tell him the whole story or something short and palatable. She decided that if she wasn't going to be available to answer questions, it was better to be brief. She wrote the letter like a newspaper obituary, with a few personal details that sounded manufactured. He died in a place he loved, doing what he loved most. He seemed to have died of natural causes. In the end, the letter read like a big lie. It didn't matter. She was just the messenger. She licked the envelope and pressed a row of Egyptian stamps above the address. She decided against penning a return address. Egypt wasn't her home, after all.

To clear her head, she began a letter to her friend Lucy Bingham, someone to whom she always told the truth. Lucy did not understand euphemism. She liked a good juicy story. When they'd been girls, Gemma had been lighthearted enough to make them up for her.

The war changed all that. No one's heart was light. And Lucy had been lost to Gemma for the duration. Early on, she found herself an American soldier safely stationed at a desk job and spent the next years more or less unaware of the devastation taking place around her. It seemed all wrong to Gemma. You didn't survive a war by falling in love. You survived by keeping your head, by avoiding acts of desperation. And Lucy and her soldier seemed desperate. The velocity with which they hurled themselves at each other was alarming. In Gemma's mind, no one could remain comfortably entwined for long; it became strangulation. Disturbingly, they remained entwined and, surprisingly, seemed happy enough.

Though Lucy in love did not have much to offer in the way of friendship, Gemma did not stop missing her. It was the first of many vanishings. For as long as she could stand it, she watched her friend spend her free time in front of her cracked mirror, making up her face with cosmetics she had pillaged in the rubble of the East End. Gemma didn't approve of her little war crimes and Lucy knew it. She thrashed around her room, looking for pretty things she'd stolen to wear for her soldier, attacking Gemma for being too virtuous. War was not a time for virtue. "Who's going to use all this lovely stuff, then? A bulldozer?"

When Lucy became pregnant, Gemma stopped visiting the Bingham house. The tension between Lucy and her parents was explosive. Light seeped weakly through the blacked-out windows as if to compensate for the harsh decibel level of the voices. The last time Gemma visited, Lucy was retching in the bathroom and screaming at her mother to leave her alone. Her mother screamed back just as loudly, telling her daughter that she had ruined her life and to get the bloody hell out of the bathroom.

Gemma took her pocket calendar from her purse and counted the weeks. Lucy would have had the baby by now, and the American soldier would have married her or been shot in the head by Lucy's father.

Dear Lucy,

If I'm calculating right, you might have a little one suckling. I hope the labor wasn't too laborious and that you had your Gerald there to help you through it. I'm still in Cairo, taking care of Dad's things. It's hard to believe he's gone. I think I won't realize it until I get home and he simply doesn't return from his latest jaunt to Egypt.

It's quite incredible here; you might like it. There are camels on the streets. And believe it or not, lots of elegant Europeans. I've been taken in by friends of Father's, the Lazars, who have been very kind to me. They have two sons, half brothers, who have become my friends.

You would want to know if I fancy them. You should be here to help me. I wonder what you would think of them, which one you would choose.

I hope you're faring well, dear Lucy. I do miss having a girl to talk to. I will pop by when I get back to London, whenever that is.

Much love to you and your family,

Gemma

Gemma capped her pen and went downstairs. The house was quiet. David was working in his upstairs office and Nailah was out somewhere. She wandered through the kitchen, taking in the dense aroma of Amad's dinner stew. She could not identify the combination of spices, what was pungent and what was acrid and what was sweet. Fish, though. It looked like perch. There was, as always, a pot of water and a bowl of uncooked rice. On the butcher block were vegetables for a dish she had grown to like: okra, cauliflower, and potatoes stewed with tomatoes and the ubiquitous garlic.

She was early for her oud lesson but she liked being in the kitchen; the only person who would find her here was Amad, who never asked questions. She sat down at the table and stared out at the garden, where today there was no dappling of sun and a breeze stirred the leaves. The time passed; Gemma did not move. Sitting there, she began to feel tired, so tired she wanted to lay her head down on the wooden table. Then the fatigue passed and there was just the stillness of the kitchen. She became aware of her breath. She followed it moving in and out of her body and felt her little universe quietly rearranging itself. Her father's discoveries rested uneasily inside of her; she understood why he had kept them to himself. They pressed up against her now, against a formidable structure she had taken for granted, that she hadn't really noticed was there. As David Lazar said, a sense of God almost preceded consciousness. She did not have to like a church that called her a spinster, that droned its condolences in boilerplate phrases, but it was still indisputably there and had been for aeons; it was an archetypal parent to rail against. Now something else was emerging; she could sense it in the periphery of her awareness, rocking gently to life.

The wind had picked up outside, whipping the leafy sycamore in the back garden, flushing birds from branches. Though the sky was clear, it felt as if a storm was coming. Gemma closed her eyes and tried to imagine rain.

At their appointed time, Gemma found Amad in the courtyard. She had learned quickly; she could now pluck out a few songs. Today she shook her head when Amad offered the instrument. "I'd rather just sit today, and listen."

"Then you give me an audience."

Amad played with his eyes closed, his fingers finding the strings and sliding up and down the neck of the oud as if they had created it. The first song meandered, trancelike. Soon Gemma also closed her eyes. She was in the leaves of the sycamore. From that height she imagined she could see the Nile and the hotels Michael loved for their bars. Farther off were the places Anthony had taken her: Al-Azhar Mosque and the Mosque of Mohammad Ali. Beyond that was a place she had not yet seen but could create from what she had read: the City of the Dead. Initially, the idea had appalled her; an underground cemetery that, for need of space, turned village for the living, where children played and car tires were patched and life unfolded as it would anywhere. This, it occurred to Gemma, captured Cairo perfectly. The vile and the pure; the hand that groped your pocket for coins one minute was praying in a mosque the next. She should have mentioned it to Lucy. As Amad's melody took an unusual turn to major notes, Gemma followed them mentally, and Cairo faded. She was back on the plane that had brought her to Egypt, flying across the sand mountains of the desert. Her eyes fluttered open, and when she closed them again, she was high over London. Below her was the destruction of the war, the rubble and the deep smolder of fire gnawing its way through mattresses and sofas and dresser drawers, leaving behind only what it could not consume, a cold graveyard of coiled springs and melted vinyl.

From her height she saw what God might see. A city of blocks tumbled by children. How many bodies had been buried under those blocks? Her mother's—and those of countless other mothers. As she had told herself many times before, she was not alone. She started to drift away from the wreckage. There was nothing more that could hurt her here. What she could lose had already been taken; she was in some way safe now. She could hear the soft voice of Amad speaking.

"Come, child," he said. "Help me cook dinner."

CHAPTER NINETEEN

Thunder

I N HIS OFFICE, Anthony rested his head in his hands. He had translated half of the text Tano had delivered. It had taken all night. Letting his mind empty, he dropped his chin on his chest and fell into a dreamless sleep.

When he woke, it was fully morning and his head was clear. Perhaps, he thought, he wouldn't feel as overwhelmed as he had in the small hours of the night. What he'd translated was like nothing he'd ever seen or read. Pages of verse spoken by a voice that had both authority and wisdom, a voice that was somehow divine in the way it traversed the distance between exploitation and empowerment, between debasement and virtue, between war and peace.

I am the first and the last.
I am the honored and scorned.
I am the whore and holy.

Phocion Tano had given him *Thunder.*

Anthony finished the last of his cold tea as his eyes ran over the translated verse in front of him, over words that were too wise to be arrogant, and yet spoke to him with such directness and candor that he felt intimate with the speaker. He felt the speaker could be in the room with him.

Thunder indeed. The words rumbled and crashed above his head. It was the most profound prose poem he had ever read, spoken by someone with no class or country, an observer of mankind and his universe and the brutal poignancy of man and woman and their life on earth.

Anthony didn't know if he was moved more by the grace and wisdom of the words or by the fact that the speaker was undoubtedly—pronouncedly—a woman.

A woman who was fearless and shameless and unapologetic about following, above all else, the clear call of the spirit.

It was, he decided, one of the most perfect sermons he'd ever heard. Anthony stretched his cramped muscles. He was exhausted. He was exhilarated.

He wondered if Tano knew what he had done.

He closed his eyes for a moment. Thunder was right there, pressing up against him.

When I am weak, don't forsake me
Or fear my power.
Why do you despise my fear
And curse my pride?
I am woman existing in every fear
And in my strength when I tremble.

What is your actual name? Anthony thought. Is it Thunder, or is that just how you sound?

. . . Take me into understanding from grief
. . . and come to me, you who know me.

. . . I am peace, and war has come because of me.
I am alien and citizen.
I am the substance and the one without substance.

He had no idea what she would look like, this Thunder, how her female voice would sound. In the vacuum of his imagination it was Gemma he saw, Gemma he heard.

> *. . . I am one you studied and you scorn me.*
> *I am unlettered and you learn from me.*
> *I am one you despise and you study me.*
> *I am one you hide from and you appear to me.*

Anthony pushed the translations away and tipped his chair back. He had come to a full understanding of Charles Bastian's urgency and of the risks he had taken. If there was a god-given purpose to his own life now, it would be to recover the other gospels his friend had chosen to embrace.

Wandering to the cafeteria for tea, he thought he could feel Charles Bastian's intent—and his hope. As mankind approached another crisis of faith, limping forward unsteadily with a ravaged heart and bloodied soul, unsure of the way—or why forward motion was even necessary—these books had the power to bring back life and direction. They might possess people to turn their heads to the heavens and feel, even just for a moment, their own divinity.

He understood it was worth dying for.

He sipped his tea, thinking about his brother and Gemma and how they were casualties of a world that had been hurt and learned to hurt itself. Of the great and unhealed wound of war.

Of which you know nothing, said a voice inside.

No, Anthony agreed.

You should feel sorry for yourself, it continued, *for while they have pain they also have love—and you have neither. You have your distance and the illusion of strength.*

It was true. And what good was distance when you were forced to deal with people?

His strength might very well be an illusion. The peace of the desert was being crowded out by violence and greed, by a war fought by men who thought they could control God. And he had joined the fight.

He knew better than to run away. Aside from the blood being shed over the lost gospels, aside from the discomfort and uncertainty growing inside of him, something important was happening to him here, something he had been waiting for. Something he had not yet named. He could not have predicted it would come this way.

CHAPTER TWENTY

EMMA SPENT THE next morning at the post office, waiting in line behind men who eyed her occasionally over their shoulders. Sunlight fell from high slat-like windows, and there was the smell of human traffic. The street delivered a thin cloud of dust.

It took most of the morning to send the letters she had written reporting her father's death. She had written them one after another, allowing no other thoughts. Not of her father, not of Michael, not of Anthony. The process had rebound her to the reality of her situation: She was parentless in a foreign country with enough money to keep her alive for half a year or so, living modestly. But what was she doing here, really? Her time was running out; she couldn't continue foraging in an office that would soon belong to someone else.

Later she stood in her father's office and felt invaded by uncertainty. Her conjectures had served a purpose: They had kept her father alive. But while he might have come up with the most incredible story history had known, he was not there to tell it. She didn't even know what that story was. What she knew had been put together with marginal notes and fragments; it was proof of absolutely nothing. The insight and strength she had gained might be all she was going to get from a search that would soon come to an end.

And she didn't know what to do next.

She turned to the boxes and the mounds of material she had almost finished sorting. The Tut material would go to the museum to be compiled someday, maybe by David Lazar. She would keep the books and the journals. The rest of it would probably be tossed out. The problem was, though the work in his office was done, she was nowhere near being ready to leave. Maybe she could stay in Cairo anyway, find a job and an apartment. If there was going to be a war, they would need nurses. The last place she wanted to be was London, her own city of the dead. She sat in her father's chair. So now what? Get an apartment in Cairo and wait for another war? Go to Upper Egypt by herself and walk around in the sand?

She imagined Anthony would be relieved if she left; he had never been truly comfortable with her. He had been a dutiful friend to her father. She could free him of that obligation anyway.

And there was Michael. Part of her wanted his company enough to risk his brokenness. They were not so different, really, fitting together with only a few rough cojoinings. Michael knew war and loss. She couldn't imagine being with someone who didn't know these things, who had not fallen into such a yawning darkness. He was an addict, but she was a nurse. She had not entirely given up on the possibility that they could climb out together.

Gemma pushed a box with her foot and spun her chair half around to face the door. Maybe the most important task before her had to do with rejoining the living. Maybe the reason she wanted to stay in Egypt was to open her heart again.

But it hurt. Every time it opened, her heart hurt.

She spun back and propped her feet back on the box, flipping absently through the pages of her father's most recent journal, the journal with which she had spent the least time.

She reread his final words, pausing this time at the line *Between Isis and Mary is the proof of woman lost.* She closed the journal and swiveled to face the lithograph of Isis. *Proof.* She thought of the folder of women, she thought of her dream of Mary. The picture had given her so much, but it had not given her proof. Had her father been speaking literally? Once again she took down the lithograph and carefully removed the back of the frame. Pressed against the cardboard backing was a thin layer she hadn't noticed the first time. Now, as she pulled one from the other, she could see there was something sealed against the backing.

She took a pair of scissors and ran it carefully along the seam. Inside were folded sheets of onionskin paper. Her eyes searched a page of lettering that was clearly not her father's. It was like nothing she'd ever seen, tall and cramped and undoubtedly ancient. Her eyes paused at a word she recognized because it was a name. An unmistakable name. This, she knew, was Coptic, complete with vowels. Gemma wrote the name on a piece of scrap paper, letter for letter: *Mary Magdalene.*

She almost ran to Anthony's office, stopping abruptly halfway there. There was a man posted outside the door, leaning against the wall and reading from an open file. Something in his stance reminded Gemma of a policeman. He looked up at her and quickly closed the file. As Gemma approached, he assumed the unnatural position of holding the folder behind his back.

"Is Anthony in?" Gemma asked.

"I'm afraid not," he said. "You must be Gemma Bastian. I'm Togo Mina, the director of the Coptic Museum."

Gemma took the hand he offered.

"How are you finding Cairo?"

"It's not like London," she said. "It's not like anywhere." She looked at the file behind his back. He actually seemed to be hiding it. "Sometimes I wish it would rain."

Mina smiled. "Sometimes it does."

Anthony appeared down the hall, raised his hand in greeting, and walked briskly toward them. There was an awkward moment when he arrived. Gemma watched his eyes find the file behind Mina's back. Typically, he made no attempt at small talk. Both men seemed at a loss. Gemma looked from one to the other.

"Shall we go in?" Anthony asked Mina.

Mina nodded his assent. "I only need a moment of your time."

After they had closed the door, Mina sat down and sighed. "Not much is lost on her, I can see that. Her eyes were like a hawk's on this file. I should have acted more naturally, but she came charging out of that office like fury itself. There I was, reading about her father's last excavation."

"What have you got there?"

"Notes from the man I sent to Nag Hammadi. Someone saw fit to return his personal belongings to Cairo. He spoke to a Mr. Bashir and learned that three months ago a leather-bound text was sent from Nag Hammadi to Cairo to be authenticated. The messenger was Bashir's cousin. He was to deliver the text to Albert Eid, the antiquities dealer."

"So it's Eid we want, not Tano."

"Yes. I've been chasing the wrong dog. I think I will pay Eid a visit. Not alone, mind you. I'll bring the police—and I'll bring Doresse. At the very least, we will persuade Eid to show it to an expert."

"So we can know exactly what we may never have."

"Don't be dour."

"There's no reason Eid should cooperate. There's no reason we should ever touch what he has in his keeping. I'd wager it vanishes within the month into private ownership."

"Could you do me the favor of feigning optimism?"

Anthony considered his pencil. "I can try."

"Good," Mina stood. "That would help."

GEMMA SAT IN her father's chair and waited for the sounds of Togo Mina departing. She entered Anthony's office without knocking.

"What was that about?"

"The building plans for the new museum. Odds and ends."

She smiled. "So you're an architectural consultant as well?"

"You could say that."

Her sarcasm eluded him. "You are a man of many talents. But if I may say so, your director looked like the cat who ate the canary. Now, why do I think that?"

"I don't know."

"You're both hiding something. It's as plain as day."

"And your imagination is active."

"So here we are." Gemma flopped down into a chair. "Deadlock. Again."

Anthony crossed his arms over his chest. "Is that what it is?"

"For whatever perverse reason, you won't tell me what you're doing. I'd be an idiot to rush into the void. So we'll just sit here."

"As you like," Anthony said.

"What irritates me is I feel like I'm being electrocuted by all this and you just sit there like some chunk of marble."

"Electrocuted by all what?"

Gemma shook her head. "You'd have made a good spy."

Anthony held up his hands in a gesture of surrender. But he surrendered nothing. Gemma stared at him, drawing on a patience she had learned during the war. She pretended for a moment that she was in a bomb shelter. There was nowhere she could go, nothing she could do but wait. She began silently counting to herself, the way they had with carpet bombs. Instantly the smell of frozen earth was in her nostrils, and her family's breath in the dark night air. And in the half-light of their candles, the faces of her mother and father.

Anthony interrupted her trance by speaking. "Have we reached a truce? Because I need to get to work."

Gemma continued to stare at him with a now aggressive sobriety. "You're lucky I'm resourceful enough to conduct myself reasonably with someone like you. I don't think you realize what a strange and difficult man you are. You might have made a good spy, but you might not have survived the war."

Anthony peered at her, squinting as if he could not see her clearly. "Why is that?"

"Because you wouldn't have known how to ask for help."

Anthony laughed. "Am I that bad?"

Gemma did not laugh. "I was thinking of showing you something. But now I don't know."

"Yes you do, Gemma. What is it?"

"First I need a favor. I need to find out more about alphabets."

"What kind of alphabets?"

"Old alphabets."

"The museum library has a good reference section on linguistics. I'm sure there's some material on alphabets."

"The problem is I will lose my privileges there. Can you fix it so I can work there for another week?"

"Give me a reason."

Gemma pulled out the transparent piece of paper. "Here's your reason."

Anthony put on his glasses. She knew from his face, and the motionless way he held the onionskin paper, that he had never seen it. It took him a long time to put it down.

"It's a tracing, isn't it?" she asked.

"Where did you find this?"

"It was my father's," she said. "I can make out one name."

Anthony took off his glasses and rubbed his eyes. "You've been teaching yourself Coptic?"

"A bit. What does it say?"

"It's from the Gospel of Philip, something I have only heard exists." Anthony replaced his glasses and held the tracing in front of him. "Give me some time."

"I'll give you all day."

Forty minutes later, Anthony raised his head. "It says,

". . . *the companion of the Savior is Mary Magdalene.*
But Christ loved her more than all the disciples,
and used to kiss her often on the mouth.
The rest of the disciples were offended . . .
They said to him, Why do you love her more than all of us?
The Savior answered and said to them,
Why do I not love you as I love her?"

Gemma was silent. Her cheeks were flushed. "There's no longer any doubt in my mind that my father was murdered." She held her hand out for the tracing. Anthony returned it reluctantly.

"What are you going to do with that?"

"Am I required to tell you?"

"No."

"Good." She stared at the floor.

"Gemma?"

"'Why do I not love you as I love her?'" Gemma shook her head. "You know, while I imagined such a relationship between Jesus and Mary Magdalene, to see proof . . . it makes me feel, I don't know, sad. Incredibly sad." She turned away. Anthony thought she might be on the verge of tears. He almost rose, almost left his chair to comfort her. Instead, he made a stiff offering of his handkerchief. But she was not crying, and she ignored the handkerchief. "Someone took her away," she continued. "His greatest love, and she barely exists in the story of his life." Gemma rose. "Philip is a sign. A sign that I shouldn't give up."

"I didn't think that was possible."

"Then you're an easy man to fool."

"Not usually."

"You and I are alike in one way," she said. "We're alone. But while I've learned it, you chose it. If the choice were mine, I'd have a different life." She held his eyes until Anthony looked away. "There's more," she said, producing the other onionskin sheets.

Anthony looked at the sheets and then at Gemma. "If you have something else to do, do it. This is going to take some time."

"I'll wait."

Anthony smiled. "You don't trust me."

"You haven't given me a reason to."

It took three hours. Gemma dozed and startled herself awake, unsure of where she was. She stared at Anthony's back and remembered. Philip's words played in her mind as she settled herself back into the chair. Nothing would ever be the same. She was visited by the hope that as she changed, the world would change with her.

"Are you all right?" he asked without turning.

"Yes."

"I'm nearly done."

Gemma waited until Anthony was ready to begin. Finally he said, "The verses read,

"If the woman and man had not come apart,
They would not know death.
Christ came to repair the split, there from the beginning
And join the two and give them life
They, who had died of separation.
Now the woman and man are one in the chamber
With the bed, and those so joined will not come apart again."

"We are talking about actual physical union," Gemma said, "aren't we?"
"Partially."
"As a metaphor or literally?"
"I don't know. Maybe both."
"Never mind. What else is there?"

"The world has become the eternal realm
Because the external realm is fullness for you.
This is the way it is: It is revealed to you alone,
Not hidden in the darkness and the night
But in a perfect day and a holy light."

"It sounds like my father's credo: *God is revealed to you alone.*"
"I agree. There's one more short verse.

"Ignorance is the mother of all evil
Ignorance will eventuate in death."

"They must have been his favorites," Gemma said. "But why seal them behind a lithograph of Isis?"
"That's where you found them?"
"Yes."
"Clearly he didn't want just anyone finding them."

"Why not?"

"Because he needed them as evidence, because—" Anthony stopped himself.

"No, don't stop," Gemma said.

Anthony closed his eyes. "Do you know the word 'gnosis'?"

"I've heard it."

"Your father once told me he regarded himself as a Gnostic, someone who seeks God through understanding, through knowledge. Someone who would, like Philip, believe that ignorance is the mother of all evil."

"Go on."

"He had been uncovering a branch of Christianity, a branch that was very much alive at the time of Christ. A branch that was later buried. He called it the Gnostic branch. As I have said, he believed that Jesus had two levels of teachings: one for ordinary disciples in public and one for an inner circle of disciples in private. Jesus spoke to his inner circle differently from the way he spoke to others; he taught them different things. He taught them to seek God through wisdom. I think Thomas, and now Philip, were members of the inner circle, the Gnostic circle.

"As far as the apostles of the New Testament, it's there for anyone to see—they continually misunderstand Jesus' words and actions. They are constantly asking questions: Which way should we go? When will the kingdom come? Their insistence on interpreting Jesus' words literally is almost childlike."

"Whereas a Gnostic interpretation would see these statements as symbolic: There is nowhere to go; the kingdom is inside," Gemma said. "So the gospels of the New Testament did not come from the closest disciples of Jesus."

"Your father didn't think so. I'm starting to agree."

"Why haven't you told me this before?"

"Maybe I didn't believe it myself."

Gemma glared at him. His reflective eyes revealed nothing of himself. He was maddening. "What about Mary Magdalene?" she demanded. "Was she in the inner circle?"

Anthony shook his head. "You are remarkable. You have your father's brain with some innate knack that allows you to leap from one point to the next, skipping the steps in between."

"My father called it the genius of the female mind." Gemma stood abruptly. The color had come up in her face. She was as strident as Thunder, as righteous and as beautifully angry.

"Who knows," Anthony said. "We might be able to bring Mary back."

At the door she turned. "If you bring her back, bring her back as an apostle."

CHAPTER TWENTY-ONE

ANTHONY KNEW HE had to talk to Mina about the tracings Gemma had shown him. Instead he sat in silence for some time trying to summon the peace of the ruins at Kharga. He closed his eyes, envisioning the dust that colored everything, penetrating every crease and crevice of skin and cloth by the end of the day; and the burning and sand-filled journey away from the ruins to Kharga's oasis, to the monastic ruins where he spent the cool mornings, and at noon the relief of the oasis and its extravagant greenness, without which he could not survive, and the feeling that he sometimes had of being on an island in a shifting sea of sand that might one day not let him cross it. If he were a stronger man, he would not need the oasis. He would live on the sea of sand. He was not like the men he studied; he was not as brave or driven. The world still held him, he thought, as he collected his things to visit Mina's office. Now more than ever.

TOGO MINA WAS barely visible behind a desk heaped with books and papers. He leaned out from a precariously stacked pile to greet Anthony. "What have you found out?"

"Gemma Bastian has shown me tracings her father made. They purport to be from the Gospel of Philip."

"Philip?" Mina jumped up. "You've found Philip?"

"I don't know we can say that. Bastian found him. He must have made the tracings from the original."

"Tell me, do you know what they said?"

Anthony spoke calmly. "One quote was about Jesus' love for Mary Magdalene—a love greater than his love for the apostles. 'Why do I not love you as I love her?' he asked."

Mina got up and poured two glasses of Scotch. "What we have here, what we finally may have, is the story we were never meant to know fully."

"I have also found Thunder. I would describe it as a gospel, though I'm not sure what ilk. It's a manifesto of the universe told by an enlightened woman."

Mina's eyes widened. "I want to see it," he demanded.

"Later. We don't have time for textual analysis now."

"At least tell me where in God's name you found it."

"It was delivered anonymously. It might have slipped off the pile somewhere, and been picked up by someone who knew where it belonged."

"Bollocks! You're not telling everything."

Anthony raised his hand at the fuming Mina. "We have a fragment of Thomas, verses from Philip, the text of Thunder—that leaves Mary on Bastian's list of four. I think when we find her, we will have the complete picture Bastian wanted to paint. I think part of that picture is determining who Mary really was. She was certainly Jesus' consort. What we haven't considered is that she too was an apostle. That there might be evidence to prove it."

"Do you know what that would mean?"

"I know just what it means. The reason women have not been ordained, have never been equal members of the Church, is that the Church claims there was no female apostle."

Mina gave a glass to Anthony and emptied his own. "I am working on an ulcer," he said, dropping a tablet into a glass of water. "You are certain of the authenticity of these texts?"

"What convinces me of the authenticity is the fact that Bastian is dead. The question is why. He didn't have the texts, as far as we know."

"My news," Tano said, "is that Eid is in possession of the Gospel of Thomas. Doresse saw it. Not only is it authentic, but he thinks it predates the gospels of the New Testament. He thinks it might have been a source for Matthew and Luke."

"It's remarkable; Bastian had suspected as much."

"Well, Eid's giving up nothing without a fight. So a fight there will be. In the meantime, he is deflecting attention to his competitor, Tano. He mentioned a name I have heard before. Dattari. An Italian woman who is somehow involved with this madness. So Eid says. But there's more to all of this, I'm sure. Bastian must have seen the texts in Nag Hammadi. He traced them there, before they got to Cairo." Mina collapsed on the couch. "We need to send someone else to Nag Hammadi. Someone needs to talk to Mr. Bashir. And we should no longer ignore the proximity of Stephan Sutton. What was he working on, do we know? What if there are more gospels yet to find? Maybe I will go myself."

"A man in your position will draw attention. You wouldn't make it halfway there before you were abducted."

"Well, I can't send someone else, knowing it might be a death sentence."

"Tell me, are you still being followed?"

"I don't know. Maybe it's my imagination. I'm not sleeping well. I think he's there and then he's gone. I feel my eyes are playing tricks."

Anthony let a moment pass. Then he said, "I'll go to Nag Hammadi."

Mina was on his feet. "I don't know, I don't know."

"I don't see an alternative."

"With your background and languages, you would have the best chance at getting to the bottom of things."

"I agree."

"I would be eternally grateful, Lazar. I think it's the only way to find out what happened there—and what is happening now. You could find out who Bastian talked to, who helped him." Mina stalked around the room, conducting the air with his arms. "You speak the dialects, could mingle with the locals."

Anthony looked down at his hands. He felt tired. "And Gemma Bastian?"

"What about her?"

"She's involved."

"Get her uninvolved. It's something we simply can't risk. Think of it: a father and a daughter both casualties, both in association with the museum. We would look responsible. That's not a position I want to be in."

"I understand. But I will uninvolve her for her own sake."

"Whatever reason suits you, Lazar."

"I'd prefer not to lie."

"Withhold, then."

"Another lie."

"Then avoid her, for God's sake. She doesn't know enough to endanger our project."

"There's no telling what she knows. I think it's best for me to leave as soon as possible. I need a few days to take care of some other business and then I'll be off."

"Take what you need, but work quickly. This is potentially more important than the museum. This is the stuff for which museums are built. God willing, we will see these gospels in ours."

ANTHONY MADE HIS way across town, keeping his eyes on the pavement in front of him. This was the second time he had heard the name Dattari. When was the first? It took him a moment to recall. It was Gemma who had mentioned her, at her father's memorial service. She had mentioned that Angela Dattari had gone back to Italy, as if Anthony would know who this woman was. The only reason for her to assume such a thing was that her father had known her.

Anthony entered his family's house through the back door, which opened directly into the kitchen. Amad was not there. The shopping had been done and two canvas bags lay on the table, vegetables and fruit spilling out. He would be preparing dinner soon. Anthony took out a string of beads from his pocket and sat down to wait, running them through his fingers.

When Amad entered, he glanced briefly at Anthony and shook an apron from a drawer.

"Amad," Anthony said, rising. He was still not used to seeing Amad as a cook. This was the man without whom his father might not have persevered. He was a man of learning and languages, and for decades he had provided the bridge over which his father crossed into lands he wouldn't have otherwise been able to enter, or perhaps even understand.

Anthony had once made the mistake of asking Amad if his new domestic position made him feel in any way demeaned. He had been presumptuous enough to suggest that he might have some idea what the old man valued.

Amad had scolded him. "I am at the time in my life where I want peace. Here, I have it. What I am doing is useful and it is quiet. No one bothers me. I can think of the things I have seen and know and be glad for the length of my life. And I can imagine you and Zira doing the things I used to do."

Now Amad tied his apron, crossed the kitchen. He took Anthony's hand in his and pressed it in both of his own, quickly inspecting the younger man's face. "You need something. Tell me."

One could speak nothing but the truth with Amad. It was why Anthony loved both him and the son he had raised. "I have a favor to ask. There are some manuscripts floating around Cairo, the same books Charles Bastian was involved with."

"At the time of his death."

"I don't need to tell you to be careful."

"I can take care of myself, child." Amad went to the table and emptied the shopping bags, taking time to arrange the contents in the order they would be chopped—garlic, then coriander, then tomatoes. "You want to know where they are?"

"Either Tano has them or they've left Cairo."

Amad crossed the room to the magnetic strip where his knives hung, meticulously clean and sharp. "And his daughter? She is involved?"

"Not if I can help it."

"She is a good pupil on the oud. A natural musician. Sometimes she helps me in the kitchen. I have come to enjoy her company, the way I enjoyed her father's." Anthony watched as Amad rapidly peeled and chopped three fat cloves of garlic. "This is what I enjoy about food. No trouble." He wiped his knife with a moistened rag and set it down. He placed his hands on the butcher block and, while he seemed to study the grain of the wood, his face lost all expression. Anthony recognized in the unannounced silence that Amad was coming to a decision. It was the Amad he knew better, not the cook but the elder who possessed a wordless understanding of most things. Finally, he looked up at the boy he had helped raise, the boy who was now a man who did not often ask for anything. "I will do what I can."

"I have a name," Anthony said. "A Mrs. Angela Dattari. An Italian woman, a private collector. Her name keeps coming up. It might be a place to start."

Amad's eyelids fluttered briefly at the name. "I will do what I can," he said again.

CHAPTER TWENTY-TWO

T HAT AFTERNOON GEMMA was reading in the den, alternately finishing a paragraph or a page and then becoming distracted by the rays of sun that sliced through the curtains, giving unimaginable life to dust. Her father's notes and tracings had brought to mind romantic notions of love that swam enticingly inside her head, diving and surfacing in a dangerous and flickering pool of hope.

She found herself thinking about Michael. She hadn't seen him much lately. Half listening for the door, she tried to quell her impatience. She wasn't sure for what. Part of her wanted to plan immediately for a trip to the place her father had worked, the place where he had discovered the astonishing words of apostles she had never heard of. She knew very well there might be nothing to see. It didn't matter. She would take the translation of Philip's words with her. She would take her fragment of Thomas. She would take her father's journals. She would search for the spirits of men who had disappeared as she had searched for women who had been lost.

The reason she couldn't leave yet was that there was one woman who it was in her power to find.

She had revisited Angela Dattari's house. The now insolent gardener, looking at Gemma as though she were deranged, confirmed that his mistress would be returning at the end of the week. She was haunting a stranger's house, waiting for a woman her dead father might have loved. During some moments, she felt the gardener was justified, that she was half crazy. In other moments, she knew she could feel her father in this place, just as she could feel the man he had been coming to life. Not just the man, she considered, a whole philosophy, a philosophy built partly on the words of lost apostles and partly on something she couldn't yet read. Gemma no longer doubted there was something in the half-legible lines of the journal pages. She was now convinced that the two colors of ink and the altered handwriting represented two entries made at two different times, one from the past and one from the present. But both entries were governed by the same strange rules: no vowels and a cohesive visual pattern of letters that was present in one line and gone the next. Either that, or the gardener was right and she was going a little mad. She took out the translations of Philip she had read now many times.

> *The world has become the eternal realm*
> *Because the eternal realm is fullness for you.*
> *This is the way it is. It is revealed to you alone,*
> *Not hidden in the darkness and the night*
> *But in a perfect day and a holy light.*

She wasn't sure why this made her so happy, or why, after reading the words of Philip, she felt temporarily released from the stranglehold of her life.

She put the tracing away and held her hand into the band of sunlight, watching the delicate universe of dust arrange itself around her fingers.

> *The companion to the Savior was Mary Magdalene . . .*
> *If the woman and man had not come apart,*
> *They would not know death . . .*

Maybe love was the point, she thought. Maybe if you knew love, everything else became insignificant. If you didn't have it, you had nothing.

Jesus had known this.

He had known it with Mary Magdalene.

Had her father known it too? She thought he had, with her mother. And after that?

Would she herself ever know it?

She wondered then whether if her father had known love, finding his God would be so important. If she had known he was happy, wouldn't that be enough? Would it?

She had designated Angela Dattari as the one person who could help her answer these questions.

She turned then from history's earliest alphabets to a tour guide of Upper Egypt. She studied the section on Luxor, the nearest major tourist destination to Oxyrhynchus. She was squinting at age-faded photographs when Michael crashed through the front door. The taxi driver who had been supporting him stood on the doorstep with a glistening brow, waiting to be paid. Gemma ran upstairs for her money. When she came back down, Michael was lying in the middle of the hall and the taxi driver was leaning in the doorway, smoking. Only one of Michael's legs was visible. She paid the driver and sat down next to Michael.

"Hallo," he said. "How are things at the museum?"

"Fine, actually."

"You spend a bloody lot of time there."

"I know."

"If you've entered the darker realms, I don't want to hear about it."

"No dark realms here. The opposite, in fact."

"That's my girl," Michael gibed. "All sweetness and light."

"Michael," she said, "what happened to your other leg?"

"I should have known. I've never done well at the races." Michael was staring at the ceiling. Gemma lay down and gazed with him at the glinting tiers of crystals in the chandelier above. "At the Windsor a pig of a German was boasting about his marksmanship. I suppose I said something to annoy him. I said Germans couldn't hit a stuffed duck with a bazooka, that was why they lost the war." Michael laughed. "That made him mad. But being German, of course, he wouldn't let it go. He had to prove himself. His bragging was unbearable. 'Hit this,' I finally said, and I held out my leg like a ruler. And hit it he did. Blasted the leg in half. Not my finest moment. He was a stupid oaf, and a Kraut, but I'm afraid he won the day."

"Where's the leg now?"

"I tossed it out the taxi window. It's brought me enough trouble. Fought me from the beginning."

"We'll have to get you another."

"No. I think I'll be what I am for a change. A worm."

"So you're going to spend the rest of the day in the front hall?"

"No, I'll crawl upstairs presently."

Gemma got to her knees. "You know, Michael, in hospital I saw better false legs than yours. They looked more functional; some even looked like real legs. If we found you a prosthesis that served you better, you might be happier wearing it. What do you think?"

"I think that was London."

"And this is Cairo, an enormous cultural center of history and learning and not so far from London by plane."

Michael yawned. "It's time to go upstairs. No help this time, Gemma. You're going to have to watch me slither." Halfway up the stairs, he rested and looked down at her. "If you could, bring me the package on the table there. My cousin Sam has sent me some books from the civilized world. I'm going to be needing a good story."

BEFORE DINNER, Gemma came down from her room and sat in the garden watching platoons of clouds march across the sky. High above the billowing, imperial soldiers were mottled pheasant wings of cirrus clouds already pink with the setting sun. Belonging to no order at all were the broad isolated strips of thick cloud, placed like mistakes on a canvas. Gemma sat under the fronds of the date palm and with her right hand fingered a simple Bach melody in the air. Some sort of falcon circled overhead and she put its soaring turns to music. A small plane crossed the sky, catching the light on its yellow wings, and she thought of Michael and how badly he needed to find the sky again. With very little trouble, she thought, she could do something to help him before she left. I've been too self-absorbed, she thought. I've been ignoring the people right in front of me. I should be trying harder to open my heart, she thought. I should attempt to love.

THE NEXT MORNING she brought Michael his toast and coffee and tolerated his sour, half-conscious silence. Then she found her way to the University of Cairo medical library. She went for herself as much as for Michael, to escape the entropy of his inaction.

The streets were quiet for noontime prayer. Halfway to the university she paid the taxi, opting to walk. They had come to accept each other, she and this foreign city. The bands of small children seemed to know she was impenetrable, her pockets empty, and she found it possible to ignore the stares of Egyptian men. She learned to walk as if she had been in the country too long to care what any of them thought. In her mind, it was Anthony she mimicked, with his averted eyes and bowed head. She wanted to be able to cut through a thick crowd as he did, moving like a fish through a river.

The woman behind the information desk at the library was sipping tea. She held a magazine in front of her face. Gemma stared at the photograph on the cover. It was the billowing mushroom cloud of the atom bomb dropped on Hiroshima. Gemma stood with her hands resting on the counter and said nothing. She had not given significant thought to the apocalyptic end of the war. She, with her sound mind and body, was preoccupied with smaller matters. Michael had thought about it, ratcheting his mind open to let in all the images of horror. He read every newspaper and magazine, stared mutely for long minutes at the photographs. But she, a nurse, could not take it in. Faced now with the mushroom cloud, she felt leaden. What did she know of war? She had hidden, safe in her nurse's superiority, imagining she could heal people by fixing their bodies. She knew nothing of Michael's wounds, not really. How could she possibly be irritated—and worse, impatient with him?

She forced her hand to touch the bell on the counter and the woman behind the magazine looked up. Though she was dark, she wore pearls and lipstick and Gemma guessed she spoke English.

"I'm looking for information on prostheses. Books, articles, mailings, anything you've got."

When the woman did not at first answer, Gemma thought she had guessed wrong. She had been as presumptuous as one of Cairo's expatriates who, while living off the riches of a poor country, both condescended to its people and expected them to speak their language. But as the woman put down the magazine, Gemma saw that she understood her well enough. It was the cloud that had distracted her.

The librarian supplied her with more than enough information. Old, timeworn history books with thin pages and medical texts with cracking new bindings. Gemma chose five books and a small stack of periodicals. Arranging them around her at the end of a long wooden table, she began making notes on her pad.

BECAUSE MICHAEL REFUSED to come down to dinner that evening, Gemma brought a dinner tray to his room. He considered her dyspeptically over one of his new books.

"It must be a good story," she said.

"It's perfect. An angry alcoholic living under a volcano in some godforsaken country and drinking himself to death. I feel I've found a friend."

Gemma set the tray on his lap and then pulled a chair to his bedside. "I've been to the medical library."

Michael held up his plate and sniffed his food. "You're a crazy little wren."

"You'll be happy to know the oldest known splint was dug up right here, in Egypt, nearly four thousand years ago."

"You don't say."

"In India the Rig-Veda describes how a warrior, Queen Vishpla, lost her leg in battle. Then she was given an iron prosthesis and returned to fight."

Michael tucked his napkin into his collar and pulled his tray closer. "What I would do for a plate of bangers and mash," he said. "Here, I've no idea what I'm eating half the time."

"There are even amputee gods," Gemma continued. "The Peruvian jaguar god, Ai Apec, lost his arm above the elbow. And the Aztec god of creation, Tezcatlitpoca, had his right foot amputated. The Celtic god New Hah had his left arm amputated."

"What an illustrious group. We should all get together sometime."

"And here's a story you might like: In Greek myth the grandson of Zeus, Pelops, was killed and cooked by his father, Tantalus, and served to the gods to see if they could tell the difference between the meat of an animal and the meat of a man."

"How civilized. What part did they serve first?"

"Demeter ate Pelops's shoulder. She was so horrified that she brought him back to life and gave him a lovely ivory prosthesis."

"Poor little goddess."

"Millions of warriors and knights and kings have lost limbs—and they had it worse than you, being dipped in hot oil or seared with hot irons."

Michael wrinkled his nose and raised a forkful of rice. "Wren, I'm trying to eat."

"The point is, you're luckier than these other amputees. Science has advanced." Gemma scooted forward in her chair. "Just last year in America they made a new prosthesis. They use something called a 'suction sock' that fits tightly. It's supposed to move almost like a real leg. And it bends. I made an inquiry to find out where we can get one, and what doctors could fit you. There's a doctor in London who has trained in America and specializes in upper-leg prostheses. I think you should go."

Michael set his fork down and took a long drink of wine. "Will you come to London with me?"

"If I did I might never come back."

"Let's go, then, and never come back."

"I can't, not yet. You go. It's not a long trip. Think how good it will feel. You won't hobble anymore. You won't thump. You might even be able to fly."

Michael looked up. For the first time in days, there was life in his eyes.

T HAT EVENING, father and son sat reading in the den. An hour passed with tentative conversation, gentle forays and retreats by the older man.

His son was tolerating a rare physical proximity, a temporary coexistence that touched the father as much as an embrace and maybe more because it was Michael. It was his gifted, betrayed, wounded son. Michael, for his part, knew he was requesting his father's presence by not driving him away. David could hear that while his son's words were not kind, he did not want his father to leave. Then, all of a sudden, it was over. Michael's eyes hardened and he put his book down. "You're terrified, aren't you?"

"Excuse me?"

"You've been whipped by guilt. That's what keeps me from forgiving you; your guilt is stronger than any love you might feel for me."

David gazed at his son in the firelight.

"It's about your vision of yourself," Michael continued. "Of how I reflect upon you. You can't stand that you've failed. I'm here as evidence and you can't stand it."

"If you truly reflected me, I'd be happy. You're a remarkable man."

Michael stared. "How? Because I had the luck to survive?"

David closed his book. "Do you think someday we'll be able to speak without rancor?"

"What could we possibly have to say to each other? We've nothing in common but a dead woman."

David shut his eyes tightly.

"Yes," his son went on. "It's like a circle of hell, isn't it? You can't get out of it as long as I'm alive. Whenever you see me, you're back in it, going round and round."

"I'm not concerned about my own circle of hell. I know it well. I'm concerned about yours."

"You needn't be," Michael said faintly.

"I have no choice. You're my son."

Michael smiled so brightly it couldn't have been genuine. But David was taken in by the hope that it was. "I'm doing quite well as it turns out. I'm getting this dandy new leg and a pretty girl to help me learn how to use it."

"You like Gemma."

"I think that's obvious."

"I like her too. I'm glad she came along, for all of us." David put his book on the table next to his chair and rose. "Well, I'm off."

Michael said nothing until his father was at the door. "Does Anthony speak about her?"

David turned. "Not to me. But then I don't seem to be the kind of father who inspires confidences."

Chapter Twenty-three

Gemma slept badly that night and came to breakfast late, feeling confused. Amad gestured diplomatically to her shirt, which was buttoned up wrong. As she was finishing breakfast, he paused in front of her. "There is a letter for you in the hall, from the Bank of Egypt."

"Thank you, Amad. Where is everyone?"

"Out."

Gemma made her way quickly to the hall and sat on the stairs to read the letter.

> Dear Miss Bastian,
>
> I came across some notes in your father's file and found out that the money transfer your father was expecting was meant to come from the Bank of England. The guarantor was the British Museum. I don't know if it means anything, but I remembered your request to inform you if I learned anything else about your father's affairs. Find below the telephone numbers and the contacts of both the bank and the museum. I hope this proves useful.
>
> Sincerely,
> A. Sadir

Gemma entered David's office and stared at the phone. She would tell him later about the long-distance expense. She requested the number and soon the phone rang its double English ring. For a moment, she was homesick. "Is there a Mr. Huffington there?" she asked.

She tapped her toe until Mr. Huffington came on the line. "Mr. Huffington," she began, "I believe my father, Charles Bastian, was involved in some sort of a business deal with you. A few months ago he was expecting a money transfer from the Bank of England, guaranteed by the British Museum. Your name was on the account."

"Only from this end. Our man Stephan Sutton was on the Cairo end."

"Stephan Sutton is dead."

"Yes, in fact."

Her thoughts raced. "Was my father selling something to your museum?"

"I'm not at liberty to discuss our acquisitions."

"But you didn't acquire anything, not from him."

"Didn't we?"

"Unless he wasn't paid for it. And both men involved are now dead."

Huffington went silent. She could hear the rustling of papers. "Then maybe this is a matter for the police."

"Do you know what my father and Stephan Sutton were arranging?"

"As I said, I'm not at liberty to go into detail."

"My father might have died for your acquisition, so the least you can do is tell me what happened."

"All I can tell you is that there was something the museum was interested in acquiring, and on the eve of acquiring it, we lost our man. As far as we know, what we are interested in is still at large, so you understand the need for discretion. That's the end of the story I am willing to tell. I'm sorry about your father." And Mr. Huffington from the British Museum hung up.

Gemma put down the phone and lost herself in the polished grain of the teak desk. Stephan Sutton and her father had been negotiating a deal. They had been negotiating at the time Sutton had died. Where had her father been when Sutton was buried alive by rocks? Had someone murdered him because he was going to help acquire the lost gospels for the British Museum?

Why the British Museum? She absently opened the desk drawer and was on the verge of invading David's privacy when she heard someone in the hall. She grabbed a travel guidebook from David's shelf. When she emerged from the office, Michael was standing by the door, going through the mail.

"Hallo," he said, glancing up. "How funny to find you here."

"Michael"—she tucked the book under her arm—"where have you been?"

"Oh, here and there."

"I feel like I haven't seen you much this week."

"I've had a little project of my own." He winked. "Jealous?"

"Terribly."

"What have you got there, a tour book?"

"I found one in your father's office; it's got lovely photographs. I'm still determined to take my trip south."

"Good for you." Michael gave a little smile. "Your slothlike patient has had a talk with the doctor in London."

"The prosthetics specialist? You called him?"

"This wooden replacement is the bloody limit. It's killing me a bit faster than I want to die."

Gemma frowned down at the leg. "The replacements are often bad fits."

"Bad, nothing. This is an appalling *mash*. I've got a little infection brewing already. So I talked to a doctor here in Cairo, another specialist. He advised me to call London directly; he thought this bloke Henderson might take me on. I guess he has a weakness for war heroes. So I thought it was worth a try. And it was. He'll see me."

"Michael, that's wonderful."

"Thank you, Gemma, for making the inquiries."

Gemma searched Michael's face for an irony that for once wasn't there. He seemed genuinely pleased. For a moment, she forgot her own complex of worries and was simply happy for him. "When will you go?"

"He's leaving for America next week. I want to see him before then. I've made a reservation on Thursday's plane to London."

"Have you really?"

"I'll just be a few days. I'll be back before any of you miss me." He gently pulled her to him and kissed her head. Gemma's thoughts returned to her father and Stephan Sutton. She was now considering the disturbing possibility that Denton had been right; her father had been planning to sell the gospels for profit. But surely they were in good hands with the British Museum? Maybe that was the problem. Maybe people like Denton didn't want the public to know about them. A museum would be the safest place to show them to the public.

"Look at you," Michael said. "You're worse than preoccupied." He caught her in a tight grasp and lifted her from the ground. "You were right, you know. They say that with a leg like this, I might be able to fly again."

"That's marvelous." Gemma laughed, recaptured by his enthusiasm.

"To think that I might have a semblance of a life," he said, twirling her in a circle. "You don't know how it feels."

He set her down and looked at her for a long moment before kissing her swiftly on the lips. "You look far away."

Gemma rested her head on his shoulder. "I'm just very happy for you."

After Michael went upstairs to his room, Gemma went back into David's office. Without thinking, she opened the desk drawer. There was a checkbook and a box of pens, a pocket-sized pad of blank notepaper, and a single lined notebook. She took out the notebook and opened it, staring blankly at first at the word inscribed inside. *Bastian.* Below was a kind of log, detailing places and dates. She studied it quickly. It was a record of her father's movements over the past five years. There were months in Dendera and then in Luxor; a series of trips to Oxyrhynchus. Sprinkled between these trips were stays in Cairo at the Lazar house. Next to these entries were short notes. Gemma studied them. It was a list of books, some of which she knew from his office—*The Catholic Encyclopedia; Iranaeus: A Life; The Pagan Myth; Isis and the Egyptian Holy Trinity; The Egyptian Book of the Dead.* David Lazar had been taking notes on her father's reading. Why?

Then there was an address for her father in Cairo and a note that he had moved, and after that, no more books were listed. Her father had stopped staying in the Lazar house. Had he known he was being spied upon?

Her eyes went back to Oxyrhynchus, where, in the margin, there was the first of a series of circled letters A. The A appeared sometimes in Cairo, sometimes in Upper Egypt.

She turned the pages, running her eyes over the dates as they brought her closer to the present. The entries were fewer, the time away from Cairo longer. She came to the last entry. *Cairo, October 1947.* Then nothing. But there were more A's. There was one in Cairo and then one with an arrow pointing to *Kharga.*

She noted the dates and sat back. A was Anthony.

Before she could stop herself, she turned the next page. Her breath caught as she saw the next heading, and another, shorter list of entries. The name at the top of this page was G. Bastian. And the books—*The Coptic Alphabet, The Divine Transformation,* the New Testament, *The Egyptian Book of the Dead.* And in the margin was a bold circled A. She turned all the pages until the end. Every one was blank except the final page, where there was a London phone number. Without hesitating, she picked up the phone.

A woman's voice answered and announced briskly, "Father Westerly's office." Gemma hung up the phone.

CHAPTER TWENTY-FOUR

WHEN NAILAH ASKED, David told her he'd decided to forgo a birthday celebration this year. He was feeling too old to feign happiness. "I'm worn out," he complained.

"You're feeling sorry for yourself."

"Perhaps. This business of getting old is wretched. You wait."

Nailah's smile was serene.

The day before his birthday David found Amad in the kitchen. They sat at the table and drank apple tea.

"It reminds me of old times." David smiled. "Do you ever think of them?"

"Often."

"Do you remember the mornings? The chill of the air at dawn—the smell of the fire and the coffee you always managed to make before I woke. I sometimes wondered if you slept. Did you?"

"Lightly."

"Because you didn't drink. You'll outlive me by a decade at least. What do you think, Amad, am I getting pickled? I can't remember when we first went into Tut's tomb. What year was it?"

"November 29, 1922."

"Blast it."

"My friend, you are prosperous and healthy and have a kind wife and two strong sons. You have lived a full life. Another year on this earth should be celebrated."

"Just so, Amad," David said. But as he finished his tea, his eyes filled with tears.

"If you lose yourself in memories, no one will have the pleasure of your company."

"Damn it." David took out a handkerchief and blew his nose. "It does overtake me sometimes."

"Fight it off. Be the warrior you've been before."

"I was never a warrior."

"We are all warriors, my friend."

David looked across the table at Amad. "Maybe we should have a little party after all. We could hire that bloke from Shepherd's to put it on if he's available."

"I am available."

"Damn it, Amad, you're not going to work. You're going to be my guest! Bring whomever you like. I'll send a courier with invitations—I'll write them myself. We'll have a ridiculous, fun party, like the old days. I'm going to enjoy myself, damn it."

About twenty people could come on such short notice, most of them colleagues from the past. The invitation had told them to dress in things they loved and would never wear in public. Most had followed the instruction, donning garments that qualified as absurdly revealing or absurdly awful. David was delighted. He wore his tuxedo with a yellow and pink polka-dotted bowtie and a flower behind his ear. Nailah wore a pink blouse and slacks, and a hat with pale violet plumes arching over her head. Gemma, in the dress Nailah had given her, needed help to get down the stairs.

"You, my dear," Nailah had told the younger woman, "will wear something I can no longer get myself into. Tonight we will transform you into a mermaid." Gemma had shimmied into a black beaded dress that hugged her body all the way to the ankles and would have sunk any mermaid. It must have weighed twenty pounds. "Is it all right that I can't walk?"

"In a dress like this, people will come to you. Would you like something fanciful for your head?"

"Why not?" Gemma had banished all thoughts of David Lazar from her mind. The matter would have to wait. In the meantime, there were other things to be cheerful about, enough to propel her through the evening. Michael was in good spirits and would soon be off to London. Angela Dattari was due to come back to Cairo the next day. She herself would be leaving for Upper Egypt within the week. Soon she would see the place where her father had worked, the place his partner Sutton had died. Soon she would be leaving the Lazar house.

Nailah pinned a close-fitting cloche on Gemma's head. It was made of black feathers that brushed the edges of her cheeks and jaw, framing her face like a dark flower. "Exquisite," Nailah pronounced.

"Are you sure I won't be locked up looking like this?"

"As long as you don't leave the house."

"Is Michael back yet?"

"He's called and left a message with Amad. He won't be coming tonight."

"Not coming? Why?"

"He had other plans, I suppose," Nailah said, wandering off. Gemma checked herself in the mirror and with irritation adjusted the feathers of the ridiculous cloche.

Anthony arrived in normal dress, claiming he did not own anything fanciful. His father, whose spirits were soaring, dragged him to the coat closet and pulled an aviator's leather cap over his head. Anthony immediately pulled it off. "This is Michael's."

"No, it's mine. Wear it or insult your father on his day of birth. Anyway, Michael won't be coming."

"I'm sorry."

David found his son's hand. "I know you are."

They emerged into the hall, where a clutch of guests had just arrived. Most noticeable was a striking dark woman with jeweled necklaces that started at her throat and cascaded all the way down to her waist. "Who is that?" Anthony asked.

"The lovely Angela Dattari."

"I didn't know you were friends."

"We're not, really. I wasn't aware I invited her. But what a nice surprise, no?" Behind Angela Dattari was a handsome younger man wearing tails and a hat with a long feather in its side. David laughed. "I haven't seen one of those in years."

"What?"

"The hat of the Australian Light Horsemen. They were here in the last war; occupied Cairo like a barrel of monkeys. Oh but they were charming, racing camels around the streets, defending the honor of the prostitutes they'd found. Nearly always drunk, nearly always happy. We missed them when they were gone."

David kept the music playing, selecting highly danceable songs and grabbing Nailah every few numbers to twirl her through the hall. Anthony stood with Amad and watched his father, whom he had not seen so jubilant in months. He nodded his head toward the woman with the necklaces. "Did you invite her, Amad?"

"Mrs. Dattari? Yes. I thought she would be a good addition. She collects art, among other things. She is a close friend of Phocion Tano's." Anthony glanced at Amad. The old man's face was inscrutable. Amad added, "It seems you are right—Mrs. Dattari is his shelter."

"She has the gospels?"

"So I have heard."

Anthony watched the Italian woman and the dark young man by her side. "Who is her chaperone?"

"That is Umar. He is the partner of your cousin Mohammad at the Giza Stables. He is the reason Mrs. Dattari came tonight. And he came because he wanted to visit again with our houseguest, Miss Gemma Bastian."

"Gemma?"

"That's right."

"You said, visit with her again?"

"I did." Amad slipped away as Anthony watched Umar approach a startled and uncharacteristically blushing Gemma, who looked as though she might topple over in her dress. She laughed and accepted the arm of the man she had clearly met before as he led her to the safety of a sofa.

Gemma did not notice Anthony circling her like a bird of prey. She was thoroughly engrossed in her conversation with Umar. She now calmly accepted his attention. It was the greatest relief to flirt, to be flattered and treated like a precious object. She was enjoying the illusion of being irresistible, of being a woman whose birthright was praise—a beautiful, mysterious woman like Nailah, not just a nice girl who could tie a decent bandage and give a clean injection.

After a few minutes of pleasantries, Umar put his hand over Gemma's. "And how is it with you, Miss Bastian?" he asked.

"Gemma, please."

"Gemma. I was hoping to see you again at the stables."

"I did come again. You weren't there."

"I know. You came to scatter the ashes of your father."

Gemma's eyes rested on the elegant older woman talking to Anthony in front of the garden windows. "She's beautiful. Is she your mistress?"

Umar's laughter was light. "I have come to enjoy the directness of women from your continent, but I think this is not the place for this conversation. Tell me"—he turned his liquid brown eyes on her—"have you ridden another Arabian?"

"Sadly, no."

"I have not forgotten the sight of you on Yoolyo."

Gemma finished her drink and looked back at Umar's woman friend.

"Come again someday," Umar urged softly.

Gemma met his eyes and felt the heat return to her cheeks. She dropped her gaze to the floor. "Maybe I will."

Umar pressed her hand. "Good. That is what I came for. Now forgive me, I must return to my friend."

Gemma searched the room for someone to talk to. She felt suddenly awkward and silly in her costume. It would not be easy to get off the couch.

She realized that she missed Michael. He would never have allowed such a flirtation. He would never have allowed her to feel so exposed.

Now, as she sat captive, she watched as Umar brought his companion to meet her. There wasn't enough time to get away, so she smiled and waited, trying to look at ease in a dress that didn't allow her to breathe.

"You are the daughter of Charles Bastian?"

"Yes." Gemma held out her hand. "Did you know him?"

The woman scrutinized Gemma, as if deconstructing her face to find his. "You sent me a letter."

Gemma grasped the arm of the couch and pulled herself to her feet. "Mrs. Dattari?"

"You may call me Angela."

"I'm sorry, I didn't know you were back in Cairo. I've been waiting to meet you."

"You have your father's mouth." The older woman's voice quavered. Gemma thought she looked as if she was going to cry. Umar took Mrs. Dattari's arm because she had started to sway.

"Shall we go?" Umar asked. Mrs. Dattari almost fell into her chaperone, who held her upright and smiled immaculately. Gemma realized that she was drunk.

"May I call on you tomorrow?"

"I've only just arrived. You must give me some time to . . . reopen my doors. I'm not entirely well." Angela Dattari rested her hand on Gemma's and briefly closed her eyes. Gemma looked down at her hand, which was long and cool and jeweled. When Mrs. Dattari opened her eyes, it was as if from a long sleep. They were solid amber, strangely undisturbed by any other color.

"How long will you be in Cairo?" she asked.

"I don't know."

"Perhaps you'll find a reason to stay forever." Mrs. Dattari removed her hand and covered it with a black glove. "I did."

"I might be taking a trip to the south."

"To Luxor?"

"And other places."

"Maybe you'll love it as your father did. For me it was a bit . . . brown. Visit me when you get back. We'll have tea. Your father loved tea."

"Please"—Gemma stepped closer to the older woman—"let me visit tomorrow. I won't stay long."

"Tomorrow isn't possible."

"I have so many questions. Please."

"I don't know what they could be."

Gemma whispered, "'If the man and woman had not come apart, they would not know death.'" When she stepped back, she saw she had guessed right.

"How like your father you are," she said. "You will not be put off, not for a day, not for a moment."

"I've been waiting for weeks."

"Are you as strong as he was?"

"I've lived through a war."

"Good, then. You will need to be strong. Very well, Gemma Bastian, come to my house tomorrow morning."

Gemma watched them leave. Did my father show you his God? she wanted to ask. Did you replace the woman he lost?

She did not notice that Anthony was standing next to her until he touched her arm.

"Having a good time?" he asked.

"That woman knew my father," Gemma said.

"Yes, I remember your mentioning her."

"But you don't know her."

"Only by name."

Gemma was suddenly tired. It seemed that not enough oxygen was reaching her brain in her mermaid dress. She turned to Anthony. "I think I have to go upstairs now. Tell your father happy birthday, will you? I don't think I can manage a formal exit."

Anthony watched her slow progress up the stairs, wondering what she had said to Angela Dattari. Even across the room, he had seen the slight collapse of the older woman's face.

✝ ✝ ✝

Gemma did not sleep. She lay listening to the party downstairs. When the last guest had left, she rose and went to the window. David was in the garden smoking his pipe, as she knew he would be. She put on her slippers and padded downstairs.

"David," she called softly.

He turned. "Gemma. You're up late."

"I can't sleep," she said.

"Nor I."

She pulled a chair next to his. "It's the haunting hour."

His smile was fleeting. "Yes."

"I need to talk to you about something I saw in your office."

David looked at her sharply.

"I'm sorry," she went on. "I used your phone. I saw the notebook in your desk. Were you reporting my father's movements to a man named Westerly?" When David stared ahead without answering, she continued. "He came to see me in London. Was it you who sent him?"

"Of course not."

"He was from the Church, wasn't he?"

"Not just any church. Your father's church."

"What was he looking for?"

David clenched the pipe between his teeth and struck a match to relight it. "I told him about the letters your father sent you."

"How did you know about them?"

"Because Charles asked Nailah to post them and she did so from here."

Gemma pulled her robe more tightly around her. "Why would you tell him such a thing?"

"It was something I had agreed to do."

"For Westerly?"

David gave a small nod.

Gemma was incredulous. "Why?"

"He contacted me years ago, when Charles first began his inquiring into early Christianity. He wrote me a letter asking if I could keep him apprised of Charles's movements, tell him what Charles was up to, the books he was reading. Little things, really. It seemed harmless enough. The church your father had left was concerned for him. They did not want to lose sight of him completely. They maintained hope that he would come back someday."

"You believed that?"

"This was a representative from the Catholic Church, Gemma."

"And so you started spying on him, no questions asked?"

"No, it took some time for me to agree. It wasn't until I became worried myself about Charles's direction that I decided to oblige Westerly."

"When he started talking about Jesus being a magician from Egypt."

"Yes."

"You were worried for what, his soul?"

"Yes, in fact."

"And so you started reporting him."

"To people who claimed to care about him, who were familiar with his spiritual history. With what your father was getting into, it didn't seem like a bad idea. I, for one, was out of my depth."

Gemma stared into the night. "Might there have been another reason?"

"Such as?"

"My father took something from you. He took someone."

"I don't know what you're talking about."

"I'm talking about Anthony. Maybe you wanted to punish him. Reveal him as dangerous or fraudulent so you would get your son back."

David was silent for a long time. "If that's so, I failed."

"Did Westerly ask you to watch me?"

David didn't answer.

"It was my father's work, not his spiritual path, that interested Westerly. You must know that. Now that he's dead, they're still not leaving it alone, are they?"

He repositioned the pipe in his mouth. "I have elected not to think about it."

Gemma watched the smoke rise into the night air. "I have been learning so many surprising things about our church." David cast her a wary glance. "Did you know that when Christ was tried for his life by the Romans, the apostle Peter was sought as a witness?" David responded by half closing his eyes as she continued. "Instead of testifying to his Savior's innocence, Peter denied knowing him three times. *I know not the man.* Even his own church admits to Peter's irresolute character. Jesus himself told him that Satan desired him, might sift him as wheat. This is the rock on which our church is built."

David stared at the ground in front of him. "I'm not a bad man, Gemma."

"Clearly, the system is relative. My father is dead and you're alive. The Church Fathers made all the apostles infallible, and so above sin. Peter, the irresolute prince of the apostles, was made a saint. It seems the rules don't apply equally to everyone. It's no wonder the sense of morality gets lost."

"Be careful, Gemma."

"I have no reason to be careful."

"Don't let your anger best you."

"Why, is that what happened to you?"

"What happened to me"—David paused—"was not as dignified as anger."

Gemma regarded him silently. "You've been doing your penance, haven't you?"

"I haven't completely ignored the accounting."

"For your sake, I'm glad."

"This business about your father. Please, don't mention it to Anthony. He might not understand as well as you."

"What is it you think I understand?"

"Human nature," David said. "How a straight path can be bent by life."

"And can be bent back, if the will is there."

"The will weakens." He held her eye with a pained gaze. "I'll ask again. Have mercy on an old man. Don't take the one son I still have."

"I have no interest in taking anything from you." Gemma rose. "And I'll ask you to take nothing more from me, not even so much as the title of a book."

"You have my word." David held out his hand. "Perhaps someday you'll accept my apology."

CHAPTER TWENTY-FIVE

IN THE MORNING the sky was festooned with thick ribbons of cloud. The sun passed through the striations and dimmed, as if in eclipse. Chilled, Gemma kept her sweater on for the length of the walk to Angela Dattari's house.

She thought about her conversation with David. It was not about God, she reasoned, it was about love. You are drawn to the people who teach you, she thought. The people who teach you set you free; you love them like no one else. That was where David had lost his son.

To her father.

She neared Angela Dattari's house abstracted and unprepared for what awaited her. She stopped at the entrance to the driveway. It was filled with automobiles, some with official insignias of the Egyptian Museum, some with that of the police. Anthony was there, and Togo Mina, as well as a few men she didn't know and four policemen. Gemma approached Anthony. "What's going on?"

Anthony led her into the garden. "We're too late."

"Too late for what?"

"The books are no longer in Angela Dattari's possession. They've been sold to a private buyer. We've been preempted." Anthony looked at her. "You didn't know. I was sure you had guessed."

"My father visited her every evening for three weeks before he died. I knew she had something he wanted. In the end, I wasn't sure. I thought they might have been in love."

"I'm afraid it wasn't romantic. Angela Dattari is what's called a shelter. She's been so in the past, for Phocion Tano. The government can't touch things in private ownership. If an artifact is thought to be privately owned, the government must back off, buying the dealer some time to find the highest bidder. We came this morning prepared to bid, but Tano's made up his mind. He didn't even want to hear our offer. Someone has given him something he wants very much."

Gemma's eyes wandered to the house. "So Angela Dattari has been posing as the owner of the lost gospels."

"We can't confirm exactly what she had in her possession, but yes."

"Is it illegal?"

"It's how things work here."

Gemma looked around for Angela Dattari. "You brought police?"

"We were prepared to exert pressure."

"You must have scared her half to death."

"I don't think so."

"Where is she?"

"Inside."

"I want to talk to her. I don't think she's well."

ANGELA DATTARI WAS lying on a sofa. A formidable man barely contained by his suit sat next to her in a chair, smoking a cigar. His eyebrows arched at the sight of Gemma. There was a sumptuous quiet in the room, born of thick rugs and fine furniture.

"Is she ill?" Gemma asked.

"She's made a big decision," the man said affably. "I think it has made her faint."

"I believe we're done, Mr. Tano, aren't we?" Angela Dattari said.

"Not quite."

"I want to talk to Miss Bastian privately for a moment. Gemma, please sit." Angela Dattari motioned to the seat Tano had vacated. "It's early in the morning for such commotion."

Gemma watched Tano leave the room and sat down. "What decision?"

"It's nothing to do with this other business." Mrs. Dattari closed her eyes.

"Can I get you anything?"

The older woman smiled weakly. "I remember, you're a nurse. No, thank you. I haven't been sleeping well. I have these headaches. The doctor has just given me pain tablets. In addition, my eyes are easily irritated by the dust here. I don't know how I've lived with it for so long; it's only when I go away that I remember how uncomfortable it is. Sometimes the only thing is to keep them closed. Forgive me for not looking at you while we talk."

Gemma studied her beautiful, patrician face. Long lashes protected the wounded amber eyes.

"You had the gospels from Nag Hammadi. It was why you knew my father."

"Yes."

"You act as a shelter for that man, Tano."

"You don't approve." Mrs. Dattari smiled to herself. "Nor do I. But I am a widow. My husband died with both debts and enemies. Doing these occasional favors affords me some protection in a country where you can't do without it, not as a woman, not alone."

"And my father?"

"Your father discovered the gospels were here, sniffed them out like a hound. He was persistent, like you. He had to see them—not just see them, learn them. My arrangement with Tano doesn't allow for such a thing. Charles, your father, swore he would say nothing to anyone. Finally I gave in. He came every evening in the safety of darkness. My house became his library. That is how I knew him."

"And you became . . . friends?"

"Friends, yes." Angela Dattari yawned and shifted the pillow beneath her head. She seemed to be drifting off to sleep. Gemma sat and waited. Angela Dattari smiled, as if in a dream. "He told me once I was his Thunder. He told me that once."

Phocion Tano reentered the room and strode to the sofa where Mrs. Dattari lay. He stood in front of her like a mountain, his black hair gleaming. "We have some final business to conduct," he said.

"Yes, I know. Give me another moment," Angela Dattari said. "Goodbye, Gemma."

Tano went to the window and relit his cigar. Gemma leaned toward the older woman. "I'd like to speak to you again."

The amber eyes fluttered open. "Have I not answered your questions?"

"There must be more to tell."

"There's no more. I cannot bring him back for you, Gemma. We were tossed together in a stormy sea, your father and I. That is all. Business brought us together. I knew him but for a moment." Mrs. Dattari raised herself from the pillows. "In any case, I won't be staying in Egypt."

"Why not?"

"Like you, I've lost everything." She pressed her fingers gently to her eyes. "These tablets really are muddling. Though I admit it's not an entirely unpleasant feeling, I'm having difficulty keeping track of things." She wandered past Tano and trailed upstairs. Gemma noticed her feet were bare. "Get all these people to leave, will you, Tano?" she called back.

OUTSIDE, Anthony was sitting on the stairs. One by one, the cars were pulling out of the drive. Gemma sat next to him. He glanced at her. "You look disappointed."

"I expected more. I don't know why. My father once said romantic love was an abstraction, like God, an ideal created in the eleventh century by the troubadours, a band of wandering poets who lived in the woods with their lutes and wrote verses of love to women they'd never even seen. Like them, I was seduced by the idea. The reality is something different."

"I'm sorry."

"It doesn't matter." Gemma put on her hat. "So the gospels are gone," she said. "Full stop."

"There's a chance they might resurface, but probably not in Egypt. I'm afraid we've lost our chance to keep them here."

"There's something I haven't told you. There is at least one more gospel out there. Albert Eid has it in his antiquities shop. My father had the receipt."

Anthony pushed gravel with his shoe. "I know about it. So does the museum. It has been authenticated as the Gospel of Thomas."

Gemma stared. "Do you think your secrecy is noble?"

"Well, now I've told you. There's no reason to keep secrets anymore. The great race is over."

"I was never in a race—and it's not over for me. I'm going to see Eid."

"There's nothing you can do there, Gemma, but antagonize him further."

"I'm going anyway."

As they left the driveway, Gemma cast a final look back at Angela Dattari's house.

"Let me go with you," Anthony said.

"Why, because you're afraid I might find something you didn't?"

"Because you never know what might happen."

"I'm having lunch with your brother. He's leaving for London, did you know?"

"I heard."

"We can meet at the museum afterward—say, three o'clock."

BEFORE THEY PARTED, Gemma said, "Angela Dattari said my father called her his Thunder."

"His Thunder," Anthony repeated, looking away.

"What are you thinking?" she asked.

"I'm thinking there is much we may never understand."

CHAPTER TWENTY-SIX

G EMMA AND MICHAEL drove through the city. Between houses, she could see the Alabaster Mosque with its three layers of gleaming white domes and needle-like towers piercing the sky. She studied Michael when he wasn't watching. She wanted to take the memory of him with her to Upper Egypt. She wanted to plant it within her and watch it like a shoot, to see what it would become.

In her pocket were the folded sheets with Anthony's script. The verses her father had traced now never left her person and often ran through her head. They were like mute companions, gems she carried in her pocket. They had become a secret source of strength. She wondered if this is how it had been for her father.

Out on the street, the British troops that had been on such rigorous patrol were nowhere to be seen. Rows of men were in the process of laying their mats on the sidewalks and streets to pray.

"Michael," she said, "where are all the police?"

"They've been sent off. To the Suez Canal region, I'm told."

"Why? Is there trouble there?"

"No. The natives just don't want them here anymore. Trade unions have been striking. The war is over, they say. What they might not be aware of is that another is on the way."

The car crawled along. Prayer time ended and the street filled with men from a nearby mosque. Michael was perspiring. He rested his head against the window and closed his eyes. The driver slowed to allow another demonstration to pass. Gemma looked away and stared absently at a woman in a robe with faded red flowers. She was talking to a vendor whose tables were piled high with miraculously stable eggs.

They were meeting a friend of Michael's for lunch at some hotel Michael had never taken her to. He explained it had been a Turkish bathhouse for the royal families in Cairo. Gemma had not yet met any friend of Michael's. She was willing to accompany him to anything that might return him to his life.

"Just so you know," Michael said, "there's no pretense at the Windsor. It's a bit shabbier than the places you've seen, but there's a jolly good bar. It was a place for soldiers to let down a bit. They've a piano—maybe you could play."

"I don't think so."

Michael had been short with her that morning, snapping at her when he thought she wasn't listening to him. His present euphoria only subdued her; she didn't know how long it would last.

WHEN THEY ENTERED the hotel bar, she knew instantly that it was not a lunch date at all. The man who was supposedly meeting them for lunch looked up at them with bloodshot eyes that held absolutely no recognition. He lived at the bar, Gemma thought, holding court at his personal table. Now, at a relatively early hour, his face had the wasted absence of an addict.

She sat numbly as the two men went through the embarrassingly superficial motions of friendship. When money and an envelope were exchanged, she stopped listening and tried to recall the melody of a song she had recently learned on Amad's oud.

She did not hear the conversation take a turn. It did not seem like an argument was building. Both men were smiling; she watched them move like silent actors. But then Michael opened the envelope and found it was empty. He half rose and swung his fist at the other man. The man staggered to his feet, blind drunk. Then somehow Michael was behind her and she was turning to look for him when a blow caught her on her mouth. She staggered, paralyzed by the pain. The man who hit her fell to the ground as if he too had been struck. Michael laughed cruelly. Gemma stared over his shoulder and was briefly transported. She was no longer in the seedy bar but somewhere above it.

Michael picked up the chairs that had fallen. Far off, she listened to him apologizing to the bartender. It wasn't until he looked at Gemma and saw the blood that had trickled onto her shirt that his face went white.

"Gemma, my God."

She gingerly touched her split lip. The bartender was by her side with a cloth napkin. "Bad business, ma'am. I'm sorry you were hurt. I've had a mind to boot this degenerate out. This is his last trick."

"Bloody bastard!" Michael kicked the fallen man in the gut with his new wooden leg. There was no sound from the floor.

"He's unconscious, Michael," Gemma said. "Leave it."

THE CAR WAS waiting outside. Michael walked as quickly as he could to open the door for her.

"Darling, I'm so sorry. It looks awful."

"Lips tend to bleed."

"I didn't mean to drag you into an altercation."

"No?"

Michael scowled.

"If you took me for protection, it worked out well for you."

"Bloody hell."

Michael instructed the driver to take them to a neighborhood Gemma had never heard of. She held the napkin to her lip and stared out the window. "It takes thirty-six to seventy-two hours," she said, "for the symptoms of morphine withdrawal to reach their peak intensity."

"Yes, I've run out."

"It makes me sad."

"Don't worry, darling. It's just a temporary affliction."

"It's an addiction."

"Call it what you will."

"It will take your life from you."

"Well, it's a pity, because nothing much else makes me feel very good."

"Would you like to stop?"

"I would like to, but not this instant. I feel too bloody awful."

"If you could tolerate a few days of feeling awful, you could be free of it."

"One hour is too long."

"I could help you."

"I would probably kill you."

"Would it help if I said it would make me happy? That I would admire you more than I can say?"

"I don't need your admiration. But I would like you to be happy. Why don't you think about some other ways I can make you happy." When she didn't respond, he reached for her hand and turned it over. His fingers ran over the lines in her palm. "Do you know what it feels like?" he asked. "It feels like being held in the hand of God. Not only is everything as it should be, but it's beautiful—and there's no pain, no pain at all."

The taxi pulled up to a house in a desolate neighborhood. Outside a coal seller in a dusty blue robe stood surrounded by piles of coal. He rested on his shovel and watched Michael get out of the taxi.

"Won't be a moment."

In the taxi by herself, Gemma was tempted to tell the driver to leave. Michael could find his own way home. She could not be a party to his disintegration. If she cared about him at all, she would not make it so easy. A bigger part of her remembered she was still a guest in his house, that he had a vile temper—that he might be in love with her. Sometimes she was half in love with him.

Her father would have asked her simply, "Tell me how it is, Gemma." In her mind she told him that she almost loved this man who was a crescent of himself. And in the shadows, sometimes, she could see the shape that had once been there, the whole that might someday be there again. She rested her head back on the seat.

When Michael returned, he was transformed. His features were pliant and a smile played on his lips, giving him the air of careless youth. He got into the taxi and moved to embrace Gemma. She held him off with a stiffened arm. "Drop me at the museum, will you?"

"More work?" Michael complained.

Gemma continued to look out the window. In one day, it seemed, everything had been destroyed. The gospels her father had spent years pursuing were gone. Angela Dattari was a businesswoman, only half-awake, with no interest in knowing Gemma. Her father's closest friend had betrayed him, and Michael, his firstborn son, was an addict, in the hand of God. She was alone.

CHAPTER TWENTY-SEVEN

ANTHONY WAS WAITING for Gemma at the entrance to the museum. His eyes rested briefly on her split lip. "Shall we go?"

They started to walk. When they reached Sharia El-Tahrir, Anthony asked, "How was lunch?"

"Delightful."

"Really?"

"Please, let's not talk."

"Shall we take a taxi?"

"No. I want to walk."

Near the palace of El-Abdi, they passed a political rally for the Muslim Brotherhood. A man in a uniform stood on a podium delivering a passionate oration. Gemma slowed. "What's he saying?"

"He's recruiting. The Arab coalition is preparing to invade Israel. They want soldiers."

"Maybe another war will make everything right."

"I think you should leave Egypt before then. It will be unsafe."

"I'll stay as long as I have to."

"Even through a war?"

"I know war better than anything."

A flock of pigeons swooped in front of the chanting throng. The crowd held signs in Arabic painted in a red that looked like blood.

"I'm afraid Farouk's days are numbered," Anthony said.

"And your family's?"

"I imagine they will survive."

"Because your mother is Egyptian?"

"Because my father would never leave this country."

"And your brother?"

Anthony glanced at her. "Maybe he would prefer England."

"Of course he would. But he's dependent on your father."

"I realize that."

"I don't know if you do, not really."

Anthony stopped when they were almost outside Eid's shop. Gemma turned. His hands were in his pockets and he was staring at the sidewalk. He looked up at her. "I am thinking that war gets to be a habit; that those who have been in one have a hard time not fighting, even when it's over."

"And with you, it's always peacetime."

Anthony stared back at the asphalt of the sidewalk. "There is always some peace in war. I believe the reverse is also true." His eyes returned to her face, passing quickly over her lip. "I'm sorry, Gemma."

"Don't be. Shall we go in?"

The door opened and suddenly a man was pushing quickly past them. Gemma stepped in his path. "Mr. Denton," she said.

"Miss Bastian, how nice to see you." Denton tipped his hat and, stepping neatly around her, was gone.

"Who was that?"

"That was Roberto Denton, the man I found in my father's office. The man who had been following me."

"So you know his name."

"We've spoken."

"You have your share of secrets, Miss Bastian."

"No more than you, Professor Lazar."

Anthony glanced in the direction Denton had gone. "What do you think he's doing here?"

"He followed me here once before. He wants these gospels maybe as much as we do."

Anthony held open the door to the shop. "Our friend Eid will know something."

They didn't at first see Eid. He was sitting on a stool at the end of the counter, bent over a ledger. It looked as if he was doing his accounts.

"Has it been a good month, Eid?" Anthony asked.

Eid looked up and blinked. "Average. And you are?"

"Anthony Lazar."

"Ah, the sons and daughters of the great men rally to seek justice."

"Not justice," Anthony said. "Just something that belonged to Charles Bastian."

"Belonging is a complex concept in Egypt. I'm sure you've noticed. What, for example, belongs to France? And to Britain? Do Egypt's greatest artifacts belong in their public squares and behind the glass cases of their museums? I ask you how something that was created thousands of years ago could belong to anyone living today?"

"This is not just any artifact. Its value reaches beyond the monetary, far beyond."

"Speaking of money, I should thank you for sending Doresse and authenticating my little treasure. It added considerable value."

"And you're going to offer it up to the highest bidder, like chattel?"

Eid's smile crept across his face. "Terrible, isn't it?"

"Think for a moment beyond the profit, Eid."

"Profit is as important as anything I can think of. If that's all you came to say, I'll ask you to leave."

"And I'll ask you to keep yourself open for discussion."

"To the monkeys at the museum?" Eid laughed and rose. "Now if you'll excuse me, I'm expecting a private customer."

"Keep in mind"—Gemma stepped forward—"that whatever god you believe in might be watching."

"The god I believe in is the god of commerce, and he is quite pleased with me, I'm sure. Now good day."

Gemma didn't move. "Who was that man who left as we came in?"

"That, my lovelies, was the highest bidder yet."

GEMMA MARCHED QUICKLY away from the shop, leaving Anthony to follow. At the intersection she turned and waited.

"I set it up for Denton," Gemma said. She peered down one street and then the other. She could not see the flame of Denton's hair anywhere. "Is there nothing we can do about Eid?"

"Sadly, Egypt doesn't have the legal infrastructure of England. In our present situation, we have little to no recourse."

"So it's over. Thomas will never be within our reach."

"To be honest, I never thought he would be."

Inwardly, Gemma shouted her protest. She did not want to show her anger to Anthony. It would be lost on him. They continued walking. They walked halfway back to the museum. Gemma's lip began to hurt. She wanted to be alone. She wanted to make peace with the Lazar family and then she wanted to get some distance from them. Their structure was increasingly sharp and fragile and she did not want to be caught inside of it. She touched Anthony's hand. "Thank you for coming with me."

"You're welcome."

"I'm sorry I've been rude."

"Not rude, exactly."

"Rude. You don't deserve it. Goodbye, then."

"Where are you off to?"

"Just a walk, and a think."

"I'll see you tomorrow?"

"Tomorrow, yes."

After walking half a block, Gemma turned to watch Anthony. His square shoulders and effortless gait were easily visible in the crowd, but only for a moment. When she lost sight of him, she took a taxi to the pyramids.

She walked toward the Great Pyramid, stopping to watch the outlines of two men descending from the top. She could hear them even at her distance, their clarion laughter ringing as they lowered themselves in tandem from the magnificent formation.

Because she was afraid of heights, Gemma didn't consciously decide to climb Khufu. She wanted to raise herself just a little ways, to see what, if anything, lay beyond Cairo. But as she began moving upward, pulling herself to the next higher level, she knew she wasn't going to stop.

The exertion of the first stones exhilarated her. She started to forget her life. The blocks were rough and uneven; the steps were a stretch. That they seemed designed for a man's legs only made her try harder.

She didn't really believe she could make it to the top, but once she established a rhythm, climbing became easy. She passed what she judged to be the middle of the pyramid without looking down. It was a simple and terrifying exercise that she instinctively felt would strengthen her.

When she stopped moving, she felt lightheaded. There was a wind at the top. She focused on her hands and crouched before looking down. The distance of the world below made her palms tingle with fear. Then came the dampness that she prayed would pass. When she was a girl, she had remained paralyzed on a mountainside, incapable of resuming a narrow traverse. Her father had come back to coax her. But she wouldn't, couldn't move. They had to wait it out. When she was simply too tired to resist, she allowed her father to take her hand and lead her along the precipitous trail.

Now she was in far worse straits. She was higher, a fall might kill her, and there was no one to talk her around. Soon she would lose her light. Instead of falling, what if she just leapt; thrust herself into the empty golden sky? In that unknowable freedom, she thought, there might be a moment of pure joy.

No. She had to stand up, pretend the land started at her feet, that everything below her was an ocean she could swim in. She imagined she was not alone in the ocean, that there were other women too, mortal women like Lucy and Angela Dattari—and goddesses like Isis and Inanna—all afloat on the same buoyant sea. It was Mary Magdalene, half mortal, half goddess, who filled Gemma's mind as she forced herself to rise.

For a moment, her fear was that the wind would be too strong. As she got to her knees she started softly singing a song she had heard the band play at the dance. She repeated the first two verses because she didn't know the third. Then the song was done and it was time to stand up. She had done far harder things.

Later she wondered how she could not have heard the plane coming, but she was sure there had been no warning drone of propellers, no distant hum. It seemed headed directly for her. When it passed by, she could see the face of the man flying it. It was a military plane, though she found no insignia to indicate country of origin. She held her hand out in salute and turned as the plane passed, deafening now and harrowingly close. For a moment it seemed she was eye to eye with the pilot. She watched him grow distant and then loop around and return. Against the sky, she saw him unlatch his door. It was a hatch, like Spitfire doors. Something shot out of the door as he crossed overhead. A ball of white. Watching it almost made her lose her balance. A long strip of fabric unfolded and floated on the wind. Gemma watched it drop below her, snagging on the stones halfway down the pyramid. A scarf. For a moment Gemma was elated. She would not fall, not today.

She clambered down the pyramid without thought or hesitation, keeping her eye on the patch of white below. When she reached the scarf, she paused to look for the plane. The sky was empty. Stars pierced the darkest patch of the dome above her. The light was leaving her, but she no longer felt any urgency to reach the ground. She sat and ran the scarf through her hands. It was silk with a fringed border. She held it to her face. It smelled faintly of cologne. She tied it around her neck and it caught the wind behind her, making her feel she was attached to something winged.

SHE ENTERED THE Lazar house with the scarf still around her neck. Michael emerged from the den. His cheeks were flushed and his hair disheveled. He'd been napping. He stared at her legs. "You're bleeding," he said.

Gemma looked down at her shins. She hadn't noticed the scrapes. "That looks like an aviator's scarf," he said. He did not come closer, but stood at an awkward distance. For a moment it was as if they'd never met.

She held up the scarf. "Does it?"

"Where did you get it?"

"I found it," Gemma said, realizing that after the events of the day, it was easy to lie.

"Found it? Where? Around an aviator's neck?"

"I was walking out by the pyramids and I found it just lying there. It's quite nice, don't you think?"

"It's a man's scarf."

"Well, I like it."

"What were you doing out by the pyramids?"

"Just walking."

"Forgive me, but in my present state it's hard to grasp the joy in walking. But if I search hard enough, I suppose I can dredge up a memory or two."

"How was your day?"

"Ghastly. I've missed you. I've been waiting patiently for my first drink. Will you usher in the evening with me?"

Gemma bounded up the stairs to change her clothes. Even Michael could not sadden her. It was the pilot, the scarf; it was the fear she had conquered.

She gave her hair a wild brushing and inspected her face in the mirror. Aside from the split lip, she was taken aback by the fact that she looked very much the same.

MICHAEL WAS WAITING for her in the den. The fire had been burning since the afternoon and warmed the room with its burgundy coals. Gemma poured herself a drink and sat down next to him in front of the low, lapping flames. He repositioned himself to look at her.

"Your lip looks better."

"Does it?"

"And I love that shade of blue."

Gemma stared at the hearth.

Michael placed his hand on the arm of her chair. "I can't tell you how sorry I am about this afternoon. It was a beastly, unforgivable display."

"Yes, well. I'd like to say these things happen, but I'm not sure they should."

"You think I care more about my medicine."

"It's the nature of it."

"You're wrong."

"Am I?"

"Because I know you. How could I know you if I weren't trying—if you didn't mean so much to me?"

Gemma turned to him. "What do you know about me, Michael?"

"I know that you like gin and tonic but not with a lot of ice. You don't like drinks that are too cold because you've got a tooth that is sensitive to the cold. I know that you sometimes still draw on your stockings with eyeliner, not because you don't have stockings but because you like the feel of your bare legs. I know you are embarrassed by your beauty but you know it's there because you know just how to avoid your own reflection. I know you are sad and maybe always have been because the creases in your face couldn't have formed in a year—and though those creases are faint, I can see what you will look like when you're fifty. It's a face I could love for a lifetime."

Gemma returned her gaze to the fire. "I don't know how you do it."

"Do what?"

"It's like a tap you turn on. But it can be turned off just as quickly. It makes it hard to listen to you."

"I think what makes it hard is that you're afraid to love. Well, so am I. I'm the first to admit I'm not perfect." He reached for her hand. "I could die trying to be good enough for you."

"I don't want you to die for me, Michael. I don't want a hero."

"What if I don't know how to be anything else?"

☩ ☩ ☩

THEY SAT IN silence until Amad called them for dinner. "Would you prefer if I lied to your father and Nailah about what happened to my lip?"

"If it's all the same to you."

"I don't care. I'll tell them I walked into a wall."

CHAPTER TWENTY-EIGHT

I N THE MORNING, Michael was gone and the house fell
into an uneasy peace. One day passed, and then another.
Gemma sorted and boxed in her father's office and spent
the afternoons in the museum library, avoiding the strained atmosphere
of the Lazar house. Preoccupied by the coming war, David scoured newspapers and magazines, taking the trouble to find the most recent editions
by daily forays to Cairo's best hotels. Nailah kept busy with a string of
social engagements, because European Cairo had hurled itself into a state
of frenetic activity. A war was coming. Life, as they knew it, might soon be
taken from them.

Gemma ate most of her meals in the kitchen with Amad, both of them
content not to make conversation. In the silence between their words, she
mentally prepared herself to leave Cairo. There was no longer any question that her time at the museum, at the Lazars', was drawing to a close.
This would not be a new home for her, as her father had intended. Not
without him. Without him, London was where she belonged.

Michael had been gone three days when she taped up the last of the
boxes from her father's office and locked the door behind her. Without
allowing herself to think about what she had done, she went upstairs to

the library to finish the last book on alphabets. One of her only comforts was in the work, and that too was ending.

She'd been alternating between alphabets and *The Catholic Encyclopedia,* which continued to fascinate and repel her. She had copied down the most shocking passages, most of them in the voluminous entry on Gnostics and Gnostic literature, which the authors of the encyclopedia described as "a stupefying roar of bombast" with "little to no intrinsic value." Citing no examples, they called the Gospel of Thomas "vulgar and foolish." At times, the emotion was so transparent, Gemma wanted to laugh. This was supposed to be an encyclopedia, a reference book, not a soapbox. As Anthony said, the vehement protest against the Gnostics was proof of their power—and their threat. She copied a last entry into her notebook:

As Christianity grew within the Roman Empire, Gnosticism spread as a fungus at its root, claiming to be the true Christianity. So rank was its poisonous growth that the earliest fathers devoted their energies to uprooting it.

She closed the encyclopedia. Maybe someday it would become clear to the public at large that Christianity had been created by men who lived hundreds of years after Jesus; that Jesus himself might not recognize the religion founded in his name; that now, in the Catholic house of God, women were not welcome as equals or teachers; that all other faiths were considered deficient; that the once preposterous notion of a single church was now gospel truth. Gemma found it physically painful to think about.

She turned back to the alphabets and the comparative charts she'd been studying. But today the rows of letters and symbols hurt her eyes. She did what she imagined her father would have done and read about the history of alphabets instead, starting with the Coptic, which seemed so central in this country.

She read that the word *Copt* originally came from the Greek *aiguptios,* meaning "Egyptian." That was shortened to *guptios,* then translated into Arabic as *qopt.* Translated into Egyptian, it became *coptos.* Coptic script replaced the hieroglyphics that had represented Egypt's language for three thousand years.

The Coptic alphabet was not original; it was adopted from the Greek alphabet almost completely. But there were sounds in Greek that didn't exist in Egyptian, so these extraneous letters were used to represent numbers. Then the Copts added five letters that they took from another script, called "demotic," that gave them representations of sounds that didn't exist in Greek.

It was like a patchwork quilt, Gemma thought. She smiled. Her father must have loved this material. He had a passion for puzzles. When solving a crossword, he pointed out, you forgot the time, which was always a measure for happiness.

Gemma continued. Unlike the three Egyptian scripts that came before, the Coptic script had both consonants and vowels. One of the earliest and greatest scripts, the script the Greeks used to create their alphabet, was called Phoenician.

Phoenician, she wrote.

Gemma stopped and reread the passage. Phoenician script seemed to be the basis for all these other alphabets. It was the starting point, the bedrock, the original. Gemma scribbled in her notebook. Phoenician script had letters only for consonants. *No vowels.*

She sat up on her knee and looked around, afraid that her excitement was visible. But no one was looking at her. She bent her head and stared at the page again. Then, marking her place, she rushed back to her father's office, to the few books she hadn't packed. Minutes later she was back in the library with his Berlin journal.

For a moment she thought she would be able to read the lines he had written, that it would all be clear. But it wasn't. There was still something missing. There was still another piece she hadn't yet found.

She reopened the book on alphabets and read ten more pages before she started to doze off. She needed coffee. She needed to eat. Instead she jiggled her legs and stretched and looked back at the paragraph in the book that had lulled her to sleep. It was about the direction of writing and how it changed over time, from right to left, to left to right, and so on. And then, she read, it became something called "boustrophedon."

"Boustrophedon," she mouthed. What a remarkable word. It was the style eventually used with early Greek, when the direction of the writing changed with every line. At first Gemma didn't understand. Then she read that the word translated, literally, to "ox-turning"; it meant reading and writing the way an ox would plow a field, turning at the end of the line. It got more confusing. With this system, the orientation of the letters themselves was dependent on the direction of the writing, so while one line would be legible, the next would be nonsense. In fact, Gemma thought, one would have to read every other line in a mirror.

She looked back at her father's journal and sat perfectly still. Then she picked up her pencil and began transcribing the words of a verse. It took her over an hour. When the verse was done, she stared at it. She was suddenly afraid to continue. She was entering the territory her father had been treading on. She realized she didn't want to do it alone. She went back to his office and packed her bag with his last journal, a copy of the Phoenician alphabet, and some loose pages and pencils. She locked the office behind her, left the museum, and started making her way through narrow streets toward the river.

CHAPTER TWENTY-NINE

A NTHONY LIVED IN an area called Kit Kat. Amad told
Gemma it was near a place called Imbaba. She was impatient; she did not want to wait for his nephew to guide her.
Amad told her that if she got lost, the word in Arabic was *awwamat:*
houseboat.

They were houses more than boats, houses with gardens and balconies
that rocked gently on the river. Gemma immediately felt she had entered
a refuge; she could not hear the city or feel its dust. All she could see was
the stretch of calm water in front of her and the far bank fringed with palms.

There was a doorkeeper at Anthony's address, a man who could have
been thirty or fifty years old. He sat on a wooden chair. In a cage on the
ground next to him was a bright green parrot. The man was feeding the
bird bits of fruit. When the parrot saw Gemma, it cocked its head and said
something in another language. The man looked up.

"I'm here to see Anthony Lazar."

"He isn't at home."

"I'm a friend," Gemma said. "Do you mind if I wait for a bit?" The man
shrugged and Gemma moved past him.

"If you would like some tea," the man said, "the door is open."

✝ ✝ ✝

SHE SAT ON the balcony of Anthony's houseboat and watched a fisherman haul in his net. Even in the late afternoon, the sun was strong. Gemma pulled the brim of her hat over her eyes and squinted at the blazing water. A felucca tacked lazily upriver, steered by a reclining captain with a pipe between his teeth. She could feel the sun burning her arms.

When she finally succumbed to the shelter of the houseboat, she stood awhile at the entrance. Anthony's house was filled with light. She walked the perimeter slowly. The scarcity of objects did not surprise her. A sofa and two chairs, a sisal rug. In the corner was a desk with writing paper and an ink blotter. Gemma sat down and picked up the pen. Pressing its nib on the corner of a white sheet of paper, she was able to draw a spot of residual ink. In the drawer below was a box of matches and a brass compass. She lit a match and then blew it out. Turning to survey the room, she decided it was like a sketch of a room; it had all the component parts but none of the ornamentation, nothing to make it overly inviting. It was, instead, peaceful.

She left the desk to inspect a collection of framed photographs on the mantel. There was a photograph of Anthony and his father and brother. Another of a smiling Nailah in a sundress under a parasol. Behind these was a third photograph of Michael by his airplane, suited up. Gemma held the photograph closer. Even in a picture, Michael was devastatingly handsome; his confidence and charm were overwhelming.

Gemma went to the kitchen and filled a sea-green glass with water, refilling it because she had walked a long way in the heat. The kitchen was orderly and well stocked with baskets of fruits and vegetables. She leaned against the counter and ran her eyes along the shelves. There were jars of grain, dates, and honey. So Anthony cooked at home, she thought. Or maybe someone cooked for him. Maybe he kept some kind of woman.

She peered into the bedroom. Like the rest of the house, it seemed to have no places to hide things, no locked drawers or closets. The open alcove where his clothes hung contained only a few shirts and slacks. On the floor below were a pair of dusty boots and a pair of dress shoes. She recognized the suit he had worn the day they met. And on the far side hung a tuxedo with his father's name stitched under the label. Gemma held up the sleeve of a shirt to her face. It smelled of nothing, really. Simply clean.

She realized she had been there too long. And on some level of her consciousness, she was aware that looking through Anthony's things was not acceptable. But instead of preparing herself to go, she sat on the edge of the bed. It was neatly made and covered with a white quilt. The Nile flowed past like a grand avenue. She lay on her stomach and watched it. How wonderful, she thought, to have a river outside one's window. She reached for the book on his bedside table. It was something called *Verba Seniorum* and it was written in Latin. She did not remember enough Latin to read it. She put the book down and rested her head on a pillow to watch the shimmering river.

ANTHONY RETURNED AT sunset. The female visitor was reported by Ebo, the doorman, but it took Anthony a moment to find her. He went back to Ebo to check that she had not left. Ebo had been known to doze. It was then that Anthony thought to look in his bedroom. Gemma lay asleep, her arm extended, her hair spread. He sat on a chair in the corner and waited. The light was almost gone. His eyes rested on her and then moved past to the Nile, where a felucca floated by, a cloth lantern hanging from its mast.

When she woke and saw him, neither of them spoke. It was dusk. She could not see him clearly. She thought to apologize and then didn't. Finally he sat forward.

"Would you like some apple tea?"

She yawned. "Yes, thank you."

"I assume you have something to tell me."

"A few things."

"Then why don't I fix something to eat. Unless you have other plans."

"I don't, not tonight."

"Michael is in London."

"Yes."

"You seem to have had a galvanizing effect."

"We'll soon see to what end. He comes back in two days."

Anthony walked into the kitchen and Gemma followed. From a shelf in the living room, she picked up a book written by his father.

"Your father blazed such a path for you," she said. "Weren't you at all tempted to follow in his footsteps?"

Anthony was slicing pita bread and arranging it around a bowl of some unknown dip. "I'm having wine," he said presently. "Would you prefer that?"

"Yes, actually."

Anthony poured two glasses. "It wasn't an issue. I don't have a passion for the pharaohs."

"How could you not? All that gold and mystery."

"I don't find them mysterious at all. They were afraid to die and they spent their entire lives preoccupied with that fear. Every temple and monument they constructed was built to ease it; every god they worshipped was meant to mitigate it. In some ways, it's a simplistic culture. Maybe the gold was meant to compensate for a belief system based solely on fear."

"So"—Gemma sipped her wine—"you aren't afraid to die?"

"I don't think about it. It will happen someday. In the meantime I'd rather spend my days thinking about something else."

"Like what?"

Anthony smiled. "You protect yourself with questions."

She looked at him over her wineglass and then picked up a piece of pita. She held it in front of her as if it were a shard of glass before she dipped it into the bowl. "And this is?"

"Baba ghanoush. It's made with eggplant."

Gemma bit, chewed, and swallowed before she spoke. "My father wrote part of his first journal in code." She leaned down to her purse and extracted the book. "What he did was take out the vowels and make it read from left to right, then right to left."

"What?"

"The Phoenician alphabet had only letters for consonants. He used it as a model. For example, the Phoenician letter aleph, which stood for a glottal stop, became the Greek letter alpha. But that was only half of it. Then I discovered boustrophedon, which literally means 'ox-turning,' the way an ox would turn when plowing a field. You start on the right of the page and write to the left, and when you reach the leftmost end, you reverse your direction and start writing toward the right."

"So you have made good use of the library."

"Now the obstacle is that I don't read Coptic, and the trick with the ox writing makes it slow going because every other line seems to have been written backwards."

"Are you asking for my help?"

Gemma gulped her wine. "Yes, I'm asking for your help. Do you have a hand mirror?"

ANTHONY PUSHED THE plates and glasses to the top of the table and waited as Gemma marked what she thought was the beginning. They sat next to each other with the open journal and loose pages of copies Gemma had made. Anthony spread her sheet of code next to them and wrote slowly in pencil above the Coptic script, following her instructions with the vowels and the ox-turns. Gemma held a mirror up to the lines so they could see them in reverse.

IT STARTS, *In this gospel there are no miracles, no prophecy, no ending of the world, no dying for one's sins, no resurrection. There are simply Jesus' words. And Jesus promises, Whoever discovers what these sayings mean will not taste death.* Anthony paused and looked at her over his glasses. "Are you ready for this?"

"I'm more than ready."

"It says, *This is the Gospel of Toma, the twin of Yeshua,*" Anthony said.

Gemma turned to him. "It's Thomas?"

"Your father writes, *It says in the Gospel of Thomas, Jesus said, Whoever drinks from my mouth will become like me. I myself shall become that person.*" Anthony paused again. "He is acknowledging the possibility of a spiritual twin."

Gemma read aloud as Anthony translated lines from the next passage.

"Jesus said to Toma,
I am not your master.
Because you have drunk,
you have become drunk from the bubbling stream
which I have measured you . . .
He who will drink from my mouth
will become as I am:
I myself shall become he,
and the things that are hidden
will be revealed to him."

Gemma sat back. She realized she had been holding her breath. "Jesus is saying his twin is Thomas." Anthony's finger moved over the next few lines. "Here, he is called 'Yeshua.' Yeshua said:

"Blessings on you who are alone and chosen,
For you will find the kingdom.
You have come from it
And will return there again.

"Seek and do not stop seeking until you find.
When you find, you will be troubled.
When you are troubled,
You will marvel and rule over all."

Gemma reached for her wineglass and thought for a minute. "It's the difference between what you would say to a child and an adult. To a child, you would say, There, there, everything's going to be all right—*just have faith.* To the adults, he says, Beware, the truth can be troubling. Is this how he spoke to his inner circle?"

Anthony put up his hand and continued reading. "Jesus said,

". . . the kingdom is inside of you . . .
When you come to know yourselves,
then you will become known, and you will realize
that it is you who are
the sons of the living father.
But if you will not know yourselves,
you dwell in poverty."

He looked up. "Therein lies a central threat. You don't need a church to find God. You don't need a priest or a rabbi—the kingdom is inside of you."

Gemma pressed her hand to her chest. Anthony watched her for a moment and turned back to the text.

"Y said,
I disclose my mysteries to those who are worthy
Of my mysteries."

Gemma held up her hand. "Only those who can understand will hear the words."

"And listen to this," Anthony said, now animated:

"Toma said to them,
If I tell you one of the sayings he spoke to me,
You will pick up rocks and stone me
And fire will come out of the rocks and consume you."

"So Thomas knew that being so close to Jesus put him in danger. Understanding more than the others put him at risk. There was so much jealousy with these disciples."

Anthony was looking at the next passage.

> *"Y said,*
> *As for you, be on guard against the world.*
> *Arm yourself with great strength,*
> *Or the robbers will find a way to reach you,*
> *For the trouble you expect will come."*

Gemma sat in silence, wondering if her father had also been on guard, if he had expected the trouble that came.

"Now we come to an older ink and a slightly different script." Anthony's pencil began scratching as the new translation began. He looked up. "This isn't Thomas."

Gemma leaned forward. "It's Mary Magdalene, isn't it?"

"Why do you think that?"

"It was her gospel that my father saw in Berlin. He was only twenty-three. I think he wrote this then."

"Well," Anthony said, staring at the lines, "this seems to be her version of the Crucifixion. I think this is a record of Jesus' last words." Over the next hour, the lines appeared, one by one.

> *"He who has ears to hear, let him hear.*
> *He who has a mind to understand, let him understand.*
> *Those who seek Him will find Him.*
>
> *"Do not lay down any rules beyond what I*
> *appointed you, and do not give a law like the*
> *Lawgiver lest you be constrained by it.*
>
> *"When He said this He departed."*

Anthony sat back and ran his hands through his hair. He looked as though he was in pain.

"If that was his last advice to his disciples," she said, "they certainly didn't take it to heart, did they?"

"By creating a controlling church rife with rules and regulations? By making access to God conditional on paying homage and obeisance, and if not that, simply cold cash? I'd say not."

"I didn't know you were so angry at the Church."

"Neither did I." Anthony drank half his glass of wine. "The next chapter is long. Perhaps you'd like to take another nap."

"No, I want to watch."

Anthony read to her after each paragraph. It took over two hours to reach the end. "This passage seems to begin after Jesus died on the cross."

"The disciples were grieved. They wept greatly, saying, How shall we go to the Gentiles and preach the gospel of the Kingdom of the Son of Man? If they did not spare Him, how will they spare us?

"Then Mary stood up, greeted them all, and said to her brethren, Do not weep and do not grieve or be irresolute, for His grace will be entirely with you and will protect you. But rather, let us praise His greatness, for He has prepared us and made us into Men.

"When Mary said this, she turned their hearts to the Good, and they began to discuss the words of the Savior.

"Peter said to Mary, Sister we know that the Savior loved you more than the rest of woman.

"Tell us the words of the Savior which you remember which you know, but we do not, nor have we heard them.

"Mary answered and said, What is hidden from you I will proclaim to you.

"And she began to speak to them in these words:

I, she said, I saw the Lord in a vision and I said to Him, Lord I saw you today in a vision. He answered and said to me,

"Blessed are you that did not waver at the sight of Me. For where the mind is there is the treasure.

"I said to Him, Lord, how does he who sees the vision see it, through the soul or through the spirit?

"The Savior answered and said, He does not see through the soul nor through the spirit, but the mind that is between the two that is what sees the vision, and it is . . .

280 · Tucker Malarkey

"It says there are pages missing," Anthony interjected. A moment later, he continued.

> *"Peter answered and spoke concerning these same things.*
>
> *"He questioned the disciples about the Savior: Did He really speak privately with a woman and not openly to us? Are we to turn about and all listen to her? Did He prefer her to us?*
>
> *"Then Mary wept and said to Peter, My brother Peter, what do you think? Do you think that I have thought this up myself in my heart, or that I am lying about the Savior?*
>
> *"Levi answered and said to Peter, Peter you have always been hot-tempered.*
>
> *"Now I see you are contending against the woman like the adversaries.*
>
> *"But if the Savior made her worthy, who are you indeed to reject her? Surely the Savior knows her very well.*
>
> *"That is why He loved her more than us. Rather let us be ashamed and put on the perfect man, and separate as He commanded us and preach the gospel, not laying down any other rule or law beyond what the Savior said.*
>
> *"And when they heard this they began to go forth to proclaim and to preach.*

"Your father's made a note. It reads, *Proof that Mary was the first disciple to receive a direct apostolic commission from Jesus by being instructed to take the news of his resurrection to the other disciples. The early Church called her the Apostola Apostolorum, or the 'Apostle to the Apostles.'*"

"I didn't know that," Gemma said.

"Because who listens to the early Church? Who even knows there was one? It goes on, *In these gospels, Mary's status is made clear. She was second only to Jesus—she, not Peter, was Jesus' chosen second in command. It was the Church formed by Peter's disciples that chose to portray Mary Magdalene as an unnamed sinner, a repentant whore.*"

Gemma put her hand over the page to stop him. Anthony sat back and poured the last of the wine as she ran her fingers over the words on the page. He glanced at the passages they had translated. "With the later material, your father is jumping around."

Gemma was silent. "Maybe he only had so much time with the new text. Maybe he copied only the passages he needed."

"Needed for what?"

"Never mind. Are you done?"

"Almost." Anthony continued,

"Y said,
I took my stand in the midst of the world,
And I appeared to them in flesh.
I found them all drunk
Yet none of them thirsty.

"Yeshua said,
One who knows all but lacks within,
Is utterly lacking.

"Yeshua said,
I shall destroy this house
And no one will be able to rebuild it . . .

"Yeshua said,
I have thrown fire upon the world,
And look, I am watching till it blazes."

"This sounds like an angry man," Gemma said. "And disappointed. You know, you don't think of Jesus as angry or disappointed. But how could he not have been? The man was doubted and betrayed and murdered. The miracle is that he was still able to love." Gemma put down the mirror and sat for a while with her eyes closed. "You seem to be someone who has always known your own heart."

"I believe that is changing."

"How?"

Anthony picked up the mirror and held it in his teeth. "The second-to-last verse:

"Y said,
Have you discovered the beginning and now are seeking the end?
Where the beginning is, the end will be.
Blessings on you who stand at the beginning.
You will know the end and not taste death."

"I would like to stand at the beginning." Gemma opened her eyes. "You're right about the jumping around. It seems like he's arranging verses in some order. That insidious man Denton told me he was making an argument that nothing in God's book was as it seems. Maybe this is the evidence he needed to prove it." She turned to Anthony. "Where would he go with an argument like this?" Answering her own question, she said, "The Vatican, The Hague, the *London Times*—the British Museum." She rested her head on the table, suddenly too tired to hear more. But Anthony persisted with the last lines.

"He said to them,
You examine the face of heaven and earth
But you have not come to know the one who is
in your presence,
And you do not know how to examine this moment."

Anthony looked up. His eyes looked black, the pupils dilated. "If you're talking about evidence, these words are damning. They not only prove your father's theory about the inner circle, they also show that Jesus is exasperated with his ordinary followers."

She glanced at her watch and began gathering her things. "It's almost midnight. In his last journal my father made sketches of a place with mountains. A place at the base of a cliff with loose rocks and a boulder with a shovel leaning against it." She reached for the journal and pointed at a boldly written word. "Nag Hammadi. That's where I'm going."

"Because he drew a picture of it?"

"Because Stephan Sutton had made a deal with my father," she said. "And he made it in Nag Hammadi. My father was going to sell something to the British Museum. Something he found in Nag Hammadi. Stephan Sutton was his contact."

"How do you know this?"

"Because I spoke with the British Museum."

Anthony looked at her, amazed.

Gemma's smile was terse. "Does that make me intelligent enough to learn what all you great men have been doing out there in the sand? Do I now qualify to hear whatever truth you are still withholding?"

He was shaking his head in the universal denial she had come to despise.

"This isn't over," Gemma said. "So stop shaking your head."

"It should be over."

"Listen to me," Gemma said. "I don't know what my mother died for, or what millions of people died for in the war. But my father died for a reason. He died searching for a God, and every step that takes me closer to that God has strengthened me. But I still haven't gotten close enough. I haven't seen Nag Hammadi—and I must see it. Maybe what he and Sutton were negotiating is still there. Now let's be civil and stop arguing. When we finish with this, we can respectfully part ways."

Anthony sat down and cradled his wineglass. Gemma returned to the journal and searched for another page. "I've translated something on my own.

"If you bring forth what is within you,
what is within you will save you.
If you do not bring forth what is within you,
what you do not bring forth will destroy you."

Gemma closed the book with finality. "Maybe that's advice we should both pay attention to."

Anthony got up and started to pace. Gemma was folding her copies of the translations and reinserting them into the journal. He stopped mid-stride, watching them disappear. "One more question," Gemma said, turning back to the journal. "Can you tell me who or what Bashir is? The word appears over and over in his journals."

"Bashir worked for your father."

"In Nag Hammadi?"

"Everywhere."

"I want to talk to him."

"He's Bedouin; you won't be able to."

Gemma looked at Anthony. "Then come with me. Translate."

Anthony looked away. "I think traveling companion is my brother's job."

For a moment this silenced her. "He won't go."

"Good. Stay here with him. As exciting as all this is, Gemma, you will soon be returned to your life. You had better make sure you have one."

"Who are you trying to protect, me or your brother?"

"Both of you!" Anthony almost shouted.

Gemma stared at the plate of uneaten food they had pushed to the edge of the table. She sat for a long time without speaking. Finally she said, "You're stronger than he is. That's why you're protecting him."

Anthony sat down again at the table and stretched out his legs. Almost resting his chin to his chest, he seemed to be preparing for sleep. Then he looked up at her. "Michael needs you."

"Yes."

"It's what you've been doing for a long time, taking care of people. Wounded people."

"That's not all I do, Anthony. That's not a destiny."

"I'm just trying to understand."

"Understand what?"

"How it is for you."

"I'm sorry it's such a challenge," she said.

Anthony steepled his fingers and did not answer.

"You're thinking that you and I have not had the right experiences to understand each other." Gemma continued, "It's Michael and I who are stuck in the same lifeboat, right?"

"Stay here with him, Gemma."

She rose to leave. Anthony didn't try to stop her. He helped her with her jacket and walked her to the street, where he hailed her a taxi. Before she stepped in, she said, "You weren't at war, Anthony. You don't know what it was like. Some of us aren't as whole as we used to be."

"You are whole, Gemma. You were born whole. I doubt anything could take that away from you." Anthony paid the driver and then closed the taxi door. He pressed his hand against her window. From inside the taxi, Gemma stared at his hand and resisted the impulse to match it with her own. Before she could change her mind, he tapped the roof, signaling the driver to leave. The taxi pulled away. She spread her hands on her knees and stared out at the raucous riverside street, seeing nothing.

ANTHONY WENT BACK to the kitchen. On the table with the spoils of their uneaten meal was a folded piece of paper. He sat down and opened it. In Gemma's writing was a labored translation of a verse she had not shown him. It had taken her some time and error; there were lines crossed out, words written in. It read,

Yeshua said,
When you make two into one,
And when you make the inner like the outer
And the outer like the inner
And the upper like the lower,
And when you make male and female into a single one,
So that the male will not be male nor the female be female,
When you make eyes in place of an eye,
A hand in place of a hand,
A foot in place of a foot,
An image in place of an image,
Then you will enter the kingdom.

CHAPTER THIRTY

G EMMA RETURNED TO a silent house. Amad was in the kitchen. "The Lazars have gone out," he reported. "Michael has returned. He was able to come home early."

"Where is he?"

"Upstairs."

"How is he?"

"Disappointed to find you away."

Gemma mounted the stairs two at a time. She found Michael lying on the floor of his room. When he saw Gemma he held out a trembling hand. "I can't fasten this new goddamn leg."

She sat on the floor and held him. Near him was a broken vial of morphine.

"Where have you been?" he asked.

Gemma banished a tremor of guilt; she had done nothing wrong. "With Anthony."

"I don't blame you, choosing him."

"I'm not choosing anyone," Gemma said. "I had to talk to him about something I found in my father's office."

"Sex would be far easier with a man with two legs."

"Don't be vulgar."

"If you like me at all, help me get this poison in my arm."

"Tell me about your trip," she urged.

He was craning to watch her. "Please," he begged. He was almost weep-ing with frustration.

She had done it a hundred times. She snapped the top off a vial and drew the syringe. Tapping it, she did not let herself think of who this was. She simply thought of him as a dying man and stuck his arm with the needle.

Michael settled his head in her lap, his body limp. Gemma absently stroked his brow and examined his new leg. There was something disturb-ing about the shape and color; it was meant to look like a real leg. After a while, Michael reached up to touch her hair, dreamily winding it around and around his finger. "Why is a woman's hair so much softer?" Gemma smiled down at him. "What if I said I want to marry you?"

"Why would you want to do that?"

"Because I can talk to you. Because you can give me my poison."

"Michael, I would not give you your poison. I would make you give it up."

He pretended he hadn't heard. "The rest would come. If we start on the road, we would get somewhere. It will be beautiful. Come with me?"

Gemma turned away. He was not with her. He was in the hand of God.

"We could start a family," he entreated. "The bad memories would be crowded out eventually."

She pressed his head to her chest and hushed him like a child. Michael clung to her as if an angry sea were trying to claim him. "When I crashed in France," he said roughly. "That old man, the farmer. He was innocent. I killed an innocent man."

"You had been shot down, Michael."

"For the first time I killed on the ground. It was not war, it was murder."

"You were wounded and probably half-blind with burn."

"But I saw him, this old man in a nightshirt. He had nothing to do with the war and I knew it."

"You were both frightened."

"No, that wasn't it." Michael gripped her arm. "For a moment I saw my father."

There was a knock on the door that startled them both. The door opened and Anthony stood at the threshold. He did not cross it. "I'm sorry," he said. "I didn't know where everyone was. Gemma, you forgot something at my house. I'll leave it downstairs."

Michael said, "You should be the first to know. I've just proposed marriage."

"Have you?" Anthony's eyebrows rose in surprise. "Congratulations," he said quietly. "I'll leave you, then."

Gemma did not look up as Anthony closed the door behind him. She did not know if it was his presence or his absence that made her go so cold.

CHAPTER THIRTY-ONE

TOGO MINA WAS jumpy. He had not changed his clothes, it seemed, in days. Empty teacups and remnants of dried-out sandwiches cluttered the available surfaces of his office. He and Jean Doresse had been laboring over *Exegesis*. Anthony stood quietly inside the door and waited for Mina to finish.

"Lazar." Mina looked up. "You won't believe this material."

"I might. Gemma Bastian has made a discovery. Her father wrote his last journal in code. She has cracked it. He has transcribed the words of Yeshua, as heard by Toma."

Mina fell into his chair. "I don't believe it."

"Yes, it's quite incredible."

"Tell me more."

Anthony quoted:

"If you bring forth what is within you,
what is within you will save you.
If you do not bring forth what is within you,
what is within you will destroy you."

He looked at Mina and continued. "Bastian has written that in this gospel of Thomas there are no miracles, no prophecy, no ending of the world, no dying for one's sins, no resurrection. There are simply Jesus' words."

"How astounding."

"Jesus goes on to promise, 'Whoever discovers what these sayings mean will not taste death.' They almost read like riddles, these verses. They have a different quality from the gospels of the New Testament altogether. Jesus himself has a different quality; he's more of a sage, more of a Gnostic."

"Do you have the transcriptions?"

"No. I think Gemma Bastian feels a certain proprietary interest in keeping them. Clearly, Bastian saw the Gospel of Thomas before Eid had it. He's copied the verses with haste, as if he only had so much time with them." Anthony paused. "What's interesting to me is the passages Bastian chose. Gemma noticed it seemed that he was forming some kind of an argument."

Mina frowned. "What are you thinking?"

"That it's the first plausible motive for murder. Gemma Bastian found out that Stephan Sutton and her father were arranging a sale of texts to the British Museum. I'm thinking they were negotiating the sale of the Gospel of Thomas; that the sale was how he was going to take his argument public."

"The British Museum! If I had known that, *I* would have tried to kill him."

"I have to go to Nag Hammadi," Anthony said. "I need to speak to Bashir. Somewhere between Nag Hammadi and Cairo is something that will tell us what happened, something that will tell us how to proceed with what Bastian has left behind." Anthony rose.

"Lazar." The older man's voice quavered and cracked. He seemed unable to speak.

"Are you all right, Mina?" Mina was shaking his head silently. "Are you sleeping any better?"

"Not sleeping, no," Mina managed. He put his hand on Anthony's shoulder. "Please take care of yourself."

"Listen, try not to worry."

"I don't want to lose you, Lazar."

"You won't."

"Good, then." Mina was patting his arm. "Thank you for everything."

Anthony left for Kit Kat, thinking it was more of a goodbye than he was comfortable with.

CHAPTER THIRTY-TWO

GEMMA LAY IN bed and watched the shadows of palm fronds cross one another like swords on the ceiling. She was attempting a mental letter to her friend Lucy. If she could explain her position to Lucy, she could understand it better herself: After she returned from Upper Egypt, she would leave behind the family that had taken her in. She would return to London. Michael's tortured heart and his brother's torturing distance would eventually fade from memory. She wouldn't be forced to understand either of them. She wouldn't have to convince herself to love.

Love would come in time.

Or not.

She sat down at the desk and tapped the nib of the pen while she considered the wording. As she wrote, she felt she had already waited too long. When she was done, she lit her lantern and opened her wardrobe. Systematically, she began removing her clothes from their hangers.

She fell asleep surrounded by her folded clothes.

WHAT'S GOING ON in that feline brain of yours?" Michael asked the next morning. He had successfully fastened his new leg and was putting a golf ball down the hall. "Are you plotting something?"

"Of course I am. It's what women do."

"Where did you disappear to after dinner?"

"I was exhausted. I fell asleep in my clothes and slept through till morning."

"I hope it wasn't that aviator that wore you out. You shouldn't romance more than one pilot at a time. It's conventional wisdom. They become spiteful and dangerous. Come, there's coffee and toast in the breakfast room."

OVER HER COFFEE cup, Gemma watched Michael read the newspaper.

"Good Lord," he said. "Cambridge is going to accept women."

"Good!"

"That will change things." He folded the paper back and held it closer. "Have you heard of this bloke Chuck Yeager?"

"No."

"He's an American pilot. Seems he's flown a Bell-X-1 faster than the speed of sound. And he's done it in level flight. Incredible! Good for him. Go where no man has gone. Someday I'll do the same. The first crippled pilot to win a dogfight."

"The war is over, Michael."

Michael smiled and raised the newspaper over his face. "That's just a rumor."

Gemma set down her coffee and addressed the newspaper. "What would happen if you had," she faltered, "an episode, and I was out? Is there someone else who can help you?"

Michael lowered the paper. "An episode, darling?"

"You know what I mean."

"Ah, that. Ever the nurse. I have a button that rings a little bell, actually. Amad answers it." Michael whispered, "He's a bit of a stiffy, though."

"But you would ring for him."

"Trust me, darling, my appetites won't go unfilled. Certain of them anyway."

Gemma stood.

"Where are you off to?"

"The museum," she lied.

"I envy that place. It sees far more of you than I do."

She leaned down and kissed one of his cheeks and then the other. Michael took her face in his hands and pressed his lips to hers. She stepped away. "I'll see you, then."

GEMMA LIED AGAIN in the letter she left for the Lazars, telling them she'd hired someone in advance to take her to Upper Egypt, that other Europeans were going along, that the trip was leaving immediately so she hadn't had time to say goodbye. She almost left without saying goodbye to Amad, because she knew she couldn't lie to him. She found him in the garden, cutting herbs. He looked at her traveling outfit, the slacks and jacket that she had arrived in.

"You are going?"

"Not forever. Just a little trip."

"To the South, I imagine."

"I need to see it."

"I understand. Your father liked it there. Do you have someone to travel with?"

Gemma hesitated. "I thought I'd find a guide at Shepherd's Hotel. I've heard they're quite reliable."

"Some of them. If you can wait an hour, I can accompany you."

"No need. I've become quite adept at getting myself around Cairo. I rather enjoy the challenge."

"Very well. Be careful. Choose wisely with the guides."

"Thank you, Amad, for everything. I think when I leave Egypt, I will bring an oud with me."

"If I begin carving one now, perhaps it will be ready by your return."

Gemma stepped forward and embraced the older man. "You've been very good to me."

He took her hand and held it briefly to his forehead. "It has been easy."

CHAPTER THIRTY-THREE

A NTHONY STOPPED BY Charles Bastian's office and found it locked. He waited impatiently in his own office with the door ajar, listening all morning for the sound of Gemma's step. His thoughts, for once, had stalled completely. As the morning wore on, he fought anxiety, the virulent specter of panic.

Togo Mina had been found dead. The knowledge had not yet been made public. There would be an inquest, but the initial word was that he had died naturally, at home in his bed.

Anthony waited until noon. Finally he packed up his things and left, hailing a cab to take him to his father's house.

He called her name as soon as he entered.

"Too late, brother," Michael called from the den. "The bird has flown." He waved a letter when his brother entered. Anthony read it quickly and then handed it back.

"When did she leave?"

"Who knows? I've only just woken from a nap."

"Is anyone else here?"

"Sorry, brother. *Seulement moi.*" Michael tilted his head and squinted at Anthony. "What are you going to do?"

"She doesn't know this country."

"She's quite capable. Or haven't you noticed?"

"You don't know what she's got herself mixed up in. She shouldn't be traveling alone."

"So what are you proposing?"

"Going after her."

"Don't tell me you're going to play the hero. I'll be sick."

"I would call it common courtesy. Unless you're willing to go."

"I could maybe, tomorrow. But my head's splitting open at the moment. I haven't had my lunch."

"But you've had your drink."

"Yes, well, I lost my lovely nurse. Bad news needs medicine."

Anthony looked at him and held his eyes for one long moment. "It's your decision."

"Go, go." Michael flicked his brother away with his hand. "Bring my damsel back to me."

Anthony found Amad in the kitchen. "Tell me what you know."

Amad raised his eyebrows in dignified silence.

"Did Gemma tell you she was taking a trip?"

"She told me, yes."

"And what did you tell her?"

"I told her to choose carefully from the guides at Shepherd's. I offered to accompany her, but she is independent, as you know."

ANTHONY RAN DOWN the streets of Garden City until he found a taxi. His sense that Gemma was in danger was growing by the moment. He did not understand what had happened to Mina. Mina, a relatively young man, should not have died in his sleep. And yet Anthony could not imagine why someone would want to kill him, not now. Had Mina shared with someone the possibility that Bastian might have been arguing for a new Christianity? Christianity rewritten—complete with a new New Testament? It might be a reason to kill, especially if Mina had boasted of evidence—evidence that only a few knew about, evidence that would die when they died.

But who would he have talked to?

The taxi slowed for construction, and Anthony strained to see their progress, hitting the back of the seat in frustration. Gemma, it occurred to him, would be a sharper thorn than Mina in the side of anyone interested in destroying her father's work, particularly when her single purpose in life was to resurrect it.

Not only did she know too much, she was blithely heading to the source of the violence. Anthony threw some bills into the front seat when Shepherd's came into view. He was out of the taxi before it had even stopped.

H E F O U N D O U T the details, such as they were, quickly. A seasoned guide reported with amusement that the Englishwoman had been in a hurry. She had hired a guide, the only guide willing to leave that day.

"A charlatan, no doubt," Anthony said.

The staff at Shepherd's didn't know the man; he wasn't one of their regular guides. One stable worker remembered they left by camel.

"By camel?" Anthony said incredulously. "To Luxor?"

He quickly navigated the grand rooms of the hotel and reached the front desk, where he scribbled a note. Outside the hotel, he found a boy and pressed some coins into his hand. "Take this to Gabbar. He has a felucca docked at Maadi, called *Ibis*. Do you know the area?" The boy nodded. "Tell him I will meet him at his mooring this afternoon. Quickly, you understand?"

PART THREE

CHAPTER THIRTY-FOUR

ANTHONY CAUGHT SIGHT of Gemma at the outskirts of the city, where houses gave way to spiny acacias that stabbed the empty sky. She was perched on the back of a bony camel. With her head and face wrapped in a scarf, he could see only her eyes, which flashed in what might have been anger. Anthony's eyes ran quickly over her guide. He got off his horse and stood below her, instructing the animal to kneel. The beast folded its forelegs in a languid collapse that threw Gemma forward, then back. "What are you doing?" she demanded.

"Get off," Anthony said. "Who knows where this man was taking you."

The young man Gemma had hired spoke enough English to be a convincing fraud, and for a while he boldly upheld the charade. Anthony silenced him by switching with fluency to his native language. A combination of confusion, shame, and fury played across the guide's face as he decided simply to plead. Gemma stepped forward, trying to intervene, but the guide refused to look at her.

"The money she paid you," Anthony said.

The guide spat and barked a command at his reclining camels.

"The money," Anthony repeated. "And I will forget your face."

With his back turned, the guide dug into the folds of his burnoose. He dropped a wad of damp notes on the ground. Without turning, he tied the camels together and remounted the healthier of the two. Gemma watched him plod back the way they had come.

"I don't know if you consulted a map," Anthony said, "but Luxor is to the south." He picked up her bag and tied it to the saddle of his horse.

"So I'm a fool."

Anthony didn't respond. He mounted his horse and held out his hand. "I suppose I should thank you," she said, allowing him to swing her up behind him. She held his waist as lightly as she could. "It wasn't you I expected to see." The horse was moving slowly enough for Gemma to take her hands off Anthony's waist altogether. She crossed her arms and looked at the scenery to the side. After a while she said, "I thought Michael might come." She chewed the inside of her cheek. "What's it like to be surrounded by fools?"

Anthony glanced at his watch. They had left the ox-plowed flats of the fellahin and were winding down a path to the river. Rocks skittered to the bank where a large felucca lay tied to the shore. The boy Anthony had sent was waiting. Anthony gave him another bill to take the horse back to Shepherd's and stepped onto the felucca. Gemma remained standing on the bank.

"What are we doing?"

"There has been an outbreak of cholera in the delta, so the railway service has been suspended. Because we do not have a plane, the quickest way to Nag Hammadi is by the Nile."

"And you've decided to take me?"

Anthony waved her onto the boat. "There are worse traveling companions, as you have discovered."

"I don't know that I want to go on your boat."

A man appeared, emerging from a trail leading upriver. "Gemma, this is Gabbar. We were lucky to get Gabbar; he's usually booked." Anthony turned to Gabbar. "Were you able to get any provisions?"

"We'll manage for the night." He turned to Gemma and briefly inclined his head. "Please make yourself comfortable."

"What's the price?" Gemma asked.

"No price," Anthony said.

"You're simply going to taxi me to Nag Hammadi?"

"I was going anyway."

"Why?"

"Togo Mina felt there was something to be learned by speaking to your father's man, Bashir, and perhaps by seeing the discovery site."

"So we will meet Bashir together."

"If that's all right."

Gemma looked away. "When?"

"As soon as we get to Nag Hammadi. I have sent word that we are coming, so he is expecting us."

"How long will that take?"

"Five more days."

"So long."

"Too long?"

"There's no choice, is there?"

The boat was low and flat on the water. There wasn't a galley as such, but a large table was affixed in a sunken area at the back of the boat. It was surrounded by cushions. On one of them sat a large red hen. Gemma relinquished her bag and went to the front of the boat while Anthony and Gabbar pushed away from the shore with wooden poles. She let her eyes slide over the scenery that began floating by, the pale, slender forms of egrets hidden among the reeds. Above, the banks were steep and sudden. Children ran along paths, shouting and waving. Women stirred buckets of wash with long sticks. A plow was dragged by a pair of oxen. The sun began to sink, laying down a burning orange path in the water. The glassy reflections of trees and the surrounding sky in the river were disturbed only by the slightest ripple. As the outskirts of Cairo slipped by, mountains came into view in the distance, blue-black on the horizon.

When Anthony came and sat next to her, she kept her eyes on his dust-covered shoes. "It's beautiful," she said.

He handed her a cup of lentil soup. "On the Nile, we practice tent cooking," he explained, "learned from the Bedouin, who eat only what they can pack: rice, beans, dates. I hope you don't find it limiting."

She raised her eyes to his. "I didn't want a companion, not in the end."

"I know. I think you'll find the boat is big enough. Dinner in an hour, then."

The soup was spiced with cumin; the lentils were just the right firmness. Gemma ate quickly. She set down the empty cup and stared at the disappearing shore, wishing she weren't still hungry, wishing she could avoid both dinner and conversation.

As it turned out, no one spoke during the meal. She should have expected it. Instead of finding relief in the silence, she was as put off as she had been when they'd first met that Anthony didn't even attempt to put her at ease. He was quite content to let her writhe. She glared at him in the half-light, wondering if she was in fact writhing, eating her *fuul* and fava paste with bread.

"Tonight you will taste a fine dessert," Anthony said. "Gabbar is a date connoisseur. Some call dates the soul of the Bedouin."

Gemma looked past the boat to the banks of the river, where a few men had gathered around a fire. "That's rather sad."

"Not when you know how much they provide. The leaves are made into sandals, baskets, rope, roofs, even bricks. The wood from the trees provides lumber, furniture, fuel for their fires. Pyramid workers were paid in dates. Along with water, they are the only true currency in the desert."

"They are also used to sweeten wine," Gabbar said. "May I pour you some?"

Gabbar's dessert was a small, warm loaf of dates wrapped in filo dough with whipped cream and sliced almonds on top. The chewy, sweet fruit and flaky pastry and cream melted together in Gemma's mouth.

"There is a story about the Holy Family's flight into Egypt," Anthony said. "They left with no food, but when they reached Egypt, the palm groves bent down to Joseph and Mary so they could pick the fruit from its crown."

Gabbar collected the plates and threw a bucket tied to a rope over the back of the boat. Gemma listened to him humming as he washed the dishes. The river was suddenly lit by a small cruise boat that steamed past, its cabins bursting with light. In the large upper level, windows and French doors were flushed with the colors of dining guests, the air filled with their smoke and cocktail conversation and laughter. And then, just as suddenly, the churning of the paddlewheel and the voices faded and were replaced by the small and lonely slap of waves against the side of the felucca and the strange music of Cole Porter played by Egyptian instruments, drifting back across the water like an afterthought. Gemma stared as the cruiser disappeared. In another life, she thought, I might have been on that boat. If Michael had come, they might have danced, played cards, sipped cocktails. They might have laughed with strangers. When the boat disappeared around a bend in the river, there was a long, dark silence.

Anthony lit a lantern. "Togo Mina is dead," he said quietly. Gemma stared at him. "They said he died in his sleep. I suppose it's possible." Anthony watched the shadows on her turbulent face. From his canvas pack he brought out a melon-colored water pipe and filled the bowl. He lit it and drew in the air. The water bubbled like a tiny cauldron. The smoke from the flavored tobacco reached Gemma. She looked up when he offered her the pipe. "*Sheesha,*" he said. "It's a bit different from the tobacco you're used to."

Gemma sucked on the pipe and for a moment dizziness softened her fear. She coughed. "I don't understand. Why would someone want to kill him?"

"We were sent two of the gospels from the Nag Hammadi find. I think Mina knew the rest were with Phocion Tano. He might have pushed his luck. Tano is prone to violence. But really, I don't know. I don't know what happened."

"Tano sent you two gospels? Why?"

"Because we are the Coptic Museum. Because he has an honor of a sort."

"What gospels?"

"One was called *The Exegesis of the Soul.* The other was simply called *Thunder.*"

"Thunder," Gemma repeated. "What my father called Angela Dattari."

"Yes, well, it's a remarkable piece of writing. I've brought the translation for you to read."

"Have you really?" Gemma said. "How kind of you to think of me."

Anthony held her eye. "I've tried to be kind through all this, Gemma."

"I know you've tried. Your effort is the most noticeable aspect of your kindness."

"Effort does not pass as kindness."

"No." Gemma paused. "I can believe that you are doing something that is difficult for you; I can believe that. I have never been sure why."

BEHIND THEM, Gabbar was tying a sheet across the width of the boat, bisecting it for Gemma's privacy. He brought her a bowl of water to wash in. When she had finished, Anthony appeared with a thin headscarf. "Use this against the mosquitoes." He unrolled two sleeping mats on either side of the deck. "It's less than luxurious, but the sheets are clean."

"It's fine."

She set a lantern by her head and lay on her stomach with the translations of *Thunder* in front of her. Her eyes began to scan the verse and then slowed. As she returned and reread, the words mingled inside of her. Everything else faded; the boat, the river, the veil of night insects circling the lantern.

> *I am the first and the last.*
> *I am the honored and the scorned*
> *I am the whore and the holy.*
> *I am the wife and the virgin*
> *I am the mother and the daughter . . .*
> *I have had a grand wedding*
> *And have not found a husband.*
> *I am a midwife and do not give birth.*

The words pierced her as cleanly and deeply as arrows, but what she felt was beyond pain. She felt laid bare. Though lying alone in the darkness, she felt she was in full view, every wound she had tried to hide open to the night air. She blew out the lantern and laid her head on her arm. Rising inside her was a tremor, a wave that was equal parts hope and despair. *I am a midwife and do not give birth.*

I am a healer who will not be healed.

Long moments later, she looked over at Anthony. She became aware of how physically close they were. Michael would not have liked it. He would have considered it a betrayal, might have called her a whore. She forced herself to return to his brother, to the boat and the river and the night that held them both. She closed her eyes to the unimaginable sky above and soon her anguish was replaced by a peace that settled inside of her like a soft, worn fabric.

IN THE MORNING Gemma stared up at the cloudless sky. Birds winged in and out of view. Turning her head, she could see the upper fringe of palms, the now exotic color green. Things seemed sharper, more defined. She closed her eyes. The sun crested a ridge and lit the morning like a bomb blast. She threw an arm over her face, blocking out the light. Against the darkness of her eyelids, she could sense what was different. There was something in front of her now, almost a physical space, something she could step into—step toward.

He called me his Thunder.

Gabbar brought her a mug of hot coffee. She sat up and watched the hen stalking around the deck, thinking about her father, thinking about Angela Dattari.

Anthony joined her, setting a plate of fruit between them. "Were you able to sleep?"

"Who is she?" Gemma asked. "Who is Thunder?"

"I confess," he began, "this gospel has pushed me to the limits of my understanding. These verses seem to have come from nowhere—but they came from somewhere, from someone. And I know nothing about it." Anthony began peeling an orange, taking care not to break the skin of the fruit. "It has not been easy to find material on women at this time in history. I have discovered that when Christianity was taking hold, women had achieved a position of power in some societies. In Egypt and Asia Minor they were property owners, they ran businesses, had wealth—sometimes lived independently. The contract of marriage was changing—it was becoming a contract of equals. In Rome, girls of the aristocracy were being educated with the boys. They had the same curriculum. Women were teachers, leaders in their communities. They were powerful, respected. I think *Thunder* was the voice of those women. I think women spoke then. They had been permitted to; they had learned how."

"And then something happened. They were silenced."

"Your father said it, but I didn't know how deep the event was, how violent the reversal. He was right; the female was cleaved from the male. Half of humanity was obscured from view." Anthony offered Gemma an orange segment. "The longer I sit with the verses of *Thunder,* the more I am sure that men have suffered its loss."

Gemma looked a moment longer at Anthony's face and had to look away. The intimacy of *Thunder* could almost not be borne. She left him and made her way to the back of the boat, where Gabbar was untying the ropes crisscrossing the mast. The sail unfurled and they were under way. Gemma let her thoughts wander. It seemed more than enough to watch Gabbar, who sat back and steered with his foot, deftly manipulating the immaculate cotton sail that looked like something a child might build, it was so primitive.

The hen dropped down to the cushions and nestled herself between them. Gemma pointed at the bird. "Will we eat her?"

"Not on this trip."

"Then we should name her."

Gabbar smiled. "As you wish."

"We'll call her Hestia. I think we need a goddess on board."

"A chicken goddess?" Anthony called from the front of the boat and threw his head back and laughed.

LATER THAT DAY the wind died. When Anthony took an oar, Gemma joined him, rolling up her trousers and dangling her feet off the deck. It provided some satisfaction, pulling the river this way. On some strokes it seemed her body pulled with an energy she didn't know she had. By midday, it had grown too hot for a hat, and the bright sun touched her hair and cheeks. They floated past lush little islands and coves where feluccas sheltered, their captains asleep in the shade of the sails. Beyond the banks of the river were distant plateaus. Closer, brown hills rose like loaves of bread. Someone on the shore played a flute. A line of goats picked its way downriver. The wind rose and Gemma rested her oar.

"Have you ever sailed on the sea?" she asked Anthony.

"No."

"It's not at all like this. The winds can be very strong; you can lose control."

"That can happen here."

"Once, we sailed across the channel to France. It's not so far, but it felt far. When you lose sight of land, it's the best and worst part. It seems there is no end to the emptiness. I always thought that if death lived on earth, it would live in such a place. It's the closest I can think of to what it might be like in the desert."

"You're not far off, though the feeling of death changes after a while."

Gemma dipped her oar back into the river. "I can't stop thinking about *Thunder*."

"Yes, I know."

We are catching up to each other, she thought, Anthony and me. We have shared our verses and now the same words are living inside of us. What does that make us? she wondered.

AT SUNSET THAT night, they tied up on a small island. Gemma posted herself at Gabbar's makeshift kitchen. "Give me something to do."

"There is nothing for you to do."

"Please," she said.

Gabbar considered her. "You can chop."

Gemma chopped three piles of vegetables and asked for something else to do.

"You are on the river of life," Gabbar said. "Maybe you should be just content to live."

Gemma's eyes drifted to the languid swirls of the river. "Like your chicken, with no clue to my approaching end."

Gabbar poured her some apple tea. "Go watch the sun set. You will see, it is never the same two nights in a row."

Gemma obeyed like a child, settling herself on the deck. Anthony appeared on the island's strip of beach, where he had waded to pick fruit. Gemma watched as he entered the river again, carrying a canvas bag heavy with oranges. She was becoming familiar with the structure of his lanky body, the sharp definition of its muscle and bone. The beauty of his face was something he was wholly unaware of. As he made his way to her, she studied him as she hadn't dared before, considering the intensity of his wide and slightly hooded eyes. Eyes that might not after all be judging her, that might just be watching.

ANTHONY PULLED HIMSELF up onto the boat.

"Tell me how it was," she said, "when Michael first came to Egypt to live."

Anthony set down his bag and sat on his haunches, staring into the foliage of the island in front of them. "He was like a wounded dog."

"But this was before the war."

"Yes. But wounded all the same. He hated us all. I think he believes our father killed his mother. To be honest, I was glad to go to Kharga."

"Is that why you started spending time there?"

"Partly, in the beginning. I didn't want to compete with Michael. I didn't want to remind him with my own mother that he had lost his—or that his father was my father too. Even the country was mine."

"Were you ever friends?"

"I have always thought so. Since the war he has made it impossible."

"I hated that bloody war. I don't think I've ever said it. I hated it with all my heart."

LATER, when they were preparing dinner, Gabbar instructed Gemma to lift the cushions in the eating area to search for the store of dates. Gemma found the dates. She also found an oud. It wasn't as beautiful or well crafted as Amad's but she held it with some happiness. She asked Gabbar to play it after dinner.

Gabbar obliged with two traditional songs, neither of which she'd heard. His style was different from Amad's, more precise and linear.

"I think Gemma plays a bit too," Anthony said.

Gabbar offered her the instrument. Gemma laughed, embarrassed. "I don't want to give you indigestion," she said.

"Don't worry about us."

The two men watched her bent head as she studied the strings in the darkness. "Try closing your eyes," Gabbar said.

Gemma looked up. "That's what my teacher does."

"It can make it easier. It stops you from thinking too hard."

Gemma smiled self-consciously and lifted her head to the sky. She laid her hands on the oud and closed her eyes. Her fingers hesitated at first but then found their way. She played well. At the end of the song she shook her head. "I must look like a fool."

"On the contrary," Anthony said. "You look like a musician."

"She has a gift," Gabbar said.

"She has a few."

Gemma smiled, glad for the darkness.

She insisted on cleaning up after dinner. Anthony sent Gabbar to the front of the boat with his pipe and the oud. He knelt next to her with a dish towel. Gemma handed him a wet plate. "Thank you for speaking honestly about Michael," she said.

"It's easier when there's some distance between us."

"Yes, I can see that." She paused. "You stop taking responsibility for him."

Anthony took the plate from her and covered it with the dish towel. "Not entirely."

Later, they laid out their mats under a sky of stars that was still unbelievable to her. It wasn't until they were settled in their blankets that she spoke.

"I was remembering something good about the war. During the Blitz, during the blackouts, you could see the stars at night. They weren't as bright as these, but there were more than I'd ever seen before."

"It seemed a barbarous way to fight," Anthony said. "Bombing civilians in the middle of the night."

"I remember in the beginning they said it would be over by Christmas. The whole war wrapped up in time for the holidays. We waited for weeks for the whistles to sound a raid. I kept thinking, if it doesn't start soon, it won't end soon. The boys on our street were going mad with impatience. They wanted the war. They were all playing soldiers. Then it began. And it seemed like there had never been another life."

A night heron screeched and took flight. Gemma raised herself and watched the span of its blue-gray wings beating in the silvery light. It glided soundlessly downriver.

"Why did you not marry?" Anthony asked.

"I don't know." She paused. "It seems absurd to think about love during a war."

"But there is always war, isn't there?"

Her eyes scanned the sky for constellations. "There was someone. But he died." After they lapsed into separate silences, Gemma addressed the darkness. "Do you think we must remember everything that came before?"

"I think we are here to learn. There are times I think it is fine, perhaps even better, to forget."

Gemma closed her eyes then and sank into a strange, animated state of rest. She didn't know if she actually slept. She seemed to be fully awake, yet simultaneously hovering over her body. It should have been frightening but it wasn't. She could see Anthony too, not far away, sleeping soundly.

THE NEXT MORNING Gemma drank her coffee and fell into a trance over a golden swath of sunlight on the blue water. She watched it dance and thought about nothing. She felt, if not peaceful, settled inside. In just a few days, she had gained a new awareness of her body. Her arms were sore from rowing. Her skin had darkened, and since she had stopped wearing her hat, her hair had turned lighter. She liked the idea of being physically changed by this country, of leaving the protection of the leaves of Garden City. When Anthony came to collect her coffee cup, she looked up at him.

"I have this sense that I just arrived here. Like when you're walking and you're not really aware that you're walking until suddenly you're somewhere else. Suddenly I'm here. I'm not sure where I was before."

Anthony squatted on his haunches. "You were too busy to know."

An ibis sailed along the shallow waters of the bank, its wingtips almost carving the still water.

"How is it, to spend so much time in a place like Kharga?"

"For me, it's quite normal."

"Such isolation seems hellish. We're alone enough as it is."

"But I'm not alone."

"Then who are you with, out there in the middle of nowhere?"

"The desert hermits, mostly. Men who lived a long time ago. Men who understood this contradiction well."

"Dead men."

"Not dead to me."

"And now?"

"Now I am with you."

LATER, the wind grew strong and the felucca sliced quickly upriver. Gemma watched the banks of the Nile, asking Gabbar the names of various long-legged wading birds. She periodically glanced at Anthony as he repaired a patch in the spare sail, making quick, neat stitches with a fat needle. At moments, he reminded her of a boy. It seemed no part of him had yet been pulled in the wrong direction; nothing had yet been broken or burned. He was still upright and strong. His body was a vehicle that had not yet betrayed him. Not like his brother; not like the men Gemma had known.

It occurred to her that Anthony did not know betrayal at all. He lived in the past, a place where betrayal did not exist. It had taken some time to understand this. She had first thought he rejected the company of people incapable of holding a stone in their mouth, of anyone weak enough to need the reassurance of civilization. She had been wrong. He lived far from others not because he had contempt for them, or because he was afraid of them. He lived in the desert because that was where he learned the most.

Now, on the river, he seemed sometimes surprised by the presence of living people, people who talked to him, offered him help. He seemed continually taken aback by her offers to cook, to man an oar, to make up the beds, to do the wash.

"You must think I'm incompetent," she finally told him.

"I've never traveled with a woman."

"That's not it. You're just not used to being around people who don't work for you."

Anthony considered this. "You're right."

THAT NIGHT GEMMA lay perched on the edge of sleep. The moon was outshining the dimmer constellations, making the sky more a village than a mecca of shimmering silver points. Anthony was nearby. Always, it seemed. She was aware of his breath, of the many types of silence between them. Sometimes the silence was a conversation. Sometimes it sat on a hot plate of frustration and simmered. Other times it was cool and dark and unbroken. Sometimes it was just sleep.

Gemma raised herself. Somewhere on the riverbank was a hissing sound, a warning or an alarm. An answer came from downriver, a high-pitched bird call. Anthony was already out of bed, crouched, listening. He strained to hear the whispering voices. "They are hunting," he said. "Crocodile, maybe. For purses and shoes." He glanced at Gemma. "You're not asleep."

"No."

"Try. We have a hard day tomorrow."

As he walked past her, his fingers brushed the top of her head. She lay back into the shadows and began listening again for his breath, keeping herself awake until she heard it slow and deepen in sleep.

IN THE EARLY morning Gabbar tied the felucca up to land. Feeling the change in motion, Gemma woke and pulled the headscarf from her face. Anthony was packing a bag with food and water. "Where are we?" she asked.

"We are in Daraw. We're going to buy some camels."

Gemma sat up and looked around. "Where?"

"The camel market. The biggest in Egypt. You can't see it from here, but there, over there, you can see the dust."

Gemma ran her fingers through her hair. "I see."

"We are nearing the area of the cholera outbreak. It's time to go inland."

AS THEY WALKED over the hill that separated them from the camel market, Anthony explained that the camels and their drivers came from as far as thirty days away, from the Sudan, to buy and sell the animals. Camels, he said, were Allah's gift to the desert peoples.

"Why?"

"Because they can survive here."

What Gemma saw was that they had padded feet that spread instead of sinking into the sand. They could close their nostrils, keeping out sand and dust. In the bedlam and dust of the open market, they were obstinately serene.

Anthony bought Gemma a native headscarf, to protect her from the sun. "And to make me less conspicuous?"

"That too."

Gemma wrapped the scarf around her head and inspected the camel that would be hers. It was closer to white than brown and had enormous brown eyes and the lashes of a girl. It, she, was chewing cud indelicately. Gemma clucked her tongue and gestured with her arm the way Anthony had taught her. The camel, which was supposed to kneel so Gemma could mount, looked away.

ANTHONY HIRED A boy to bring the camels to Al-Qasr, where that afternoon they would leave the river. Gabbar would sail past Luxor and restock. He would meet them back in Al-Qasr in five days.

Gemma looked at Anthony. "Five days?"

"You can't move quickly in this part of the world." He was studying her. "Is it all right?"

"It has to be, doesn't it?"

"We can turn back."

She rested her hand briefly on his arm as she stepped past him onto the boat.

GABBAR'S ABSENCE WAS noticeable as they made their first inland camp. Gemma missed him, as she missed the river, and Hestia and the boat. She sat on a blanket in the sand while Anthony cupped his hands around a cluster of paper and twigs to light a fire. He would not let her cook. He would not let her do anything. She was grateful; the day had been long and dry, and riding a camel had been a curious and difficult exercise. She pressed down on the sand under the blanket and felt it shift beneath her hands. They had made camp near a tree that had long been dead, its limbs like licked bones. Her eyes traversed the landscape, searching for a smudge of color. There was no place for greenery here, no crack deep enough to reach moisture; not even a shadow relieved the insistence of rock and sand. She closed her eyes and tried to remember the parks of London. She didn't know what she hoped to find in Nag Hammadi. The thought of reaching the place she had been longing for filled her with anguish now. As uncomfortable as this place was, she wanted to pause, to stop time from slipping away from her. She did not want to arrive in Nag Hammadi only to leave. She did not want to hurtle toward more endings.

She watched as Anthony stirred a pot of couscous over the open fire, tossing in pinches of mixed spices from a dented tobacco tin. He glanced at her as he sat back from the fire. Soon her eyes met his.

"What happens tomorrow?"

"We go to Nag Hammadi."

"And after Nag Hammadi?"

"We return to Cairo."

Gemma hung her head and traced the sand with her fingertip.

"What is it?" he asked.

"I'm not sure what comes after that." Strands of hair had fallen in front of her downturned face. She spoke quietly. "I feel myself . . . between worlds."

Keeping his eyes on her, Anthony rearranged the sticks in the fire. "A great Gnostic teacher, Monoimus, said, 'Abandon the search for God and the creation and other matters of a similar sort. Look for him by taking yourself as the starting point. Learn who it is within you who makes everything his own and says, "My God, my mind, my thought, my soul, my body." Learn the sources of sorrow, joy, love, hate. . . . If you carefully investigate these matters you will find him *in yourself.*'"

Gemma made him repeat the quote and then returned to her sand design. "Maybe you could write that down for me."

"With pleasure."

"And how," she asked, "in this system, does one go about finding someone else? Or doesn't that work?"

"Love is primary, always, even to the desert hermits. When one truly loves, they believed, the self dies for the other."

"Then how does one continue? How does one have a relationship if the self is dead?"

"I think it's something you understand only by experience."

"Maybe it's just for hermits, this strategy. Maybe they're talking about love of God."

"Maybe. Maybe there's no difference."

✝   ✝   ✝

AFTER DINNER, they laid their mats close to the fire. Gemma hugged her knees under the blankets, feeling the chill of the desert air. Across the fire Anthony's eyes were already closed.

"I think your brother misunderstands you," she said softly.

"Our relationship is complex."

"He thinks you're incapable of love."

Anthony was silent.

"Are you?" Gemma said.

"I think I have known love, though it's a love my brother might not recognize."

"Love for whom?"

Anthony was quiet for a long time. "It's difficult to answer. To put words to it. I have love for the past," he said slowly. "For the stars. For beautiful verse. For the sight of Kharga after three days in the sand—or the taste of water, or Zira's laugh—or my mother's grace."

"I think Michael means for a woman."

"Yes." Anthony smiled faintly. "I know."

THE NEXT MORNING they were joined by a boy Anthony had sent to bring provisions and water. He arrived at dawn and sat on his camel, chin jutted, waiting for them to rise.

"Hanif will come with us to Nag Hammadi," Anthony explained. "He knows this territory well."

Their small train of camels wound its way through the rocky terrain toward Nag Hammadi on a path that was steep and never straight. In the distance, the great cliff of Jabal al-Tarif rose like a wave, its surface pitted with depressions. Other than the occasional skitter of rocks dislodged by the camels' hooves, there was no sound at all. Gemma's neck was damp with perspiration. She lifted her hair from her back and piled it into her hat. She fought to stay awake. The rolling rhythm of the camels lulled her;

she found herself nodding forward and jerking awake as she almost lost her balance. Then Anthony was no longer behind her, but beside her with his hand on her saddle. "You can learn to sleep this way," he said, "but you might fall a few times first." He handed her a leather bag of warm water and she drank enough to moisten her throat. It tasted of dirt.

"I don't think I could manage it," she said. "Living out here."

"It's only the first day," Anthony said. He added, "Any courtship takes time."

"There is a country in the far north. The sun doesn't rise there for months. It's closer to my home than this place."

"You would miss it," he said. "You would miss the sun."

She wiped the grit from her face with her shirtsleeve. "Tell me, what do you know about Bashir?"

"He's Bedouin," Anthony said. "He was devoted to your father."

"I remember hearing stories about the Bedouin in the war against Rommel. They seem quite fierce."

"The Bedouin are like no other people. They are not, as some Europeans think, barbarous."

"My father told me they live in tents."

"They are nomads, so they move from place to place depending on the season, water, and the needs of the tribe. The women weave the fabric for their tents out of the fur of black goats and sheep."

Gemma had closed her eyes. "But they are fighters."

"They will fight when they have to. But they are not interested in dominating others. They want to hold their own, nothing more. They are a free people. I have found more nobility in them than in some of the princes I have met."

"You've met princes," Gemma echoed.

"Everyone comes to Egypt, it seems. And when one's father holds the keys to the treasures of the old kingdom, one dines with royalty, heads of state. They would come to our house to be educated. I was just a boy. No one thinks about what they say around little boys. I suppose that's when my respect for my father's culture began to wane." Anthony cleared his throat. "As a schoolboy I was made to memorize poems. Some of them have stayed with me." He recited,

"If you can talk with crowds and keep your virtue,
Or walk with kings—nor lose the common touch,
If neither foes nor loving friends can hurt you,
If all men count with you, but none too much . . ."

But none too much, Gemma thought. "You've left out the beginning."
"You know it?"
"It's a standard school poem."
"So we were learning the same verse thousands of miles away."
"The difference is, you remembered it. Can you recite the other verses?"

"If you can dream—and not make dreams your master,
If you can think—and not makes thoughts your aim,
If you can meet with Triumph and Disaster
And treat those two impostors just the same . . ."

"Maybe Kipling was what started it all. Maybe he was your first desert hermit." She glanced at him and smiled. "I'd wager you've achieved these things. You should be proud."

They continued on, Anthony dropping back when the path narrowed. Gemma found herself in the haze of a waking dream, thinking about the possibility that Anthony had shaped his life by a philosophy, by a few lines from a poem. That the reason he was so often awkward and staid was that his companions in life hadn't been people but ideas. She understood why he and her father had been friends. Sometimes she felt she and Anthony had become friends. But he was not like any friend she had known. He did not try to reassure her of anything, ever. On the long days they had spent together, this was something she had begun to value. It created a space between them in which she could breathe and move, in which she was never able to forget herself. He was not responsible for her, nor she for him. But there was a care taken. It was the opposite with Michael, who made her feel she was melting into him, that he could not live without her, that at the same time, she was utterly, tragically alone.

WHEN THEY NEARED Nag Hammadi, Anthony drew up next to her. "Tell me," he said, "what do you hope to find here?"

"You're worried I will be disappointed. Don't be. My expectations are not your responsibility."

Anthony considered her. "I wanted to remind you that it may not be a very safe place to be, but I imagine you're aware of that." Gemma kept her eyes on the path in front of her, which was widening into a small road. They were entering the outskirts of Nag Hammadi, passing mud-brick dwellings and goats. Sometimes a child in a doorway. The sky had turned a violent red and they could smell meat cooking in the narrow street.

Hanif slid off his camel to find someone who knew Bashir. As they followed a local man through the town, the silence was ruptured by the sudden, rasping drone of an airplane engine. They watched, heads tilted, as a biplane invaded the magenta sky, circled, and angled back toward Luxor.

Anthony touched Gemma's shoulder. "I don't know how long it will be possible to stay here."

"Why? Is that someone you know up there?"

"They flew directly over Nag Hammadi. We should assume they're coming this way."

When they reached Bashir's tent, the color in the sky was extinguished like a flame. All at once, it was dusk. A small bearded man who had been sitting motionless outside the rectangular tent rose when he saw Gemma and Anthony. "I have been waiting for you." Bashir held out his hand for Gemma. "Welcome to my home, my *beit sha'ar*."

The furrows on Bashir's forehead began at the arched peaks of his eyebrows and extended up like ripples. His eyes were deep-set and warm, his nose as sharp as a falcon's. "Everything is ready for you inside," he said. Bashir followed her into the tent. The floor was laid with rugs and patterned cushions. Smoke curled from a cooking fire. Gemma stared absently into the embers. Bashir motioned her to a large pillow. "You are tired."

Gemma smiled. "I am happy to be here." The wind buffeted the cloth walls. She felt she was inside a lantern. "This is where my father stayed," she said.

"Yes."

"I have been waiting to meet you, Bashir."

"I feel I have already met you. When your father spoke about you and read your letters, it seemed you were sitting here with us."

Gemma accepted a cup of tea. "I know so little about you. I don't even know how you met."

Bashir shook his head. "It's some years ago now."

"Where?"

"Not far. My people were traveling; our seasonal journey. My wife was with child. She was not well, and began her labor early. We had to leave our caravan. She did not live."

"And the child?"

"I stayed behind to bury both of them. A small expedition passed us. The only person who looked at me was your father. He helped me bury my family and then brought me with him. He gave me a job."

"That would have been the year my mother died."

"It was something we shared." Bashir went to a small table where a single framed photograph stood. He brought the photograph to Gemma. It was a dusty, crinkled, sepia print of a child. She held it closer. The child was her. "Why do you have this?"

"Your father asked if Bashir would be his daughter's Bedouin father. He said the more people who had you in their heart, the better. He was far away. You were unprotected, without a mother."

Gemma dropped her eyes.

"Behind the curtain," Bashir said, "there is water for washing. There is soap and a towel."

She washed in privacy, smiling at the feeling of water. She rubbed soap into her dusty, tangled hair and scrubbed her scalp. She took a rough washcloth to her brown ankles, poured water down her neglected back. Afterward she changed into clean clothes and sat on the cushions and worked through the snarls in her hair. Incense burned and mixed with the wood smoke. There were covered pots warming in the embers of the fire. She thought of nothing at all until she realized that for the first time in days, she was hungry.

Anthony and Bashir returned with more wood. Anthony paused at the sight of her.

THEY SAT ON cushions around the fire. Bashir spooned servings of lamb and couscous and bread spread with clarified butter.

Gemma copied Bashir and Anthony and ate with the three fingers on her right hand. "I didn't expect you to speak English," she said.

"Your father taught me."

"And you have met Anthony before."

"Of course."

"In Oxyrhynchus."

"Yes. You remember, Anthony, we left in the night."

"I remember."

"That was when word came from Nag Hammadi. Though we came straightaway, some of the books were already lost."

"Lost how?" Gemma asked.

"First I must tell you who found them. Then you might understand better how they would be lost." Bashir passed a bowl of dates. "To grow anything in this rocky soil, one needs sabakh," he began. "It is a soft, rich soil found near the base of Jabal al-Tarif. Mohammad Ali from the al-Samman clan went with his brothers for their annual collection of sabakh. Their father had just been killed by a man from Al-Qasr. It started a blood feud. The brothers were planning their revenge as they dug for sabakh, when their shovels struck something hard. Digging farther, they found first the skeleton of a man. Then they saw a large jar. The jar was sealed and very old. The brothers were worried there might be jinn, evil spirits, inside. But there might also be gold. So Mohammad Ali raised his mattock and smashed the jar. There was no gold. There were books. Mohammad Ali took them back to his home in Al-Qasr and left the books there. No one knew what they were; if they were of value—if they would bring bad luck. Some were used by Mohammad Ali's mother to fuel the fire."

"She burned them?"

"She cannot read. The books meant nothing to her." Bashir wiped his fingers on a cloth. "When the brothers avenged their father's murder, eating the heart of the man who had killed him, there was an investigation. The police came to Mohammad's house every day to look for weapons. For safekeeping, Mohammad gave the books to a priest, Basiliyus ʿAbd al-Masih. It was the brother of the priest's wife, a history teacher who read Coptic named Raghib, who recognized that the books might have value.

"That was when we came. We were known to these people; we had been here before, looking for such books. Your father believed that the monks of Saint Pachomius hid the books many years ago."

"Why would he have believed that?"

"Because the monks loved them," Anthony interjected. "And they had been outlawed by the Church. It was another of your father's theories. Another that proved to be right."

Gemma looked at Anthony for a long moment and then turned back to Bashir. "So this teacher, Raghib, knew what the books were?"

"But not as well as your father," Bashir said. "They sat for many days looking at them. Then your father sent for Stephan Sutton back in Oxyrhynchus. When Raghib advised Mohammad Ali to send one of the books to Cairo to find its worth on the black market, Mohammad chose the book your father loved best. Your father begged them to take another, but Mohammad refused. 'It is your favorite; it may bring us luck.' He allowed your father to spend three days with the text, copying it onto other pages. Then Mohammad sent it with a messenger to Cairo. 'If these books are of worth,' Mohammad said, 'this one will be my gift to you.'"

"The Gospel of Thomas," Gemma said.

"The same. Then Stephan Sutton arrived, and they arranged with Mohammad Ali to buy the books. Your father went back to Cairo to collect the Gospel of Thomas. Stephan Sutton stayed here to gather as many of the books as he could find. Your father instructed me to stay with Sutton, and help him back to Cairo. Then a terrible thing happened. The books were stolen."

"By whom?"

"By Bahij ʿAli, a criminal and an outlaw. A man with no soul." Bashir bit into a date. "We were on our way to Cairo. There was a rock slide. Stephan Sutton was killed. I thought it was an accident, but then Bahij ʿAli was there with his knife. We lost the gospels. We lost them all."

"There was nothing you could do." She turned to Anthony. "I don't think my father knew about Stephan Sutton until he read it in the newspaper. I think it was a complete surprise."

"Bashir," Anthony said, "do you know how the books got to Phocion Tano?"

"Bahij ʿAli took them to Cairo. Tano bought them all and then came here to look for more." Bashir rose and crossed to the far end of the tent. He was reaching to untie an inside flap. "When Tano came, he searched everywhere, all the houses. He frightened people. I did what I had to do to protect what your father had left behind. A gift from Mohammad Ali. Come." Anthony and Gemma stood next to Bashir. In the lamplight they could see the faint script of papyrus pages that had been sewn into the fabric of the tent. "Everyone was looking for books," Bashir said. "So I took this one apart. The leather cover is buried in the dirt under my sleeping mat. You'll see the translations your father made behind the papyrus pages. It's called *The Dialogue of the Savior*."

Gemma sat and skimmed the translations. She read out loud,

"If one does not understand how the fire came to be, he will burn in it, because he does not know its root. If one does not first understand the water, he does not know anything. . . . If one does not understand how the wind that blows came to be, he will run with it. If one does not understand how the body that he wears came to be, he will perish with it. . . . Whoever does not understand how he came will not understand how he will go. . . ."

She paused.

"The Savior said, The lamp of the body is the mind. . . . More than all the other disciples, Mary Magdalene understood."

From a leather bag behind his bed, Bashir extracted two large envelopes. "He also left these." Each envelope bore an address. One to St. John's Seminary, Surrey, England, and one to the British Museum.

"But the envelopes are empty. Do you know what they're for?" Gemma asked.

"He left me no instruction."

Gemma looked at Anthony. "They're not big enough to hold the original book. Were they for the translations?"

"Or for something we haven't yet seen," Anthony said.

"Now it is late," Bashir said. "And you have traveled a long way."

As they sipped their tea, Bashir tidied up and put wood on the fire. "Tonight you will take my tent, Miss Gemma. The men will sleep by the fire outside."

"Then I will also sleep by the fire outside," Gemma said.

"The woman needs the cover of the tent," he argued.

"But the woman wants to sleep outside. She has gotten used to it. She wants to see the stars. Please. Tell him it's safe, Anthony."

The two men talked rapidly. Bashir was not pleased.

"He says he will have to send for someone to stand guard. He says it's not safe."

"That's absurd."

"You may not understand the nature of Bedouin hospitality," Anthony said. "While you are here, you are under Bashir's protection. Even if you just ate dinner here and left, for three days following, he would be responsible for your well-being. I think you could show him the courtesy of sleeping in the tent."

"Oh, all right."

A moment later she was outside. Anthony looked up from the fire. "I want to look at the sky first," she told him. "Just a short walk."

"Bashir will not let you go alone."

"Then come with me."

They walked away from the orange glow of the fire into the silvery night. Gemma's voice was hushed. "You told me Bashir didn't speak English."

"To discourage you from coming."

She turned to him. "Are there more lies? If there are, I'd like to know now."

"No, there are no more lies."

"It's hurtful."

"I know."

"They haven't protected me."

"I'm sorry," Anthony said, adding, "I didn't expect to know you so well."

He returned her to the entrance of the tent, briefly touching her hand before she left him.

THE MORNING WAS cold. Gemma's breath appeared before her, a tiny tempest of warmth. The floor was covered with a soft pattern of light that pressed through the weave in the cloth. She waited for Anthony before eating.

The three of them breakfasted on bread Bashir had cooked in the embers of the fire. Like a magician, he produced a small glass jar of strawberry preserves. "This was what your father liked to spread on his bread."

Gemma smiled, accepting the offering.

"When you are ready, I will take you to Raghib," he said. "He has also been waiting to meet you."

"Do we have to go so soon?"

"A plane has come," Bashir said. "A small caravan is making its way to Nag Hammadi."

"So that means we must rush?"

"Think, Gemma," Anthony said. He turned to Bashir. "Were you told who's on it?"

"A single European man with two guides."

Gemma glanced at Anthony. "Did they mention the color of his hair?"

"No, they did not."

They walked through the town of Al-Qasr in silence. A baby goat trotted after them, its bell tinkling. Heat was already softening the ground, the infertile soil that needed sabakh.

Bashir led them to a small mud-brick house. Its walls were heat-cracked, baked to a dark brown. The unmolested blue of the sky was already being assaulted by the sun; the color bled from the anemic edges. The only real blue was straight above.

Word of their arrival had already reached Raghib, and the door opened before Bashir could knock. Both men smiled. "Here is Raghib," Bashir announced. "And this is Professor Bastian's daughter, Gemma. She has come from England."

Raghib had a round, untroubled face. He reached for Gemma's hand and grasped it warmly. "Welcome, welcome."

"Raghib is an educated man," Bashir said proudly. "He has been to school in Cairo."

"Please, come in. I am happy that you have come. I have been keeping something for your father." He laughed. "Rather, my house has been keeping it." Inside, the light was dim. An oil lamp burned on a desk. The morning shone in through cracks between the bricks. When her eyes adjusted, Gemma saw that Raghib was reaching above the desk to remove a seamless square that had been cut from the wall. He removed a wrapped bundle and set it on the desk. Wrapped with thick oilcloth were pages covered with her father's script. Raghib's fingers twisted the lamp to swell the flame. He unwrapped the pages and motioned for Gemma and Anthony to come closer. They stood next to him and pored over the script. "It looks like a letter," Gemma said.

"You'll see there is a copy of the same letter behind it," Raghib said. The letter read:

To the Abbot of St. John's Seminary,

I write to not only settle an old argument, but to offer a story. But first we must go back to the beginning.

I have asked myself many times, since I first saw the Gospel of Mary as a young man, since I argued with my superiors at St. John's and was asked to leave the seminary—I have asked myself this question: Did God create man, or did man create God? I have spent my life in search of the answer. I know now, and like the apostle Thomas, I am troubled.

If I could ask one question and have it answered it would be how and when the Church Fathers decided to make Jesus' resurrection a physical event, an event of flesh and blood—how the bright light of his spirit that so many witnessed was reported to take on a human form that only twelve men witnessed, men who later testified to his humanity. They said, in fact, that Jesus was so alive, so physically real, that he ate boiled fish. These men, these so-called witnesses, were to become the sole inheritors of The Faith, and with their testimony, they formed the most exclusive club on earth. Soon, if you did not agree with this literal interpretation of the resurrection, you were branded a heretic.

If we are to tell the truth, we know it was Mary Magdalene who first saw the risen Christ—it was she who rallied the dispirited and disbanding disciples to spread his teachings. She shared her vision with the other disciples. Peter in particular both mocked and doubted her. But by that evening Peter claimed the vision as his own. Mary was not going to have the sole connection to the Savior. Soon the story took shape. It was Peter who had first seen the risen Christ, Peter who was designated by Christ himself to inherit the flock.

I do not mean to cast doubt on Jesus—the man himself was a miracle—only on the convenience of the story of the resurrection, of how perfectly it suited the politics of the time. Because how many others witnessed the spirit of Jesus risen? Countless others, among them the troublesome Gnostics—Thomas, whom Jesus called his twin, who doubted the physicality of Jesus' return but never that of his spirit. Why was this symbolic resurrection not viable? Because it would have opened the doors to too many witnesses. The Fathers would not have been able to maintain control. They would have been forced to form a democracy.

That was never a possibility. While exclusivity has been the Church's most powerful weapon, I am sure it is not what Jesus intended. How quickly the Church lost sight of what their Savior believed, of what he both taught and practiced.

Then came the wars of the Christianities. Peter went to Rome. When the emperor Constantine converted and claimed Roman Christianity as the only authentic faith, the Jews of Jerusalem contested Rome's self-proclaimed authority and went to war three times for it. Three times Rome's army was too strong. Finally the Jews were expelled from Jerusalem. Then there was no one left to argue who was the orthodox Christianity. Military might had answered that question definitively.

If I were to offer a gift that would help you survive, I would give your church strength instead of rigidity. I would undo two knots tied early, knots that should never have been tied, knots that have become like deformed ganglia, cutting off circulation, leaving the church in a fatal state of isolation. I would return women to the place Jesus gave them, a place in the religion, the teaching and leadership. What jealousy his love and respect for women caused in the imperfect hearts of men—in the gospel Pistis Sophia Mary confesses, "Peter makes me hesitate: I am afraid of him, because he hates the female race." How unguided that a personality like this founded a religion.

Then there is the fallacy that there is but one path to God, and your church is its sole proprietor. How, out of all the religious traditions in the world, could only one be authentic? Is your God only God to those who come to the church you built? Is his love so conditional? Your rejection of other faiths is a sin of ignorance that has led to bloody crusades and inquisitions, intolerance and death, death, death. In the name of God.

Is this what Jesus would have endorsed? Jesus, a man who never once referred to himself as the son of God? Jesus, whose closest disciples believed that there was truth in all religions, that all sacred texts should be celebrated? Jesus, who admired and respected women?

Jesus, who loved. *Who loved.*

You will find all of this detailed in the gospels your forefathers attempted to destroy, gospels that will now be returned to the people. In them we have an opportunity to forgive and heal the grievous human errors of the past. I do not hesitate to call it God-given. It is a chance to go back to the start, to what was true at the beginning. It is

a chance to reclaim the original content and spirit of Jesus' teachings.
Read these gospels and find a chance to rebuild a faith that could be a
home for so many. Find in their resurrection a resurrection for your
dying church.

Light poured in from the outside. Gemma felt herself swimming up
as if from a great depth. Bashir said, "We have a visitor. I found him outside, listening." In the doorway the silhouette was not at first discernible.
Gemma moved from the table as it came into focus. She knew the voice
instantly.

Roberto Denton stood smiling as his eyes adjusted to the thin light. "In
fact, I was riveted. Who would not be? Your father was an excellent
writer," he continued. "He could convince anyone of anything. You don't
see that ability every day. He was also a natural leader. Men followed him
without hesitation. It would have been dangerous had he been possessed
by darker forces. But he was good. He simply lost his way." Denton
reached out his hand. "I think you have something that belongs to me."

Bashir stepped in front of Gemma protectively. "It's all right, Bashir,"
she told him, glancing at the letter on the desk. "I do not see your name
here, Mr. Denton."

"But you see my community's name."

"St. John's," Gemma said softly. She felt neither annoyance nor surprise. She was still intoxicated by her father's vision, protected by the
beauty of a world that might have been. Roberto Denton was incidental.

"Now I will collect what your father has left for me—for us."

She looked at him for a long moment. His pale skin gleamed in the
heat of the airless room. "Am I to believe you are the designated representative for St. John's?"

"I have spent more than half my life there and the early part of it with
your father. How sorry we were to lose him. Few who choose a path with
God possess such light. If only he had used it to illuminate his faith."

"What do you know of his faith?" Gemma asked.

"At one time, I was quite touched by it. Later, alas, learning took prece-
dence."

"And this was a transgression?"

"Think of where it led him. After his time in seminary, your father, who desired community, was forced into isolation. After having a small family, he chose to work abroad. He spent most of his life alone in a foreign country. It is in isolation that we lose our way, creating entire new worlds for the ones we have lost. This is what your father did after he left us—after he left you."

A moment of silence passed. Gemma set her jaw. "So my father was a lonely fantasist?"

"He was, perhaps, too educated for a man so alone."

"I don't believe there can be too much education. What does it matter that he was alone?"

"Because we are relational creatures. We understand the world in terms of one another. We find our way together."

"That hasn't been my experience."

Denton smiled. "I'm not surprised."

Gemma ignored the comment. "On whose authority are you here now?" she asked evenly.

"That requires more of a story—a story you, Miss Bastian, might benefit from knowing."

"Gemma?" Anthony asked.

"It's all right." It was her father who had told her to listen. *Let him show you who he is.* She watched as Denton crossed to the table and pulled out a chair. When she refused his offer, he took the chair for himself. "After he left us, your father kept up a written correspondence with St. John's. He maintained a relationship with us. He was, as I said, an 'intellectual.'" Denton pronounced the word acidly. "Though preparing for a life with God, your father never lost his hunger for the world. With his weekly scourings of newspapers and periodicals, he made himself our informant, retelling stories he had read, summarizing the news of the world." Denton smiled, warming to the small congregation. "One day he reported a discovery, a text purchased in Cairo by a German scholar. The article said the text included original gospels—gospels other than those we knew by rote. One of them purported to be the Gospel of Mary Magdalene." Denton surveyed their faces, looking beyond them as if to a vaster audience. "From that day on, the questions began. At every Bible reading with scenes of Christ and the apostles, your father asked us what might have been taken out. Had Mary Magdalene once been there too? Had her words and presence truly been erased? And why?

"He was irresistible. A true charismatic. Many of us would have followed him through fire. However, he made that impossible when he brought the matter to our superiors, asking for permission for leave to go to Berlin. He wanted to see the gospels with his own eyes. When permission was not granted, he went anyway. The door of the Church slammed on him. It would never reopen. God tests us, Miss Bastian, and sometimes we fail. In choosing knowledge over faith, your father failed. He lost his entire world." Denton peered at Gemma in the faint light. "Do you begin to understand? The poor man was heartbroken. *He was lost.*"

Gemma looked away.

"A few years later," Denton continued, "we read an article he published; it ran like brushfire through the seminary." Denton clapped his hands in mock celebration. "Charles Bastian had become an archaeologist. He continued to send us articles about the missing pieces of Jesus' life. They had gone missing, he said, because men made them go missing. God had nothing to do with it."

Anthony interrupted. "Have you heard enough, Gemma?"

"No. I want him to finish."

Denton offered her a small nod of appreciation. "We found later that he had gone to Egypt. There were letters every year or so. Finally, last year, he wrote us about a great discovery, said he could finally make his case. He would make it first to us, the order that had shut him out. It seems we had gotten a few things wrong. Jesus would have wanted women in his church, he would have honored other faiths, he would not have created a closed system of power. Your father's final report would make us see that the book of Christianity needed to be rewritten. Of course, we should not think of it as a harmful thing. The books were beautiful, he said. He wanted to share them with us—and then with the world."

"And that was not acceptable," Gemma said. "Was it, Mr. Denton?"

Denton stared back at her, his eyes like flint. "What do you think, Miss Bastian?"

"I think it wasn't. I think you were sent to stop him. Or maybe you volunteered."

"I came to retrieve what he had promised us."

"This letter—the case he had made."

"Yes."

"And the gospels he had found."

"Heretical gospels belong in the protection of the Church."

"It's quite clear why you would think so."

Anthony cleared his throat, his eyes on Gemma. She glanced at him, shaking her head slightly in response.

Denton's next words were delivered with painful slowness. "Do you understand it would be an act of cruelty to shake people's faith at such a time?"

"Who are you to judge that?"

"People have such little comfort."

"Then comfort them with a truer god."

"And the truth shall set you free?" Denton laughed. "Not so. The last thing people want is to be challenged by the truth."

"How does a man of God get to this point?"

"You're young yet. In time you may see."

"What will I see?"

"That men cannot govern themselves. They need order. They need a father."

"The pope? A figurehead created by men?"

"You are an atheist, as he was." Denton pressed a handkerchief to his brow. "And you preach as he did."

Gemma continued. "I think you also came because you wanted to make sure my father wasn't right."

"But he wasn't." Denton's smile was resolute. "Your father wasn't right. Have I not made it perfectly clear? Your eminent, learned father had lost his way."

Gemma studied the man across the room in silence. "Or perhaps he had found it," she said softly. "Perhaps it was your heart that was broken, Mr. Denton. Did you almost follow him into the fire? Mr. Denton?"

Denton burrowed his gaze briefly into the earthen floor. When he raised it, a strange smile was playing on his lips.

"In any event," Anthony interjected, "yours is not the only letter."

The flinch in Denton's face was almost imperceptible.

"No," Gemma added. "In case you thought you had sole rights to my father's final statement."

Denton turned to the desk and moved his chair closer. The oil lamp threw flickering shadows on the open pages. He lifted one letter to see the next and nodded. "I know this writing well." As he bent to read the words, Gemma glanced at Anthony.

"I think you should leave," Anthony said. "Now, Mr. Denton."

"Just another moment. Oh yes, here he is, at the height of his intellectual powers. *If I were to offer a gift that would help you survive . . . I would return women to the place Jesus gave them; a place in the religion, the teaching and leadership. What jealousy his love and respect for women caused in the imperfect hearts of men . . .* What presumption your father had, Miss Bastian."

Something between a smile and a grimace twitched on Denton's lips as he turned away from the desk, his right arm partially extended like a broken wing. He was watching Gemma as his arm brushed against the kerosene lamp, tipping it onto the open pages, where it smashed. The last image she had before the room went dark was Denton smiling.

The darkness lasted for an instant before the pages and the oilcloth ignited, exploding in a searing light. Flames leapt to Denton's jacket, scurrying after the kerosene that had splattered his body and spread up his body like a torch to his face. His scream split the silence and released them from where they stood watching, paralyzed.

At once, Bashir ripped off his robe and threw it on the flaming desk. A moment later, Anthony pulled up the rug from the floor and tackled Denton with it, rolling him up in the smoking fibers while the smaller man struggled against him. The airless room filled with the odor of burned flesh and hair.

"Open the door, for God's sake," Anthony ordered.

The beam of light that sliced into the house blinded Gemma. She could see only what lay in its path, the wrapped midsection of Roberto Denton, Anthony's hands holding him down, the bare floor and papery ashes floating silently to the ground. The room was silent except for the moans of pain from Denton.

Bashir had drawn a sword and stood over Denton like an executioner. Gemma raised her hand as she leaned over the burned man. "His jacket was made of nylon fibers," she said. "It has melted to his skin. Have you any medical supplies?"

"You will treat this animal?" Bashir asked.

"It's my training." She turned to Anthony. "I have a small medical kit in my bag. There is some burn ointment and gauze. There's also morphine. He's going to need it."

GEMMA CLEANED DENTON's wounds with what to Anthony looked like tenderness. When she had gingerly stripped the half-melted clothes from his upper body and tended to the minor burns, she put her tweezers and burn ointment and gauze down. "Are you allergic to morphine?"

Denton mutely shook his head.

"I'm going to give you an injection that will ease your pain and allow me to tend to the more severe burns."

LATER, Anthony and Gemma stood outside in the dusk. The air felt clear and soft after the scorched, acrid room. Raghib had gone to his sister's. Bashir had posted himself like an avenging angel against the house only after Gemma entreated him to let her stay inside with Denton. "He cannot hurt me now," she told him, adding, "It's what my father would have wanted."

"There is a man," Bashir said, "a Bedouin healer. He could tend to him."

"Tomorrow. Tonight I will stay with him."

✝ ✝ ✝

DENTON WOKE IN the night weeping. Gemma had set up her mat on the other side of the room. Anthony slept outside the door. She held Denton's head and tipped water into his mouth. The burns were bloody and raw. One of his eyes was swollen shut. "I'm going to give you more morphine," she said slowly. "So you can rest."

Denton stared at her with his one seeing eye as she searched in the half darkness for an unburned place on his arm for the needle. She felt his body relax and laid him back down. She did not know how much time passed before he spoke.

"I need a witness." The words were slightly stronger than breath.

"Not now."

"God has chosen you, the daughter of the man who brought me here."

She pulled her blanket more tightly around herself and stared back at him. "If it's guilt you're feeling, absolve yourself. I won't forget the words my father wrote; I understand them too well. They are written inside of me. They will never be lost." She moved away from Denton and leaned against the wall. A sudden anger made her want to deprive him of a confession. But Denton dozed off. Gemma had closed her eyes when he spoke again. "Your father made the mistake common to many educated men," Denton added softly. "He forgot that people are lazy. They need to be led."

"Maybe they've never been given the chance to govern themselves; they've never been given the tools." Gemma reached for her medical kit and removed another vial of morphine. "They've been told to replace thought with faith. A good Christian does not question. A good Christian accepts what he is given. It does not matter if he understands it." Denton offered his arm with relief. Gemma waited for the opiate to take hold. She did not move back to the wall but stayed close to Denton. She wanted to see his face. "Here's what I believe. The walls of your faith were shaken by my father. That is why you are here. My father stirred doubt in you. He made you think. Even though you are not trained to think, you cannot shut out the doubt. It has started to eat you alive."

It took Denton some time to respond. When he spoke, his words were slurred. "Doubt is a minor sin." He smiled loosely. "Your father's sin was cardinal. It was fatal. He was proud, from the beginning. He had to let his superiors, the fathers who rejected him, know that he was right. He said the book of Christianity would be rewritten," Denton sputtered. "There were quotes."

"From the Nag Hammadi find."

"Yes."

"Evidence worth killing for?"

Denton's fist slammed weakly on the floor. "He was naïve!"

"Who killed him?"

"Does it matter? Your father came up against a force that was stronger than he was."

"And what force have you come up against? You're a burnt prisoner confessing to someone who has no mercy for you."

"But you do have mercy." He smiled thinly. "It's in your eyes."

"What you see is disgust." Gemma rose.

"Don't go."

"I have heard your story. You do not even have the conscience to confess."

"I did not volunteer," he said. Gemma turned. "It was because I knew him. They thought I could change his mind. They thought I could bring him back."

"Westerly," Gemma said. "Your instruction came from Westerly."

"I was not as brave as your father." Denton winced at the pain of tears. "But I followed him into the fire after all," he said. "He did not suffer," he whispered.

She froze. Then she knelt down next to his charred face. "What did you say?"

"I said your father didn't suffer. He said he understood." Denton smiled weakly. "He said he was glad it was me, someone he knew. The circle of his life had been completed."

Gemma, barely breathing, remained motionless. "What circle?"

"He was being returned to God."

A long moment passed in silence. "Whose God?"

In the barely audible words was a note of insistence. "*Our* God."

She hovered above him, scenarios racing through her head. She wanted to lay her hands on him; she wanted to commit violence. Instead she backed away. Denton strained to see her, his single eye bulging. It was, she realized, what he wanted. Absolution, rescue. Someone else to end it for him. She collected her medical kit, leaving some ointment, three vials of morphine, and a syringe. He followed her with his naked eye. She would not give him what he wanted. She would not hate him.

"Where is your Bible?"

"I left it." Denton had squeezed his eyes shut. "I cannot feel him anymore. I cannot feel God."

Before she left, she forced herself to bend over him and, looking straight at his burned and detestable face, she touched his forehead with her lips. In his ear she whispered, "It's what Mary would have done."

CHAPTER THIRTY-FIVE

O UTSIDE, Anthony was waiting. Gemma looked at him briefly and then folded herself onto the ground. Anthony sat next to her. "Someone else needs to tend to him now," she said.

"Someone will."

"I left him enough morphine to kill himself," she said. "But I don't want him to die. I want him left alone with his thoughts."

"Come," Anthony urged. "Let's leave this place."

"He said my father came full circle. He tried to make it sound poetic. I'm afraid—I'm afraid I will never be strong enough for forgiveness."

"It's too soon for that."

She looked up at him. "But there's never enough time, you see. People are there and the next moment they're gone."

WHEN THEY GOT back to Bashir's, their bags had been packed and were sitting outside the tent. There were two horses standing, heads hung in the heat. The sun was at its brutal zenith. Bashir emerged from the tent. They stood there, shadowless, on the baking dirt.

"You are ready," Bashir said. "There is food in the saddlebag. Water enough to get you to the Ibrim well."

"What's happening?" Gemma asked.

"We've had a message from Gabbar," Anthony said. "We're to leave immediately. I've arranged for horses this time."

Gemma looked at Bashir. "I'm not ready to go."

"We don't have a choice. Gabbar won't wait forever."

"I'll go later. Bashir can find me a guide."

"No, Gemma." Anthony held her eye. "We go together."

She turned to Bashir. "We've only just arrived."

"It is God's will."

"I will come back," she told him. "Will you be here?"

"I will be here."

"Then I will write to you."

"Write me as you would have written your father."

"Thank you, Bashir." She hesitated. "For keeping me in your heart."

"I hope your difficulties are over." Bashir inclined his head. "Go with God, child."

THE RIDE BACK to the river was fast and hard, the air like a hot bath. Conversation was impossible. Gemma felt enveloped, bereft. Every mile took her farther away from Bashir, farther from her father. Ahead of her she could sense nothing of substance. The future was as thin and vague as a vapor.

She grasped her reins and pressed her leg against her saddlebag. Inside, she could feel the shape of *The Dialogue of the Savior,* the one thing she had taken away from Nag Hammadi. She had lost much more, precious things she had had for just a day. Her father's letter, the beginnings of a friendship with Bashir, the realm of Nag Hammadi.

If one does not understand how the fire came to be, he will burn in it. . . .

Denton's blackened face floated against the empty landscape. No one would come for him, she realized. He would never leave Nag Hammadi. She focused on Anthony's back and the dark band of perspiration down the middle of his shirt. His right hand was wrapped in gauze, singed from his embrace with Denton's burning body.

They dismounted at the Ibrim well to water the horses. Anthony threw a leather bucket down the well and pulled it back up, sloshing, letting her horse bury his muzzle to drink.

Gemma sat on her haunches, pulling her hat over her eyes. "What did Gabbar say?"

"It was more the language he used. I think something's happened."

"What more could happen?"

Anthony wet a handkerchief and returned the reins of her horse. Kneeling in front of her, he gently removed her hat and passed the handkerchief over her dusty brow. "I'm sorry we had to leave that way."

Gemma closed her eyes to the coolness of the cloth. "Perhaps it's the only way to leave."

GABBAR'S FELUCCA WAS tied in the shade of a date palm. He leaned against the rudder, dozing. While Gemma washed in the river, Anthony untied the bags and dropped them onto the boat. It took him half an hour to deal with the horses. When he returned, Gabbar was waiting on the bow of the felucca. "I came as soon as I heard," Gabbar said.

"Heard what?"

"Cairo is being bombed. The Arab-Israeli war started two days ago."

"The Israelis are bombing Cairo?" Gemma asked.

"I have been told there have been many surprises. It seems their air force is stronger than anyone knew."

"My God," Anthony murmured.

Gabbar untied the sail and pushed the boat back into the current. As the bow swung into the wind, Anthony briefly caught Gemma's eye.

"So," she said quietly. "Another war."

The trip back was quick; the wind blew steadily from the south. Anthony and Gemma sat on different sides of the felucca, watching separate banks of the river. Gemma glanced periodically at Anthony, but he remained posted resolutely, his back to her.

✝   ✝   ✝

THEY SAW THE planes from Helwan. Puffs of smoke rose silently where bombs fell. As they neared Cairo, people gathered on the banks to point and watch. Children were excited. Adults stared. Neither understood the danger that was encased in such silence.

Late in the afternoon, Gemma sat at the front of the boat, unable to move. Her eyes were trained on the horizon. Anthony rested on his knee next to her. "Come and have something to eat."

"Why can't we hear anything?"

"It's sometimes the way sound travels in the desert. It's a kind of mirage of silence."

"I climbed to the top of the Great Pyramid," she told him. "The day we went to Eid's shop. A plane flew by, so close I could see the pilot. It was a military plane, but not one I recognized. He must have been reconnaissance. I thought— I took it for something else. An omen, maybe."

"Come, sit. Have a meal. Who knows when we'll have another."

They sat across from each other, their eyes occasionally holding. It would be their last meal on the boat. Gabbar had fixed a cold salad of grains with cucumber and tomato and mint. There was little to say.

"Gabbar doesn't want to enter the city," Anthony told her. "We will make our own way from the Nilometer. We can find a water taxi to take us north."

"And then?"

"And then I will take you back to my family's house."

"To Michael."

"To Michael, yes."

IN THE CITY, there were no water taxis. The ancient steps of the Nilometer were filled with people. Gemma could not tell if they were climbing up or down to the river. She watched as they pushed past each other, arguing loudly, their confusion mixing with panic.

"This is chaos," Anthony said. "We need to make our way north."

They traveled by foot through the bomb-hit streets, Anthony reaching back occasionally to touch Gemma's hand, to make sure she had not been swept away. Whole blocks had been sealed off. Policemen struggled with barricades and frantic citizens trying to reenter their demolished homes. Anthony stopped to talk to one of them, and Gemma watched as the policeman gesticulated, his hands becoming planes, bombs. Anthony rejoined her and took her by the elbow.

"No one knows how many have died," he told her. "All communication systems are down. The great city has become an island."

Farther into the old Coptic quarter were chimneys of black smoke and choking clouds of dust and the alarming sight of people running. They had no difficulty hearing the planes now. The bombers swooped and dove above, dispensing their lethal charge like Christmas packages. Gemma was momentarily transfixed, scanning the sky.

"It's so strange," she said, "to be able to see them." Two planes flew in tandem high overhead. It seemed that they were leaving. A flyer and his wingman, she thought, going home. Behind them, flying lower and with greater intent, was a third plane. It seemed to arrive from nowhere. Anthony pulled Gemma to a doorway for shelter.

They saw the bomb dropping in the face of the man across the street, who looked from his window. Even from a distance, Gemma could see his disbelief. Anthony pulled her to the ground and covered her with his body. The building across the street flashed white and then red. A fierce wind blew debris and glass across the street. Anthony felt the shards sprinkle on his back. He tried to cover Gemma's exposed skin, her forearms and shins and face. Beneath him, he could feel that her body was softly wracked with sobs. When it was over, they rose together, she still in his arms. Then they were pressed into oneness as Anthony held her tightly to him, hugging the length of her body to his, sheltering her, feeling every part of her he could, limb to limb. Her knee hit his calf, his hip fell into the softness of her abdomen. He encircled the fragile width of her neck under her head-scarf, the neck that supported that strong head. Such a slender neck for such a strong head. He had never noticed.

They left the doorway and walked quickly from the burning building. Anthony pressed his lips to Gemma's hair, holding her close to him as they made their way through the square near the Church of Abu Sefein.

Another plane appeared suddenly, flying just overhead. Gemma's body tensed as she strained against Anthony's hold. She wanted to run but he did not let her go. As they made their way together across the square, he kept his eyes on the plane, but there was no bomb. After it passed, the plane returned and then swooped upward at an impossibly steep angle. They watched in silence as it climbed higher and higher, the drone of the propellers growing fainter and finally stalling out altogether. The plane hovered like a cross in the sky before it turned, nose down, plunging for the ground. They waited for the fire and smoke but the plane had landed in the middle of the Nile, the river of life.

Gemma turned to Anthony. "Did you see that?"

Anthony looked stricken. Neither of them spoke. As they made their way through the city, he grasped her hand tightly in his.

In the sudden and complete silence of the Lazar house, they stood close, as if physically connected. It took them a moment to separate, to realize they could. The house had the feeling of desertion. The doors and windows were closed, the air inside stale with the scent of old flowers. Gemma ran upstairs. Anthony found David in the garden, sitting with a blanket over his legs, suddenly an old man.

"Father," Anthony said. "What are you doing?"

"Watching," David said. "It's as good a place as any."

Gemma appeared, breathless. "Where is everyone?"

"Nailah has gone to her mother's. Amad is with Zira. And your brother"—David looked up at Anthony—"has found the sky again."

"What do you mean?" Anthony asked.

"He's flying for the enemy. He could be up there now."

There was a moment of stunned silence. Gemma did not let herself look at Anthony.

"No," she argued. "He wouldn't."

"Oh, I don't know." David sighed. "I think bombing this country might give him great satisfaction."

"How can he fly?" she demanded.

"They've fitted a plane for a cripple. When the Israelis heard about Michael's Distinguished Service Medal, they asked no questions. Offered to pay his fare and off he went. He'd been arranging it for weeks."

Finally Gemma looked at Anthony, who had not yet spoken. His features were rigid with absence, his skin white, as if even his blood was leaving him. Suddenly she knew exactly what was going to happen, how it was all going to end. She watched it as if it had nothing to do with her. He was leaving her, leaving all of them. Anthony was already as far away as his brother. Farther even.

"He may be flying over Cairo right now," David said. "Sherut Avir. They have Spitfires, I guess. And Harvards and Mustangs and B-17s. Michael was like a little boy talking about it. I have word that eight Israeli planes have been shot down."

"Already?" Anthony asked.

"Already." David rose. "Now Michael can't accuse me of never being close to war."

When David left the garden, Gemma and Anthony did not look at each other.

"It was him," Anthony said. "Above the Nile."

"You don't know that."

"I know." Anthony put up his hand to stop her protest and then turned away.

"You're taking responsibility."

Anthony glanced at her. "He loved you."

"No," she said. "He wanted my help."

"Then I think you didn't know Michael."

"I know Michael. He lived for other things. I was . . . a consolation."

"You were strong enough for both of you." Anthony's eyes rested on the scattered petals beneath the rosebushes. "He told me to bring you back to him."

"Then he should have waited."

He raised his eyes to hers. "I might not have."

Gemma stepped toward him. The distance between them was unbearable. "Wouldn't you have?"

"Every day must have felt like a week."

"Why? Because he knew—he thought there might be something between us?"

"We were gone too long."

"You haven't been listening to your father. He'd been planning this for weeks."

Anthony pointed to the sky above the Nile. "Planning that? I don't think so. No, that was for us."

She touched his hand. "Don't do this."

"I'm not doing anything. You were his."

"You don't believe that. You don't *think* like that."

"It's how he thought—and I knew it."

"I am not a possession, not a thing. You cannot give me to a dead man." He was shaking his head. "Don't let death win—not after all this," she said, grasping his hand. "You have been here with me."

He pulled away gently. "But I cannot be with you now."

Chapter Thirty-six

S HE HAD NOT been alone for weeks. She had not been without Anthony. Disembodied, Gemma wandered the empty house, forcing herself to remember how it had been before. She summoned the lilt of Michael's voice, the uneven rhythm of his step. It took a few hours to know she couldn't stand it.

She left the house and started to walk. With all that she could not bring herself to think about, it was Roberto Denton that filled her mind. His terrible loneliness, his abandoned Bible. She allowed herself to imagine that he was dead, and it was she who had given a broken man of God the means to kill himself. She had left him in a living hell. Where he was, there would be no one to lay him to rest. It was, perhaps, the worst sentence. A life that ended without love, human or divine.

She made her way to Kit Kat, not caring anymore about the planes. She did not know how she reached the river, only that the city was filled with images without sound. She walked in perfect silence.

The doorman and his parrot were gone. The river was full of debris, turbulent and brown. She paused to watch a woman's shoe float by.

Anthony was in his room, duffel bag half-packed.

"You are leaving."

"Yes."

"For Kharga?"

He pressed his clothes down and zipped the duffel. "Yes."

She stood in front of him to block his way. "Will you listen to me?" Anthony paused but did not meet her eye. "You are like one of your lost cities. But you have allowed me to glimpse you. Perhaps you did it by mistake. But I can't forget what I've seen."

Anthony turned from her and sat on the edge of the bed. "An hour ago a man came to the house. He was from the city police. A body was fished out of the river not far from here. A pilot from a plane with unexploded bombs. It was Michael."

She knelt in front of him. "I'm so sorry." He looked at her for a long moment, taking her in with his great green eyes, eyes that were already looking beyond her. He pressed a kiss onto her forehead. She spoke from under his lips. "People have become unbearable to you. I have become unbearable."

He would not look at her again. "I've become unbearable to myself," he said.

"But you will bear your hermits."

"They will bear me."

"I would bear you."

"I'm not asking you to."

"Stop it." She pulled away. "Stop asking for nothing."

Anthony half smiled. "Then I will ask for everything. I ask you to accept both my love and my leaving."

"No."

Anthony spoke gently. "I thought you might understand."

Gemma was shaking her head. Tears filled her eyes. "I don't understand."

"Close your eyes. You are strong enough to believe in what you cannot see." He pressed her hand to his chest. "You cannot see my love. But it is there. It will be there as I make peace with my brother. I cannot do it here. I cannot do it with you."

Anger stemmed Gemma's tears. "How long will peace take?"

"I don't know."

She squeezed her eyes shut. "It will take forever." The tears spilled onto her cheeks. "You can't leave. I am still learning you."

"You know me," he said, taking her hands and putting them on his face. As her fingers traveled his features, he kissed her closed lids, her cheeks, her lips. "And yes, I have been here with you," he whispered into her ear. "We have been together."

She stood on the dock as Gabbar's felucca sailed away in the murky churned water, the tilted mast arching against the sky like a dancer's arm. The sky was bright behind it; she could not see anything but outline. Anthony's head and frame, standing still, faced her.

CHAPTER THIRTY-SEVEN

THE NEXT DAY Gemma moved out of the Lazars' house and booked a room at the Palace Hotel. The room had a balcony from which she could see the pyramids and the edge of the Sahara. But the room faced east, away from Kharga.

She did not unpack her suitcase. She did not leave her room for dinner. She sat there listening to the airplanes. She did not take cover, but sat at the open window.

After dark she went down to the front desk. "Is it possible to leave Cairo—" She faltered. "Is it possible to fly out of here?"

"There are planes leaving, yes."

"To London?"

"Every two days. Would you like me to see if there are seats available?"

"Please. If you find one, reserve it. It doesn't matter when. I could leave tomorrow."

"No planes, not tomorrow."

"The next day then."

SHE SLEPT IN her clothes and in the early morning walked numbly through the desolate city to the river. The river of life had become the river of death. It had taken both brothers from her. She looked around. There was no one about. A brindled mutt dragged itself from its sunny patch to sit next to her. She rested her hand on its mangy head. Turning to face the rising sun, she opened the letter that had been sent to her at the Lazars'. She scanned the page to the end and saw it was from Angela Dattari.

Dear Gemma:

I feel there is no longer any time. War has fallen upon us again. Bombs are dropping as I write this; I don't know if I can survive another war.

When I met you I knew you were like your father; you are strong and intelligent and you deserve the truth. I was not honest with you. I loved him. We loved each other. I believe he was happy when he died. I was wrong not to speak of this to you. I know your life has not been easy. I will be in Cairo until the end of the month, if you wish to speak.

Sincerely,

Angela Dattari

Gemma wove her way through a city filled with ghosts, stepping recklessly on shards of broken glass and wood splinters. No one looked at her. Maybe she had disappeared with all the people she had loved. Maybe she was a ghost now too. She had never traveled through Cairo so quickly.

The lights of Angela Dattari's house were extinguished, the shutters closed, as if the house itself were mourning. The doorbell echoed inside and Gemma turned, believing no one would come. When Angela Dattari opened the door, she caught her breath.

"I'm glad you came." Angela Dattari was wrapped in a shawl that she hugged closer to her. "Would you like to come in? I can make tea."

"Yes, please." Gemma found herself both flooded with relief and closer to the brink of total despair.

Angela Dattari led her to a comfortable chair in the living room, where a fire burned. "You're shivering," Angela Dattari said. She unfolded a blanket and tucked it around Gemma. "Has something happened?"

Gemma mutely shook her head.

Angela Dattari turned to tend to the fire, sending a swarm of sparks up the chimney. "When you rang I was listening to opera," she said. "Verdi."

"I don't know opera."

"Neither did your father. I taught him how to listen to it."

"Then please, keep it on."

"Rest and I'll bring the tea."

The music started and Gemma closed her eyes. She couldn't follow it. "It's a story," Angela Dattari said, setting down a tea tray. "Imagine the north. Imagine snow falling, the short dim light of winter. Now listen and you can hear the voices speaking to each other—to us. You don't have to understand the words. Listen to the emotion. They are calling out in their isolation, in space and time, they are asking, Am I alone? They are calling to see if anyone will answer."

"It's a love story."

"Every story is a love story."

"Tell me about your story with my father."

Angela poured herself some tea and sat across the fire from Gemma. "Like you, he came to my door. He doesn't seem to notice doorbells so he banged like a madman. I suppose he was a bit mad."

"Why?"

"Because I had something he wanted more than life itself. Because he couldn't stand being so close to the thing he had worked for all his life."

"You had the gospels."

"Of course I wouldn't show them to him."

"But then you did. You gave up Tano's protection."

"Because I had found something better."

Gemma sipped her tea and felt the warmth migrate down her body. She looked around. "Where did he sit when he came?"

"He sat on the floor. Just there, in front of the fire, with pages spread all around him."

"And where did you sit?"

"Where you are now. I watched him at first because I did not trust him. Why should I? Then he began talking, telling me what he was reading. Then it was terrible; I caught his disease. I began to think about the books and what they said. I looked forward to his coming. He told me the most astonishing things. A long story about the Garden of Eden, told from the serpent's point of view! Can you imagine? What craziness. But it was quite beautiful. Quite poetic. And your father was like a boy, so joyful. He taught me to read a bit of Coptic. I got down on the floor with him like a silly schoolgirl. He was so excited that I wanted to learn. He didn't want to leave me behind, he said. I should take the journey with him—we had been placed in each other's path for a reason. He was superstitious in that way. Then I started making him dinner. I gave him some of Antonio's old clothes because he was so threadbare. Somehow I fell in love with him. It was a great surprise." Angela stirred her tea absently. "Now he is gone."

"And you are leaving."

"It's time to go home."

"Isn't this your home?"

"It was. Now I want to live in a place that is closer to the water, with not so much dust. A place where no one will come banging on my door asking me to love again."

"My father loved again," Gemma said quietly. "He loved you."

"I think now"—Angela hesitated, her eyes on the floor—"that I only loved once."

"You did not love your husband."

"Oh, Gemma." Angela faltered, searching for the words. "I don't know if you can imagine the loneliness of marriage. It is so—unexpected. For me it was a prison. I thought my husband had put me there. But when he died I stayed locked up. I was too weak to leave. It was in this state of shame and hiding that your father found me. He took me by the hand. With him I was able to walk away."

Gemma stared into her tea. "It doesn't seem right that I won't know you. It doesn't seem fair."

"What terrible person told you that life was fair?"

"I think he used the word *just*."

"That's very different. That can take a long time. Fairness is for children."

Gemma held the older woman's eyes. "Your love was the most impor-tant thing to him in the end. I am sure of that."

"Are you?" Angela Dattari turned away and then held her silk scarf to her face. "I am waiting for him to tell me how this is just," she said.

Gemma set down her teacup and pulled the blanket around her feet. "When did you first know that you loved him?"

"If I am to be honest, I would have to say it was quite soon, before I even saw him. The way he knocked on my door. There is something about people who demand entry. To those of us in the locked houses, they are our only means of rescue."

Gemma turned from Angela and stared into the fire. Long minutes passed in silence.

When Angela spoke again, Gemma followed her voice like a melody. "He told me once that isolation was not the answer. We must be braver than that, Angela, he said. God exists in the space between us, when we reach out for each other. We find him when we seek each other. I don't know if I believe in God, but he made me want to be brave."

Gemma did not turn from the fire. "You are brave."

Angela kept her eyes on Gemma as she began clearing the tea tray. "What will you do now?"

"Please, don't worry about me."

"If I don't, who will? There's no one left."

Gemma turned to her. She could not speak.

"I know this sadness," Angela said.

Gemma shook her head, her eyes pooling with tears. "I'm just tired."

"Rest here. Perhaps tonight we can worry about each other."

GEMMA DID NOT feel she was falling asleep, simply sinking from the world. It was a light, dreamless state. When she awoke, she was alone. On the table next to her was a note and at her feet a leather valise. *Do what he would have done. Finish his work.*

Gemma unlatched the valise and opened it slightly. A slice of stale air escaped from the thick papyrus pages; she could smell the antiquity. Tentatively, she reached to touch the pages her father had held. Then she hugged the valise and wept.

Angela Dattari watched her from the doorway. "Tano always liked my jewel collection."

Gemma looked up. It took her a moment to understand. "That day you bought the gospels with your jewels?"

"It doesn't seem fair, does it? Trading stones for God—and for love. I got the better deal by far." She paused before she went upstairs. "Take them," she said gently. "As with your father, they were only meant to be mine for a moment. It was enough."

CHAPTER THIRTY-EIGHT

NAILAH FOUND GEMMA in the garden sitting on the ground with her arms wrapped around her legs. She sat down next to her.

"You are leaving," Nailah said.

"I wanted to thank you, for everything."

"I'm sorry David isn't here."

"You must tell him how sorry I am."

"He will miss you," Nailah said. "The house will feel so empty."

Above, the sky was momentarily empty, the day strangely still. "Anthony is leaving for Kharga," Gemma said.

"I know."

"He's leaving because he blames himself for Michael's death."

"That's silly. He's leaving because he prefers the desert. We cannot hold him here."

Gemma looked at Nailah. "I wanted to hold him here."

Nailah gently touched Gemma's hair. "Michael left you a letter. I found it in his room this morning."

My dearest Gemma,

You are out there somewhere, I don't know where. I know you are safe because Anthony galloped after you like the bloody cavalry.

I am missing you! You are the only person I want to tell—I am going to fly again. I am going to fly! It has changed everything. I feel myself now for the first time since my accident.

You would be angry; I have had my medicine. I write you as I descend from the hand of God. Soon I will be back on miserable earth. Nothing, none of the good things, remain. The love I felt a moment ago is already slipping away.

I think now I could not have made you happy. There is one thing I have wanted. To finish the war the way it should have been finished. With dignity—not shame.

I want you to be free too. Not bound by your training—not bound to bring people back. Not bound to me. I won't be coming back. Not this time.

I think the last time I was happy was in the sky.

How good you've been to me. How kind. I hope you have the life you deserve. I am smiling because I think it is my little brother who will take care of you now. The little boy with the big eyes. The little boy I wanted to hate.

I am smiling.

Your, Michael

That night Gemma slept with the gospels but she did not dream of them. She dreamt of her own life, of the sequence of events that, since the war, had joined together like beads in a crazy necklace. Now there was nothing more, nothing to gain or lose. There was no one. Within the necklace was a void, and she was in the middle of it. For a time, Michael had floated within its boundaries, and Anthony. It was so quiet now, this sphere of silence. With her eyes closed, she traveled its perimeter and found it sound and sealed. No doors had been left opened, no beads left unstrung.

Isolation is not the answer, her father had told Angela Dattari.

To step out of it required more than she had, more than the strength that remained. She laid her hand on the stack of bound books. She had wrapped them with a sheet; they looked as if they were going to be laid to rest, returned to the earth they had lived in for so many years.

She rolled away from the books. They would never be buried again. They would be seen. She sat up. She did not have to step out of her isolation. She could crash out of it, shatter it like glass.

It was not possible to sleep then. She lay with the shrouded books, imagining. As she lay there, a future almost came into being. Her father's voice was inside of her, pushing her like a horse into gallop. *Rise, always rise. Strength to your sword arm!*

No. She shook her head to the empty room. The next thing would require a courage she had not felt. But already in the imagining there was more than there had been.

As she waited for daylight to press against the curtains, she reminded herself she was not the first woman to be alone. Mary Magdalene had been alone, never more so than after the death of her teacher, her love.

It wasn't the end. After witnessing his suffering death, she had done something even more. She had followed those who left the place of pain, who could no longer bear being physically close to the crucified body of their Savior. She had gone after them and brought them back.

CHAPTER THIRTY-NINE

ANTHONY HAD SET up camp at the outskirts of the oasis, at Al-Bagawat. He was without Zira, kilometers away from Kharga, at the edge of the desert. The winds had started. They had scoured away a layer of dirt from the western wall of the Necropolis. He had found a new painting. He did not know what it was. In the beginning, there were only colors.

He had visitors. Word got back to Kharga that he had returned. The locals who knew him were curious, offered to work for him. They could not believe a European could take care of himself. When Anthony refused, they brought him things to eat and drink. Fruit, dates, water.

In the cool mornings, he focused on the painting, coming to it like a meditation. He stood in front of it with his brushes, some stiff, some soft, and began the slow process of uncovering the picture. He did not try to guess what it was. He stayed close to it so his eyes would not try to make sense of the shapes. Later, he would step away from it.

At night, the moon had been enormous and yellow. He slept sporadically, often waking to watch it move across the sky. He lay there and silently spoke to his brother, saying things he had not said in life. Sometimes Michael's mocking laughter rang in his ears, out of nowhere. He had not listened in life, he was not listening now. Still Anthony talked to him.

Gemma came to him unbidden. She came in dreams, when he could not keep her out. He woke with the memory of her clear eyes. Of what he had known of her touch. In daylight, he coaxed her back into the darkness of his heart.

IT WAS SUNSET when he saw the small caravan from a distance, approaching from the east. The winds had begun in earnest. The camels floated toward him in a storm of sand. Their riders were undefined, merging into the beasts that carried them. Three camels, three riders. They seemed to be coming straight for him. He stood motionless outside his tent, his eyes fixed on the smallest rider. He walked to the caravan as it began to angle toward Kharga. He was wrong; it wasn't coming to him. It was a supply caravan, on its way to the city. He walked toward it anyway. He had been alone too long. Finally, he saluted the mirage of hope and turned away, looking back a last time to see if it had been real at all. He stopped and squinted because one of the riders had slowed and raised a hand. He walked toward it, quickly now. As he closed the distance between them, the wind blew sand into a cloud. His eyes stung as they searched. Then he saw it. On the rider with a raised hand, a strand of escaped hair. His eyes locked onto its fluttering motion as it whipped through the grit and cloud. He held his hand to his eyes in an attempt to block the sand. *Gemma.*

She disappeared from him then. As he moved blindly forward, he thought he saw her hand raised again in protest. He kept his eyes on it, pushing against the wind. Suddenly she was there in front of him. He laid his hand on her ankle and she reached down, almost falling from her camel. He caught her in his arms, caught her easily. She was looking at him then, with eyes he remembered. He held her gaze as he steadied her on the ground before him and reached for her hand.

Epilogue

LBERT EID smuggled Codex 1 to America in 1949, where he attempted to sell it for as much as $22,000. When he failed, he took it to Belgium, where he placed it in a safety deposit box. A Dutch professor, Gilles Quispel, urged the Swiss psychoanalyst Carl Jung to buy the codex. Jung had been fascinated by the Gnostics for years, and the availability of this new material eventually allowed him to write extensively about Gnosticism. The codex was finally purchased by Jung and brought to Zurich. It is now referred to as the "Jung Codex."

The largest portion of the texts was for years in the care of Maria ("Angela") Dattari. With the help of Phocion Tano, Dattari made various attempts to sell and smuggle the books from Egypt, all of which failed. When the texts were finally seized by the Egyptian government in the early 1950s, Dattari demanded $100,000 for them. She was paid nothing. The collection was nationalized in 1952 and can be seen today in the Coptic Museum in Cairo.

For the next twenty years another great race took place: the race among international scholars to gain access to the codices. Dr. Pahor Labib, the new director of the Coptic Museum, greatly restricted access to the texts. Only a handful of people were allowed to see them, and they were sworn to secrecy about what they had seen. It wasn't until the 1970s that a facsimile edition of the Nag Hammadi codices became available to the public.

The journey of the Nag Hammadi gospels has been, from the beginning, beset by a series of bizarre circumstances. One after another, obstacles have arisen, beleaguering the gospels' path to recognition.

TIMELINE

DATE	ARCHAEOLOGY	EGYPT	EUROPE
1896	Archaeologists Bernard Grenfell and Arthur Hunt discover first papyrus fragments at Oxyrhynchus site in Egypt. Four Coptic papyrus texts are purchased in Egypt by German professor Carl Schmidt, including the Gospel of Mary.		
1898	Grenfell and Hunt publish their first volume of findings from the fragments at Oxyrhynchus.		
1923	British archaeologist Howard Carter discovers tomb of Tutankhamen in the Valley of the Kings, Egypt.		
1936		Anglo-Egyptian Treaty is signed.	
September 1940– May 1941			Tens of thousands die, and more than a million homes are destroyed, in the London Blitz.

DATE	ARCHAEOLOGY	EGYPT	EUROPE
1945			
January			Soviets liberate Auschwitz.
April			Hitler dies in his Berlin bunker.
May			Allies and Soviets defeat Germany.
August			United States drops atomic bombs on Hiroshima and Nagasaki.
November			Nuremberg War Crimes trials begin.
December 1945– January 1946	Nag Hammadi texts are discovered by Bedouin peasant Mohammad Ali.		
1945–1946		Anti-British riots break out in Cairo.	
1947	Dead Sea Scrolls are discovered by Bedouin goat herders in a cave along the Dead Sea in what is now Israel.		
June			Marshall Plan for reconstruction in Europe is announced
August			India and Pakistan declare independence from Britain.

DATE	ARCHAEOLOGY	EGYPT	EUROPE
1948	Nag Hammadi Gospel of Thomas is matched to the three Greek fragments found in Oxyrhynchus.	Egyptian prime minister Mahmoud Nugrashi Pasha is assassinated by a member of the Muslim Brotherhood.	
January			Indian leader Mahatma Gandhi is assassinated.
February			Communists take power in Czechoslovakia.
June			Soviets cut off ground transportation to West Berlin; Berlin Airlift begins.
May			State of Israel is founded; first Arab-Israeli War begins. Newly elected National Party of South Africa introduces apartheid.
July			President Harry Truman orders desegregation of all U.S. armed forces.
1949		New government is formed in Egypt. British troops open fire on Egyptian protesters.	

DATE	ARCHAEOLOGY	EGYPT	EUROPE
January			Chinese Communists win civil war.
April			NATO is founded.
September			Soviets test their first atom bomb.
January 3, 1950		Wafd Party wins a majority; King Farouk promises social reforms.	
1952		King Farouk is toppled in a coup d'état led by army officers including Gamal Abdul Nasser and Anwar Sadat.	
May 10, 1952	Jung completes purchase of Albert Eid's codex.		
1953		Clashes worsen between Egyptian and British troops in Suez Canal zone.	
1955	Walter Till, a German scholar, publishes texts purchased in 1896 by Carl Schmidt.		
1956		Last British troops leave Suez Canal region and Egypt. Egypt declares independence from Great Britain.	

Who Is Real

Togo Mina: Director of the new Coptic Museum until his death in 1949 at age forty-three. Focused and determined, Mina was repeatedly frustrated in his attempts to acquire and secure the safety of the Nag Hammadi find.

Pahor Labib: Replaced Mina as director of the Coptic Museum in 1950.

Albert Eid: Belgian antiquities dealer who came to possess the texts found at Nag Hammadi. He had no interest in cooperating with Togo Mina or the Egyptian government; he envisioned greater profit by selling the texts elsewhere. Though warned by Mina not to remove the manuscripts from the country, Eid smuggled them out of Egypt in the winter of 1948, taking them first to New York City, where he failed to find a buyer, and then to Belgium. Eid died in 1951, and his widow, Simone, sold the texts to psychoanalyst Carl Jung the next year.

Phocion Tano: Antiquities dealer who claimed to be Maria Dattari's business manager.

Jean Doresse: Young French graduate student specializing in the history and writings of early Christianity. He was perhaps the most dogged in attempting to uncover the story of the Nag Hammadi texts, the details of which were not complete until 1975.

Angela Dattari: Her real first name was Maria; I changed it because my portrait of this enigmatic woman was more "angelic." An Italian widow who conspired with Phocion Tano to obtain as high a price as she could for the texts, she photographed them and sent the pictures to France, where they attracted the attention of Jean Doresse. Doresse went to Egypt to see the collection and teamed up with Togo Mina, but they couldn't raise the money to buy the texts (government funding vanished when Prime Minister Nugrashi Pasha was assassinated). Dattari was detained at the Cairo airport when she tried to smuggle the texts to present them to the pope. Offers by the Egyptian government to buy the manuscripts fell through. Eventually, the codices were placed in the protection of the Egyptian Department of Antiquities. Incredibly, the collection sat for the next seven years in a suitcase in department offices before being declared national property.

CARL SCHMIDT: Purchased four Coptic texts in Egypt in 1896. He devoted great effort into translating the texts and getting them into print, but mishaps and wars prevented this from happening until 1955. By this time, Schmidt had died, leaving the project to a colleague, Walter Till.

MOHAMMAD ALI: Bedouin who came across the buried texts when digging at the cliffs of Jabar-al-Tarif.

RAGHIB: Local history teacher in Nag Hammadi who could read Coptic and understood the potential value of the texts Mohammad Ali had found.

SAINT PACHOMIUS: Born a pagan, he founded a monastery in the Egyptian desert in the fourth century A.D., the ruins of which sit a few miles from the discovery site of the Nag Hammadi gospels.

A note on geography: While the papyrus texts were found near an ancient town called Chenoboskia (near Hamrah Dum), the discovery was linked to the nearest known town of Nag Hammadi.

TERMINOLOGY

Apocryphal: Hidden or secret; not included in the New Testament. Some of the Nag Hammadi texts bore this label.

Codex: A manuscript volume, especially if a classic work of the scriptures.

Coptic: One of the oldest forms of Christianity. Established in Egypt by the apostle Mark in the middle of the first century A.D.

Dogma: An uncontestable belief or doctrine held by a religion or any kind of organization. In the Catholic Church, dogma is understood to be truth revealed by God and transmitted by the apostles.

Gnosis: Greek for "knowledge."

Heresy: Opinion, doctrine, or philosophy held to be contrary to Catholic Church teachings.

Isis and Horus: Respectively, mother and son Egyptian deities whom some believe to be precursors of the Christian Mary and Jesus.

Mithra: Originally a Persian deity; thought to have been the son of God, conceived by a virgin and born on December 25. According to the myth, God sent his son to defend humanity from evil. Mithraism entered Europe after the conquests of Alexander the Great and spread rapidly throughout the Roman Empire.

Phoenician alphabet: An alphabet of twenty-two consonants and no vowels, developed from the proto-Canaanite alphabet and dating from around 1400 B.C. The Phoenician alphabet is thought to be the basis for most modern alphabets, including Greek, Latin, Hebrew, Cyrillic, and Arabic.

A Word on Gnosticism

The Gnostic movement encompassed numerous forms of religious thought in the Roman Empire between the first century B.C. and the fourth century A.D. Gnostics existed long before Christ and were spread throughout the world. There were Manichaean Gnostics in Europe, North Africa, and China; Islamic Gnostics in the Muslim world; Mandaean Gnostics in Iran and Iraq; and Cathars in Western Europe. There were correspondingly different Gnostic traditions, writers, and bodies of literature (such as Valentinius, Seth, Mandaean, Manichaean, Islamic, Cathar). Not all of the Nag Hammadi texts are considered "Gnostic" per se.

The primary concern of Gnosticism addressed a duality between the material, which was rejected, and the spiritual, which was thought to be attained through gnosis, or knowledge. For Gnostics, ignorance was considered the greatest sin. Gnostic thought was declared heretical by the Church.

ACKNOWLEDGMENTS

I have first to thank Elaine Pagels, for being such a cogent and wonderful writer. It was her book *The Gnostic Gospels* that inspired me to attempt this novel. I am incredibly grateful for her work, and that she is on this earth, building such crucial bridges of understanding. I also want to thank John Dart, whose research came to me late but was extremely valuable. He provided factual detail that I didn't know existed and was ultimately unable to fully incorporate. His excellent reporting on the Nag Hammadi find and its protracted story helped me to understand better what happened in Cairo in the late 1940s. Thanks to the wonderful translations in *The Gnostic Bible,* edited by Willis Barnstone and Marvin Meyer, and to Bart Ehrman's work in *Lost Scriptures.* I found guidance in the writings of Thomas Merton, particularly *The Desert Fathers.* I made great use of *The Nag Hammadi Library in English,* revised edition by James M. Robinson, as well as *The Catholic Encyclopedia* and the Gnostic Society Library website (www.webcom.com/gnosis/library.html).

A very deep thank-you to my first editor, Cindy Spiegel, for wanting to publish this book, and to my second editor, Jake Morrissey, for inheriting it so gracefully. I am indebted to Ed Stackler for his editorial genius and incredible book smarts.

Thank you to Thomas and Nicole Newnham Malarkey and the friends who were kind enough to read early drafts and offer invaluable suggestions and support: Ann Banchoff, Chris Boas and Claire Ferrari, Julie Colhoun, Jinx Faulkner, Joanna Goodman, Alice Koehler, Vivian Prinsloo, and Lee Rahr. Thank you to Deida Garcia for helping me keep things together on the home front. A special thank-you to my mother, Brent Malarkey, who listened to this tale from the start, and to Dan Geller and Dayna Goldfine, whose warmth, creativity, and friendship have long provided a mainstay for me. And for my sister, Sarah Malarkey, whose fine mind, spirit, and sense of humor contribute greatly to my general stability.

Thanks for the love and support of Mark Becker and his father, the late David Becker—whose excitement about this book was unflagging. In many ways, this book is for him.

I am deeply grateful to Svetlana Katz at Janklow and Nesbit, who has assisted me in every possible way in the writing and publishing process. No one has helped me more on a day-to-day level.

Finally, a profound thanks to my agent, Tina Bennett, for being the one constant in the inconstant world of publishing—and for pushing me always to a higher level. I am indebted to her unfailing instinct, her vision, and her perseverance. She has been an outstanding editor and an incomparable ally.